The Skulduggery Pleasant
GRIMOIRE

Dear weirdo,

The *Grimoire* is a reference guide to the Skulduggery Pleasant series – as such, each individual book should be read before you read the *synopsis* of that book.

Proceed with caution, is what I'm saying.

The *Grimoire* tracks a slightly different timeline than currently exists in the Skulduggery universe. Mistakes have been made over the last fifteen years and shall be corrected in future editions of the series. The *Grimoire,* therefore, contains the new, improved timeline.

I owe a huge thanks to Lassie, Luca and Ivy for helping to sort it all out, and I don't think we should blame any one person/author for those mistakes. We're better than that.

Thank you for your time. And sorry I called you a weirdo. You're not a weirdo. You're a totally normal person.

Totally. Normal.

Sincerely yours,

Derek

BOOKS BY DEREK LANDY

The Skulduggery Pleasant series

SKULDUGGERY PLEASANT
PLAYING WITH FIRE
THE FACELESS ONES
DARK DAYS
MORTAL COIL
DEATH BRINGER
KINGDOM OF THE WICKED
LAST STAND OF DEAD MEN
THE DYING OF THE LIGHT
RESURRECTION
MIDNIGHT
BEDLAM
SEASONS OF WAR
DEAD OR ALIVE

THE MALEFICENT SEVEN

ARMAGEDDON OUTTA HERE
(a Skulduggery Pleasant short-story collection)

THE SKULDUGGERY PLEASANT GRIMOIRE

The Demon Road trilogy

DEMON ROAD
DESOLATION
AMERICAN MONSTERS

DEREK LANDY

The Skulduggery Pleasant

GRIMOIRE!

HarperCollins *Children's Books*

First published in Great Britain by
HarperCollins *Children's Books* in 2021
HarperCollins *Children's Books* is a division of HarperCollins*Publishers* Ltd
1 London Bridge Street
London SE1 9GF

www.harpercollins.co.uk

HarperCollins*Publishers*
1st Floor, Watermarque Building, Ringsend Road
Dublin 4, Ireland

2

SPECIAL EDITION ISBN 978-0-00-849227-4
HB ISBN 978-0-00-847240-5
EXP ISBN 978-0-00-847241-2
ANZ ISBN 978-0-00-847242-9

A CIP catalogue record for this title is available from the British Library.

Typeset by Sorrel Packham
Printed and bound in the UK using 100% renewable electricity at CPI Group (UK) Ltd

This book is dedicated to the men, women, and individuals of the Archive Department.

These days, more than ever, it is important to shine a light into the darkness, to uncover truth in lies, and to separate fact from falsehood.

This is our mission. This is our calling. This is our duty.

Also, to Flopsy.

FOREWORD

This edition is the result of the hard work and dedication of four members of the Archive Department and any mistakes/errors/omissions are solely the editors' responsibility and not the fault of the authors. In an effort to publish this book on time, we have made the decision to compile entries from all four Archivists, and include original notes, interviews and comments supplied by relevant parties as they appeared.

The Archive Department

INTRODUCTION

What you hold in your hands is the secret history of the universe.

This history reaches from the very beginning of time (in fact, if the legends are true, it reaches back *even further*) up to the very recent past. In these pages you'll find the obscurest of God Myths standing shoulder to shoulder with confirmed, provable fact – and you'll find that one is as impressively outrageous as the other.

As part of the High Sanctuary's drive to catalogue the many occasions where the world has been threatened by sorcerers (and subsequently saved by other sorcerers), we have come, inevitably, to the tale of Skulduggery Pleasant.

I do not claim to know him well and I certainly do not claim to be his friend – I've met him only three times over the years: the first two times he insulted me, and the third time he insulted me *and* my wife. Suffice it to say, I do not like the man. I find him arrogant, insufferable and rude. You may be wondering, therefore, why I have insisted on writing this introduction.

To put it plainly, this is an opportunity to tell him what I think of him in a medium in which he cannot immediately reply with a sarcastic one-liner or a supposedly witty observation about my taste, my intelligence, or the underlying motivations for my bias.

I have no bias against Skulduggery Pleasant. I simply don't like him.

I admit, somewhat grudgingly, that he has saved the world on occasion. I admit that he has put a stop to people even worse than himself. I haven't read the book you hold in your hands, save for the interesting bits about the gods and such, because reading an entire tome about the fabled "Skeleton Detective" is more than I could possibly handle. The only redeeming factor about this entire enterprise is that the contents of these pages will only ever be used as a reference tool, perhaps to check dates, or deaths, or as a quick reminder of a "madcap" escapade he had once upon a time. But mostly it will be put on a shelf to gather dust, and no one but those on the Council of Elders will have access to it.

I don't know why the story of Skulduggery Pleasant garners such secrecy. I'm a sorcerer, and I'm over four hundred years old, and no one wants to file any of my adventures in the Top Secret Section. And I have had some hair-raising adventures, believe you me. Maybe they're not as obvious as his, though. Maybe they don't have the same kind of mass appeal. Perhaps if I'd made more jokes while I was engaged in fisticuffs, or if my enemies had been a little more flamboyant in their appearance or ridiculous in their ambitions. Maybe then I'd be a household name.

But, of course, he isn't alone, is he? He has a partner. Astonishingly, however, Valkyrie Cain is every bit as reckless, irresponsible and sarcastic as he is. When she first burst on to the magical scene, she was a precocious twelve-year-old who hurtled into danger with her head down and her eyes closed. Now that she's in her mid-to-late twenties, the only difference I can see is that she's in her mid-to-late twenties.

I'm not even going to mention what she did. I'm not going to even say *that* name. It's all here in these pages, presumably. If you don't know, you can find out for yourself. Far be it from me to spoil the surprise.

The editors have asked me to mention the layout of the book and explain and excuse the haphazard approach they've taken. Apparently, this was all a bit of a rushed job by the end. They won't say why. Maybe the Archivists (four! Four of them! Why did it take four?) found their subject to be as irritating as I do. Maybe each one of them walked away in disgust.

I hope you walk away in disgust, I truly do. Books

like these should be used to record the exploits of honourable, decent sorcerers, to secure those stories in our vaults for future generations to look back on and learn from. I don't think anyone should learn from Skulduggery Pleasant and Valkyrie Cain. He's a bad influence on her, she's a bad influence on him, and they're probably a bad influence on you, dear reader.

Do yourself a favour. Put this book back on the shelf and go about your life. You'll be happier without the darkness in these pages, I swear to you.

Austere Wycherly

NOT TO BE REMOVED FROM
THE SANCTUARY ARCHIVE

"Doors are for people with NO imagination"

A NOTE FROM THE ARCHIVIST

I have been asked to introduce myself and to explain the decisions I am set to make over the course of this book as I make them. The intention, I believe, is to give you, the reader, supposedly valuable insight into the process of collating all the information before me and how I arrive at the finished product.

I find this a ridiculous prospect as I am merely an Archivist, and as such I should be invisible to the reader, and am in no way involved in the stories I am about to relay.

But the Archive Department has been cultivating some rather grand ideas as of late – ideas that seek to elevate it above its station – and so I have little recourse but to comply.

With great reluctance, therefore, allow me to tell you that I am Archivist Palaverous and I will be doing my best to provide context and explanation (where needed) to the history lesson you are about to receive. Apologies for the shocking lack of professionalism in this approach.[1]

1. In our continuing efforts to make seamless the reader's travels through the assorted sources, interviews and essays contained in this edition, these footnotes will provide necessary guidance and explanation – the Editors

A SHORT GUIDE TO THE LIVING AND THE DEAD

ADEPTS: those who have chosen non-Elemental disciplines of power, such as Teleporters and Necromancers. Sometimes known by colloquialisms (for instance, Arbokinetics are known as "Energy Throwers" and Vitakinetics are known as "Healers".)

DARK SORCERER: a colloquial term as apt as it is vague, usually denoting a mage who has used magic for nefarious purposes.

ELEMENTALS: those with the ability to manipulate earth, air, fire and water.

HOLLOW MEN: bloated bags of noxious gases with papery skin. They obey orders, and little more.

MORTAL: a person without magic.

NEOTERIC: a sorcerer who has discovered their magic beyond the point of their Surge. Lacking proper instruction, and without the necessary focus, their magical ability forms around their subconscious needs and/or desires.

SORCERER/MAGE: a person with magic. The constant use of magic rejuvenates the sorcerer, leading to a much longer lifespan. The physical signs of ageing are slowed, the rate of which can vary wildly from mage to mage.

VAMPIRE: human by day, their true nature quelled by the sun; by night they are uncontrollable monsters. Stakes and crucifixes do nothing to harm them, though they are deathly allergic to saltwater, and fire and beheading will kill them.

The Infected undergo two to three days of "mindless slavery" to the vampire that bit them, or constant, debilitating pain – sometimes both. Assuming they survive the physical and psychological changes that occur within those forty-eight to seventy-two hours, they will then have no choice but to shed their human skin, hair and human qualities every night, and become a vampire.

WARLOCK: a catch-all term for a variety of mages whose disciplines do not conform to the standard/recommended/healthy branches of magic.

WITCH: a female-centric avenue of the mystical arts, categorised into the Maidens of the New Dawn, Brides of Blood Tears and Crones of the Cold Embrace.

WRETCHLING: a flesh-and-blood version of the Hollow Men. Stronger. More vicious.

ZOMBIE: a person raised from the dead and sustained by magic. They cannot use magic from this point on, and feel an unnatural level of devotion to their new "Master". This zombie, the Alpha, can transmit the infection through bite. The subsequent zombies will decay faster and, unlike the Alpha, lose all control if they taste human flesh.

VAMPIRE

Extract from *Straight from the Source: Understanding Magic* by Galliday Monfreak (a textbook for First Years used in Corrival Academy):

The Source of All Magic is a theoretical universe that encompasses all other universes.

Imagine that our universe is a box of cereal, standing on a table. And beside our box is another box of cereal. It's the same cereal, but it's not the same box. It has, maybe, a different number of flakes in there, or maybe it's less sugary or more sugary or less healthy or more healthy. Whatever. This isn't really about cereal. Cereal is a metaphor. A metaphor is like a simile, only sneakier. So in the metaphor, in the box, we're the cereal, or rather we're a part of the cereal, just one of the flakes, or a grain of a flake, not even a grain, a part of a grain on a part of a flake. The flake itself is a galaxy, and the grains are the planets, and we're on one of those planets, only we're really small.

So, as we've established, beside our box is another box, and it's a little different from ours, and beside *that* box is *another* box, and that's different again.

Now, imagine that this table is ridiculously big. And it has an infinite number of cereal boxes on one side of our own box, and it has an infinite number on the other side, and an infinite number in front, and behind, and even above us and below us.

That's a lot of cereal boxes, right? A lot of *alternate* cereal boxes. A lot of *parallel* cereal boxes.

Now I want you to imagine holes that have been punched in these boxes so the air can get in. I don't know why you'd punch air holes in cereal boxes – they'd make the cereal go stale – but that's what I want you to imagine. Some of these boxes have many holes in them – called *rifts* – and some only have a few, and I suppose some even have no holes at all. For cereal, that's probably good, but for the metaphor that's pretty awful.

So, taking all this into account, do you know what the Source is? Have you worked it out? Is the Source the table, perhaps? The floor the table stands on?

No. The Source is the kitchen. The Source is around all of these cereal boxes. It contains them. And the air in this kitchen passes through those rifts and allows the people inside the cereal boxes to be sorcerers.

And that's where magic comes from.

THE FACELESS ONES AND THE ANCIENTS

Extract from the *Book of Tears*:

As the infinity of universes burst into being, the Faceless Ones were already old.[1]

They watched, with a billion blinking eyes,[2] this universe, as suns formed and planets spun, as matter found the laws to which it would be wed. They witnessed the birthing of creatures of immense power – power, they saw, that could grow to rival their own.

Among these creatures, these gods,[3] were the Deathless, the Cythraul, Gog Magog and the Sathariel.

1. Contradicted by the *Book of Shalgoth*, page 106

2. Unsure how beings without faces could have eyes to blink, but the *Book of Tears* is not known for its steadfast accuracy, nor even its internal consistency.

3. See *The Pantheons*, page 25

But, as the universe settled and matter took shapes more solid, the Faceless Ones did not suffer these lesser gods to live, and they took from them their power and their light, and they killed and were most savage, until the universe was awash with the blood of the lesser gods.

Through dimensions the Faceless Ones began hunting, for their hunger was towering, and could not be fathomed.

They found a world and stood upon it and were its masters, and demanded fealty from the animals of that world who grasped at knowledge. Those animals did worship, and that worship gave strength, and those animals did offer their souls, and those souls gave power. Some of the Faceless Ones took the form of these animals, and went among them and bred.[4]

But the animals, who were called the Ancients, rose against their masters and used their weapons of death against them (*see* GOD-KILLERS). The Faceless Ones, showing mercy and compassion and love above all,[5] stepped from this universe into another, and the way back was lost to them.

And the Ancients, consumed now by greed and a hunger of their very own, discovered murder and found that it was good. Shorn of an enemy to rail against, the Ancients killed each other[6] and the eons passed, and new animals grasped at lesser knowledge and became that which we call humankind.

4. It is generally accepted that the Faceless Ones used human beings as vessels, and there are stories of them actually taking human form.

5. The Faceless Ones, by all other accounts, left this universe kicking and screaming.

6. Once the gods were forced out, bitter rivalries surfaced among the Ancients, and they used the weapons against each other until they had been virtually wiped out.

The Last of the Ancients, appalled by what he and his people had done, hid the Sceptre deep underground so that no one could ever use it again.

But within the veins of some of these humans there ran the blood of the Ancients, and there ran the blood of the Faceless Ones.

The natural way, which they named magic, and sorcery, called to some, and glimpses were stolen of the true history of the universe. The Faithful saw the Faceless Ones and they recognised their claim to this planet and this universe, and wars were fought to bring them home.

The Six Bloodlines

From what our research has shown, there have been six distinct Faceless Ones bloodlines, only one of which was strong enough to produce the Child of the Faceless Ones.

The first bloodline produced no one of any note.

The second bloodline was cut short during the war with Mevolent.

The third bloodline produced Temper Fray.

The fourth produced Damocles Creed and the Unveiled.

The fifth produced the Darklands family.

The sixth produced the Edgley line.

The tens of thousands of Kith have been drawn from the first five bloodlines over the centuries.

THE PANTHEONS

Extract from the *Book of Shalgoth*:

In the Time Before Time, in the Space Before Space, there were the First Gods, whom we now call Those Who Slumber, Whose Names We Dare Not Speak Lest They Rouse To Waking. They drifted through Nothing and all was calm, and all was quiet.

Then there was Existence, and with Existence came the universe, and life, and other gods: the Deathless, the Cythraul, the Faceless Ones, Gog Magog, the Sathariel, Acht'kawhl, Illom, the Arok, the Arok-Nar, the Rakhirrians and more of both scant and many numbers. But Those Who Slumber, Whose Names We Dare Not Speak Lest They Rouse To Waking were the strongest and most ruthless of all the gods, so the others banded together to destroy them in what we call the Scourge.

And when the First Gods fell, and the allies were weakened and wounded, the Faceless Ones took to them a slaughter called the Great Betrayal, which saw the survivors fleeing into darkness and obscurity, and the universe belonged to the Faceless Ones.

ACHT'KAWHL: Our knowledge of this race is limited.

AROK: Our knowledge of this race is limited.

AROK-NAR: Our knowledge of this race is limited.

CYTHRAUL: Our knowledge of this race is limited.

DEATHLESS: "And they sat in Judgement, and judged fairly, and they found the Balance in the Universe and watched over it."

GOG MAGOG: "There was one god without a race, a god alone, and he was called Gog Magog and he was named the God of the Apocalypse, and he was named Destruction."[1]

1. In an interesting side note, I may have found a further reference to Gog Magog. The *Great Book* mentions the God of the Apocalypse, also known as He Who Is Called Destruction, and details his – frankly annoying – habit of waiting until the other gods have built up a civilisation to worship them, and then coming in and destroying everything. He does this again and again until the gods group together and strip him of his power and cast him out of their cosmic pantheon.

It was this moment of co-operation, it seems, that made them believe they could band together to strike against Those Who Slumber, Whose Names We Dare Not Speak Lest They Rouse To Waking. This led directly to the Scourge and then, obviously, to the Faceless Ones slaughtering them all in the Great Betrayal. So, basically, Gog Magog continued to wreck everything even when he wasn't even around.

THE FACELESS ONES: See the *Book of Tears*.

ILLOM: Our knowledge of this race is limited.

RAKHIRRIAN: "Sixty-eight there were, of Demons and of Princes and Princesses, of Dukes and Commanders and Governesses, and they did follow their god, the Great and the Terrible Tunnrak Rakhir – the Pandemonia Daemonum."

SATHARIEL: Our knowledge of this race is limited.

A HISTORY

Across a Dark Plain

SKULDUGGERY: You just want to talk about what happened?

ARCHIVIST: We have precious little information about the Dead Men's[1] exploits during this part of the war. If you wouldn't mind...?

SKULDUGGERY: There isn't much to tell. It was 1861, and it looked like we were about to win the war. Mevolent was hurt, in hiding somewhere, and there was talk of a Truce and an Amnesty, and we had tracked Serpine from Wyoming to South Dakota. He had a Necromancer with him, name of Noche, who was leading him to a temple. There were zombies. We got Noche.

ARCHIVIST: But not Serpine.

SKULDUGGERY: No. We almost got him, but Solomon Wreath denied us the opportunity.

ARCHIVIST: Is that why you don't like Cleric Wreath?

SKULDUGGERY: That has a lot to do with it, yes.

1. A special operations team consisting of Skulduggery Pleasant, Ghastly Bespoke, Erskine Ravel, Anton Shudder, Hopeless, Saracen Rue and Dexter Vex. At various times, Larrikin Fetter substituted for both Hopeless and Ravel when their other commitments took them off the field. Larrikin later became a full-time Dead Man upon Hopeless's death.

The Horror Writers' Halloween Ball

VALKYRIE: You attended the last ever Horror Writers' Halloween Ball? I didn't know that.

SKULDUGGERY: Gordon's date had dropped out and I happened to be in between cases at the time – and I wasn't going to pass up the chance to be in a room full of horror writers.

VALKYRIE: Those were the parties hosted by Sebastian Fawkes, weren't they? What was he like?

SKULDUGGERY: Insufferable, but I wasn't surprised. Every single book he'd ever written was designed to make the reader care deeply about the characters on the page, just so he could kill them in increasingly cruel and heartless ways.

VALKYRIE: Isn't that what Gordon did?

SKULDUGGERY: Yes, but Gordon at least had the decency to enjoy it. A sorcerer – what is commonly known as an empathy vampire – had shown Fawkes how to siphon energy from the trauma he inflicted upon his readers.

VALKYRIE: Whatever happened to Sebastian Fawkes?

SKULDUGGERY: I don't know. I think he fell off a cliff.

He had a look the ladies
Would say did smoulder,
It's a pity he couldn't
Avoid that boulder.

The Age of the Maggot Part One

On 30 June 1908, an explosion flattened 80 million trees in 830 square miles of forest near the Podkamennaya Tunguska River in what is now Krasnoyarsk Krai, Russia. The occurrence is attributed to an asteroid impact – or air burst – five to ten kilometres above the Earth's surface. This is what mortals believe.

Voracious Kurakin of the Sanctuary in Moscow was sent to investigate. Skulduggery Pleasant, who was in Russia to follow up on reported sightings of Baron Vengeous and an unknown collaborator, accompanied Voracious to the scene on 1 July. They discovered what they described as a radial pattern of felled trees leading up to a distance of five kilometres from the centre, at which point the trees remained upright, but were scorched and devoid of branches.

The source of the explosion was a bare patch of blackened ground. There were strong – yet rapidly fading – traces of magic in the immediate area. And a pair of footprints in the soil.

The footprints were the only part of the ground that had not been scorched, indicating that someone had been standing there – and had remained upright – while the explosion occurred. Before the footprints was a piece of bone, 11.46 centimetres long, twisted into the shape of a hook.

Further examination of the Tunguska Bone (or Hooked Bone, as it also became known) revealed it to be from neither human nor animal – but rather to be fused from a form of exoskeleton. Neither Voracious nor Pleasant could identify where it came from, and Pleasant was soon called back to continue his pursuit of Baron Vengeous. Similarly, Voracious was reassigned to duties pertaining

Baron Vengeous

to the ongoing war with Mevolent, and the Tunguska event dropped quickly down their list of priorities.

A century passed.

Voracious, now a detective for the German Sanctuary, received a call from Hosanna Fortune, a sorcerer who had devoted her life to learning more about the various gods of the universe. She had recently come across the Tunguska report and claimed to be able to identify the Tunguska Bone.

When Voracious visited the following day, however, he found Hosanna Fortune dead and her office in disarray. It was at this moment that Voracious was attacked.

VORACIOUS: Monsters. Bipeds. Humanoid, but... Have you ever seen a larva, up close? With that pinched face? Ugly, man. Very ugly. Maggots, I call them. They came at me, shrieking, Hosanna Fortune's blood all over their claws. I couldn't get out of there, couldn't run, so I unleashed the Gist and let it do its thing.[1]

But when they were down, after I'd pulled the Gist back in, I heard more Maggots coming. I grabbed what I could off the desk and got the hell out of there. The next morning, I learned someone had burned down her office, so what I'd taken were the only things that remained of her work. I got so, so lucky.

1. The dark essence of a sorcerer, formed from their own fears and hatreds, that emerges from their torso as a twisted, screaming version of themselves. Attached to the body by a stream of light, to lose control of the Gist is to allow it to take over.

One of the items Voracious procured was Hosanna Fortune's notebook, its pages stuffed with scribbled notes. Included was an interview Fortune had conducted with an unnamed Sensitive who had experienced a vision of the event in Tunguska as it happened.

SENSITIVE: His name was Bemmon, the demon who was killed.
FORTUNE: Demon?
SENSITIVE: That's what they refer to themselves as, yeah.
FORTUNE: As in a demon from... hell?
SENSITIVE: As far as I know? Not hell. They're offspring, I guess, of a god called Tunnrak Rakhir, the head of the Order of the Maggot.[2]

2. See "The Order of the Maggot", page 107

FORTUNE: Tell me about your vision. What did you see?
SENSITIVE: I saw him – Bemmon. He was standing in a forest, talking with someone. Arguing. I couldn't see who he was with. Couldn't even hear their voice. But I could see Bemmon. He was a demon. A man with the head of a... I don't know. Not a fly, exactly, but close. He was strong. Powerful. Important. I mean, he was the Overseer of the Enduring Way. He was in charge of making sure evolution happens as it's supposed to happen. He wasn't used to feeling... threatened. Or scared.
FORTUNE: Is that how he was feeling?
SENSITIVE: He was feeling angry, and the anger was covering up the fear. Or maybe he didn't understand that it was actually fear he was feeling, so the only way he could think of it was as anger. I don't know. It's hard to figure out how he thought of normal human things. I've read stories of gods who came here and had children, and some of the children are demi-gods, and some are completely human, and some are monsters... But the children of Tunnrak Rakhir, they're different. They're demons. It's hard for me to process what they're processing, you know?

FORTUNE: I think so. Please continue.

SENSITIVE: The argument, or the discussion, or whatever it was, it came to an end and... and finally, I think, Bemmon recognised fear. It was too late to do anything about it, though. Far too late to run. He was killed. I don't know how – I didn't see that. All I saw was him dying. It was over in a heartbeat. One moment he was alive, the next he wasn't. But the release of energy as he died, this explosion of... I don't know. His soul, maybe? It burned everything. It flattened the forest. It scorched the very air itself. The only thing it didn't kill was the killer.

FORTUNE: And Bemmon? What became of his remains?

SENSITIVE: It was all... condensed, I guess is the word for it. The only thing left of him was a piece of bone, shaped like a question mark. Or a hook.

Skulduggery Pleasant

Gordon Edgley's eventual death was reported as a heart attack by the media. His funeral was attended by family, other writers and various celebrities. Skulduggery Pleasant was also in attendance, albeit in disguise.

VALKYRIE: Let's talk about this disguise.

SKULDUGGERY: What about it?

VALKYRIE: It was rubbish. A wig and sunglasses and a scarf? Seriously? You went out like that?

SKULDUGGERY: It was a very convincing wig.

VALKYRIE: It really wasn't.

SKULDUGGERY: Then it was a very convincing scarf. There is no way you could have looked at that scarf and thought to yourself that it was anything but a scarf. Do you know who knitted me that scarf? Grace Coolidge.

***VALKYRIE:** Who?*

***SKULDUGGERY:** Incredible woman who did sterling work for the Red Cross, helped Jewish refugees during World War Two and worked a lot with the deaf. And, of course, she knitted wonderful scarves.*

***VALKYRIE:** That's incredibly fascinating.*

***SKULDUGGERY:** You're being sarcastic, aren't you?*

***VALKYRIE:** Duh.*

Gordon's mansion, Grimwood House, was left to his niece Stephanie Edgley, who lived in the coastal town of Haggard with her parents, Desmond and Melissa. Stephanie also inherited Gordon's business and writing estate.

Desmond (Gordon's youngest brother) and Melissa received Edgley's French villa, and his other brother, Fergus, and Fergus's wife, Beryl, were left a boat, a car and a brooch. Fergus and Beryl's twin daughters, Carol and Crystal, were reportedly unhappy with this arrangement.

***VALKYRIE:** "Unhappy." Ha!*

According to testimony delivered to the Council of Elders, Stephanie was attacked while alone in Grimwood House late at night. Her attacker, whom we have since identified as Vindick Leather, demanded from the girl a key. He did not specify what this key would unlock, or indeed what kind of a key it was.

At this point, Skulduggery Pleasant made his presence known

by causing structural damage to the door.

In the ensuing struggle, Pleasant's disguise, such as it was, became dislodged. Vindick Leather was forced to flee, but by this stage Stephanie had already seen that Pleasant was not a flesh-and-blood man but was, in fact, a skeleton.

Stephanie proceeded to faint.

VALKYRIE: *I did not faint.*
SKULDUGGERY: *Yes, you did.*
VALKYRIE: *I did not.*
SKULDUGGERY: *You swooned and fainted and I caught you.*
VALKYRIE: *I didn't faint – I blacked out. There's a difference.*

Pleasant informed Stephanie of his theory – that her uncle had been murdered by the red right hand of Nefarian Serpine – and Stephanie promptly decided to assist in the investigation.

SKULDUGGERY: *"Assist." Ha.*

They discovered that Edgley had found evidence of the existence of the Sceptre of the Ancients, and that it was now sealed within the maze of caves underneath Grimwood House. The key that Vindick Leather had demanded, they realised, was the brooch that was now in the possession of Stephanie's aunt, Beryl.

Why did Edgley entrust the key to a woman he barely liked? Fault must be laid squarely on Edgley's own sense of the dramatic. As a writer of predominantly lurid pulp tales, he would invariably have found it entirely reasonable to hide the key with such a person, as it furthered both the "mystery" and the "journey", as proposed in the ridiculous riddle that was read out during the reading of the will.

Pleasant took Stephanie to meet China Sorrows, a woman of extraordinary grace and beauty, who offered Stephanie her help should she ever need it.

Mr Bliss travelled to Nefarian Serpine's castle, informing him that Clement Arden and Alexander Slake, Sanctuary operatives who had been assigned to watch Serpine, had been murdered. Serpine extended his condolences and denied any involvement.

Pleasant and Stephanie visited Bespoke Tailor's. The family of the owner, Ghastly Bespoke, had amassed an impressive collection of ancient books of artefacts, now housed in the Vault, in the Dublin Municipal Art Gallery. Bespoke, however, disapproved of Stephanie's involvement in a case so dangerous, and refused to allow them access. Pleasant decided to break into the Vault.

Mr Bliss approached Tanith Low and asked for her help. He explained that Serpine was about to break the Truce, and he needed Low on his side when that happened.

Pleasant marked Stephanie's mirror with the Ator sigil, and released her reflection,[1] allowing Stephanie to accompany Pleasant to the Sanctuary.

In the Repository, Pleasant showed her the *Book of Names,*[2] protected by the Will of the Elders.[3]

1. See "Reflection", page 216

2. Constructed by the Faceless Ones, containing the three names of every living sorcerer, and the two names of every living mortal.

3. A protective shield that fills a prospective thief with apathy the closer they get to the Book, ensuring that they give up before they reach it.

To get the Elders to move against Serpine, Pleasant needed to prove that he broke the Truce, and so he needed to prove that Serpine was actively searching for the Sceptre.

Pleasant and Stephanie slipped by patrolling vampires[1] and broke into the Vault. They activated the Echo Stone,[2] imprinted with the consciousness of a monk and scholar named Oisin. Oisin told them that the black crystal – what we now call the katahedral crystal – was forged into a weapon by the Faceless Ones, and that there was nothing that it could not turn to dust. The crystal reportedly sang whenever an enemy neared.

But, when a group of Ancients crept up and stole it, the crystal remained silent. The Ancients spent a year forging the Sceptre, of which the katahedral was the main part. Asked by Pleasant where he thought the Sceptre might be hidden, Oisin suggested that Gordon may have hidden it in a similar environment to which it was found.

Pleasant realised that the best place Gordon could have hidden it was in the caves below Grimwood House.

They travelled to Grimwood and searched the cellar, finding a lock that needed an unusual key. They were interrupted by Serpine and a group of Hollow Men, who abducted Pleasant and proceeded to torture him.[3]

1. See "Vampires", page 18

2. See "Echo Stone", page 102

3. Inflicting pain upon Skulduggery Pleasant is an easier prospect than one might imagine. His skeleton is held together by his life force – what could also be called his soul, his spirit or his consciousness. This life force can be detected by certain Sensitives on the visual spectrum, and appears as auras of varying colours.

His life force has formed a shell of integrity round his skeletal structure, allowing him to speak, whistle and even sigh. It also allows him to feel pain, though scholars still debate whether this is actual pain or merely the memory of it, as Pleasant has no nerve endings or pain receptors. It has been proposed that much of his ability to detect physical discomfort could be due to the so-called phantom limb phenomenon, which is the sensation that a missing limb is still attached. Consensus has been reached that the pain he feels is probably psychosomatic, but that any attempt to relieve him of this hindrance could, in fact, destabilise his entire sense of being – which might lead to total discombobulation.

Stephanie went straight to Miss Sorrows. Understandably concerned that the sudden rush to action could jeopardise her own plans, Miss Sorrows used Stephanie's given name to command her to stay in the building.

It was at this point that Stephanie decided on a taken name, in order to break free from Miss Sorrows's influence.

Because of her late uncle's insistence on calling her his "little Valkyrie", plus the repeated references to the phrase Raising Cain, Stephanie took the name Valkyrie Cain.

Cain went to Bespoke, who took her to the Sanctuary to petition the Elders. Meritorious finally decided to send a small team, comprising Bespoke, Tanith Low, two Cleavers and Cain herself. They stormed Serpine's castle and rescued Pleasant. One of the Cleavers was captured alive.

That Cleaver was later resurrected by Serpine using Necromancy and, from that day until years later, he would don the uniform of the White Cleaver.[4]

4. There have been both White Cleavers and Black Cleavers in Cleaver lore going back centuries, oftentimes used as a warning to new recruits. Further research suggests that these are more than mere legends, and would indicate a greater unknown force at work. Thus far, there has only been one recorded mention of a Red Cleaver.

CLEAVER

Pleasant worked out that the brooch Gordon had left for Beryl in his will was the key to the caves, and he talked Cain into stealing it from Beryl.

VALKYRIE: Whoa. Whoa there. I borrowed it. Didn't steal it.

SKULDUGGERY: Have you given it back?

VALKYRIE: It was destroyed.

SKULDUGGERY: You do realise that borrowing something without telling the owner and then never returning it is classified as stealing, yes?

VALKYRIE: Why are you fighting me on this?

While waiting for Pleasant to get to Haggard, Cain spoke to her father.

VALKYRIE: He said my great-granddad believed that the Edgley family were descended from a sorcerer called the Last of the Ancients. He used to tell all kinds of fantastic stories that my dad and Fergus learned to ignore, but Gordon never did.

Cain delivered the brooch-key to Pleasant and Bliss. It was Bliss's opinion that Serpine planned to use the Sceptre as a stepping stone to get what he wanted. Bliss then revealed that he was working with Serpine by pushing Skulduggery off the cliff and taking the key.

Serpine used the key to unlock the entrance to the caves in Grimwood House. Pleasant and Cain followed him down but, delayed as they were by various creatures, they failed to prevent Serpine from finding the Sceptre of the Ancients.

Pleasant attempted a silent approach, but the katahedral crystal started singing, alerting Serpine to his presence. Pleasant attacked, but Serpine healed himself and chased Pleasant and Cain from the caves. They were subsequently rescued by China Sorrows, demonstrating a courage that was matched only by her unnatural beauty.

Back in the Sanctuary, the Elders apologised for not taking Pleasant's concerns seriously. Only Elder Tome remained sceptical.

Pleasant, however, had noticed that while the katahedral had sung when he approached, it hadn't sung when Cain had neared – lending credence to the Edgley family legend. If Cain was, indeed, descended from the Last of the Ancients, then she was the gap in Serpine's defences that Pleasant needed.

Serpine recognised Pleasant as the real threat, and so he sent the White Cleaver to kill Cain, in an effort to force Pleasant into an emotional response that Serpine could predict – using the same methodology as when he killed him the first time.

Acting on information that Serpine had been spotted in a Dublin warehouse, Pleasant, Bespoke, Low and Cain searched the premises.

Now seemingly loyal only to Serpine, the White Cleaver attacked, proving himself a match for their combined might. To save himself from death, Bespoke called on the earth element, and turned to stone before he could be killed.

The others removed themselves from the situation.

VALKYRIE: I went to the beach, thinking heavier thoughts than any twelve-year-old should have to think, and my dad came over and started talking about Gordon and Fergus and his own dad and granddad. He told me his grandfather had told them stories when they were kids, about magic and sorcerers and stuff, and that the Edgleys were descended from a great sorcerer called the Last of the Ancients.

Using the Sceptre, Serpine killed Grand Mage Meritorious and Elder Crow, which weakened the Will of the Elders protective shield that surrounded the *Book of Names*.

With the aid of the traitorous Elder Tome, Serpine and the White Cleaver – and a small army of Hollow Men – invaded the Sanctuary. Now that he was no longer useful, Serpine killed Tome, which deactivated the final security measure around the Book.

Low took on the White Cleaver. The battle took them into the Sanctuary Gaol, a room of dangerous sorcerers, confined to cages that hung from the ceiling. Badly injured, Low managed to lock the White Cleaver out, before she collapsed from her injuries.

Before Serpine could read from the Book, Pleasant attacked him. The struggle, in which Cain received a broken leg, saw her glimpse her own column in the Book – but glimpse it too fleetingly to make out her True Name.

In a reversal that surprised nobody who knew him, Mr Bliss revealed that he had been working as a triple agent in an attempt to limit Serpine's hostile actions. His attempt to apprehend Serpine, unfortunately, came too late, and Serpine incapacitated him.

Serpine retrieved the Sceptre and proceeded to use it on Pleasant, who held the *Book of Names* before him as a shield. The Book, which had proven impervious to all damage before now, was turned to dust.

Furious, Serpine tried to kill Cain with his red right hand before Pleasant obliterated him with the fallen Sceptre – in the process destroying the katahedral crystal that powered it.

The Lost Art of World Domination

While closing in on Rancid Fines and the Crystal of the Saints, Skulduggery Pleasant stumbled into a trap laid by Scaramouch Van Dreg.

> *VALKYRIE: This was embarrassing. There are some bad guys you just don't want to face. Not because they're scary or powerful, but because they're cringe-inducing. I didn't know it at the time – I'd barely turned thirteen – but Scaramouch Van Dreg was one of those. The man wore a cape, for God's sake, and not in an ironic way, either.*

Van Dreg planned to drain the magic from sorcerers everywhere – making him the most powerful being in the world – with the aid of the Channard Box,[1] one of the Lost Artefacts.[2]

1. A small wooden box, protected by twenty-three spells by twenty-three sorcerers. Contains an insect that drains magic with a bite.

2. See *The Lost Artefacts* by Remy Sayce, published by Twelve Eyes Books.

Pleasant tricked him into opening the box. The insect flew out and Pleasant knelt on it. Cain's subsequent arrival led to Van Dreg's arrest.

Rancid Fines got away.

Playing With Fire

After ten months of continuing her training/apprenticeship/ partnership with Skulduggery Pleasant, Valkyrie Cain encountered Vaurien Scapegrace and successfully subdued him.

VALKYRIE: I can't believe I once viewed Scapegrace as an actual threat. I mean, he was always an idiot, but he's about as threatening as toast.

Thurid Guild, the new Grand Mage and sole member of the Council, had little time for Pleasant and Cain's escapades. He informed them that Baron Vengeous had been broken out of his Russian prison, and assigned them to the task of tracking him down.

Vengeous arrived in Ireland, and was soon joined by the vampire Dusk and the killer-for-hire Billy-Ray Sanguine, who was responsible for his escape from his cell. In the latter stages of the 300 Year War, Vengeous had been assigned the task of resurrecting the humanoid remains of a Faceless One. In order to achieve this, he combined those remains with body parts and organs from other creatures, forming a hybrid being, what he called the Grotesquery, that would be capable of bringing the Faceless Ones home.

China Sorrows, as wise as she was graceful, informed Pleasant and Cain that Vengeous had required only two more ingredients to successfully resurrect the creature. She knew that the first ingredient was Necromancer magic but, through no fault of her own, did not know what the second ingredient was.

But Vengeous didn't get a chance to collect those ingredients. Eighty years ago, he hid the Grotesquery in an undisclosed location

GROTESQUERY

mere days before Skulduggery Pleasant found and arrested him – and that is where the Grotesquery had lain ever since.

Pleasant knew that Vengeous had been searching for the armour[1] of Lord Vile, so that he could wield the Necromancy he needed. He did not know that Vengeous was now using Dusk's Infected to search a cave system where he believed Vile had abandoned his armour when he walked away from Mevolent's army.

1. Necromancy is too unstable a magic to wield without protection, so practitioners store their power in an object. Lord Vile stored his magic in the armour he wore.

The Grotesquery had the heart of a Cú na Gealaí Duibhe (in English, Hound of the Black Moon). The Hounds of the Black Moon were ruthless, savage creatures who were at their strongest during a lunar eclipse – and there was just such an eclipse in two days' time. If ever there was an ideal opportunity for Vengeous to bring the Grotesquery to life, it was now.

TANITH: I was in London while all this was going on, oblivious and preoccupied with tracking down Springheeled Jack. Odd individual. Nasty tendency to eat babies. Once I'd put the shackles on him and delivered him to the Sanctuary in London, I got a call, and took the next flight to Dublin.

Knowing that Pleasant's weakness was the people around him, Vengeous instructed Dusk to abduct Cain.

VALKYRIE: Insulting.

Dusk, along with two Infected, attempted to do just that. Pleasant's arrival forced him to retreat, but not before Dusk had accidentally dropped a syringe.

Upon taking this syringe to the magic-science facility located in what used to be the Hibernian Cinema – and operated by Professor Kenspeckle Grouse – the detectives discovered that it was what is commonly referred to as "vampire serum" – a mixture of wolfsbane, hemlock and various other herbs. The serum works to subdue the more bestial side of the vampire's nature.

VALKYRIE: I stopped by China's apartment to wait for Tanith to show up. We were chatting, talking about unimportant, everyday stuff – jewellery, vampires, the fact that China used to be a bad guy and worship the Faceless Ones – and then Baron Vengeous arrived.

Vengeous attempted to recruit China Sorrows to his side, knowing that her network of contacts and the quiet power she wielded would be a significant asset. China, as noble as she was beautiful, declined his offer, and when Dusk and Sanguine entered the apartment, violence ensued.

VALKYRIE: Violence definitely ensued.

In an effort to draw their attention away from the selfless Miss Sorrows, Cain made her presence known. Sanguine pursued her and she managed to take his straight razor, his signature weapon and item of great sentimental value. Tanith arrived and Sanguine was forced to leave with Vengeous and Dusk.

Cain went to Grimwood House to search for any books or notes her uncle may have had concerning the Grotesquery. Instead, she discovered a secret room that held an Echo Stone imprinted with Gordon's personality.

VALKYRIE: I don't think I have the words to explain to you how much that meant to me. To see Gordon, to talk to him... Yes, I know, it wasn't the real him, technically, but... it was enough. When he died, I didn't have a chance to say goodbye. Now I had a chance to say everything I'd ever wanted to say and ask everything I'd ever wanted to ask. Which, y'know, included a lot of stuff about monsters.

Gordon informed her that a Child of the Spider,[1] known as the Torment, might know where the Grotesquery was hidden.

1. See "Children of the Spider", page 115

SKULDUGGERY: Valkyrie was doing great work without me, I have to admit, and she hadn't got herself killed, which was a nice bonus.
ARCHIVIST: And what were you doing while all this was going on?
SKULDUGGERY: Not anything of note, I assure you – just a slight bit of breaking and entering and the mild theft of confidential documents.
ARCHIVIST: To what end?
SKULDUGGERY: The location of the prison in Russia that had held Vengeous was known only to a very few people – and somebody would have had to have leaked this information to Billy-Ray Sanguine. I suspected Grand Mage Guild, because of the years I had learned not to trust him, so I had a playful snoop around.

ARCHIVIST: Did you find any evidence of his involvement?

SKULDUGGERY: I'm sorry, those documents I stole were marked *confidential* for a reason.

In order to don Lord Vile's armour, Vengeous needed to wear specially treated garments underneath that would protect him from the Necromancer power within. It was Sanguine's job to procure these garments, which he did, without incident, mere hours before the armour was found.

With the Torment as their only lead, Pleasant and Cain questioned an associate of his that they already had in custody.

SCAPEGRACE: They threatened me. That's not allowed, surely? They said they were going to suck my brains out if I didn't lead them to the Torment. I need my brains. I use them for thinking.

Scapegrace led them to Roarhaven.

SKULDUGGERY: A friend of mine once described Roarhaven as a dark, suspicious town for dark, suspicious sorcerers.

Scapegrace had once owned a pub there, and had converted the basement into a living area for the Torment. He led the detectives into a back room, where a group of hostile mages congregated. Scapegrace goaded them into attacking.

SCAPEGRACE: They walked right into my trap. You know why? Because they underestimated me. No one should *ever* underestimate me!

VAURIEN SCAPEGRACE

Pleasant and Cain emerged triumphant.

SCAPEGRACE: They were probably right to underestimate me.

When they found the Torment he agreed to reveal the location of the Grotesquery – provided Pleasant kill Cain in front of him.

VALKYRIE: From the very first moment, the Torment didn't like me. This was a surprise because usually people adore me when they meet me, and they quickly grow to love me. It's because I'm a delight. Ask anyone. No, seriously, ask anyone. Apart from the people who don't like me, of course.
ARCHIVIST: Maybe explain why the Torment didn't like you.
VALKYRIE: Because he was a bad judge of character? Oh, also? He was a giant spider. Will you be explaining that bit? That he could turn into a giant spider?
ARCHIVIST: I think that will be made clear, yes.
VALKYRIE: That's important, though, in order to convey the full ickiness.
ARCHIVIST: But just to get it down on record—
VALKYRIE: Yeah, yeah, fine. Right, so, the Torment didn't like me because he said he could smell my blood, which is gross. I think he meant more, like, he could *sense* my blood. At least, I hope that's what he meant. Man, I'm hungry.
[Irrelevant discussion on sandwiches removed.]
VALKYRIE: He said that Faceless Ones and Ancients alike have this special kind of blood, and because, you know, I'm descended from the Last of the Ancients, he hated me. But we tricked him – because we're smart and he's a giant spider – by summoning my reflection. It was the reflection that Skulduggery shot and so the Torment, thinking the reflection was me, told Skulduggery where to find the Grotesquery. And all we had to do was put the reflection back into the mirror and boom! I could use it again with absolutely no side effects

or repercussions whatsoever! Though, later on, when the reflection returned to the mirror, I thought I sensed a kind of... resentment. But I put it down to my imagination.

The Torment revealed that the Grotesquery's remains were located at the ruins of Bancrook Castle.

Sanguine tunnelled into Springheeled Jack's jail cell in the London Sanctuary, and offered to free him if Jack agreed to kill someone that Sanguine needed killing. Jack – no fan of the Faceless Ones – would only participate if this murder had nothing to do with the Dark Gods. Sanguine assured him that it had not. This was a lie.

Sanguine then returned to Ireland in time to join Baron Vengeous as he recovered the Grotesquery's remains from Bancrook Castle. Pleasant and Cain attempted to take the Grotesquery for themselves. In the altercation that followed, however, Cain slashed Dusk's face with Sanguine's straight-razor – the scars from which never fade.

Vengeous escaped with the Grotesquery's remains, and Sanguine brought Cain to him at an abandoned church. Here, Sanguine told Cain that she wasn't a hostage – she was the missing ingredient.

VALKYRIE: I thought I was a hostage and that really annoyed me, because I hate being the hostage. It's insulting. Demeaning, even. But then Sanguine told me that I was the missing ingredient that Vengeous had been waiting for – and that annoyed me even more.

Vengeous donned Lord Vile's armour, and Sanguine cut Cain's right palm with his razor. Her blood mixed with the shadows that Vengeous was pouring into the Grotesquery.

VALKYRIE: Sanguine told me that blood with a certain type of power was required. Since they weren't likely to come across any fresh Faceless Ones' blood any time soon, the blood of someone descended from the Ancients would do just as well. That's what Vengeous had been missing eighty years earlier. Someone like me.

While this scene of amateur theatrics was ongoing, Pleasant had located the church. He enacted a ridiculous rescue mission that, somehow, worked.

SKULDUGGERY: Ridiculous, or genius? The line between the two has been scuffed many times over the years, mostly by me.

Cain escaped with Pleasant and, crucially, the remains of the Grotesquery. They took the remains of Kenspeckle Grouse – unaware that the resurrection process had been a success, and all that was needed for the Grotesquery to waken was time.

Knowing that they needed to get to the Grotesquery as quickly as possible, Sanguine and Vengeous – still in the Vile armour – interrogated Argus Dolent, who had fought under Vengeous's command during the war. Dolent told them about Professor Grouse before he exploded.

Various members of various Sanctuaries around the world were targeted by Vengeous's killers in an effort to delay their efforts to support the Irish Sanctuary. Before Springheeled Jack killed his target, he discovered that Sanguine had lied to him – that this was, in fact, to aid in the return of the Faceless Ones.

As Jack travelled to Ireland, the blood-and-shadow mix finally had its desired effect and the Grotesquery awoke. Tanith Low was injured in the ensuing violence, and Professor Grouse's assistants, Civet and Stentor, were killed, along with three Cleavers.

VALKYRIE: And then Vengeous arrived and took the Grotesquery away.

With nine hours until the lunar eclipse increased the Grotesquery's strength enough to allow it to open a portal to the Faceless Ones, Pleasant produced one of the files that he had stolen from Guild's office. The file detailed meetings the Grand Mage had taken with officials from the Russian Sanctuary.

SKULDUGGERY: Those meetings were about security matters, which would include the location of top-secret prisons. We knew that somebody had told Sanguine where Vengeous was being held, so in a spirit of playful banter, I accused Thurid Guild of being the traitor.

This resulted in Pleasant's immediate dismissal.

VALKYRIE: You are so, so clever.

Springheeled Jack caught up with Sanguine and made his displeasure at being lied to known – but when Sanguine departed, Jack's need to get his own back, as it were, remained unfulfilled.

Later that same day, Miss Sorrows was viciously attacked by Vengeous himself. Zephyr and Sev, whose honour it had undoubtedly been to serve as her bodyguards, were killed, and Miss Sorrows was cruelly abducted.

Pleasant and Cain visited noted Sensitive Finbar Wrong to retrieve an item that Pleasant had left with him for safekeeping – a so-called "spike bomb". While there, they became aware that Dusk was following them – or following Cain, to be more precise.

Pleasant seized upon the opportunity to draw Dusk into a trap, and encouraged Cain to attend the Edgley Family Reunion event being held that night at Haggard Golf Club. Once Dusk made himself known, Pleasant and Low would apprehend him and force him to give up the Grotesquery's location. Or that was the plan.

VALKYRIE: Because we all know that Skulduggery's plans always work out.

The plan didn't work out. Dusk had brought over a dozen of his Infected with him, and when Cain saw them approach the golf club she ran, drawing them away from the oblivious mortals.

VALKYRIE: And if that wasn't bad enough, the Torment had figured out that I wasn't dead, so he went after Skulduggery and Tanith.

TANITH: He vomited spiders. Did you know he could do that?
ARCHIVIST: I have read that they have the ability to—
TANITH: He vomited this blackness that became spiders and he commanded them, these big, fat, click-clacking *things*. And then? Then he turned into one. The Torment. He turned into a huge big spider, bigger than a car. Have you ever fought a spider bigger than a car?
ARCHIVIST: I can't say that I have.
TANITH: It. Was. Awesome.

Cain led the Infected off the end of the pier and let the saltwater take care of them. When she swam back to shore, however, Dusk was waiting for her.

VALKYRIE: He was really mad at me for giving him that scar. He definitely would've killed me if it wasn't for Springheeled Jack.

Sensing an opportunity to disrupt Vengeous's plan, Jack defended Cain and subdued Dusk, who was later taken into custody. Jack then told Cain that Vengeous was keeping the Grotesquery at the abandoned Clearwater Hospital. Satisfied now that he'd had his slice of revenge, Jack departed.

Pleasant, Cain, Low, Mr Bliss and several Cleavers travelled to Clearwater, where they overheard Sanguine talking on the phone to an unknown individual. It quickly became apparent that Sanguine's loyalties lay not with Vengeous, but with this mysterious employer who – they surmised – had also been behind Guild's rise to his position as Grand Mage.

The lunar eclipse was set to occur at ten minutes past midnight.

They attacked the Grotesquery. Despite its astonishing strength and resilience, it began to falter under the sustained assault. When Bliss called in the Cleavers, it faltered further.

VALKYRIE: I don't mind saying – I was feeling pretty confident at that point. Didn't last long.

Baron Vengeous appeared, still clad in Lord Vile's armour, carrying the unflappable Miss Sorrows with him.

He attacked, and quickly bested the assembled warriors. Pleasant, however, managed to get close enough to dismantle some of his armour, and finished the fight with a gunshot to the chest.

Wounded, Vengeous sought out the Grotesquery in his final moments – and the Grotesquery killed him.

The Torment arrived to finish the creature off, such was his hatred of the Faceless Ones, but the Grotesquery defeated him. It fell to Cain to stab the Grotesquery through its heart with Tanith Low's sword. As it died, it screamed.

VALKYRIE: We didn't know it right there and then, but that scream? It pretty much woke up the Faceless Ones and told them where we were. So... not cool.

Gold, Babies and the Brothers Muldoon

Three babies were abducted by goblins and ransomed back in exchange for gold.

According to the stories told about them, the Muldoons were once powerful sorcerers who, because of a family legend that they were descended from the Ancients, believed they should be ruling the world. After reports of the Muldoons attacking mortals, the Sanctuary sent a team after them. In the ensuing battle, they were turned into goblins.

VALKYRIE: OK, stop, wait. What?
SKULDUGGERY: You know this.

VALKYRIE: Yeah, but this was told to me by, amongst others, a corpse. I never really thought it was true. Is it true? Can people be turned into goblins?

SKULDUGGERY: No.

VALKYRIE: Then how did they turn into goblins?

SKULDUGGERY: They didn't. They were born goblins, but their memories were altered so that they thought they were people who had been turned into goblins.

VALKYRIE: Why? I mean, who altered their memories?

SKULDUGGERY: I don't know. Probably someone who didn't like them very much.

They spent the next few decades amassing a collection of gold – gold being the only thing that could turn them back into humans. Kidnapping and ransoming babies was the latest scheme in a long list of schemes to gather more of the precious metal.

VALKYRIE: So this part isn't true either, right? But if gold WASN'T gonna turn goblins into humans, what WOULD it have turned them into?

SKULDUGGERY: I don't know. Goblins with gold, presumably.

Pleasant and Cain rescued the three mortal babies and, when a double-cross was attempted, they apprehended the goblins. Only the goblin sister, Peg, was allowed to leave.

VALKYRIE: She was sweet. I liked her. She liked you.

SKULDUGGERY: Obviously.

The Slightly Ignominious End to The Legend of Black Annis

TANITH: There isn't really much to say about this. A creature called Black Annis lived in a ditch and ate people. She had blue skin and big fangs and if the sun hit her she'd turn to stone, so… pretty standard. There was some fighting and… and that's it.

Sorry. Don't know what else to say.

You want me to tell a joke, or something?

Beneath this dirt
Is our dear friend Clive,
Whose screams shall haunt us,
Since he was buried alive.

The Age of the Maggot Part Two

When Hosanna Fortune's office burned down, Voracious Kurakin got in touch with Skulduggery Pleasant, telling him about Fortune's death, the attack on Voracious himself, and the notebook he had managed to take from Fortune's desk – a notebook that turned out to be a fascinating study of the various gods[1] that had fled to Earth after the Great Betrayal.

1. The notebook also references "the Great Destroyer", which made me hopeful that I'd picked up the trail of Gog Magog, but it turned out to be the name some had given Abrogate Raze, a particularly disruptive sorcerer who was roaming through (what is now) the Middle East in the fourteenth century. Despite this error, I believe I may have inadvertently stumbled upon something extraordinary, and tasked a junior researcher with looking into Abrogate Raze (see "Abrogate Raze", page 146).

Pleasant and Valkyrie Cain travelled to Berlin to meet with Voracious and view the notebook.

VALKYRIE: We met in this huge, wide-open café that looked like a museum more than a coffee shop. Plenty of mortals around, basically. Voracious showed us the notebook, told us he wasn't even a quarter of the way through it. I wasn't surprised. The writing was so small, all this information just crammed on to every line, and bits of notes and scraps of paper were falling out of it... Anyway, that's when the Maggots attacked.

Security camera footage showed that the Maggots – six of them, the same species that had attacked Voracious – came through the fire exit and inflicted only superficial wounds on the mortal customers before focusing on the sorcerers.

SKULDUGGERY: They had an agenda. With all the shrieking and the hissing and the sheer ferocity of their attack, one could be forgiven for dismissing them as mindless creatures obeying simple instructions. But they came straight for us, their attack a mere distraction, until one of them could grab the notebook and leave. Once it was out, once it was in the clear, the others followed. There's an intelligence there. It would be a mistake to underestimate these things.

The area was cordoned off as per standard protocol, and Sanctuary operatives adjusted the memories of the mortal witnesses and wiped all footage from electronic devices. All traces of the creatures, however, vanished the moment they left the view of the security cameras.

VALKYRIE: We were stumped.

SKULDUGGERY: We were not stumped.

VALKYRIE: What would you call it? Baffled? Bewildered? Dumbfounded?

SKULDUGGERY: We were at a momentary loss.

VALKYRIE: We were befuddled.

SKULDUGGERY: Not all investigations go smoothly. Not every investigation proceeds from start to finish in an orderly fashion.

VALKYRIE: We didn't know what to do, basically, but we figured that killing a demon would be almost as difficult as killing a god, and, because the only thing that can kill a god is a God-Killer, we started looking for God-Killers.

In 1908, when Bemmon was killed, the Sceptre of the Ancients was still in the caves beneath Grimwood House, and the dagger and the sword were in private collections – which left the spear and bow.

SKULDUGGERY: I didn't know where the bow was, but I knew that the spear was in the possession of a mage called Crab, who lived in a cave by the Baltic Sea. So that was to be our first port of call.

The detectives travelled to Poland and met the famously reclusive mage on the beach.

VALKYRIE: Yeah, Crab was... I mean, he was a hermit, right? The hermit Crab. He lived in a cave, he had a really long beard, he didn't wear an awful lot of what might be considered clothes... But he said he didn't kill Bemmon, said he didn't even know who Bemmon was, and that he had no reason to kill anyone, and I believed him.
SKULDUGGERY: He told us he had sought out the spear because of a vision he'd had in his youth where the gods returned, and he wanted to be ready to fight them when they eventually showed up. He told us he'd already killed one monster the previous week and he was ready for more.
VALKYRIE: So we were, like... you killed a monster? Could we see it? And he was, like, cool, yeah, follow me. He took us back to his cave and the moment I stepped inside the stench of rotting flesh almost made me throw up.
SKULDUGGERY: There are times, as a detective, when not being able to smell anything is a hindrance. This was not one of those times.
VALKYRIE: The word I'm looking for is "festering". The festering corpse of a giant monster – must have been the size of an elephant – lay at the very back of this long, dark, ridiculously smelly cave.
SKULDUGGERY: From what we could ascertain, this creature shared distinct similarities with the Maggots that had attacked us in Berlin –

although this one was much bigger, it had an elongated body, and a lot more legs. It was something we started to call a Bull Maggot. Crab was waiting for it to rot enough so that he could move its remains off his bed.
VALKYRIE: "Writhing". That's the other word I'm looking for. It was writhing with maggots. Not the monster types, but tiny, ordinary maggots. It had been lying there for two weeks with great big open wounds and the flies had come in and laid their little eggs and... There was just this carpet of white, writhing, undulating... grossness. So that was bad enough. What happened next was way worse.
SKULDUGGERY: Then the flesh, this rotten flesh, started to move, and bulge, and it tore open and out came a stream of our good friends, the human-sized Maggots.

Pleasant described the ensuing battle as "intense", while Cain went into far too much extraneous detail concerning "grossness". The end result, however, after close to ten minutes of continuous engagement, was that Pleasant, Cain and Crab emerged relatively unscathed, and finally the Sanctuary authorities had bodies to study.[1]

1. Official report concerning the autopsies/origins/genealogies can be found in Addendum 18(b)7.

While the detectives were travelling back to Ireland, Voracious checked with the private owners of the sword and dagger God-Killers. Both admitted to having experienced "monster attacks" over the previous two weeks.

SKULDUGGERY: Which confirmed what we already suspected: that

someone was sending the Maggots after the God-Killers. Which told us that whoever was behind this was actually scared of these weapons – indicating that they were, in fact, a god themselves.
VALKYRIE: It also made us doubt whether a God-Killer was used to kill Bemmon. I mean, if you already have a God-Killer, why not use it to kill whoever has the other God-Killers, so you can expand your collection?

Because the Maggot attacks did not happen simultaneously, Pleasant theorised that there was one single person behind it all – someone who would have been present at each scene. In their examination of the security footage, the detectives managed to find and identify one such person – a former disciple of the Faceless Ones named Remember Me, long thought dead.

VALKYRIE: You're still annoyed about that, aren't you?

SKULDUGGERY: I don't know what you mean.

VALKYRIE: You think she stole your name.

SKULDUGGERY: My name is not Me.

VALKYRIE: It's the name you give mortals when they ask who you are. Chief Inspector Me. Captain Me. Agent Me. Honolulu Me.

SKULDUGGERY: It's just a silly pseudonym. She is well within her rights to call herself whatever she wants. Do you think I'm the only sorcerer who took Pleasant as a surname? Do you think you're the only Valkyrie?

VALKYRIE: I bloody better be.

SKULDUGGERY: My point is, she can be Me if she wants.

VALKYRIE: It makes no difference to you that she's Me? What about you? Are you going to keep being Me?

SKULDUGGERY: I'll be Me when the situation calls for it.
VALKYRIE: That's surprisingly mature. Well done.
SKULDUGGERY: Thank you.

A notice for Remember Me's arrest was circulated between Sanctuaries, and her trail immediately went cold.

The Faceless Ones

Due to a variety of technological/socio-economic reasons, the two centuries leading up to the early part of the twenty-first century saw a decline in Teleporter numbers. As such, there were only five registered Teleporters left in the world, and their skills were in high demand.

It was of great concern, therefore, when someone started to kill them all.

Despite the fact that Skulduggery Pleasant and Valkyrie Cain hadn't worked as Sanctuary detectives in approximately eighteen months, Mr Bliss called them in when a fourth Teleporter, Cameron Light, was murdered in his home. During their brief inspection of the crime scene, Pleasant and Cain concluded that a) Light had known his killer, and b) the killer had not used magic while committing the crime.

Emmett Peregrine, the "last" Teleporter, had been moving around for weeks, never staying in one place for long. He told them that the only new acquaintance he'd made in the recent past was Fletcher Renn, a seventeen-year-old natural-born Teleporter from England. Pleasant reasoned that Renn could be the killer's, or the killers', next victim.

Peregrine also mentioned the last time a Teleporter had been murdered was fifty years ago, when Trope Kessel's blood was found beside the Upper Lake, in Glendalough. His body was never recovered.

The detectives travelled to the Upper Lake, where they encountered the Sea Hag.[1]

1. Used to be a Maiden of the Water. It is unclear how she reached her current state of being.

VALKYRIE: *"Encountered the Sea Hag," it says here. "Encountered the Sea Hag." Like it was a friendly conversation we had over coffee, and not this gross fish-woman being grumpy with me for no reason.*

SKULDUGGERY: *Fish-woman?*

VALKYRIE: *Eel-woman, serpent-woman, whatever. The fact is: horrible creature, grumpy for no reason.*

SKULDUGGERY: *Well...*

VALKYRIE: *What?*

SKULDUGGERY: *You had insulted her bell.*

VALKYRIE: *How can you insult a bell? It was a summoning bell, so I thought it'd be bigger, that's all. More impressive. I didn't think it'd tinkle. I was expecting this massive, clanging, church bell kind of thing, and it turns out to be a teeny-tiny little bell that barely makes a sound.*

SKULDUGGERY: *You should never, ever, insult a Sea Hag's bell. That'd be like insulting a Sand Giant's pottery collection, or a Wood Nymph's ukulele. There are just some things you don't do.*

VALKYRIE: *Sand Giant? Wood Nymph? What?*

The Sea Hag was persuaded to let them speak to the corpse

of Trope Kessel, whom she had kept underwater since he'd been murdered. In exchange for their help in bringing his remains ashore, Kessel told the detectives that he had been killed by a man called Batu.

Kessel was a Teleporter whose passion was researching the mechanics of how the Faceless Ones had been exiled from this reality. During his research, he met and befriended a man named Batu, sharing with him the process one would go about to enable a Sensitive to pinpoint the possible location of a gateway that could be opened between this dimension and the dimension in which the Faceless Ones currently resided.

Kessel told them that two things were needed for such a gate to be opened – an Isthmus Anchor[2] and a Teleporter.

2. See "Isthmus Anchor", page 102

The Sea Hag proved resistant to the idea that Kessel's remains be buried in dry ground.

VALKYRIE: She tried to kill me.
SKULDUGGERY: She did.
VALKYRIE: Are there really Sand Giants?
SKULDUGGERY: We'll talk about this later.
VALKYRIE: What's a Wood Nymph?

The question remained, however: if this mysterious Batu person was responsible for the recent Teleporter murders, why was there a fifty-year gap between those killings and Kessel's?

Pleasant and Cain visited with the peerless China Sorrows, who had information about Fletcher Renn's whereabouts. The detectives travelled to the hotel Renn was staying at, encountering Billy-Ray Sanguine. Sanguine was there to recruit Renn for his employer – Batu. Renn chose to side with the detectives, and Sanguine was forced to retreat.

The detectives explained to Renn that Batu was after him so that he could open the gateway and allow the Faceless Ones to return. They eventually convinced him to go somewhere safe, and took him to Kenspeckle Grouse and his facility in the Hibernian Cinema.

Emmett Peregrine, the only registered Teleporter left alive, was put into protective custody under the care of Tanith Low. A phone call with Frightening Jones of the English Sanctuary revealed that the Irish Sanctuary knew she was protecting Peregrine in one of his apartments in London. At that moment, a gang of killers murdered Peregrine and attacked Tanith. Injured, she was forced to flee, with the killers in pursuit.

Pleasant and Cain visited Finbar Wrong. At Pleasant's request, Finbar went into a trance, following the lines of energy on a map to the point where they weakened due to pressure from the Faceless Ones on the other side. Finbar identified this spot as the location of the gateway: Aranmore Farm.

Solomon Wreath informed the detectives that their investigation covered some of the same ground as his investigation into the Diablerie.[1]

1. A group of Mevolent's sickest fanatics that China founded and led. When she left, Baron Vengeous took over. It's been 120 years since they were considered a threat, and 80 years since they were heard of last. Jaron Gallow, Gruesome Krav and Murder Rose reunited two years ago.

SOLOMON WREATH

He doubted Batu even existed, and believed Jaron Gallow to be the Diablerie's new leader.

VALKYRIE: I still didn't understand why Batu was killing the very people he needed, until I realised –

SKULDUGGERY: By which you mean, I explained it to you.

VALKYRIE: – that Batu needed someone powerful but inexperienced to open the gate – which is why Fletcher was perfect for the job.

SKULDUGGERY: He also couldn't afford to allow any of the older Teleporters to remain alive because they'd be able to close the gate without much effort.

VALKYRIE: The big question, though, the big and massive question that everyone still needs answered, is, you know... are Sand Giants a thing? And why do they collect pottery?

SKULDUGGERY: You're going to be obsessing about this, aren't you?

Despite the Necromancer policy to not involve themselves in Sanctuary affairs, Wreath pledged his support, and the support of three other Necromancers. Pleasant accepted that support by striking Wreath across the jaw.

SKULDUGGERY: I really didn't like him.

The detectives travelled to Aranmore Farm, where they encountered the elderly farmer who lived there, Paddy Hanratty.

It struck Pleasant that the Isthmus Anchor was probably the Grotesquery – this explained why there was a fifty-year gap between murders. Batu needed Vengeous to recover the Grotesquery.

But, while Bliss had destroyed the Grotesquery's internal organs and the parts that had been grafted on to the creature, its torso was from the human vessel that a Faceless One had occupied, and that was proving harder to destroy. It was currently being kept in the Sanctuary.

The Diablerie had tattooed themselves with sigils that Batu said would mark them out as true believers, and so protect them from the wrath of the Faceless Ones.

The detectives made their way to the Sanctuary, only to find the Repository – where the remains of the Grotesquery were being kept – was guarded by Cleavers. They released Vaurien Scapegrace from the holding cells, using him as a distraction.

SCAPEGRACE: They knew I was a threat. It's why they picked me. They knew the Cleavers would leave their posts in order to chase down the greatest killer who'd ever lived.

ARCHIVIST: And have you ever killed anyone, Mr Scapegrace? Mr Scapegrace? Did you hear what—

SCAPEGRACE: You don't get to define me.

ARCHIVIST: I'm sorry?

SCAPEGRACE: Only I get to define me. I am an artist. I use blood as my paint, and corpses as my canvas. I make messy art.

When the Cleavers gave chase, the detectives slipped into the Repository. The Grotesquery's remains were held in a cage protected by a death field.[1] Before the detectives could dismantle the field, Sanguine and Krav attacked them. In the course of the struggle, Sanguine was shot in the leg.

1. The state of death, or un-life, occupying a physical space.

SKULDUGGERY: Sanguine knew how to deactivate the death field – proof that the traitor inside the Sanctuary was helping him.

VALKYRIE: At the time, I wasn't entirely sure that you weren't just bitter because he'd known how to do something that you didn't.

SKULDUGGERY: You thought I was that arrogant?

VALKYRIE: I really did. (LAUGHTER)

SKULDUGGERY: But you've since changed your mind, yes?

VALKYRIE: Hmm?

SKULDUGGERY: You no longer believe that, yes?

VALKYRIE: I like your hat.

SKULDUGGERY: Thank you. It's new. The brim is slightly wider on account of the – wait. You're changing the subject.

VALKYRIE: Hats are nice.

Sanguine and Krav managed to escape with the remains, and Pleasant and Cain were forced to run from the Cleavers.

Stinging from his continuing failure to apprehend Pleasant and Cain, Remus Crux tried to force the radiant Miss Sorrows to use her network of spies to find them for him. He informed her that a Necromancer had told him a story about how Pleasant and his family had died – and included details of Miss Sorrows's involvement in those deaths.

Professor Grouse repaired Cain's broken tooth and, while in the Hibernian Cinema, they discovered that Ghastly Bespoke had emerged from his statue state.

Bespoke told Cain that his mother had been a Sensitive, and she had glimpsed a future where she saw Cain becoming Pleasant's partner.

VALKYRIE: Ghastly's mum said there was an enemy I had to fight, a "creature of darkness". Skulduggery was at my side for some of the battle, and she sensed that the world was on the edge of destruction. And then I died, apparently. So, like… there's that to look forward to.

Hanratty called Pleasant and told him he had spotted someone on his farm. When they arrived at Aranmore, they told Hanratty about the existence of magic and sorcerers.

VALKYRIE: He took it pretty well.

Preparing for the worst – the actual return of the Faceless Ones – Pleasant and Cain decided they needed to replace the (now inert) katahedral crystal in the Sceptre.

VALKYRIE: I went to Grimwood, activated the Echo Stone and asked my uncle. Gordon told me that the man who'd built Grimwood was a Conjuror named Anathem Mire who had disappeared during his last expedition into the caves below the house. He had left a map, though – to the vein of black crystals he'd discovered. It was Gordon's theory that, because of my Ancient heritage, the crystal wouldn't kill me on touch. That was enough for me, so off we went.

In a vast cavern within those caves, the detectives discovered a near-perfect copy of Grimwood House, conjured by the ghost of Anathem Mire, who haunted its rooms. Mire showed them the vein of katahedral crystals, out of which Cain was able to chisel a usable chunk. As they attempted to leave, though, Mire tried to keep her with him in his house, recognising a power within her. Cain escaped.

Guild led a team of Cleavers to the Hibernian Cinema, where he planned to take Fletcher Renn into custody. They were interrupted, however, by the arrival of the Diablerie, also there for Renn. When Renn couldn't be located, the Diablerie took Guild with them, demanding an exchange the following day at noon – Guild for Renn.

As gracious as she was exquisite, Miss Sorrows allowed the detectives access to the Sceptre. Cain replaced the katahedral crystal, and the Sceptre once again bonded to her.

Pleasant and Cain, along with Bespoke and Low, met up with Wreath, two other Necromancers, and the White Cleaver.

SKULDUGGERY: Because Serpine had used Necromancy to bring the Cleaver back to life, it was with the Necromancers that his loyalty lay. When he'd walked away from Serpine in the Sanctuary almost two and a half years earlier, that had been because the Necromancers were calling him home.
VALKYRIE: He still creeped me out, though.

A plan was made.

VALKYRIE: My folks were heading to Paris for their anniversary weekend, and I went home to see them off. So I was delighted to have Remus bloody Crux knock on my front door.

Crux believed that Pleasant was responsible for Guild's abduction – that he was, in fact, Batu, and that he was the mysterious leader of the Diablerie. According to the report he filed, he was able to arrest Valkyrie Cain without incident.

VALKYRIE: So he didn't bother including the part where he chased me across Haggard and assaulted a mortal? No? Oh, that's nice.

Crux, in a clear breach of protocol, had confined Cain to a cell already occupied by Vaurien Scapegrace.[1] Cain proceeded to batter him into unconsciousness.

1. Crux was suspended for two months after Grand Mage Guild found out about this. In my opinion, he should have been fired immediately.

Crux had the temerity to attempt to arrest Miss Sorrows, but was forced to jump out of a window by the arrival of Jaron Gallow. Gallow offered the Diablerie to Miss Sorrows to lead, claiming that, while Batu had many fine qualities, the true leader of the Diablerie was, and always would be, China Sorrows. Miss Sorrows declined to answer, and instead escaped.

The exchange on the Ha'penny Bridge took place, and Renn was taken by the Diablerie.

VALKYRIE: Who's writing this? No mention at all of the huge battle that was held there, a literal stone's throw from hundreds of mortals heading home after work? No mention of the Cloaking Spheres or the double-crosses or even the Sea Hag snatching Fletcher off the bridge? That's the stuff people want to read about! The fighting! The drama! The witty things people say when they're being punched! They don't care about boring things like who went where when!

SKULDUGGERY: I beg to differ.

VALKYRIE: Yeah? Well, have you noticed that he hasn't included any of the hilarious things you've said?

SKULDUGGERY: I'm assuming he's going to put all that in later. Maybe we should ask someone... Hello? Excuse me? (faint voices) I'm just wondering if I should approve the quotations you're going to be using.

ARCHIVIST: I'm sorry?

SKULDUGGERY: All the funny lines, the dry-yet-hilarious things I say that really set the tone.

ARCHIVIST: I'm not aware of any plans to include things you'd said on the day.

SKULDUGGERY: I'd like to speak with the publisher, please.

ARCHIVIST: I'll be sure to pass the message on.

SKULDUGGERY: Where are you going? Why are you walking away? I haven't finished complaining yet.

Deceiving Staven Weeper into releasing her from her cell, Cain and Scapegrace escaped into the Sanctuary, where they witnessed Bliss being led into a trap set by the Administrator.

VALKYRIE: She was the traitor, working for Batu the whole time. She'd told Sanguine where Vengeous's cell was. She'd told him how to deactivate the death field in order to steal the Grotesquery's remains.
SKULDUGGERY: I knew he'd cheated.

It was Cain's actions in that moment that saved Bliss's life, and within moments the Cleavers arrived and the Administrator died in her own ambush.

Cain met up with Pleasant, and they drove to Aranmore.

The battle was already underway by the time they arrived – Bespoke, Low, Bliss and the Necromancers, plus Paddy Hanratty –

against the Diablerie. Taking cover in the farmhouse, they returned fire and watched Renn being dumped into a circle beside the remains of the Grotesquery.

VALKYRIE: All this red and black smoke began to billow up round the circle. The gate was opening. Things were looking bad. Real bad. Thankfully, I'd just changed into a brand-new set of armoured clothes that Ghastly had made for me so, if I was gonna die, I knew I'd look cool doing it.

As an army of Hollow Men descended, Pleasant led the others out, taking the fight to the Diablerie. Cain stayed in the farmhouse with Hanratty.

VALKYRIE: He told me this sob story about whatever, asked me to wear his mother's wedding ring. I thought it was weird, but I've always liked old people, so I said sure, why not?

The farmhouse was close to being overrun by Hollow Men when the Cleavers arrived, along with Miss Sorrows and Mr Bliss. The tide seemed to be turning.

Tanith Low was injured, and retreated to the farmhouse.

VALKYRIE: Then Sanguine was there and I didn't know what else to do, so I grabbed Tanith's sword and, kinda, slashed him. Across the belly. It went deeper than I thought it would, and he got the hell out of there. And then, amazingly, things got even worse.

Three Faceless Ones emerged from the gate, causing shockwaves that threw all the combatants to the ground.

VALKYRIE: I couldn't think. The world went dull. I wasn't even outside at the time, and it still made my brain buzz. I can't even imagine what it would have been like to have seen them.

Renn managed to get himself away from the circle and, without his power to keep it open, the gate collapsed.

Gruesome Krav was the first vessel that the Faceless Ones took over. According to the reports of eyewitnesses, his hair fell out and his face melted away. Mr Bliss moved to try to put down the Faceless One – now in human form – but was killed with a gesture.

SKULDUGGERY: Our only chance now was the Sceptre.

Cain went to retrieve the weapon, and Hanratty attacked her. She tried to defend herself, using magic, but her magic was bound.

Patrick Hanratty was a mortal who came from a family of sorcerers, and who had always envied their power. As a young man, when Trope Kessel had told him about the gateway, he saw his chance to seize some for himself. He re-formed the Diablerie, guiding them with his vision.

VALKYRIE: He was Batu, see? He planned to offer himself up as a vessel to the Faceless Ones so that he could finally know what it was to have magic. That'll teach me to trust old people.

Realising that the ring he had given her was binding her power,

Cain threw it off and retaliated. Batu fled.

The Faceless One inhabiting Krav caught sight of Cain and seemed to forget about everyone else.

VALKYRIE: China figured it recognised me as being an Ancient, one of its old enemies. So it came for me. It ran.

Batu had buried the Sceptre in the ground and carried on, but Crux, who had seen the Faceless Ones and was now delirious, recovered the weapon. It passed from him to Miss Sorrows, and from Miss Sorrows to Cain – and Cain used it to destroy the Faceless One.

The second Faceless One found its vessel in Murder Rose, and it came for Cain. In the struggle that followed, the Faceless One was destroyed, but the Sceptre was damaged beyond repair.

SKULDUGGERY: And there was still one Faceless One out there.

Batu got his wish, and the Faceless One inhabited him.

Renn returned to the Grotesquery's remains and reopened the gateway. Throwing everything they had at it, they managed to drive the Faceless One towards the portal. Wreath was injured, but Cain used his cane to attack the Faceless One with shadows, and then Pleasant gave it the final push it needed before sending the remains of the Grotesquery in after it.

SKULDUGGERY: I had, perhaps, three seconds to enjoy that familiar sense of triumph before the Faceless One sent out a tentacle to grab my leg and drag me into the portal after it.

SKULDUGGERY: You must have been devastated.

VALKYRIE: I was mildly upset, but then Wreath told me that we could use your skull – your actual skull, the one that had been stolen by those goblin things years ago – as an Isthmus Anchor of our very own in order to get you back.

SKULDUGGERY: Still, though... The emotional trauma alone...

VALKYRIE: It really wasn't that bad.

SKULDUGGERY: You're so brave.

VALKYRIE: Oh, shut up.

Friday Night Fights

During her hunt for Skulduggery Pleasant's skull, Valkyrie Cain became trapped in an arena where mortals forced vampires and assorted creatures to fight each other. Cain was thrown in and forced to fight two vampires.

VALKYRIE: OK, wait, that's not strictly true.

ARCHIVIST: You weren't forced to fight two vampires?

VALKYRIE: I mean... yeah, OK, that is true, but earlier I'd befriended one of the vampires in the cells—

ARCHIVIST: Caelan.

VALKYRIE: Yeah, Caelan, so it was, really, like, the two of us against the other vampire.

ARCHIVIST: So Caelan didn't attack you or try to attack you at any stage? Valkyrie?

VALKYRIE: Right, no, he did, but then he helped me, so I suppose it evens out. Listen, the end result was that we escaped, and he helped set up a meeting with Thames Chabon, so… I don't know. The moral of the story is that it's good to help people.

ARCHIVIST: Not long after that, didn't he try to—?

VALKYRIE: It's good… to help people.

Dark Days

Eleven months had passed since Skulduggery Pleasant was dragged through the gateway.

SKULDUGGERY: It must have been awful for you.

VALKYRIE: It wasn't a fun eleven months, I'll admit that. I was spending too much time away from my family, which meant the reflection was spending too much time out of the mirror, which meant that its behaviour was just getting weirder and weirder.

SKULDUGGERY: I meant it must have been awful for you to be apart from me for so long.

VALKYRIE: Yeah, that was bad too.

In that time, Valkyrie Cain, Ghastly Bespoke, Tanith Low and Fletcher Renn had been working to locate the Murder Skull to act as an Isthmus Anchor.

VALKYRIE: Y'know the best part about this whole magic thing? It's the cool names that everything is given. I mean, the Murder Skull. How cool is that?

Dusk had been held in a Siberian prison – but Billy-Ray Sanguine broke him out of his cell. Due to a botched medical procedure intended to heal the injury he'd sustained at Aranmore Farm, Sanguine could only burrow in – and had to fight his way out. The Russian Sanctuary delayed alerting the other Sanctuaries around the world.

Two hundred years earlier, Mevolent had sent his top assassin, Dreylan Scarab, to kill Esryn Vanguard, an ex-soldier who was trying to find a peaceful resolution to the war between the sorcerers. Scarab assassinated Vanguard, but days later he was tracked down by Pleasant and Thurid Guild and jailed for two centuries, where his animosity towards Eachan Meritorious, Thurid Guild and Skulduggery Pleasant was allowed to fester.

Surveillance footage showed that, upon his release, he was picked up by his son, Billy-Ray Sanguine.

Cain met again with the vampire Caelan, who arranged a meeting with Thames Chabon. Caelan gave his assistance because of the fact that Cain had scarred Dusk, a vampire he loathed.

VALKYRIE: It was around this time that Remus Crux sneaked into my house and tried to kill me. After catching sight of the Faceless Ones, he'd started worshipping them and, because I'd killed two of his gods, his feelings towards me were not very friendly.

Solomon Wreath intervened, forcing Crux to flee.

SKULDUGGERY: *I still can't believe you were taking Necromancy lessons from that man.*

VALKYRIE: *I'm quite thankful that I was. He saved my life – and where were you?*

BILLY-RAY SANGUINE

SKULDUGGERY: I was being tortured in a—
VALKYRIE: Nowhere to be seen, that's where.

Scarab convinced Dusk to join their so-called Revengers' Club. They recruited Crux and Springheeled Jack, and also Vaurien Scapegrace.

Cain's meeting with Chabon did not yield the Murder Skull, as Chabon had already sold it. Davina Marr, the Sanctuary's new Prime Detective, and her subordinate, Pennant, had offered three times the asking price, and had delivered the skull into the possession of Thurid Guild.

VALKYRIE: We knew Guild wouldn't loan it to us, on account of that decree he'd issued that forbade the opening of the gate at Aranmore ever again. So we decided to steal it.
SKULDUGGERY: And how did that go?
VALKYRIE: Brilliantly.

They walked into a trap and were immediately arrested.

Marr offered Cain a plea deal: she and Renn would go free, so long as she implicated Bespoke, Low and China Sorrows in the plot to steal the Murder Skull and reopen the gateway. Cain refused.

Marr escorted Cain back to her cell. Although the security footage has been deleted, Cain later reported that Marr assaulted her. Cain fought back, reclaimed her Necromancer ring, and overpowered Marr. She took the Murder Skull from Guild's office, and Renn teleported them both to the safety, security and understated stylishness of Miss Sorrows's library.

Cain, Renn and Miss Sorrows teleported to Aranmore Farm, where Renn opened the gateway and Cain entered the world overrun by the Faceless Ones. While Miss Sorrows bravely held off Pennant and the squad of Cleavers, Cain found Pleasant.

> *VALKYRIE: At first, I thought you were dead. Properly dead, like. You weren't talking. You weren't moving. And then you shouted, "Boo!", right in my face.*
>
> *SKULDUGGERY: In my defence, I thought you were yet another hallucination. And also it was really funny.*

Once Cain had convinced him she was real, she led him back to the gate.

SKULDUGGERY: I'd spent eleven months being tortured by the Faceless Ones and their pets, which wasn't as bad as you'd think, but far worse than you'd imagine. They pulled me apart every day and I'd have to put myself back together again. It gave me a lot of time to think, to reconnect with who I was, to ponder the great mysteries of life and death. Also a huge amount of time to scream. I do remember screaming a lot. Screaming seems to be my overriding memory of that period.

I also taught myself how to fly. I didn't have anything else to do, once I'd accepted the fact that I couldn't escape and I couldn't fight, and the fine art of flying had been lost to Elementals for over a thousand years. Flying and hallucinating was how I spent the time that I wasn't screaming.

VALKYRIE: I had to convince him that I was real, and there was a gateway waiting to take him home, but first we had to get away from the Faceless Ones' pets.

SKULDUGGERY: I miss them, even now. They were my friends.

VALKYRIE: They hated you and tortured you.

SKULDUGGERY: It was a troubled friendship.

VALKYRIE: China came through the gateway to help us.

Upon their return to their own dimension, Pleasant continued to exhibit unusual behaviour. Discovering they were being watched by Staven Weeper, Pleasant responded with an unwarranted act of violence.

VALKYRIE: Well?
SKULDUGGERY: Well what?
VALKYRIE: You're not going to argue with that assessment?
SKULDUGGERY: You seem to have mistaken me for someone who doesn't admit when they've made a mistake. I happen to love admitting whenever I make a mistake, simply because it happens so rarely.

Pleasant requested that Weeper pass on to Guild a demand that Bespoke and Low should be released from custody, and then accompanied Cain to the Necromancer Temple, where Wreath told Cain of the Passage, when a Necromancer will emerge that is powerful enough to take on the title of Death Bringer. The Death Bringer will then break down the barriers between life and death, allowing the energy of the dead to live alongside the living, and allowing the living to evolve to meet it.

There were a handful of Necromancers who were thought to be the Death Bringer – the latest being Lord Vile.

There had been a recent break-in at the Temple, and a Soul Catcher had been stolen. Pleasant found evidence that the thief was Billy-Ray Sanguine.

It was at this point, we think, that Scapegrace was killed and brought back to life as a zombie.[1]

1. See "Zombie", page 18

Intrigued by reports of Sensitives around the world having visions of the same person, Pleasant and Cain visited Finbar Wrong, who took them to Cassandra Pharos. Projecting her psychic vision on to clouds of steam in her cellar, Pharos allowed the detectives to see what she had seen: a devastated city, still burning, and the battle that raged.

They saw future versions of Bespoke and Pleasant himself, and also Cain, aged approximately eighteen years old. She had a tattoo down her left arm and a black metal gauntlet on her right hand, and she was injured. Just before they saw the world end, they watched Cain's parents, Desmond and Melissa Edgley, burn in black flame – all the work of the mysterious sorcerer called Darquesse.

VALKYRIE: That's when the headaches started.

Cain was reminded of the fundamental rule concerning prophecies and visions of the future: the very fact that the future was seen is almost always enough to change that future.

VALKYRIE: That wasn't particularly reassuring at the time. I went home, feeling pretty depressed about absolutely everything, and then my folks told me their big news. Mum was pregnant. I was going to have a little brother or sister.
ARCHIVIST: That must have brightened your day.
VALKYRIE: I suppose. I don't know. I'll tell you what it did do – it gave me something new to fight for.

Scapegrace had been ordered to form a zombie horde, and so he began recruiting.

SCAPEGRACE: I renamed everyone I turned, starting with Thrasher, Dasher, Slasher, Crasher, Basher, Slicer, Dicer, Wrecker and Boiler. Then I got bored and started calling them Zombie One and Zombie Two, and then I got bored of that and just let them keep their names. It was around that time that I started sleeping in a giant freezer to stop my bits from falling off.

The detectives visited the Sanctuary, to find that it had been infiltrated by Dusk and an army of vampires. Footage of the assault is available to view, but is not advised. The contents are quite graphic.

VALKYRIE: There were dead sorcerers and dead Cleavers and dead vampires everywhere. The holding cells were still secure, though, so we freed Ghastly and Tanith, then went and saved Guild's life because we're nice people.

Marr reported that while the attack was ongoing, Dusk himself had gone to the Repository and stolen the Desolation Engine.[1]

1. A weapon of mass destruction designed and built by Kenspeckle Grouse as a theoretical experiment in his younger days. Capable of obliterating every living thing, building, tree and stone within a 200-square-metre radius, it resembled two glass containers held in a stone hourglass. When the liquid was green, the bomb was live. When the liquid turned red, the bomb was armed.

The bomb had been decommissioned and made safe.

VALKYRIE: I visited China, who was still recovering from her gunshot wound. She told me that Dreylan Scarab was Billy-Ray Sanguine's dad,

which explained a lot. She also told me about how Mevolent had sent Scarab to kill that pacifist guy, Esryn Vanguard, two hundred years earlier. But Skulduggery had some further thoughts about that, as it turned out.
SKULDUGGERY: It's true. I did.
VALKYRIE: He reckoned that it wasn't Mevolent who'd had Vanguard assassinated. He reckoned it was our side.

A full, unredacted report on the assassination of Esryn Vanguard is available in the Sanctuary Archives (Clearance Level Elder).

Esryn Vanguard believed the way to ensure peace was to allow Mevolent and his followers to worship the Faceless Ones undisturbed, and not try to curtail their religious practices.

Thoughts of peace, however, to a soldier in wartime were a dangerous distraction. Pleasant suspected that Meritorious assigned the task of eliminating this threat to the morale of the Sanctuaries to Thurid Guild and his Exigency Programme.[2]

2. Exigency Mages are highly trained operatives skilled in assassination and sabotage.

SKULDUGGERY: If my suspicions were correct, it meant that I imprisoned the wrong man. Scarab was still an assassin, and I have no doubt he deserved 200 years in a prison cell – but, for this particular crime, I came to believe that he was innocent. Which meant he wanted revenge – not just on me, or Guild, but on everyone.

The decision was made to track down Dusk, who would in turn lead them to the rest of the Revengers' Club. To do this, Caelan took Pleasant and Cain to speak with Moloch, the vampire lord of Ireland. Moloch, in turn, directed Cain to speak to one of the Infected, who was bitten by Dusk. All he could say was that there had been a "castle", and then Dusk himself appeared, tried to kill Valkyrie, and left before he could be apprehended. He had visited Moloch to recruit new Infected to his cause.

The detectives regrouped with the others at the Hibernian Cinema, but were too late to stop the Revengers' Club from abducting Professor Grouse. As they gave chase, Tanith Low was also snatched.

SKULDUGGERY: Events were accelerating at a decidedly unhelpful pace. We reasoned that they abducted Kenspeckle so that he could repair the Desolation Engine – but, in order to convince him to do that, they needed to put someone else in the driving seat. Or something else.
VALKYRIE: It's why they stole the Soul Catcher. They needed to transport a Remnant.[1]

In 1892, hundreds of Remnants possessed the people of a small Kerry town and burned it to the ground. The Sanctuary constructed a giant Soul Catcher – called the Receptacle – in the MacGillycuddy's Reeks (a mountain range in County Kerry) and dragged the Remnants out of the people. The Remnants were then transferred to the Midnight Hotel.[2]

1. A dark spirit, capable of controlling whoever it possesses.

2. See "Midnight Hotel", page 100

Pleasant and Cain travelled to the Midnight Hotel and encountered Sanguine, who had arrived with the Soul Catcher, intending to take one of the Remnants from Room 24. He threatened Shudder with a zombie horde, led by Scapegrace, until he realised the zombies had been eating human flesh, thus rendering them uncontrollable. The zombies attacked and, in the battle that followed, Sanguine trapped a Remnant and escaped.

Scarab released the Remnant from the Soul Catcher and it possessed Professor Grouse, who was presented with the Desolation Engine and all the spare parts he'd need to repair it. Once he had finished, he was given Tanith Low to torture.

The detectives visited an information broker named Myron Stray,[3] who was able to pass to them a piece of vital information – that there had been some recent activity reported in Serpine's old castle.

3. An information broker for the Sanctuary, whose true name – Laudigan – had been uncovered by Bliss during the 300 Year War and used against him.

Remus Crux had been spotted attending a ramshackle church run by Jajo Prave, on the outskirts of Dublin City. China paid a visit, encountering Crux outside. He once again threatened to reveal that Miss Sorrows had led Pleasant's family into the trap that killed them, which proved to be a monumental error in judgement, as Miss Sorrows was armed with a handgun. Her finger pulled the trigger and the bullet happened to find its way into Crux's chest, preventing him from living any longer. Miss Sorrows, who was obviously innocent of any crime, left the scene, probably due to the distress.

Pleasant and Cain, plus Bespoke and Shudder and Renn, searched Serpine's old castle. Battling Hollow Men along the way, they spoke briefly with Scarab and Sanguine before Detectives Marr and Pennant arrived with Cleaver reinforcements. The Revengers' Club escaped, but Low was rescued, Professor Grouse was apprehended, and the

Desolation Engine was recovered – and promptly confiscated by Marr.

Using Gordon Edgley's research (supplied by Cain), Miss Sorrows was able to drive the Remnant out of Professor Grouse, proving once again that beautiful people are wonderful at everything. They trapped it in the Soul Catcher, which was returned to Wreath, who had plans to study the Remnant before depositing it back in the Midnight Hotel. Despite having no memory of his actions when he had been possessed, Professor Grouse suggested the possibility that Scarab had not only made him repair the existing Desolation Engine, but had also got him to build a brand-new one.

Because Caelan had assisted the detectives, Moloch lifted his protection – meaning that Caelan was now fair game to other vampires. He turned to Cain for help, who arranged for him to stay at the Midnight Hotel.

In figuring out what Scarab's target might be, the Sanctuary was the first obvious choice. But, as an act of revenge, detonating the bomb in a public place – killing innocent mortals – would alert the world to the existence of magic and dismantle the very core idea behind the Sanctuary – to protect the mortal population from the destructive capabilities of sorcerers.

Skulduggery reckoned that Scarab would go for a densely populated environment, such as a sports arena.

VALKYRIE: Then it was obvious – Scarab was going to set off the bomb at the All-Ireland Championship, in the stadium at Croke Park. He was going to kill 82,000 people live on air.

Renn teleported Pleasant, Cain, Bespoke, Shudder and Thurid Guild to Croke Park. With Caelan joining them, they searched the stadium while the game played on.

SKULDUGGERY: When we found Scarab, he seemed pleased to see us. He made a good point about the other Sanctuaries around the world wanting to see us fail so they could swoop in and take over. Maybe that was true; maybe it wasn't. The only thing we cared about was getting our hands on the bomb.
VALKYRIE: That's not the only thing Dusk cared about, though. He wanted me. He wanted to drain my blood or turn me into a vampire, one or the other, just because I gave him a cool scar that time. Anyway, he bit me, then immediately backed off. Which was weird.

In all the confusion, Scarab himself took the bomb towards the pitch, but he had never intended to detonate it himself.

SKULDUGGERY: He'd had it designed to arm itself once it was in Guild's hands. Guild took it, felt triumphant for all of ten seconds, and then realised that the liquid had turned red.
VALKYRIE: Scarab wanted Guild to walk out in front of all those cameras and kill 82,000 people – and, if he didn't, Sanguine would kill Guild's family. Guild was going to do it too.
SKULDUGGERY: He was going to trade the lives of two people he loved for 82,000 people he didn't even know. He was going to trade his wife and child for the war between mortals and sorcerers that was sure to follow. I couldn't let him do it. I tried to stop him. But, in the end, it was Fletcher who saved us all. He grabbed him, teleported him to the middle of the ocean, dropped the bomb into the water, then teleported back before it exploded.

VALKYRIE: And I went to save Guild's wife and daughter. Sanguine had me, though. He could have killed me and there would've been nothing I could do about it. But he'd just been talking to Dusk, who told him that he'd sensed something in my blood when he'd bitten me. He told me I had some dark days ahead. Then he left.

Guild was sentenced to 289 years in prison for the assassination of Esryn Vanguard and the subsequent cover-up. Two days after the events at Croke Park, he was due to be transferred from the Sanctuary to prison. Davina Marr contacted the detectives, relaying the message that Guild had requested that they take him.

VALKYRIE: A happy ending! I love happy endings! The bad guys were stopped, the innocent people were saved, and nothing bad happened after that ever at all. Just don't read on.

At the same time as they took custody of the prisoner, Myron Stray entered the Sanctuary with the second Desolation Engine. Marr had used his true name to instruct him to set it off.

VALKYRIE: I told you not to read on.

Pleasant took Cain and Guild and flew, barely staying ahead of the explosion that destroyed the Sanctuary, killing twenty-one Cleavers and twenty-nine sorcerers – including Marr's own subordinate, Detective Pennant.

VALKYRIE: And that is definitely the end. Yep. Nothing more to add. What? What are you looking at?

SKULDUGGERY: Aren't you going to tell them about the dream whisperer?

VALKYRIE: I don't know what you... Oh, you mean that weird, creepy-looking thing that Cassandra gave me? Yeah, what a great present that turned out to be. Right, so, whoever's reading this – remember when we were fighting Serpine, back when I was just starting out, and I caught a glimpse of the **Book of Names?** *I saw my given name and my taken name, but I didn't really see my true name – at least, not consciously. But, after what Cassandra told us about this Darquesse person coming and killing my parents and then destroying the world, it dislodged that part of my subconscious that recorded what I didn't notice. So, yeah, it turns out I had seen my true name, and—*

SKULDUGGERY: She was Darquesse.

VALKYRIE: Seriously?

SKULDUGGERY: What?

VALKYRIE: That's my story.

SKULDUGGERY: You seemed hesitant.

VALKYRIE: I was obviously getting there, though. My hesitancy showed the reluctance I had to admit to... OK, we'll see how you like it. We'll see how you like your big moment ruined. That's cool. That's how we're playing this. Fine with me.

SKULDUGGERY: I'm sorry for spoiling your big moment.

VALKYRIE: Too late.

Darquesse

Myosotis Terra

VALKYRIE: Who?

THE MIDNIGHT HOTEL

The most well-known example of a Cursion Structure – a building that travels – the Midnight Hotel was built by Anton Shudder as a refuge from the bureaucracy of the Sanctuary system. A new hotel grows in a different location every twelve hours, instantly teleporting the occupants within while the old hotel wilts away to nothing.

HOW TO GROW A NEW HOTEL:

Seeds must be harvested from the bushes that grow at the base of the hotel. Once these seeds are planted in a new location and watered, the hotel sprouts and grows over a matter of minutes. The hotel occupants are instantly transported into it as they would in a normal growth cycle, although the first sprouting of a new hotel is a slower process, so they get to witness the somewhat jarring effects from the inside as it grows to full size.

THE THREE NAMES

Human beings are born with a True Name, a name hidden deep in their subconscious that acts as a conduit through which magic enters their system. For some, the magic they have access to is so slight it could barely be said to exist at all. For others, it is so strong that they become sorcerers.

The True Name, it is thought, expresses the true essence of a being, and so the knowledge of this name gives one complete control over one's own power. It has been proven that is no insignificant matter (see Argeddion, Darquesse, etc.).

Conversely, discovering the True Name of somebody else – before that individual has discovered it for themself – immediately limits that individual's potential for attaining mastery of their own magic. Furthermore, it puts that individual in permanent thrall to the one who now commands them, and dominates their will (see Myron Stray, etc.).

Mortals are presented with a Given Name – for instance, John Smith. This name, then, is accepted by the mortal as an expression of themself, and so it can be used – by sorcerers with the appropriate knowledge – to gain a low degree of mastery over that mortal, compelling them to obey small, simple commands.

Sorcerers – and mortals who wish to protect themselves from outside influence – adopt, therefore, a Taken Name. This relegates the individual's Given Name to a lower status, as it is no longer seen to act as an expression of the self. The Given Name can be whatever the individual wishes, and can be changed without limit from that moment on.

Children from magical families are generally prescribed temporary Given Names as placeholders until they are old enough to decide on a Taken Name (the average age to make such a decision is eleven years old). These temporary Given Names tend to be traditional names used and reused in each family.

ECHO STONE

A crystal, imprinted with a user's consciousness, capable of generating an interactive image. The user must keep the Stone close for three days and three nights in order to successfully complete the transfer. Some Stones, once imprinted, cannot be changed. Others can be wiped clean, ready for a new consciousness.

ISTHMUS ANCHOR

An object belonging to one reality, currently residing in another. Animate or inanimate. Magical or otherwise. Casts an Isthmus Stream, linking realities through dimensional portals.

THE SCEPTRE OF THE ANCIENTS

One of the most powerful God-Killers.

According to the *Book of Tears*, the Faceless Ones created a new type of mineral, resulting in black crystals – what we now call katahedral crystals – that they used both as a weapon against other gods (and themselves) and an alarm, to warn them when an enemy got too close.

The katahedral, however, did not warn the Faceless Ones when the Ancients approached. Whether this was due to some sort of immunity or merely to the fact that the Ancients were not viewed as a significant threat, remains unknown. The Ancients stole one of the katahedral crystals and forged it into a golden Sceptre.

When in their raw form, the katahedral crystals could be handled by both Faceless Ones and Ancients without incident (an act which would destroy any other god or mortal) – but once one was embedded in the Sceptre, its energy could be focused into black lightning, powerful enough to turn the Faceless Ones to dust.

SANCTUARIES

Inititally set up as a refuge for sorcerers fleeing Mevolent's wrath before the 300 Year War, the Sanctuaries became each country's independent government for magical affairs, presided over by a Grand Mage and two Elders – commonly known as the Council of Elders.

Each Sanctuary consists of a contingent of Cleavers and agents/operatives.

CLEAVERS

Specially trained warriors used as soldier, sentry, and law enforcer. Sorcerer children – usually those with lower-than-average levels of magic – can enter into the Crucible (the Cleaver training institute) from between eight to twelve years old (with some notable exceptions). Training lasts nine years. During that time, the self is broken down and subdued, and each trainee's magic is redirected to serve physical ends. Cleavers are therefore stronger, faster, and more agile than they would otherwise be.

Their uniforms are armoured against assaults, both physical and magical.

A Cleaver's career is short – they must "hang up the grey" at age thirty-two, at which point their personalities begin to reassert themselves.

Ex-Cleavers can struggle to acclimatise to civilian life. A high percentage become Rippers.

Further information on White Cleavers, Black Cleavers, and Red Cleavers strictly prohibited.

THE BOOK OF SHALGOTH

The *Book of Shalgoth* was one of dozens of grimoires that was destroyed by Mevolent hundreds of years ago, after they'd been studied by scholars. It told of where the Eye of Rhast had come from – but Oisin told them that its name had changed down through the years, and that it was sometimes known as the Crystal of the Saints.

The *Book of Shalgoth* contradicts the *Book of Tears*, which states that the Faceless Ones existed before the birth of the universe. The *Book of Shalgoth* claims that Those Who Slumber existed before the Big Bang, and that the Faceless Ones, and all the other races of gods, came after.

The gods went to war with each other until, a few survivors notwithstanding, only the Faceless Ones remained. The Faceless Ones found that Earth was to their liking, but when the Ancients rebelled, the Faceless Ones created a new species of monster – the Shalgoth – and sent them to punish the Ancients.

The Faceless Ones then sculpted lesser monsters out of clay and rock and meat – the Shalgoth Reth – and sent them forth to feed off magic of the Ancients – but once they'd been released the Faceless Ones ignored them, and so these lesser monsters retreated to the underground.

Rhast was the First of the Shalgoth. His eye had been cut out one night as he slept, and became a jewel of tremendous power, but despite this, Rhast was the strongest and the most cunning of his brethren. He watched the Faceless Ones abandon the Shalgoth Reth and he knew that once the Ancients were gone, his gods would abandon him and his brethren, also. So he led a rebellion against his masters, but that failed, and so he was imprisoned along with his fellows, deep within the Earth.

THE ORDER OF THE MAGGOT

The hierarchy of the Order of the Maggot is either based on the European courts of the time or, as is more likely, the European courts of the time were based on the Order of the Maggot:

- Tunnrak Rakhir (He Who is God): Supreme Lord of the Rakhirrian Empire, and founder of the Order of the Maggot
- Shevennu: Grand Collar of the Order, and Princess of Death
- Wutt: Grand Collar of the Order, and Prince of the Rot
- Byshio: Grand Cordon, and the Prince of Suffering
- Hallick: Grand Cross, and Chief Commander of the Armies of the Maggot
- Sunas: Grand Cross, and Governess of Souls
- Bemmon: Grand Cross, and Overseer of the Enduring Way
- Tarron: Chief of the Executors, the secret police

The maggot is seen as a symbol of regrowth. Maggots, or larvae, are hatched in the festering rot of the dead, and so new life springs from the remains of the old. The Order's role, as they see it, is to facilitate "advancements" in evolution, when evolution has stalled. They have been responsible for the existence of entire civilisations on other worlds, and claim responsibility for various "missing links" in the evolution of *homo sapiens*.

"The SPARROW flies south for winter"

A NOTE FROM THE ARCHIVIST

Hi there. I'm Archivist Rux, and I don't know what happened to the last guy.

Only yesterday, I was neck-deep in Necromancer history, just about coming to terms with who was who and what was what, and now I'm reassigned to a topic where I have no idea who anyone is. I walked into this damn room an hour ago and I was confronted with a table full of books, notes and transcripts. And it's a big table.

So apologies to all the future historians reading this and expecting more of Palaverous's professionalism, but it's just me here with my trusty audio recorder, so excuse if I ramble or backtrack or whatever. I'm sure somebody will be along, at some stage, to edit my transcripts. I mean, they have to, right? They're not going to just print what I say without checking it, are they? Here's an experiment: if you can read me saying "cantaloupe" right now, that means nobody has edited me, and this book was rushed into print without the proper checks!

Cantaloupe!

But that's not gonna happen. I'm pretty sure the Archive Department has standards. Although they did hire me, so... Anyway! Peace out!

Mortal Coil

First of all, I'd just like to say that my maths is awful. Numbers, to me, are like tiny little acrobats on a page — all jumping around, tumbling, doing backflips, standing on each other's shoulders, and sometimes disappearing completely until you get to the end and you think you're done and then they pop out and go "Hey there, you forgot about me!" The point is, I'm not good at maths, but I think I'm right in saying it was three months after Davina Marr had blown up the Sanctuary, and Skulduggery Pleasant and Valkyrie Cain were finally closing in on her.

They went to chat to Ephraim Tungsten, a master forger who could also set you up with a brand-new life anywhere in the world. And I mean *anywhere*. I had a friend once who needed to get out of the country due to, shall we say, a disagreement over the best way to dispose of an incriminating amount of—

Never mind. Anyway, according to the report I've got in my hand, they figured that Davina Marr, after being responsible for the destruction of the Sanctuary in Dublin, would want Ephraim's help in getting the hell outta Dodge, so they paid a visit to the place he was sharing with a few friends. They didn't find him, but they did find a house full of dead people, so yay. There was also one living witness, name of Ranajay. He told them that his friends had been killed by a large man in a metal mask, and the only reason he spared Ranajay's life was because he knew the safe house Tungsten had set up for Marr.

The guy in the metal mask was Tesseract, the Russian killer-for-hire. If you've never heard of him, that means you're doing something right with your life, so well done you! Tesseract is a scary, scary dude, and a bonebreaker (I don't know what the technical term for that is. Probably something in Latin), so he had the potential to cause our heroes quite a bit of bother. And, like, he *did*, so...

Where was I? Yes, yeah, the Marr thing. So our heroes got to the construction site beside the safe house just as Tesseract was about to finish Marr off. They rescued her and took her to the Hibernian Cinema, where Kenspeckle Grouse set about fixing her broken bones.

SKULDUGGERY: We couldn't bring her to the Sanctuary forces because they'd execute her on the spot.

VALKYRIE: And we figured her friends, whoever was really behind the destruction of the Sanctuary, had hired Tesseract to make sure Marr didn't divulge any names, so we didn't have time to waste.

You already know that Valkyrie recently discovered that she was Darquesse, right? She was the one all the Sensitives were seeing, the one who was going to kill Desmond and Melissa Edgley and then destroy the world? (If not, Major Spoiler Alert!) This, understandably I think, had freaked her out.

VALKYRIE: I needed someone to talk to, but I didn't want to tell anyone. I figured that somebody found out that my true name was Darquesse at some point in the future and would somehow use it against me, forcing me to do these awful things. I didn't even tell Skulduggery.

So she talked to the Echo Stone version of her uncle Gordon. Echo-Gordon (as I'll be calling him from now on) advised her to visit a banshee to find out how to seal her true name.

All right, so while all this was going on there was trouble brewing in the Necromancer Order. The Necromancers, under High Priest Auron Tenebrae, had been searching for the Death Bringer for years, and Solomon Wreath thought that Valkyrie might turn out to be the one they were looking for. Tenebrae decided that they should use the Remnant — the same Remnant that had possessed Kenspeckle Grouse — to possess Finbar Wrong, and use him to peek into the future to check if Valkyrie was a serious contender. This was a hilariously stupid idea, as once the Remnant possessed Finbar and saw the future, it realised the importance of Valkyrie becoming Darquesse and figured that Darquesse was, basically, the Remnants' very own messiah. So Remnant-Finbar escaped from Wreath and made his way to the Midnight Hotel, where it switched from Finbar to Shudder. While no one had ever been able to accurately count the Remnants trapped in Room 24, some conservative estimates put the number at 2,000. And Shudder released every last one of them.

Oh, remember when Dusk had bitten Valkyrie months earlier, and he'd tasted something special in her blood? Now Valkyrie was asking Caelan to have a taste, to see if he could explain things.

SKULDUGGERY: Anything you want to add to that?

VALKYRIE: Nope.

SKULDUGGERY: Nothing at all?

VALKYRIE: Nothing important, no. Nothing relevant.

SKULDUGGERY: You say that, but your face tells a different—

VALKYRIE: He kissed me.

SKULDUGGERY: The vampire kissed you?

VALKYRIE: Of course he did. That's what vampires do. They bite some people and they kiss other people, and sometimes the biting turns to kissing and sometimes the kissing turns to biting.

SKULDUGGERY: But you were asking him to bite you, not kiss you. Did he miss?

VALKYRIE: He didn't trust himself to bite me. He said he had a tendency to become... infatuated.

SKULDUGGERY: You mean obsessed.

VALKYRIE: Listen, he was a very hot vampire, and I suppose I was into bad boys, and it was all very confusing and there was a lot of poor judgement going on. Can we just move past this, please?

SKULDUGGERY: Weren't you dating Fletcher at the time?

VALKYRIE: Like I said, bad judgement.

SKULDUGGERY: I'm going to tell him you said that.

VALKYRIE: I was joking! Jeez!

It's around this time that Scapegrace discovered Skulduggery's house.

SCAPEGRACE: Is this on? Do I just speak into it? Then what happens? Do I have to transcribe it? OK, good. My spelling isn't the best. So, hello, listeners. My name is Vaurien, and when this all happened I was a zombie, and bits had started to fall off. I was worried that I would decay altogether, so I was researching methods of staying in one piece. I visited two funeral homes on Cemetery Road, concerning questions I had about the practicalities of being stuffed. As it turned out, neither funeral director took me seriously, even though my cover story was flawless and they didn't suspect a thing. But then I recognised Skulduggery Pleasant's car, and realised I'd stumbled across his home. I'd found where he relaxed, where he was vulnerable. I thought there were definitely people who would pay for information like that.

A meeting was called in the Great Chamber[1] in Dublin, to decide on the next Grand Mage.

1. Built in 1451, the Great Chamber is decorated with murals depicting events in history, such as the Ancients defending mortals from the Faceless Ones, the rise of the Warlocks, the arrival of the Unnamed, and the War of Splinters.

Gathered together with Sanctuary officials and operatives were the creepy-as-hell Children of the Spider — represented by Madame Mist and the Torment — the almost-as-creepy Necromancers, represented by Auron Tenebrae — and the not-creepy-but-kinda-dumb Four Elementals. Corrival Deuce was also there, but Corrival's cool, and so was Geoffrey Scrutinous and Philomena Random, and Erskine Ravel.

I mean, there were other people there, too, but I don't want to bombard you with names, you know?

The vote was taken, and Corrival Deuce was elected Grand Mage. He wasn't exactly jumping for joy at that prospect, but he nominated Ravel and Skulduggery as his fellow Elders on the Council. The Torment suggested that instead of building a new Sanctuary in Dublin, they should just use the one already built in Roarhaven. So that's what they did.

I've seen footage of a conversation outside the Great Chamber between Valkyrie and Melancholia St Clair, a twenty-year-old Necromancer. There's no audio, but it's pretty obvious Melancholia didn't like Valkyrie, and Valkyrie thought this was hilarious.

VALKYRIE: It was so much fun to annoy her.

I mention Melancholia because Craven wanted a Death Bringer that he could control, and so he started carving sigils into Melancholia's skin that would take the power she experienced during her upcoming Surge and loop it around, building up her magic. A clever process, but insanely painful.

Scapegrace was figuring that if anyone could help him with his decomposition problem, it would be Kenspeckle Grouse. Together with Thrasher, he arranged an auction of sorts in a sorcerer pub in Dublin, and promised the location of Skulduggery Pleasant's home in exchange for the location of Kenspeckle Grouse. The day went downhill, however, when Tesseract killed everyone there and forced Scapegrace to tell him where Skulduggery lived.

And wouldn't you know it? Marr had just been moved to Skulduggery's house for safekeeping. Skulduggery and Valkyrie were there to guard her, as were Ghastly, Tanith and Ravel. It didn't matter, though. Tesseract knocked the hell out of everyone and killed Marr.

SKULDUGGERY: The only bit of information we could get out of her before she died was that she couldn't actually remember the names or faces of the people she was working for. Whoever convinced her to destroy the Sanctuary had somehow erased themselves from her memory.

When Tesseract went to collect his fee for killing Marr, he learned that the Torment was displeased with the fact that a few Roarhaven citizens had died in the bar fight he'd started. One of Madame Mist's spiders bit him, and Tesseract was buried alive. The end, right?

Well, not quite. That cool mask of his saved him. The same fluids that kept the necrosis under control acted as a cure to most ailments and an antidote to most poisons. Tesseract dug himself out of the grave (which is pretty badass, you have to admit) and went after the Torment – but, when he confronted him, the old guy had Madame Mist with him, as well as her protégés, Portia and Syc. The Children of the Spider attacked, but Remnant-Shudder appeared on the scene. Mist and the Torment fled, and the Remnants possessed Portia, Syc and Tesseract himself.

Did I mention all this was happening in December? Damn it, sorry. Yeah, so, Valkyrie had got in touch with the banshee, and the banshee went off and arranged for the Dullahan[1] to swing by. On Christmas Day, the Dullahan brought Valkyrie to Doctor Nye.

1. Headless rider of the Coach-a-Bowers, the Dullahan collects those who have heard the cry of the banshee and delivers them to their fate.

Nye operated from a warehouse with a modified[1] death field, meaning that nothing living could stay alive. Nye, being a Crengarrion,[2] was the apparent exception, though I have to admit I'm not sure why. Crengas freak me out and I don't know a whole lot about them.

1. This death field was modified in such a way as to "suspend" life, so that you're dead when you go in, but you're alive once you leave. This was due to the Dullahan's expertise, according to a Necromancer friend of mine. The Dullahan, for this part, was unavailable for comment. Thank God.

2. For more information on Crengarrions (colloquially Crenga), read ***Creatures that Creep Me Out: A Study of the Freakiest Non-Humans*** by Norman Odd, published by Twelve Eyes Books.

It operated on her, and inscribed three sigils into her heart, which sealed her true name.

VALKYRIE: Nye did all this while I was conscious, by the way. I mean, yeah, I was in a dead state and I couldn't feel it, but I could see every single thing it was doing. It cut me open, cracked my – it basically gave me an autopsy. It took out my heart and started carving into it.

And then? Then it tried to keep me there because it wanted to experiment on me, the creepy daddy-longlegs weirdo.

ARCHIVIST: But you escaped.

VALKYRIE: But I escaped. I hallucinated big time, forced Nye to put my heart back where it belonged and stitch me up, and then I got out of there. When I was back in the land of the living, I told Skulduggery what I'd done, and told him about the whole Darquesse thing. He took it very well. Too well, actually. I didn't even think to wonder why.

Following up on information that Scapegrace had been the one to tell Tesseract where Skulduggery lived, the detectives tracked down the zombies but, instead of putting a bullet in their squishy-squashy brains, they felt sorry for them, and took them to Kenspeckle. The professor was curious to see if he could return them to full life, and took them on as an interesting experiment.

VALKYRIE: And then I went dancing. There was this nightclub, right by the water, and they were having this under-eighteen Christmas dance kind of thing. Fletcher came by, picked me up, met my parents – a proper date. It started out so well.

Skulduggery, meanwhile, was having a quiet night in with Ghastly and Ravel until Corrival Deuce, Solomon Wreath and Anton Shudder — all possessed by Remnants — attacked them. Ravel was taken, and Skulduggery and Ghastly escaped.

VALKYRIE: That's when the Remnants swarmed the nightclub. I was having a perfectly nice conversation with a bunch of lovely girls in the toilets, and the next moment they're all possessed and calling me Darquesse, telling me they love me, they worship me, telling me they're going to help me kill the world. I ran. Everyone in that place was taken over by Remnants. I was fighting a cop outside when – yay – Carol and Crystal saw me. Fletcher teleported us all away but, well, it was too late. They'd seen me use magic.

Over the next few hours, the Remnants sought out and possessed sorcerers and mortals in positions of power.

Skulduggery and Valkyrie met Ghastly, Tanith, Fletcher and China at the Hibernian Cinema. The last time the Remnants had been loose, the Receptacle had been used to drag them from the bodies of their hosts and trap them. Seeing no reason why this wouldn't work a second time, Valkyrie and Tanith went to St Peter's Church to recover the piece of the key that would activate the Receptacle. Ghastly was dispatched to drive Fletcher to MacGillycuddy's Reeks, while Echo-Gordon taught him everything he'd learned about teleporting from the research he'd conducted while writing *Into Thin Air*. Skulduggery and China went to Burgundy Dalrymple to recover the second part of the key.

Valkyrie and Tanith broke into St Peter's Church and beat up a priest. They found the first half of the key, then beat up an old woman.

Skulduggery and China engaged Burgundy Dalrymple in a swordfight in which they did their very best to cheat. Despite being forced to play (relatively) fair, they emerged triumphant and retrieved the second half of the key, then picked up Valkyrie and Tanith. The key now complete, they returned to the Hibernian Cinema – moments before the Remnants surrounded the building.

VALKYRIE: But that was the plan, you see. They'd surround us, come in after us and, when all the Remnants were inside the building, I'd use my Necromancer ring to link everyone with shadows. Once everyone was connected, Fletcher would teleport the lot of us to MacGillycuddy's Reeks. It was a risky plan, but it was the only one we had.

GHASTLY BESPOKE
1
2
3
14
15
16
17
18
19
20
21

SKULDUGGERY: So of course it went wrong.

A Remnant possessed Fletcher. Another possessed Clarabelle and, using her, killed Kenspeckle.

VALKYRIE: That hit hard. You get used to people dying in this game, but usually it's people you barely know or you don't like. When it's someone you like, someone you depend on... it reminds you how close we all are to death.

Billy-Ray Sanguine – hired by Roarhaven mages to aid in the struggle against the Remnant threat – arrived to help Valkyrie, and they joined Skulduggery, Ghastly, Tanith and China in Ghastly's van. With their Teleporter now working against them, they decided to drive to the Receptacle.

They spent the night avoiding road blocks and evading pursuers, all the time making their way closer to MacGillycuddy's Reeks. Before they got there, China revealed that she had been taken over by a Remnant, and allowed Ghastly to be taken next. Together, they grabbed Valkyrie and left the others behind – but, in the struggle, Sanguine managed to steal the key from China.

Burgundy Dalrymple arrived to try and get possessed again, and they followed him to the hidden door to the Receptacle. They passed through, into a cavern, where the Receptacle lay.

SKULDUGGERY: We used the key. Then the Receptacle started warming up. It hadn't been used in over a hundred years – it stood to reason it would be a tad sluggish.

Valkyrie was brought before the gathered Remnants, and one slid down her throat.

VALKYRIE: It tried to possess me but, in doing so, it put me in danger. And the part of me that was Darquesse couldn't allow that, so... yeah. Out she came.

The other Remnants professed their adoration and Darquesse, being Darquesse, proceeded to kick their brains out of their heads. Literally. Like, I heard she actually did that to one guy. She killed a whole bunch of them before Skulduggery managed to convince her to burn out the Remnant inside her and allow Valkyrie to come back.

SKULDUGGERY: And then I threatened to kill her.
VALKYRIE: Oh, that's right, you did.
SKULDUGGERY: Did you forget about that part?
VALKYRIE: Amazingly, yeah.

Threatening to kill the Remnants' messiah forced the Remnants out of their hosts as the Receptacle became active. It dragged them all into the mountain, trapping them in the huge globe.

Every one of them, except for the Remnant that latched on to Tanith.

VALKYRIE: Yeah. What a happy ending, eh? We stop the Remnants, save the two thousand people, manage to fool the world into thinking that all these weird events were down to a virus... and we lose Tanith.
SKULDUGGERY: We almost lost a lot more than Tanith. While we were busy

with this, the international Sanctuaries were getting ready to come in and take over. We'd regained control just in time.
VALKYRIE: So we had our new Sanctuary, which was cold and grey and depressing, waiting for us in Roarhaven, and we had our new Council.

Corrival Deuce had been killed in all the chaos, so Erskine Ravel became Grand Mage in his place. In order to bring the Roarhaven mages onside, he accepted Madame Mist as one of his Elders, and Ghastly Bespoke reluctantly agreed to become the other.

VALKYRIE: And, just when you think it's over, Tesseract tracks down the Torment for the earlier double-cross, and kills him. And then Tesseract himself is killed by Lord Vile, who everyone thought was dead. And what does he want to do? What is Lord Vile's primary goal after spending, like, two hundred and seventy-five years being dead? He wants to kill all Necromancers, starting with the Death Bringer, who everyone thought would be me. Because of course he does.

The Wonderful Adventures of Geoffrey Scrutinous

VALKYRIE: Have you met Geoffrey? Has he come in here to record his commentary?
ARCHIVIST: I don't think he's scheduled to come in, no. We're on a horrendously tight deadline, so we can only bring in the main players, as it were.
VALKYRIE: That's a shame. You'd have liked him, I think. You share a similar style.
ARCHIVIST: So he rocked the sandals too? That's cool. I've always said you can tell a lot about a man who's willing to show you his toes.

VALKYRIE: What happened to the last guy, by the way? Palaverous?

ARCHIVIST: Ah – they won't actually tell me, if you can believe that. He just stopped coming in one day. I know it doesn't look it – especially compared to what you do – but this job is pretty intense. Lot of pressure, lot of stress. Some people just can't handle it.

VALKYRIE: Well, I hope you last longer! ***(laughter)***

ARCHIVIST: Thank you! Now, what were we saying? You were talking about Geoffrey...

VALKYRIE: Oh, I was just gonna say he's the lovliest guy. He's convinced so many people that they didn't see what they actually saw over the years. It's because of mages like him that magic's still a secret, you know?

ARCHIVIST: And this case in particular...?

VALKYRIE: Oh – cursed pen. Shark. That's pretty much it.

ARCHIVIST: I like stories with sharks.

VALKYRIE: I didn't see it. Only he could see it. All I saw was him seeing the shark that I couldn't see.

ARCHIVIST: Oh, well... OK then! Let's get Skulduggery back in and we can move on to the next report.

Just Another Friday Night

SKULDUGGERY: Sorry, I had to take that.

ARCHIVIST: Totally fine. Some calls are too important to miss, right?

SKULDUGGERY: Indeed, Mr Rux, indeed. Now then, we were talking about Geoffrey...?

VALKYRIE: We've moved on.

SKULDUGGERY: We have? To what?

VALKYRIE: Remember Hayley Skirmish and Tane Aiavao?

SKULDUGGERY: Ah, the Doherty zombies and the pit where you fell into that pile of guts.

VALKYRIE: I was washing my hair for a week.

ARCHIVIST: Actually, I was hoping we could move on to the Death Bringer report, if you wouldn't mind?

SKULDUGGERY: Not at all, Mr Rux. We are here to share our insight, after all.

VALKYRIE: Do you have anyone else coming in to talk about this one?

ARCHIVIST: I do, actually – Kenny Dunne is dropping by.

VALKYRIE: Ah, Kenny. Will we be doing the commentating together?

ARCHIVIST: Afraid not. The editors will be splicing all the commentaries together when we're done.

VALKYRIE: That's a pity.

SKULDUGGERY: Tell him Detective Inspector Me says hello. He'll know what you mean.

Death Bringer

DUNNE: You're not going to make me forget again, are you? You swear? Because it didn't work the last time. Or the time before that. I can't remember if it worked the time before that, though, so... Well, my name's Kenny Dunne and I'm a journalist. I specialised in the weirder side of life, and I'd arranged an interview with Paul Lynch, who I'd heard was some sort of genuine psychic. He'd had all these visions of the apocalypse happening in seven days, the so-called Passage. I didn't take it seriously, of course, but when I arrived he was dead. His throat had been cut.

I was interviewed by a Detective Inspector Me, who I later discovered was Skulduggery Pleasant, and his teenage assistant, who I later discovered was Valkyrie Cain. I told them the only other person Paul had talked to about his visions was this sweet little old lady, Bernadette Maguire.

VALKYRIE: My little sister, Alice, was three months old, so I was at her christening when Fletcher arrived and told me Skulduggery had found Bernadette's cottage. We teleported over, but we were too late. Bernadette was already dead. Whatever Paul Lynch had seen in his vision, whatever he'd told Bernadette... it was big enough to get killed over. We saw her murderer running off, but he left behind the Jitter Girls[1] to keep us busy.

We didn't know how to beat them. We were in deep, deep trouble. They, uh, they put their hands through my head and came very close to killing me. And because of that... out came Darquesse.

1. The Bailey triplets, warped by an unknown trans-dimensional entity. Skulduggery Pleasant and Alabaster Crawl trapped them in a thrice-charmed box after they returned from death.

SKULDUGGERY: Using extreme violence, Darquesse persuaded the Jitter Girls to return to their box and, using words, I persuaded Darquesse to allow Valkyrie to regain control of her own body. I managed, for a second time, to get through to her. I think she respected me. There was a bond there. An understanding. A kinship. She saw something in me that she responded to, a certain darkness maybe, an affinity for—
VALKYRIE: She looked at you like a pet.
SKULDUGGERY: Or she looked at me like a pet, whatever.

There are a lot of reports here concerning the Necromancers, and that's great, but most of it is pretty dull. There are notes taken at meetings, details of protocol and rules and things that I'm not too interested in. It does lead to some interesting events later on, though, so it's not a complete waste, but I won't be boring you, dear reader, with any of the non-essential stuff. The only thing you should know at this stage is that the Necromancer dudes were pretty convinced that Valkyrie was going to be the Death Bringer. All apart from Vandameer Craven, who sounds extraordinarily punchable. In secret, he'd carved all these sigils into the skin of Melancholia St Clair to make *her* the Death Bringer. She was experiencing her Surge, and the sigils kept that Surge going on a loop. This built up her power to a huge degree but, from what I've read, it meant she was in constant agony for days at a time. I don't think Craven cared.

From what I've been able to piece together, it was around this time that China Sorrows visited the Church of the Faceless Ones to meet up with Eliza Scorn. Eliza had learned about China's part in the death of Skulduggery's family and had come to, basically, blackmail her. A little bit after this, China told Skulduggery and Valkyrie that the Necromancers had found their Death Bringer in Melancholia.

(China Sorrows declined to be interviewed for this edition.)

(Oh, you'll notice that I'm not exactly fawning over China Sorrows like Archivist Palaverous did. I mean, China's beautiful and everything, but I kinda get the impression that Palaverous, for all his professionalism, had a *teensy-tiny* little crush on our favourite librarian, wouldn't you say?)

Skulduggery and Valkyrie had a meeting with the Elders in the Roarhaven Sanctuary, which had its own Administrator — Tipstaff — and, at least initially, an emphasis on the proper way of doing things. Because Erskine Ravel was Grand Mage and Ghastly Bespoke was an Elder, our heroes were given the necessary resources to find out what they needed to know about the Passage. The other Elder, the extraordinarily creepy Madame Mist, wasn't particularly fond of the Necromancers, so she didn't exactly object.

One thing you've got to remember about the state of the Sanctuaries is that no one was happy. Most of the international Sanctuaries — with the exception of Africa and Australia — were concerned about the constant threats coming out of Ireland for the past few years. They were also preparing to deal with Darquesse, whenever she decided to show up. Even the Irish Sanctuary was preoccupied at the time, and so not enough attention was given to the onrushing problem that was the Passage. Nobody really cared about what the Necromancers were up to — nobody except Skulduggery and Valkyrie.

The detectives spoke to Solomon Wreath at the Necromancer Temple in Dublin. Continuing the policy of not explaining what the Passage actually was, he did, however, tell them the name of the killer they were after – a Necromancer they frequently used for "black ops" missions, Bison Dragonclaw.

VALKYRIE: Bison Dragonclaw.

SKULDUGGERY: Bison Dragonclaw.

VALKYRIE: The thing is, right, if you're a dumb teenager and you take a dumb name, you don't have to be stuck with it for the rest of your life. You can change it at any point. So the fact that Bison Dragonclaw the adult still thought Bison Dragonclaw was a good name is all the proof you need to know that Bison Dragonclaw was an idiot.

SKULDUGGERY: Also, it doesn't matter how often you say Bison Dragonclaw, the name doesn't get any better.

They encountered Dragonclaw (yeah, that name really does not grow on you) and chased him out of the Temple, into the streets, where they were intercepted by a Warlock.

Following a brief struggle, the Warlock self-destructed.

VALKYRIE: First the Jitter Girls, then a Warlock... Dragonclaw really didn't want us to find out what Paul Lynch had seen.

Valkyrie returned home and was set upon by Melancholia.

VALKYRIE: I was nearly killed that night. Melancholia St Clair turned up at my house and shadow-walked me away, where she attacked me. If I hadn't been able to call Fletcher, I'd be dead right now.

Records at the time show that Doctor Nye had recently become the Sanctuary's Head of Medicine, appointed by Madame Mist, as Valkyrie discovered when Fletcher teleported her in for treatment.

VALKYRIE: That caused a bit of a stir, I have to say. Ghastly stormed off to argue with Ravel, who told him Nye had been punished for its war crimes and repented, and its search for the soul might even turn out to be useful in the future. Ghastly wasn't happy, but...
SKULDUGGERY: No one was happy – but there was no denying that Nye was an excellent surgeon. It saved Valkyrie's life that day.
VALKYRIE: Coming close to death like that, it makes you value the important things. I started thinking about my family, and then I started thinking about Skulduggery's family, and I asked him why he abandoned his family crest, and he said it was because he hadn't lived up to the high standards set by his parents, brothers and sisters.
SKULDUGGERY: I fail to see what that conversation has to do with the events we're here to discuss.
VALKYRIE: Oh, I just wanted to point out the fact that I specifically asked you about your family and you said it didn't matter because they were all dead.
SKULDUGGERY: And they were. Can we get back to the task at hand?
VALKYRIE: Sure.

Vaurien Scapegrace and Thrasher sought out Nye to try to get it to return them to life. They hooked up with Clarabelle, who was looking for a job. Nye found the idea amusing, and hired her, but sent the zombies away. They stayed at Scapegrace's old pub while they figured out their next move.

Ever since the Faceless Ones had come through the gateway on Aranmore Farm, Jaron Gallow – ex-leader of the Diablerie – had been a changed man. Recognising them for the horrors they were, Gallow turned away from the Dark Gods, and looked for ways to ensure that they stayed out of our reality. He recognised the threat that Eliza Scorn posed, with her plan to spread the Church of the Faceless around the world once more, so he approached China Sorrows and they came up with a plan of their own. At the upcoming Requiem Ball, Scorn was due to meet twelve powerful sorcerers who could help get the Church back on to its feet. China needed those twelve names so that she could have them killed, and watch the Church crumble.

Skulduggery led the Sanctuary forces that laid siege to the Necromancer Temple. Internal security footage showed Melancholia experimenting with the so-called "death bubble", a personal, more localised version of the death field.

Necromancer reinforcements flew in from London, and Bison Dragonclaw and his stupid name was sent to bring them straight to the Temple. Valkyrie managed to get them apprehended at the airport, and Skulduggery forced Dragonclaw to agree to show them a secret way into the Temple. They sneaked in, and split up.

SKULDUGGERY: This turned out to be a bad idea, as we were both captured soon after. We did, however, learn from our mistake, and since that moment we have never split up again.
VALKYRIE: We split up yesterday to search that spooky house in Galway.
SKULDUGGERY: Fine. We're always splitting up. For one thing, it saves time

and for another, if someone has gone to the trouble of laying a trap, I like to know what kind of trap it is and if it would really have trapped me if I hadn't known about it.

VALKYRIE: So you walk straight into it?

SKULDUGGERY: How else are you going to find out if it would have worked?

Valkyrie encountered Solomon Wreath first, who finally explained what the Passage was.

According to Necromancer beliefs, when we die, our souls become energy that joins the stream of life and death. It's a pretty nifty concept when you think about it. The stream flows from this reality into another, and from that reality into another, and then it loops back and flows through this one again, where our souls are once more born into human bodies. Isn't that nice? Kinda reassuring to think that you'll be constantly reborn. Of course, our memories and personalities die each time we do, so you're not gonna remember any of it. That's not necessarily a bad thing, though. I went to a Billy Joel concert once. I can't wait till I forget about that one.

The point was, Necromancers weren't worshippers of death, like some people imagined — instead, they feared death so much that they sought to control it. A sudden, massive influx of souls would dam up the stream. No more births. No more deaths. Everyone alive would stay alive forever. They just needed a way to kill three billion people in one moment — which is why they needed the Death Bringer. Spreading the death field around the world would kill roughly half of the planet's population (as it was at the time).

VALKYRIE: I mean, up until this point, I was seriously considering Necromancy as the discipline for me, y'know? After this, I had a change of heart.

Now in shackles, Valkyrie and Skulduggery were visited by High Priest Auron Tenebrae.

VALKYRIE: Tell them.
SKULDUGGERY: I don't think they're interested.
VALKYRIE: Tell them.
SKULDUGGERY: Fine. Tenebrae told Valkyrie that he had been the one to train Nefarian Serpine in the Necromancer technique that would eventually kill me. Knowing that I was Serpine's primary target, he added a little something to enable me to return in this form, if I had enough hate in my soul. Obviously, I did. I came back, I fought on, I grew increasingly angry, increasingly lost, and one day the hate proved so strong that I found myself at a Necromancer temple and—
VALKYRIE: He's Lord Vile!
SKULDUGGERY: Wow.
VALKYRIE: There! How do you like it when your big moment is stolen by someone else? Not cool, is it?
SKULDUGGERY: Did that make you happy?
VALKYRIE: Deliriously.

I totally get that, as an Archivist, I'm supposed to be cool and detached and everything, but *Skulduggery Pleasant was Lord Vile*? I mean, *seriously*? How many people knew this? Did everyone know it and nobody bothered to tell me? I know people who know people who were *killed* by Lord Vile! He was the ultimate bad guy, and Skulduggery's the ultimate good guy!

LORD VILE

How does something like this even *happen*?

OK, deeeeeeeeep breath. Let's be professional.

(Ohmygodohmygodohmygod.)

The Lord Vile that was on the loose at this time — the same Lord Vile that killed Tesseract — was actually the armour, and it was powered by Skulduggery's subconscious. Which is, let's face it, a little weird, but not any weirder than any other part of this.

According to Melancholia's statements, High Priest Tenebrae visited her soon after this point, where he discovered Craven's manipulations.

MELANCHOLIA: He said I wasn't the Death Bringer, so I killed him. What? It seemed like a reasonable response at the time.

Melancholia was messed up. I kinda dig that.

Skulduggery and Valkyrie escaped from their shackles and found the corridors of the Temple littered with dead Necromancers — most of them killed by Melancholia's death bubble.

VALKYRIE: She wanted an energy boost. So she drained the lives of thirty-eight people and then came after us.

Their lives were saved when Lord Vile's armour flowed out from within Skulduggery's skeleton (how cool is that?), where it had been hiding. It did enough to drive Melancholia off, and then it shadow-walked away.

VALKYRIE: This was quite a traumatic day for me, I don't mind telling you. To find out that your best friend used to be one of the uber-bad guys? See, now I realised why he was so cool with me telling him I was Darquesse.

SKULDUGGERY: Because I'd gone through the same thing. I had tasted the darkness.

VALKYRIE: You'd "tasted the darkness", had you?

SKULDUGGERY: I'm allowed to have some poetry in my life, Valkyrie.

VALKYRIE: "Tasted the darkness", I swear to God... What, did you have a darkness sandwich, or was it a whole plate? What did you have for dessert? Was it pretentiousness? Did you have a bowl of pretentiousness for dessert?

SKULDUGGERY: I used to be happier before I met you.

VALKYRIE: Lies.

Upon returning home, Valkyrie learned that her mother had been mugged earlier that day. The attacker, James Gavin Moore, was being held in the local police station. Valkyrie made her way inside without being detected, and attacked Moore in his cell.

VALKYRIE: I hit him a few times, told him to never come back, and I got out of there and then... then Caelan arrived. He made sure I got home OK. He did a little more of his weird vampire obsessive thing, and I went to bed. All I wanted to do was put that day behind me. Of course, the next day wasn't much better. Fletcher was being a good boyfriend and I was too messed up to appreciate it so I told him I'd been seeing Caelan behind his back and that we were breaking up. It was a horrible thing to do.

Then the twins were asking me to teach them magic, and Fergus arrived and

sent them away and basically told me that he'd always known about magic and how dangerous it was and how it damaged people and how he didn't want me teaching his daughters and... I don't know. It was a lot to take in. I went to Grimwood House and talked to Gordon about all of it – about Fergus, about Skulduggery keeping this massive secret from me – and he helped put it in perspective.
SKULDUGGERY: And I was instantly forgiven because I'm so lovely and everybody adores me.
VALKYRIE: Whatever.

Melancholia, Craven, Wreath and the surviving Necromancers regrouped in a closed-down retirement home, Willow Hill. Craven blamed Vile for Tenebrae's murder, and appointed himself the new High Priest, with the White Cleaver as his bodyguard.

VALKYRIE: That's when Wreath arrived at the realisation that Craven and Melancholia were both too unstable, so he came to us and told us where they were.

Sanctuary forces mounted an assault on Willow Hill. During the battle, Craven accidentally killed Melancholia.

VALKYRIE: His shadows, like, chopped her in half. It was not cool.

Craven, the White Cleaver and seventeen other Necromancers shadow-walked away, taking Melancholia's body with them.

And, just in case Valkyrie thought all the drama was over, Moore had been released from jail, and he immediately went to Valkyrie's home to pay her back for attacking him.

VALKYRIE: He took me by surprise, stunned me, but I had a secret weapon – I had another me. I let the reflection out and it finished him off. And then it suggested that we should kill him – which is when I started to suspect that something had gone seriously wrong.

SCAPEGRACE: I'd just reopened my pub, but I was having a customer-flow issue that I couldn't seem to resolve, most likely caused by Thrasher, whom nobody liked. High Priest Craven came to me and kind of told me that he was my master and, as a Necromancer, he was. So, when he ordered me to recruit twenty zombies, take them into the caves underneath Grimwood House, and make our way to the secret door into the cellar, I didn't have a choice. I had to obey. Really, none of what followed can be blamed on me.

The Requiem Ball[1] was hosted by Echo-Gordon at Grimwood House. Guests included Dexter Vex, Arthur Dagan and Hansard Kray.

1. A celebration that has been held every ten years since the end of the 300 Year War.

VALKYRIE: I wore a dress. There was dancing. Not, like, my kind of dancing, but the old-fashioned kind of dancing. Even so, it was cool. I was introduced to a load of people.
SKULDUGGERY: Like Arthur Dagan, who threw up in your hair.
VALKYRIE: Only a little bit. And I met his son, Hansard Kray, who didn't throw up in my hair and, I think, actually kinda fancied me a bit.

China was due to meet Gallow at the ball so he could pass

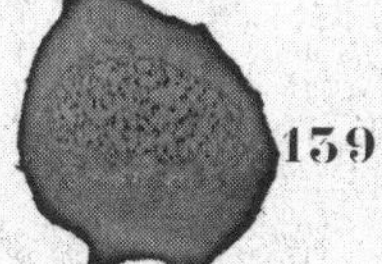

over the list of the twelve Faceless Ones' supporters, but found him dead by Eliza Scorn's hand.

The Necromancers, however, weren't finished with the Passage just yet. It wasn't Melancholia who had been killed at Willow Hill, but her reflection, who had been whisked away before anyone got the chance to spot the fake.

Now the Necromancers crept into Grimwood House, congregating in the cellar. All Melancholia had to do to be strong enough to implement the Passage was drain the life from the 300 people attending the ball. The death bubble expanded around her, enveloped the sorcerers above, and then retracted, taking their lives with it.

Valkyrie and Skulduggery, who were fortunate not to be there at the time, tracked the Necromancers into the caves, where Melancholia bested Skulduggery easily.

SKULDUGGERY: Easily? I take issue with that. I wouldn't say she bested me "easily".
VALKYRIE: She didn't even have to touch you. She drained your life and you fell apart. I'm the one who was fighting her. And then Vile's armour joined in.
SKULDUGGERY: So, in a way, I was by your side the entire—
VALKYRIE: You weren't anything. You were a pile of bones on the ground. I fooled her into releasing the life she'd taken from you. I put you back together—
SKULDUGGERY: And then I shot Craven in the head.
VALKYRIE: Oh, well done, you. And what was the next thing you did? Can you remember? Oh yeah – you joined up with your armour, you became Lord Vile again, and the White Cleaver and I had to drag Melancholia deeper into the caves to avoid getting killed by you.

SKULDUGGERY: I seem to remember something about that, yes.
VALKYRIE: Scapegrace had lost all but one of his zombies to the creatures who lived down there, and when he saw us he charged and the White Cleaver cut his head off. He did manage to tell us how to get out of the caves, though, so finally a bit of luck. Luck for us, of course, not for Scapegrace, who'd had his head cut off. Then Thrasher ran off with it. The head, I mean. Kind of a weird moment all round. Anyway, then Vile caught up with us and tore the White Cleaver apart and we got the hell out of there.

Valkyrie and Melancholia emerged from the caves, into the countryside.

VALKYRIE: And I figured the only person strong enough to stop Vile was Darquesse. So I got Melancholia to drain my life force, because I knew Darquesse would take over once my life was threatened. And I was right.

The battle that followed resulted in extensive damage to buildings and roads in central Dublin.

SKULDUGGERY: Even as Vile, I could see that Darquesse was only getting stronger with each moment that passed. This realisation allowed me to regain control and remove Vile's armour. I was confident that once I no longer posed a threat to her, Darquesse would relinquish control as well. She did, and Valkyrie re-emerged.
VALKYRIE: Let's just say, that was a very risky move.

All security footage of the battle was erased, as were the memories of any who witnessed it.

VALKYRIE: A few days later, Eliza bloody Scorn beats the hell out of China, and tells us that it had been the Diablerie who'd abducted Skulduggery's wife and child, way back when. China had gone after his wife herself.
SKULDUGGERY: I knew China was, technically, an enemy back then, but I had no idea she'd been involved in any way in my family's death.
VALKYRIE: We walked away. Didn't look back.

But the drama wasn't over. Caelan didn't respond well to Valkyrie breaking up with him, and proved to be the ultimate jilted boyfriend. He attacked her. Fletcher arrived to help and the situation escalated, resulting in Valkyrie drowning Caelan in saltwater. No less than he deserved, the whiney little psycho.

DUNNE: I saw the whole thing. I saw this one kid with fangs, for God's sake, and this other kid, the one with the ridiculous hair, appearing and disappearing all over the place. I got it all recorded too. I had plans. Big plans. Books and TV specials and... I was going to tell the world about Valkyrie Cain.

The End of the World

VALKYRIE: This was a sad one.
SKULDUGGERY: Very sad.
VALKYRIE: Most cases we're on, we beat up the bad guys and make jokes. But this... this one broke my heart a little.
SKULDUGGERY: It was very emotional.

VALKYRIE: I even cried a bit.

SKULDUGGERY: I didn't.

VALKYRIE: But you were still really sad, right?

SKULDUGGERY: Tremendously.

ARCHIVIST: Maybe if you tell me a bit about what happened...?

SKULDUGGERY: There was a machine—

VALKYRIE: A Doomsday Machine.

SKULDUGGERY: —and a group of unsavoury characters wanted to use it to destroy the world.

VALKYRIE: Vincent Foe, Mercy Charient, a guy called Obloquy, and Samuel, a vampire. They were working with a Sensitive called Deacon Maybury –

SKULDUGGERY: Who specialised in implanting false memories and false personalities in the minds of irredeemable criminals.

VALKYRIE: – only Deacon planned to betray them. The machine was activated by a key, and he was gonna sell that key to the highest bidder. Foe found out, came for him, and Deacon, kinda...

SKULDUGGERY: He disguised himself as a fifteen-year-old boy called Ryan – disguising himself so convincingly that even Ryan didn't know he was really Deacon.

VALKYRIE: It's complicated.

SKULDUGGERY: Ryan helped us dismantle the Doomsday Machine and prevent Foe and his group of nihilists from destroying the world.

VALKYRIE: Because Ryan was cool.

SKULDUGGERY: And Deacon was not.

VALKYRIE: And when it was over, and Deacon didn't need the Ryan personality anymore, Ryan went away, and there was only Deacon.

SKULDUGGERY: Who, as we have established, was not cool.

VALKYRIE: And I cried.

Get Thee Behind Me, Bubba Moon

VALKYRIE: Long story short, a dead guy called Bubba Moon possessed this kid years ago. Bubba's followers brought him sacrifices every month. We happened to be in America and we were sent in to take a look around, and we saved the day.

ARCHIVIST: Who was Bubba Moon offering up the sacrifices to?

VALKYRIE: If we answer, it's no longer a long story short, is it?

SKULDUGGERY: The sacrifices were made to a "being of wonderment and awe" that appeared to Moon in a dream, telling him that he was an integral part of the anti-Sanctuary.

ARCHIVIST: And did you know at the time what the anti-Sanctuary was?

SKULDUGGERY: I'd heard rumblings about it over the years, but no – not at that point.

ARCHIVIST: And the "being of wonderment and awe?"

SKULDUGGERY: An interdimensional entity called Balerosh. Abyssinia reached out into the ether, found him, they agreed terms, and divided up the power they received each time a sacrifice was made. We killed Balerosh when we found him but by then it was far too late. Abyssinia had already recruited her army.

ARCHIVIST: Valkyrie? Do you have anything to add?

VALKYRIE: What part of "long story short" do neither of you get?

Poor Elena was dragged
Out of her bed,
And burned at the stake
Until she was dead.
They called her demon,
They called her witch,
They called for their mothers,
When she began to twitch.

ABROGATE RAZE

PART ONE BY TAWDRY HEPBURN

Quinlan Forte is my personal hero.

The more I read about her, the more badass she becomes. Her journals portray her as humble and unassuming, but her actions paint a picture of a glorious powerhouse of awesomeness with an astonishing intellect. Seriously, I want to be her when I grow up.

From what I can work out, she was born in the 1360s in Ireland, decided on Elemental magic, and by the end of the century she was battling pirates on the high seas.

For reasons she doesn't go into, the Necromancers declared her A Most Hated Enemy – the worst thing you could be as far as Necromancers were concerned, which basically meant she was to be hunted and killed. They never did manage to kill her, and called off the hunt in 1418 after just about every single Necromancer who went after her ended up dead.

When the dark sorcerer Dragora formed an alliance with the Warlock High Chieftain to conquer the world and then split it between the two of them, Quinlan took it upon herself to infiltrate both Dragora and the Warlock's armies. She turned them against each other, resulting in the nine-year-long War of Splinters that left the High Chieftain dead, and Dragora alone and on the run.

Captured in 1453 by agents unknown, Quinlan was sold into slavery and spent six years serving Adelard the Mesmeriser.

Adelard was a Sensitive who specialised in making people obey him through sheer force of will. Though his talents could have delivered him a far greater prize, he was seemingly satisfied to rule the criminal underworld in Brigadoon due, perhaps, to a chronic lack of imagination.

Quinlan acted as Adelard the Mesmeriser's enforcer until she built up enough of a resistance to his influence to end his dominion over her and his small band of sorcerers by, in the words of Umfrey the Poet, "depriving him artfully of his limbs". She left Brigadoon soon after and was recruited into what was to become the Arbiter Corps.

The journals detailing her work as an Arbiter for the next thirty-four years are off limits to me, and the only thing I've been able to find so far is a mention of a love affair with a Mongol Khan and, simultaneously, her exploits involving the Golden Horde – though whether she fought with or against them remains unclear. She left the Arbiter Corps for a time and, from 1493 to 1541, all I can find is that she worked as an "adventurer".

Upon returning to both the Arbiter Corps and Ireland in 1541, she encountered Abrogate Raze, describing him as, "fair of countenance but dark of demeanour". He told her that he was old enough to have forgotten where he'd come from, and in her journals she described him as someone "in search of a greater meaning, yet turned bitter at having yet to find one".

Quinlan and Abrogate were to meet eight more times over

the next four years, fighting side by side against the Cazadores de Demonios[1] (once), Estrilda Gaut[2] (once), and the King of the Darklands (twice), until they married in 1555.

From 1573 to 1602, the couple had ten children.[3] Quinlan's journals describe this period as "happy" and "fulfilling" (it should be noted that she continued to work as an Arbiter during this time).

1. The secret unit within the Spanish Inquisition, who specialised in tracking down and eradicating sorcerers. Formed in 1536, and particularly busy in Catalonia, the Cazadores de Demonios lasted until 1631, almost a hundred years later.

2. Estrilda Gaut (1370–1691 approx.) was a notorious serial killer with a penchant for bathing in the blood of her victims. She was Quinlan Forte's younger sister.

3. Carver Gallant (1573)
Skulduggery Pleasant (1580)
Confelicity Divine (1582)
Fransic Catawampus (1584)
Petulance Ruin (1588)
Uther Peccant (1595)
Mirror Grace (1597)
Bayard Muchly (1597)
Apricity Delight (1599)
Respair Kempt (1602)

By 1604, it all changed. The five oldest children had left to forge their own lives, and Quinlan quit the Arbiters, took the remaining children, and ran from her husband. Her journals – by this stage rather sparse affairs – described a darkness growing in Abrogate that he was refusing to acknowledge. The final entry is dated April 17th 1604:

> *He leaves such havoc in his wake, such wanton destruction of both body and spirit, that his enemies seem to prefer a label of cowardice and disgrace than risk further confrontation. I have seen his eyes in such a moment of violence and I rightly fear that this is no longer the man I married. His terrible wrath has changed him. His bitterness has poisoned him. The empty place inside his soul is plain to me on occasions such as this. I fear for my life. I fear for the lives of my children. I fear for us all.*

I haven't been able to find a single mention of Quinlan Forte for the next three years, but the following appears in a report filed by an Arbiter, Languish D'Airelle, dated December 2nd 1607:

> *Upon our arrival at the house, it was clear that a great violence had taken place here. The roof was consumed by flame and the furniture turned to kindling. We found the children outside, huddled together, the eldest holding the youngest. We found Quinlan Forte inside, her blood spilled, her body broken, her life extinguished.*
>
> *When asked to describe the calamitous events as they occurred, the eldest, a boy, said simply, "It was Father."*
>
> *I recommend with utmost gravity that we apprehend Abrogate Raze wherever he may run to, and we do so in all haste and without compunction.*

Trick or Treat

SKULDUGGERY: We don't know quite what happened here, but it would appear that Tanith Low and Billy-Ray Sanguine killed a Sensitive named Jerry Ordain in Ohio.
ARCHIVIST: Do you know why Mr Ordain was killed?
SKULDUGGERY: Dexter Vex had gone to him a few weeks earlier, asking if he'd had any psychic flashes concerning the arrival of Darquesse. Jerry Ordain, however, was a supremely dreadful Sensitive who knew nothing about anything.
VALKYRIE: But we think he told Tanith about Dexter's plan to collect the four God-Killers to use against Darquesse – or, y'know, against me.
ARCHIVIST: And that put Tanith on the road to collect the God-Killers before them?
SKULDUGGERY: Indeed it did.
VALKYRIE: Stupid Jerry.
SKULDUGGERY: Stupid Jerry.

The Maleficent Seven

The biggest threat the world faced at this moment was, obviously, the upcoming arrival of Darquesse. Since the Sceptre of the Ancients had been destroyed, the decision was made by Grand Mage Ravel to gather together the other four God-Killer weapons that were widely known to exist: the sword, spear, dagger and bow. However, because of ongoing international tensions between the Supreme Council (boo!) and the Irish

Sanctuary (hurrah!), it was firmly believed that any request for these weapons would be denied.

The following account of what happened is not as detailed as it should be, due to the "off the books" nature of the assignment, but that suits me just fine.

We know that a team led by Dexter Vex and Saracen Rue — comprising Gracious O'Callahan, Donegan Bane, Frightening Jones, Aurora Jane and Wilhelm Scream — were dispatched to "borrow" the God-Killers.

VEX: I've always been a fan of seven members in a team, and what a team that was.
SARACEN: Frightening, Aurora, the Monster Hunters... Good people. Warriors.
VEX: Six warriors who'd march bravely into battle, and Wilhelm, who'd have to be dragged in, screaming.
SARACEN: Not a fan of Wilhelm.

Also after the weapons — in order to prevent them being used against Darquesse — was Tanith Low, still possessed by a Remnant and responsible for the murders of, most recently, Grand Mage Quintin Strom of the English Sanctuary. Her plan was to steal the weapons, replacing them with exact duplicates to prevent the alarm being raised, and destroy them.

Aided by Billy-Ray Sanguine who, by this stage, had developed strong feelings for Tanith, she set about recruiting a team for a series of "heists", as she called them. In order to secure their help, she promised each of them something they wanted and/or needed.

Dusk — promised the name of the vampire who turned him.

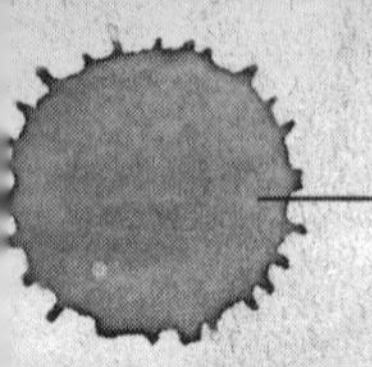

Springheeled Jack — promised information about who and what he was, suggesting that perhaps he wasn't alone in the world.

Black Annis — promised a cure for the curse that turned her into a monster.

Sabine Adorn — promised that all her debts would be forgiven and all misdeeds would be forgotten.

Sabine, in particular, was vitally important to Tanith's plan. She was a Magiphage, commonly known as a Leech, capable of draining other sorcerer's magic to use for herself, and also to temporarily transfer magic to other people/objects. Sabine would, therefore, "charge" each duplicate weapon so that it would stand a higher chance of passing for the authentic item.

The various reports suggest that Tanith wore a disguise and infiltrated a party hosted by Johann Starke, an Elder in the German Sanctuary. She switched the daggers and escaped without incident — save for one dead Ripper.

VEX: We sneaked into Starke's place a day after he'd held this grand party.
SARACEN: Although we could have been sneakier.
VEX: Really? I thought we sneaked in just fine.
SARACEN: It wasn't flawless, though, was it? For a start, we got caught, which would imply that we totally failed as far as the sneaking went.
VEX: Yeah, maybe. Anyway, we were surrounded, and Starke told us that a beautiful woman in a red dress had attempted to steal the dagger the previous night.
SARACEN: None of us knew that the woman was Tanith, and none of us knew that she'd actually succeeded in her attempt.
VEX: We managed to get out of there before they could throw us in jail, but

now we knew there was someone else after the God-Killers. And it was a race we intended to win.

SARACEN: That's very dramatic.

VEX: Thank you.

SARACEN: We didn't win that particular race, though, did we?

VEX: Dude, don't spoil it.

Jackie Earl, a crime boss in Chicago, was in possession of the bow. He may have been mortal but he knew enough about magic to have both a vampire and a Necromancer on staff. I can't find the name of the vampire, but the Necromancer was a man called Kaiven, who had abandoned the Order when the Passage failed. Like all Necromancers, he kept his power in an object. In his case: a wand.

VEX: A wand.

SARACEN: How embarrassing.

Although there is no way of verifying this, Tanith must have reached Jackie Earl's office and swapped the bows before Earl realised she was even there. Believing that he still possessed the real bow, he allowed her to leave — although she did warn him that Vex's team were also going to try to steal the bow.

VEX: When we arrived the next night, Earl had five Necromancers and a bunch of gunmen waiting for us – but they didn't last too long. We cleverly got him to tell us that it was Tanith who was leading the other team –

SARACEN: Very, very cleverly.

VEX: – and then we took what we thought was the bow.

SARACEN: Not so cleverly.

Tanith and her team travelled to Poland, where a thousand-year-old sorcerer named Crab lived in a cave, just off a beach. Crab had the spear. Tanith went to get it. She fought him and won.

Vex's team, meanwhile, were landing on a private airstrip when their plane was attacked by Sanguine and the others.

VEX: We flew straight into an ambush, which is one of the worst things you can fly into.

SARACEN: After a mountain.

VEX: Yeah – after a mountain, an ambush is one of the worst things you can fly into. We sustained a few injuries here and there – I got shot, and so did Aurora – but we fought them off.

SARACEN: We'd been betrayed. That was obvious. The thing was, six of us knew each other and trusted each other, but no one really knew or trusted Wilhelm. And guess who the traitor turned out to be?

VEX: It was Wilhelm.

SARACEN: It was Wilhelm, yes.

His cover blown, Wilhelm panicked and Sanguine extricated him from the situation.

VEX: It was around then that we realised the bow we had was a fake, and that Tanith had the real one, and probably had the real dagger, and definitely had the spear. The last God-Killer was the sword, which was locked away in the London Sanctuary.

SARACEN: So we decided to steal it.

Tanith, of course, had already decided to steal it. We know, thanks to testimony provided by one of Thames Chabon's men, that she went to the black-market dealer to get him to show her the secret way into the London Sanctuary that he used, on occasion, to deliver his goods. In return, she gave him something he had been after — Sabine, the thief who had conned him two years before.

Both teams entered the London Sanctuary within six minutes of each other — although their methods of entry couldn't have been more different.

Vex's team walked right through the front door, using non-lethal means.

Tanith's team needed a distraction to draw the sentries away from the secret entrance, and so Tanith cut the head off Springheeled Jack and threw his body down into the street.

Once inside, Dusk allowed his vampire nature to take over, allowing Tanith, Annis and Wilhelm to get to the Repository, where the sword was kept behind a reinforced case — arriving at the same time as Vex's team.

Before the two sides could decide who was going to leave with the God-Killer, the alarm sounded and the Sanctuary went into lockdown, sealing off whole sections and exits. Elder Palaver Graves walked in, backed up by sorcerers and Cleavers. He'd been expecting them.

VEX: I didn't like him.

SARACEN: I didn't like him, either.

Once he was assured of victory, Graves ordered the lockdown lifted, but Tanith had anticipated such a trap and, using knowledge the Remnant inside her had retained from its time possessing Kenspeckle Grouse, she had concocted a rage-virus that she arranged to have pumped in through the ventilation ducts during the building's lockdown. Now that the lockdown was lifted, all of the so-called "rage-zombies" came running in.

VEX: It was chaos. We were fighting Cleavers, we were fighting sorcerers, we were fighting rage-zombies, we were fighting alongside Tanith and her lot – some of the time, anyway. The Dusk-vampire was killing whoever got close. One of the Cleavers killed Black Annis.

And Tanith used the confusion to reveal why Wilhelm was on her team — his uncle had installed the reinforced case that held the God-Killer sword. Despite his protestations, she cut off Wilhelm's finger and used the blood to deactivate the security system, then took the sword.

The plan had been for Sanguine to tunnel up and take Tanith and the sword to safety, but there were creatures in the ground that later became known as razorworms that meant he couldn't take Tanith *and* the sword — he had to take one, and leave the other. Tanith gave him the sword, instructed him to destroy it along with the other God-Killers, then made him leave.

As the fighting abated, Vex and Saracen took down Tanith and delivered her to Elder Graves, before surrendering themselves.

Elder Graves, along with Elder Illori Reticent and Grand

Mage Cothernus Ode, accepted that Vex's team acted to save lives, and allowed them to leave without charge. Tanith and Wilhelm were to be transferred to prison. Dusk had managed to escape.

Tanith Low and Wilhelm Scream escaped their cells before they were transferred.

SARACEN: It seemed Tanith had had a guardian angel throughout this whole thing, taking down threats before she even knew they were there.
VEX: His name was Moribund. A psychopathic killer who Tanith had actually let out of his cage back in the old Sanctuary in Dublin, the night Skulduggery killed Serpine. Looks like he was repaying the favour.

Tanith met up with Sanguine, and told Dusk that Moloch had been the vampire who'd turned him. They destroyed the God-Killers.
VEX: Except they didn't.
SARACEN: Sanguine, in his own way, genuinely loved Tanith, but he was not a fan of letting Darquesse destroy the world. So he'd had a second set of fake weapons made, and destroyed them to keep Tanith happy while he stored the real ones away, in case of emergency.
VEX: And that emergency was on its way...

Eye of the Beholder

After Tanith Low had murdered Grand Mage Quintin Strom of the English Sanctuary, the American Grand Mage, Bisahalani, sent three old associates of Billy-Ray Sanguine – Gepard Voke, Persephone Grief, and Barnaby Skulk – to bring him in, dead or alive.

After Sanguine had killed them, he took the three razorworms they were training – the same razorworms that had caused him so many problems underneath the London Sanctuary not long before – and adopted them as pets.

Their current whereabouts are unknown.

Kingdom of the Wicked

Exactly one year earlier, the Passage had narrowly been averted — yet another crisis that could have doomed the world occurring right here on Irish soil. Perhaps understandably, many of the other Sanctuaries around the world were getting kind of worried about this trend, and united to form the Supreme Council. Representatives from the Supreme Council — Quintin Strom, the English Grand Mage, and Bernard Sult, the Junior Administrator for the American Council — were dispatched to Ireland to pressure Grand Mage Ravel, Elder Bespoke and Elder Mist into accepting their help — if by "help" the Supreme Council really meant "guidance", and if by "guidance" they really meant "instruction". Either way, the Irish Sanctuary wasn't going to agree to any of that. Damn right.

The pressure they were under, though, wasn't being made any easier by seemingly ordinary mortals suddenly displaying magical abilities and causing havoc. Skulduggery Pleasant and Valkyrie Cain learned that all of these mortals had one thing in common: a dream in which a man called Argeddion promised them a "Summer of Light" and blessed them with power.

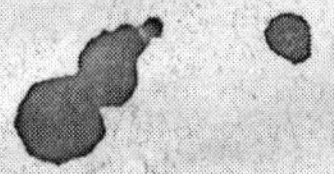

Four mortals affected proved especially troublesome: Kitana Kellaway, Doran Purcell, Elsie O'Brien and Sean Mackin — all seventeen years old, all students at St Brendan's Secondary School in Carrickbrennan, in Dublin (for the purpose of clarity, this group will be referred to as Argeddion's Teens, because I don't know what else to call them).

ELSIE: We weren't really friends or anything. I mean, I was friends with Sean – I'd known him since we were kids – and Sean knew Doran, and everyone knew Kitana, but we didn't hang out together or anything.
ARCHIVIST: Tell me about the magic.
ELSIE: I don't really know much about it, but I'd been having these dreams, we all had—
ARCHIVIST: About Argeddion?
ELSIE: Yeah. Yes. He promised us magic and wonder and... Anyway, we all got sick. It felt like the flu, only worse. And the next day I woke up and I could do magic. We all could.
ARCHIVIST: And Patrick Xebec?
ELSIE: That was an accident. I think. We were practising, just seeing what we could do, and this guy comes along, said he was going to report us. I was scared. I didn't like getting in trouble, not even in school, and this sounded a lot more serious than getting detention or whatever. But Kitana and Doran, they... I don't think they meant to do it, not really, but they killed him.

The detectives searched through Sanctuary records but couldn't find any mention of someone called Argeddion — and then Argeddion's ex-girlfriend arrived and asked to speak with them.

VALKYRIE: I love old people. Well, not all of them. Some old people are horrible. A good few of them have tried to kill me. But most old people I've met are lovely. Greta reminded me of my nana.

Greta informed them that Argeddion used to be Walden D'Essai, a sorcerer whose passion was research and the expansion of knowledge. A little over thirty years ago, he achieved his greatest wish of discovering his True Name. Once he had grown acclimatised to the increase in power, he talked about a forthcoming "Summer of Light".

The Council of Elders at the time feared what Argeddion would do with his power, and assigned Detective Tyren Lament to deal with the potential problem. Lament had a particular interest in science-magic, and his team specialised in dealing with global threats in as quiet a manner as possible.

VALKYRIE: "Black Ops in peacetime", Skulduggery called them.

A Sensitive on Lament's team saw a future of death and destruction, with Argeddion in the middle of it all — a vision that Greta Dapple ridiculed, as Argeddion was an avowed pacifist. After Lament's team went to meet with him, Argeddion was never seen again — which would indicate that the "problem" had indeed been dealt with. Lament and his team were never seen again, either.

But if Argeddion was actually dead, as Greta believed, then why was he appearing in people's dreams and handing out super powers like a magical Willy Wonka handing out candy?

Our dynamic detecting duo decided that Tyren Lament was the key to finding out what had happened to Argeddion, so they needed to know more about him — starting with the names of the other sorcerers on his team. They travelled to Hammer Lane Gaol in order to speak with notorious, dimension-hopping serial killer, Silas Nadir — one of the last people arrested by Lament.

Hammer Lane Gaol had garnered a reputation as an exceptionally well-run prison since Delafonte Mien took over as warden. The security measures he introduced meant the entire facility cycled through eight different dimensions per second, making escape virtually impossible.

Upon arrival, Skulduggery and Valkyrie discovered that Nadir was hooked up to the facility, which was using his Shunting ability to move through realities. Then there was a jailbreak.

VALKYRIE: That was scary.

SKULDUGGERY: Very scary.

VALKYRIE: You were scared, were you? From the other side of the impenetrable barrier, away from all the bad guys?

SKULDUGGERY: Maybe "scared" is a bit strong.

VALKYRIE: I'd imagine it would be. As for me? I really was scared. I was crawling through air vents with hundreds of convicts after me.

SKULDUGGERY: On the upside, you did manage to find Silas Nadir, so... silver lining.

As they cut Nadir free of the cables that held him, he grabbed Valkyrie's arm.

VALKYRIE: I didn't think anything of it.

Believing he had cut a deal with the Sanctuary, Nadir gave them the names of the others in Lament's team – Vernon Plight, Kalvin Accord and the Sensitive, Lenka Bazaar – all of whom were missing and presumed dead.

VALKYRIE: You'd think that after surviving a prison riot, I'd be due for a day off, right? Me too. I went to get a coffee and this middle-aged assassin came ridiculously close to killing me. It was only because of Tanith that I'm still here today.

The assassin had been sent at Christophe Nocturnal's behest but, knowing that Valkyrie's death would put Skulduggery on the warpath, somebody close to Nocturnal sent Tanith Low and Billy-Ray Sanguine to protect her.

That "somebody" turned out to be Eliza Scorn, who was quite pleased with how things were turning out. Nocturnal was arrested and brought to Roarhaven to be questioned and, because of that, his church – the Divine Order of the Faceless Ones – pretty much collapsed overnight, and all of those worshippers switched over to the Church of the Faceless. As payment for protecting Valkyrie, Scorn had promised Tanith that she'd find out where the God-Killer dagger was being kept. It turned out that only Nocturnal himself knew this, which meant Tanith now had to break into the Sanctuary, get the dagger's location, and kill Nocturnal while they were at it. Result!

Skulduggery and Valkyrie examined a crime scene where seventeen-year-old Michael Delaney and his parents were slaughtered in their home. Sickened by what she saw, Valkyrie asked that they leave this particular murder to somebody else and focus on Argeddion — even though it meant reading through even more Sanctuary files.

VALKYRIE: The Sanctuary was filling up with operatives from the Supreme Council by this point, here to "help". We met Bernard Sult. Really didn't like him.

Upon reviewing their files, however, Skulduggery found enough evidence to support a new theory: that Lament had been working on a containment system — a prison strong enough to hold Argeddion.

VALKYRIE: This was huge. Beyond huge. This meant that if and when I became Darquesse, there would be a way to trap me so that I didn't hurt anyone. This was brilliant.

All of which meant that both Argeddion and Lament and his entire team were probably still alive, and were probably located in a facility in the Alps.

VALKYRIE: I like how this report skips straight over the boring detective bits and cuts right to the Alps. This is someone who appreciates a good Yeti fight.

SKULDUGGERY: There was nothing boring in how I deduced

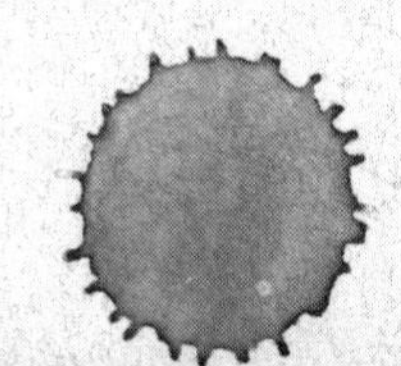

the location of Lament's facility. There was an invisible train, for God's sake.

VALKYRIE: Oh yeah! I'd forgotten about that! Hansard Kray and the train full of Hollow Men. He was so into me.

SKULDUGGERY: Didn't you ask him out and he said no?

VALKYRIE: That's not how I remember it.

SKULDUGGERY: I'd wager it's how he remembers it.

VALKYRIE: Anyway, the Yeti fight. That's the kind of stuff people want to read about – me, punching the Abominable Snowman!

SKULDUGGERY: Who do you think is going to read this?

VALKYRIE: I don't know. Everyone?

SKULDUGGERY: Historians, maybe, at some stage in the far future, will find this book on a shelf in the Sanctuary somewhere. This isn't a book that's going to be published for the sorcerers of the world to marvel at our adventures. This is purely for academic purposes.

VALKYRIE: So, no book signings? Gordon was always doing book signings. He loved them. He always talked about how weird his readers were.

SKULDUGGERY: Even if this was a book that the average mage was interested in reading, why would you be doing a signing? You're not writing it.

VALKYRIE: But I'm contributing.

SKULDUGGERY: Providing sarcastic comments in the margins is not enough of a contribution to warrant a book tour.

VALKYRIE: Well, that sucks.

Tanith and Sanguine sneaked into the Sanctuary, where Tanith insisted that Doctor Nye opened Sanguine up and repair the damage that had been originally caused by Valkyrie at Aranmore, and then botched by a terrible surgeon afterwards. While Nye worked, Tanith reached Christophe Nocturnal in his cell and persuaded him to tell her that the God-Killer dagger was in the possession of Johann Starke of the German Sanctuary. Tanith then killed Nocturnal.

Scapegrace refused to spend the rest of his un-life as a head in a jar, and persuaded Clarabelle to set up a meeting with Doctor Nye. A deal was reached — Nye would transfer Scapegrace and Thrasher's brains to new bodies, and in return, Scapegrace would give it the remains of the White Cleaver.

The throb in Valkyrie's arm, where Nadir had grabbed her, was getting worse.

VALKYRIE: And I shunted. We found out later that Nadir had passed me some kind of delayed shunt, called echoing, where the energy would build and build until I'd shunt into this parallel Earth and then back again. In the next four days, I'd do this three times. I really didn't like him.

The first of these shunts transferred Valkyrie to the Dublin ("Dublin-Within-The-Wall") on an alternate Earth, where Mevolent had won the war and had been ruling over the mortals for hundreds of years. After a brief skirmish with Alexander Remit, a Teleporter loyal to Mevolent, she shunted home again.

Deciding to focus on Argeddion, Skulduggery and Valkyrie travelled to the Alps, where they had a huge fight with some Yetis. From the report I read, the battle was harrowing and brutal, and Valkyrie discovered some things about herself as she fought. I'm no psychologist, but I feel that this experience surely reinforced her "never say die" attitude. It was, in all, a terrific learning experience and everyone should read that report. I'm pretty sure it changed my life for the better.

Once inside the mountainside facility, they met Tyren Lament and his team, who explained how they had apprehended someone as powerful as Argeddion.

When Walden D'Essai was a child, his mother was murdered in front of him, and the killer spoke three words to the boy. Lament used those three words, this traumatic phrase from his childhood, to stall Argeddion, and they trapped him, put him into an induced coma, and held him in a cell called the Cube, powered by a Tempest, where he still sleeps today.

The facility needed constant monitoring and the Tempest needed to draw magic from sorcerers, which is why Lament's entire team gave up the lives they were living to watch over him.

But now that the detectives were here, Lament suddenly had a chance to change things. He told them about Doctor Rote, who had built a machine called the Accelerator, capable of boosting a sorcerer's magic for a limited period of time. The Accelerator, kept deep in the bowels of the Roarhaven Sanctuary, could be repurposed to power the Cube indefinitely.

Skulduggery called Ghastly, told him about the Accelerator, and asked him to keep it between himself and Ravel.

SKULDUGGERY: Something like the Accelerator could change the course of history if the wrong kind of sorcerer got their hands on it.

Ghastly and Ravel went looking through Sanctuary corridors that didn't appear on their maps. They found the Accelerator, and minutes later were attacked by three Roarhaven mages.

VALKYRIE: We figured that Mist had listened in on the phone call. If this was her first time hearing about the Accelerator or if she'd already known it was there, she'd have wanted to keep it all to herself.

Fletcher arrived to teleport everyone back to the Roarhaven Sanctuary — including Argeddion, still sleeping in the Cube.

VALKYRIE: It all worked smoothly. The Cube was hooked up to the Accelerator and Lament's team were brought back to the world they thought they'd left behind. Oh, and I met Fletcher's girlfriend, Myra. A mortal. She seemed sweet.

Although Argeddion was still sleeping peacefully, Argeddion's Teens were wide awake and killing. This time it was Doran's own brother. When a Sanctuary team arrived on the scene, they found that Tommy Purcell had been literally pulled apart. This sent Elsie running.

The detectives found a possible link between the murders of Patrick Xebec, Michael Delaney and his parents, and Tommy Purcell. A conversation with Doran positioned him at the top of their suspect list, and they followed him, hoping he would lead them to his accomplices. He did, and things turned violent.

VALKYRIE: Title of your autobiography, right there. *Things Turned Violent.*
SKULDUGGERY: We weren't quite as sneaky as we thought.

VALKYRIE: They beat the hell out of us before we managed to escape. They had all kinds of magic, all directed towards inflicting pain. Oh, and they took my jacket. That Kitana one... she took my damn jacket.

As Nye worked on healing Sanguine, it revealed that Madame Mist was giving it its orders, and that the debt they owed Nye was now owed to Mist. And Mist wanted them to kill someone.

Shortly after Skulduggery and Valkyrie were discharged from the Medical Bay, Lament erected an energy field, cutting off a section of the Sanctuary — that included the Accelerator — from the rest. He announced that his team were preparing to use the Accelerator to shock Argeddion awake.

VALKYRIE: They'd been under his control for years – they just didn't have anything powerful enough to get him out of that coma.
SKULDUGGERY: And we'd brought them right to it.
VALKYRIE: Because we're clever, and apparently we hate it when things go well.

The only good guys inside the energy field were Skulduggery and Valkyrie, so they rushed into the Accelerator Room to stop all this from happening.

SKULDUGGERY: But it had already happened. Argeddion was already awake.
VALKYRIE: He talked to us. Told us all these mortals waking up with magic, they were an experiment. He was teaching himself the best way to make everyone magic, every single person. With the Accelerator boosting his power even more, and someone he called his "surprise guest", he'd be able to do that.

SKULDUGGERY: He thought that if he gave everyone magic, they'd all be like him. Good. Noble. Peaceful. He didn't listen to us when we told him people are flawed, scared, greedy creatures, and that instead of a Summer of Light and wonder, it would result in a Summer of Darkness and terror.
VALKYRIE: And before he kicked us out, he made sure we couldn't use our darker selves to fight him. He found the case that held Vile's armour and made it disappear, and then he blocked off my access to Darquesse's power. She was too violent, he said. Too unstable. I mean, he wasn't wrong, but even so... Harsh, you know?

Valkyrie returned home, when she once again shunted into the parallel word — but this time, she accidentally took her reflection with her. Having been mistaken for a member of the Resistance, she was captured by Baron Vengeous, who was still alive in this reality and married to Eliza Scorn.

VALKYRIE: I think I envied the dead one more.

Her reflection, meanwhile, had been discovered by two members of the actual Resistance — Dexter Vex and Ghastly Bespoke — and taken to safety.

Valkyrie was brought to the Palace, where she realised they had their own Sceptre of the Ancients in a glass case. And she met Mevolent.

VALKYRIE: He was kneeling beside a pool of black sludge, surrounded by the Redhoods. They stuck their spears into him. Killed him. He was dragged into the pool by Nye – because of course it was Nye – and then a moment later, he climbs

MEVOLENT

out of it, without even a wound. Vengeous told me that Mevolent did this every day – died and came back – to teach death a lesson, basically.

Mevolent questioned Valkyrie, believing her to be part of the Resistance.

VALKYRIE: I told him the truth, that I hadn't a clue about any of it, but in the back of my mind I was half expecting the door to crash open and for this reality's version of Skulduggery Pleasant to come crashing in to get me out of there. Instead, in walked Lord Vile.

Now that Argeddion was busy elsewhere, Lament and his team found that his control over them was weakening, little by little.

They took Valkyrie to the dungeon, where Eachan Meritorious had been shackled up for decades. The Resistance came and got her out, and Valkyrie met the leader — China Sorrows. Unfortunately, Lord Vile had tracked them down, and a battle broke out in which Ghastly was killed and Valkyrie and the reflection were separated once again — and Valkyrie shunted home — alone.

Valkyrie reported back to Skulduggery and the others, telling them about the Sceptre. Immediately, they zeroed in on that as a way to stop Argeddion, and Skulduggery was instructed to stick by Valkyrie's side so that the next time she shunted, he'd go with her.

There was the teeny-tiny issue of the Sceptre being deadlocked, of course, meaning it could only be used by its owner, but Doctor Nye pointed out that, in theory, trans-

dimensional travel would effectively act as a "short circuit", meaning the Sceptre would arrive in our reality with a clean slate, ready to bond with a brand-new owner.

VALKYRIE: I wasn't too keen on the idea of killing Argeddion, so I proposed that next time we shunt, we go find Walden D'Essai, find out what the traumatic phrase from his childhood was, and we use it against Argeddion just like Lament did – taking him peacefully, without having to physically hurt anyone.

The Elders gave the detectives three objectives: Steal the Sceptre, find the traumatic phrase, and rescue Valkyrie's reflection — though they didn't much care about the third one.

Cassandra Pharos constructed a shield around Valkyrie's thoughts so that if Argeddion tried to read her mind he wouldn't learn anything about the Sceptre.

Argeddion's Teens killed five Sanctuary sorcerers who were guarding their school. Skulduggery and Valkyrie went in, determined to stop them from hurting any of their teachers or fellow students — but Argeddion saved them, let Kitana and Doran walk away.

Sean was taken into custody and Elsie helped question him. After Ghastly looked at him sternly, he broke, and told them that Kitana and Doran were hiding out at a friend's house.

VALKYRIE: So we were about to go straight there, and then Grand Mage Strom and that Sult guy start going on about how our presence at the school risked the exposure of sorcerers, and Ravel isn't a real Grand Mage, and then – this is my favourite part – he told us he was taking over.

SKULDUGGERY: So Ravel arrested him and threw him in a cell.
VALKYRIE: Which was incredibly satisfying to see.

But Strom's interference delayed them, so by the time they got to where they were going, Kitana and Doran had moved on.

And then Valkyrie shunted again – and this time she took Skulduggery with her.

They found the Resistance, and once Skulduggery convinced Anton Shudder and China that he wasn't the Skulduggery that they had once known, he told them of their plan. China quite liked the idea of Mevolent's most powerful weapon being stolen from him, so she loaned our heroes a prisoner to sneak them into the palace – Nefarian Serpine.

(I love this parallel-world stuff. You thought this person was dead? Boom! Standing right there! You thought that person was a good guy? Boom! Totally evil! It's like all those mirror-universe episodes of *Star Trek,* you know? Where Spock has the goatee? I should grow a goatee.)

VALKYRIE: It was weird, seeing Serpine again. I can't imagine how Skulduggery felt.
SKULDUGGERY: I felt fine about it. He wasn't the same Serpine who had murdered my wife and child – I'd killed that one. I was perfectly fine with equipping him with a pain regulator to make him an obedient little puppy. I quite enjoyed pressing that button, actually.

Argeddion returned to the Sanctuary and took his magic back from each of the mortals he'd infected, absorbing the information and refining the process. He told Elsie that she and her friends were still an ongoing experiment, that when he took his magic back from them, it would be used to help make the world a better place.

Before he left, Argeddion was confronted by Tyren Lament and his team, who had broken free of Argeddion's mind control. They were determined to try to stop him, even though they didn't stand a chance. He took his magic back and they died instantly.

Kitana was hidden nearby, and she saw it all happen. Realising how effortless it would be for Argeddion to take their magic away from them, how easy it would be for him to kill them just like he'd killed Lament's team once his experiment was over, she figured that she and her friends would have to kill Argeddion first.

Serpine got the dimension-hopping detectives into Dublin-Within-The-Wall, and Valkyrie used the alternate world's version of the internet – the World Well – to search for Walden D'Essai's address.

Walden was a Sewage Maintenance Engineer who helped sneak Resistance fighters in and out of the city. Like his counterpart in our reality, he was a pacifist whose mother had been killed in front of him – but there was no traumatic phrase that his mother's killer had uttered, no three words that would have frozen him in his tracks.

SKULDUGGERY: I realised it had been a ruse.

VALKYRIE: OK, you ready? This gets complicated.

SKULDUGGERY: The love of Argeddion's life, Greta Dapple, had been the one

to set us on the road that ultimately led us to Silas Nadir.
VALKYRIE: Nadir had been asleep for fifteen years – plenty of time for Argeddion to slip into his mind and plant the impulse to shunt me into the parallel world.
SKULDUGGERY: And Argeddion was also in the head of Tyren Lament when Lament told us that the key to subduing Argeddion was this non-existent traumatic phrase—
VALKYRIE: —which, in the parallel world, led us to Walden's front door. Boom.
SKULDUGGERY: As my partner says, boom. Boom indeed.
VALKYRIE: Even boosted by the Accelerator, Argeddion wasn't yet powerful enough to share his magic with every single person on the planet – but he'd mentioned a surprise guest.
SKULDUGGERY: He was his own surprise guest. He wanted Walden to become Argeddion, and then the two Argeddions would change the world.

The footage was mysteriously corrupted, but somebody released Sean Mackin from his cell in the Sanctuary and allowed him to rejoin Kitana and Doran. From the single report that was filed, a sorcerer called Staven Weeper saw somebody enter Sean's cell but could not, even under psychic probe, remember who it had been.

Skulduggery, Valkyrie, and Serpine entered the palace through a secret tunnel, but Baron Vengeous and Eliza Scorn interrupted them before they could take the Sceptre. Valkyrie unlocked the glove that kept Serpine from using his red right hand, and removed the pain regulator before heading down into the dungeon to free her reflection, who had been badly tortured.

VALKYRIE: Alexander Remit tried to stop us, but my reflection slapped the pain regulator on him and suddenly we had our very own pet Teleporter.

They teleported back to the fight, and Valkyrie grabbed the Sceptre as Lord Vile and Mevolent stormed in. The good guys teleported to the Resistance right before they got horribly, horribly murdered.

VALKYRIE: My arm was hurting, so I knew we were about to shunt... but China wouldn't give us back the bloody Sceptre. So we left without it.

Back in Haggard, the reflection told Valkyrie that it would be hiding certain memories of the torture it had endured. Valkyrie, it said, didn't need that trauma. It passed into the mirror and healed.

Argeddion's Teens turned up at Roarhaven, offering to join with the Sanctuary forces to destroy Argeddion, and Skulduggery agreed with the proposal.

SKULDUGGERY: I had reason to believe that when Argeddion died, the power that he'd passed to them would die with him. They didn't know that, of course.
VALKYRIE: But in order to make sure that they'd be able to kill him, we'd have to use the Accelerator to boost their magic. So we'd basically be making three unstoppable psychopaths even more unstoppable. Unstoppabler? Is that a word?
SKULDUGGERY: It most certainly is not.
VALKYRIE: Anyway, the fact was, we couldn't trust Kitana, but apparently we didn't have much of a choice.

Skulduggery and Valkyrie went to Greta's cottage, and realised she'd been in on it the whole time. She had complete faith in what Argeddion was doing. The detectives used Greta to draw Argeddion to them. Everything was proceeding as planned, more or less, but then Kitana and her friends double-crossed them.

VALKYRIE: Big surprise there. Who would've seen that coming, eh? Who, I ask you? I'll tell you who – me. I saw it coming. I warned everyone. No one listened.
SKULDUGGERY: Everyone listened.
VALKYRIE: No one listened to paranoid little Valkyrie Cain. Oh no, they said, she's too pretty and cute and cool and she's been right about everything all along, there's no way she could be right about this too!
SKULDUGGERY: You're still annoyed you won't be doing book signings, aren't you?
VALKYRIE: All I want to do is sign one little book.
SKULDUGGERY: The point is, they were smarter than we gave them credit for. Well, maybe not Doran. And I don't think Sean was making any important decisions. But Kitana... Kitana had figured out that killing Argeddion would return them to normal, so their plan now was to beat the hell out of Argeddion and then trap him in the Cube forever. Which is what I would have done.

During the battle, Kitana killed Greta, and Argeddion was kicked into unconsciousness.

Kitana and her friends brought Argeddion back to the Sanctuary, where they tried to work out how to activate the Cube. Skulduggery and Valkyrie followed them.

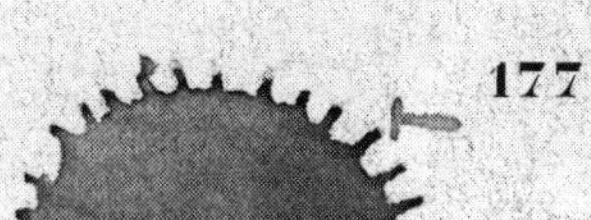

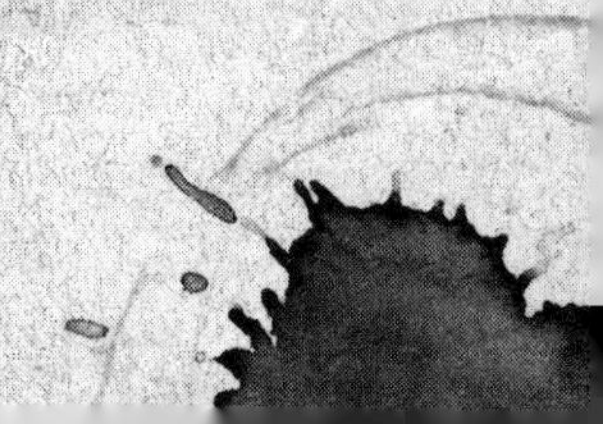

VALKYRIE: Skulduggery had found Vile's armour, so at least he had a chance fighting them. I didn't have a hope, and Kitana pretty much killed me. Or she would have, if Argeddion hadn't let that psychic block crumble, because suddenly I was Darquesse again.

In the past, that's where this would have ended. Once Darquesse emerged, it was all over.

But not today. Argeddion's Teens seemed to be getting stronger. Vile and Darquesse started to falter. Security camera footage showed Darquesse's jaw disintegrating. Her hand was burned off. The footage shows her staggering away, around the corner, trying to find a moment to heal.

Around the corner is where she met Argeddion. In the final stage of his experiment, he was pouring his power into Kitana and the others, just to see how they'd handle it. He also gave a little boost to Darquesse, activating the shunt, and accompanied her to the parallel world.

VALKYRIE: He could replicate a power. He just had to experience an ability, and he could do it. He could shunt home whenever he wanted, but first he had to go get Walden D'Essai.

Darquesse had one shunt left — the shunt that would take her back home. Before that happened, she wanted the Sceptre.

By the time she got to Dublin-Within-The-Wall, it was a warzone.

VALKYRIE: The Resistance were attacking and everything was on fire. I fought Mevolent. It was a hell of a thing. I punched him through buildings and he kicked me through walls. There were people running everywhere, screaming and crying. I think at one point I started plucking people from the crowd and throwing them like darts, but I may be misremembering that part. Maybe it was fence posts. I don't know. What I do remember very clearly is Mevolent pulling my head off. Now that was something. I knew I only had a few seconds to reattach everything before I died...

SKULDUGGERY: You OK?

VALKYRIE: I don't think about this stuff much. Is that a good thing or a bad thing? He pulled my head off. My head. He decapitated me. Maybe that's why I find it hard to relate to people. I mean, who the hell else has had their head pulled off and they're still walking around now?

SKULDUGGERY: I've had my head pulled off.

VALKYRIE: And do you relate to me?

SKULDUGGERY: ...No.

VALKYRIE: Anyway, it ended in a kind of stalemate, though I'm pretty sure I won, but I was about to shunt home so I found China, took the Sceptre, and in those last few moments, Serpine arrived. Killed China and blasted me and then I was home, back in this reality – empty-handed.

Furious, Darquesse flew back to Roarhaven and killed Kitana and Sean and Doran. The footage of the deaths is graphic and upsetting. I showed it to my nieces and they started crying.

SKULDUGGERY: Argeddion returned, with Walden D'Essai by his side. Darquesse couldn't beat him now. All his magic had been returned to him. He was a god again.

Argeddion resurrected Kitana and her friends, but when Walden realised what Argeddion's plan was, he was appalled. Human beings, he argued, were not the wholesome, decent souls that Argeddion seemed to think they were. Giving them all magic would lead to untold levels of violence, horror and death. The two men argued and Argeddion lost his cool for a moment, for a single, solitary moment – and he turned Walden to ash.

VALKYRIE: Apparently, it's a hell of a lot easier resurrecting a flesh-and-blood corpse than it is a pile of ashes.

SKULDUGGERY: At which point, I induced a slight seizure in both Darquesse and Argeddion using a rapid light pattern that short-circuited their brains. When Valkyrie awoke, she was herself again. When Argeddion awoke... well. He didn't wake.

Sanctuary Sensitives implanted a false identity in Argeddion's mind, circumventing both his memories and his magic. Kitana, Sean, and Doran were sent to prison for the rest of their lives. Elsie went home.

SKULDUGGERY: Grand Mage Strom was allowed out of his cell. He was, quite understandably, annoyed at being incarcerated, but he understood why we did it. And he recognised the fact that, while we may have had our problems, we stopped Argeddion. We got the job done.

Strom intended to report back to the Supreme Council and assure them that Ravel had everything under control – but before he could do that, Tanith Low killed him.

VALKYRIE: And we were pretty much on a path to war.

Valkyrie didn't know this, but Darquesse had actually brought

the Sceptre of the Ancients back with her when she shunted home that last time — she just lost it when she arrived. The only person to realise this was the reflection, who remembered every single thing. The reflection recovered the Sceptre, but needed somebody magic to charge it up — so she picked her cousin, Carol, who had enough magic in her blood to do the job.

The reflection killed Carol and instructed Carol's very own reflection to take over her life. Then Valkyrie's reflection took the name Stephanie Edgley and ownership of the Sceptre.

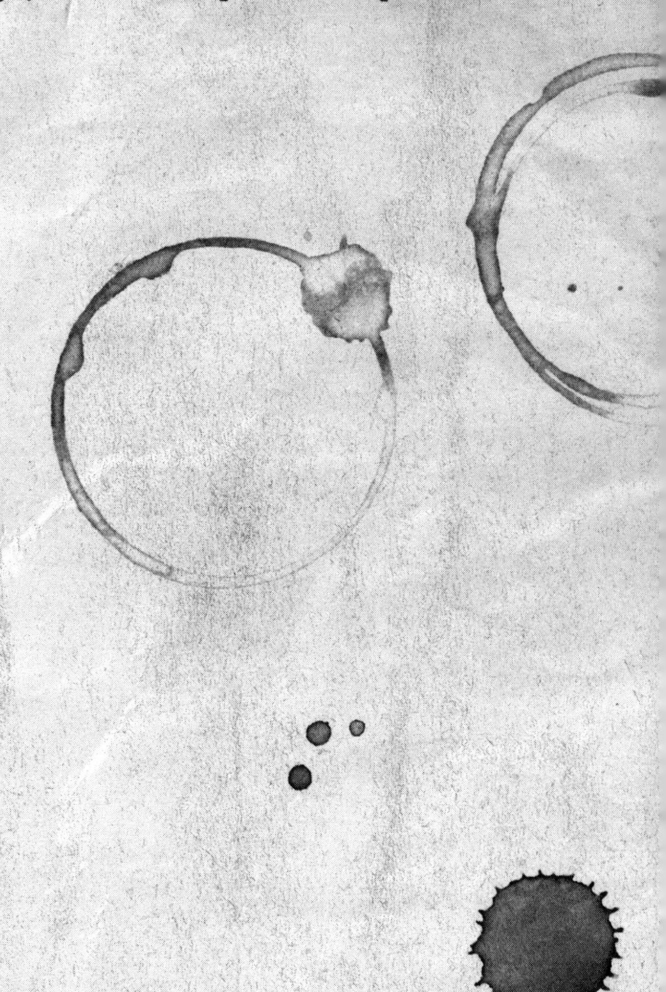

In memoriam, Enola Quirk,
Whose head popped off
With a sudden jerk.

The Age of the Maggot Part Three

By the time Valkyrie Cain had recovered from her brief time as Darquesse, Voracious Kurakin had been missing for three months. The Russian and German Sanctuaries had both assigned operatives to the search, but they found nothing to link Voracious's disappearance to the investigation into Bemmon's murder.

Then Skulduggery Pleasant received a garbled phone call from Voracious that ended before any information could be exchanged. Within four minutes, Skulduggery had the call traced back to a farm in County Kerry, and within ten minutes he and Valkyrie were on the road.

The events that followed were witnessed — psychically — by a Bulgarian Sensitive as they happened. Working in a trance state, he transcribed the events into sequential art at his studio, 3,500 kilometres away.

Those pages are presented overleaf.

ALL THESE POOR ANIMALS.
WHAT DID THIS? VAMPIRE?
THERE ARE BITE MARKS, BUT NO ATTEMPT TO EAT THE FLESH.
THIS WAS SOMETHING ELSE.

LET'S CHECK THE HOUSE.

VALKYRIE.

VORACIOUS?

STAY BACK, SKULDUGGERY.

WHAT HAPPENED HERE?
WHERE HAVE YOU BEEN?

I HAD A... A THEORY.
I THOUGHT MAYBE THAT BEMMON HAD BEEN KILLED BY A GOD FROM A RIVAL PANTHEON.
THOUGHT HOSANNA WOULD'VE HAD THE DETAILS IN THE NOTEBOOK THAT REMEMBER STOLE.

I TRACKED DOWN SABELINA BRIGHTEN, REMEMBER'S MOTHER. TOLD HER TO CALL ME IF... IF REMEMBER TURNED UP.
NEXT DAY –
UNN
– NEXT DAY GOT A MESSAGE. INSTRUCTIONS. WALKED RIGHT INTO REMEMBER'S TRAP.
BEEN THERE EVER SINCE.

SHE'S KEPT YOU PRISONER FOR THE LAST **THREE MONTHS?**

"EVERY DAY, SHE'D SIC THOSE THINGS ON ME."
"I MUST'VE KILLED HUNDREDS OF THEM. THOUSANDS, MAYBE."

"EVERY DAY MY GIST WOULD GET THAT LITTLE BIT STRONGER."
"LITTLE MORE UNCONTROLLABLE."

SHE LET ME GO TWO DAYS AGO, AND I... I DID THIS.

VORACIOUS, WE CAN HELP YOU. WE CAN–
UGGGH... GO. RUN.

NO, PLEASE

I'LL KILL YOU RIP YOU TEAR YOU APART

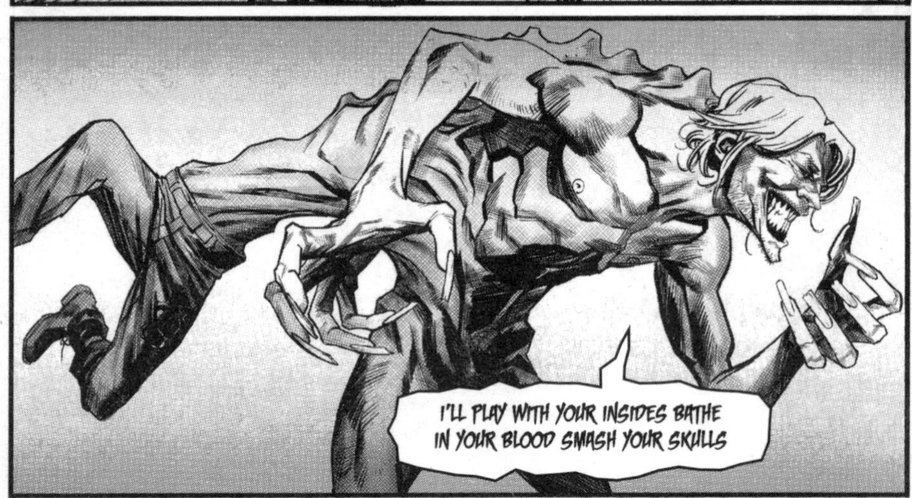
I'LL PLAY WITH YOUR INSIDES BATHE IN YOUR BLOOD SMASH YOUR SKULLS

THIS IS GOING TO HURT

HUK
YOU FIRST, SKELETON.

KRA-KRAK
HEY!

WHY DON'T YOU PICK ON SOMEONE YOUR OWN SIZE?
NNN!

LIKE A BEAR?

OR SOME KIND OF GIRAFFE?

UGH!
SO EAGER TO DIE?

YOU'LL GET YOUR CHANCE, GIRLY.
WHUFFF

AH AH.
NO BEATING UP VALKYRIE.
NUMBER ONE RULE.

VORACIOUS, NOW WOULD BE A WONDERFUL TIME FOR YOU TO REGAIN CONTROL.

OH, I AM IN CONTROL, SKULDUGGERY.
REMEMBER ENSURED THAT'D HAPPEN, THEN SHE SENT ME HERE TO KILL YOU BOTH.

FIGURED IT WAS THE LEAST I COULD -
UGH!
STOP HITTING US, DILLWEED!

WHACK
OOOH, I'M GONNA ENJOY TEARING YOUR ARMS OFF.

NO BEATING UP VALKYRIE, I SAID.
WHY DOES NOBODY EVER LISTEN TO ME?
FWOOOSH

OH, I GET IT.
YOU WANT ALL THE PAIN FOR YOURSELF, THAT RIGHT?

HAPPY TO OBLIGE!

HOW LONG WILL YOU LAST ONCE I BREAK EVERY SINGLE ONE OF YOUR BONES, DO YOU THINK?
OH DEAR.

LET'S FIND OUT!

HEY.

WHANNG
SHOVEL!

"SHOVEL"?
MIGHT BE MY NEW CATCHPHRASE.
KILL YOU... KILL...

WHANNG
I LIKE IT.

SHOVEL!

With Voracious receiving care — under heavy sedation and twenty-four-hour guard — at the Roarhaven Sanctuary, Skulduggery and Valkyrie followed his lead and visited Sabelina Brighten, Remember's mother, at her home in East Sussex, England.

SKULDUGGERY: Sabelina is, shall we say, a free-thinker.
VALKYRIE: Um.
SKULDUGGERY: A very nice lady all round.
VALKYRIE: Very... welcoming. She's a painter, and she sculpts, and makes music. She's, y'know... weird.
SKULDUGGERY: Not religious at all, which is in marked contrast to her daughter, who apparently possesses a deep-seated need to worship one god or another. For most of Remember's life, that meant the Faceless Ones.
VALKYRIE: Then she died.
SKULDUGGERY: Then she faked her death.
VALKYRIE: Didn't even bother to tell her own mum. That sounds weird, though, calling her that. Remember looks, what, twenty-three? Twenty-four? But so does Sabelina.
SKULDUGGERY: I know plenty of people who look older than their parents. It all depends on how much magic each person uses, and how it affects them.
VALKYRIE: It freaks me out a little, to be honest.

Sabelina claimed to know only a handful of sorcerers, and to not concern herself with the affairs of either mages or mortals. She did admit, however, to passing on Voracious's details to Remember, as per Voracious's request. When she tried calling her daughter in the presence of Skulduggery and Valkyrie, however, Remember's number had been disconnected.

The Button

SKULDUGGERY: Conor Delaney's family had been plagued by the design of a box for generations. In the hospitals they ended up in, they'd draw gears and cogs and schematics on the walls. They were conduits for an idea that was planted centuries before. This compulsion infected each and every one of them, and only got stronger as they got older.

But none of them saw the box so clearly as Conor. He was the last one. He was the one who saw the design clearly enough to build it.

VALKYRIE: We tracked him down. He was sitting in his kitchen, the box on the table in front of him. We told him what the Sensitives had told us: if he pressed that button, the world would end. You should have seen his face. His entire life he'd been plagued by this thing, and now it was complete and all he had to do to end his torment was to press the damn button. He didn't, though. He decided to live with the suffering.

Last Stand of Dead Men

When the Accelerator, in the bowels of the Sanctuary, was turned on in order to boost the powers of Argeddion's Teens, it needed to be turned off again within four weeks or risk a catastrophic meltdown that would set in motion a chain of events that would ultimately lead to billions of deaths. With this in mind, it might have been useful to maybe write this little fact down somewhere — on a sign, perhaps, to be stuck next to the TURN ON button.

"But surely something as advanced as the Accelerator would have come with an instruction manual!" I hear you cry. Well, it did, but in a clear case of people being far too clever for their own good, the instruction manual came in the form of a magical-and-mechanical robot that had got bored and wandered off.

The moral of the story? Never give your instruction manuals feet. Never.

The Engineer had been built thirty years earlier to safeguard against exactly the kind of catastrophic meltdown that was now firmly on the cards. For most of that time, it stayed out of sight in the Roarhaven Sanctuary and didn't do a whole lot. Then – I'm assuming – it went slightly stir-crazy and decided it could really do with a nice long walk. Can't really blame it. I've been sitting down here for weeks and I swear to you, I think I'm starting to hear voices. If I could head off and explore Italy, like the Engineer did, then I'd already have my hiking boots on.

I would, however, try to avoid getting hit by that truck.

Five months after the Accelerator had been turned on, fallout from the assassination of Grand Mage Strom continued, as Illori Reticent, of the London Sanctuary, met with the Irish Council of Elders. Grand Mage Ravel, Elder Bespoke and Elder Mist were unimpressed with Reticent's suggestion that the Supreme Council should establish a Council of Nine to "help" the Irish Sanctuary. Reticent also requested that the Accelerator be shut down, as they were nervous about the fact that it could be used to supercharge sorcerers. Ravel wasn't keen on that idea, either,

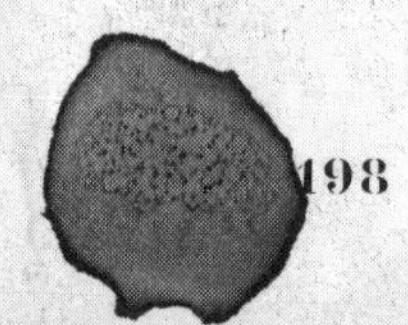

as the Accelerator was the only thing that could power a cage strong enough to contain Darquesse (whenever she appeared). The fact that the opportunity had passed to simply turn off the Accelerator didn't occur to any of the folks in charge.

This refusal of the Supreme Council's request obviously wasn't met with understanding nods, as Bernard Sult and a few other Supreme Council members were sent in to sabotage the Accelerator. Ghastly discovered them and, even though the bomb went off as planned, the explosion left the Accelerator undamaged. Sult and the mages were arrested.

While all this political intrigue was going on, Skulduggery Pleasant had been investigating why the witch Dubhóg Ni Broin had been seen associating with the Warlock who had gone on to try to assassinate Skulduggery and Valkyrie Cain. Skulduggery failed to report in, and so Valkyrie, accompanied by the Monster Hunters, Donegan Bane and Gracious O'Callahan, knocked on the witch's door and the witch's granddaughter, Misery, led them down to the cellar.

After a brief skirmish, Dubhóg explained that the Warlock had tried to recruit her and her fellow Crones to join Charivari's army in an upcoming war. He had been tasked, by Bison Dragonclaw, to kill Skulduggery and Valkyrie in exchange for a name that the Warlocks needed from the Necromancers.

VALKYRIE: I'd just like to point out that I was celebrating my eighteenth birthday while all this was happening. I got an orange car from my folks.

The detectives met up with Solomon Wreath, who told them that, five years earlier, a Necromancer — Baritone — had heard three mercenaries boasting about killing Warlocks. These mortals supposedly worked for Department X.[1]

1. Department X would appear to be little more than an urban legend: a joint Irish-British military force dedicated to hunting sorcerers.

This led them to believe that someone was working to make the Warlocks believe that they were being attacked by a mortal organisation. Baritone reported that the mercenaries had received their orders from two men: one of whom matched the Torment's description, and the other was a man they couldn't quite remember.

VALKYRIE: This guy no one could remember, he was popping up a lot. Five years ago, he arranged for a bunch of mortals to kill a bunch of Warlocks. Three years ago, he got Davina Marr to blow up the Dublin Sanctuary. And only five months ago he released Sean Mackin from his cell. All this, and the only thing we knew about him was that he'd hung around with the Torment.

Vaurien Scapegrace, now in a new female body, was being trained in combat by Grandmaster Ping, a Kung Fu master born and raised in Bristol, England, who had made a career out of teaching martial arts to people who wanted an "authentic" experience. After being attacked by a creature that may have been shunted in from another dimension, Scapegrace decided to become a masked vigilante, defending Roarhaven from evil. Thrasher volunteered to be his sidekick. I think they were just bored.

Valkyrie visited China Sorrows to enquire about this man who could erase himself from people's memories. China informed her that the amnesia is brought about by a rare type of amethyst crystal, one of which was located in the Repository.

VALKYRIE: Skulduggery wouldn't come with me to talk to China.
SKULDUGGERY: I was still dealing with anger issues and other homicidal impulses.
VALKYRIE: At the time, my folks were trying to convince me to apply to university and stuff, so I was debating whether or not to tell them the truth about me and magic and everything. I needed someone to talk to about it, and China was there, so... She talked about something called the Second Lifetime Syndrome, where mages watch their mortal loved ones grow old and die. She advised against telling them.

Our heroes found an amethyst crystal in the Repository, realising that the crystals were so rare that this was probably the exact one that their target used – meaning that he could very well be a Sanctuary Mage. Another traitor in the Sanctuary, you ask? Very possibly...

OK, I've completely forgotten about the journalist guy! Remember Kenny Dunne? He'd hooked up with a cameraman, Patrick Slattery, and they'd been tailing Valkyrie for months by this stage. They had big plans to expose the world of magic and monsters. Don't worry, we'll come back to them.

Our daring detectives visited Moloch to ask for the vampires'

China Sorrows

help should war break out, as was looking increasingly likely, because tensions were ratcheting up. The Supreme Council demanded the release of Sult and retaliated by arresting the Irish mages currently in their jurisdictions, including Dexter Vex. An Irish sorcerer, Caius Caviler, was actually killed while in custody. The American Grand Mage, Bisahalani, promised a full investigation, but stopped short of an apology.

In retaliation to *that*, Portia and Syc, two Children of the Spider, killed Bernard Sult in a live broadcast on the Global Link network, broadcast to every sorcerer around the world. Ravel immediately ordered that a (supposedly) impenetrable shield dome be raised around the country, stopping mages from entering.

VALKYRIE: We'd gone to see Cassandra (Pharos) while all this was happening. She'd had a new vision she felt she needed to share with us. It was pretty horrible.
SKULDUGGERY: The vision was a slightly altered version of the one we'd already seen. We saw a city in flames, and Ghastly and Tanith, we saw Ravel in agony, we saw Valkyrie in distress... and we saw Darquesse killing Desmond and Melissa and Alice. And then killing me.
VALKYRIE: So that was a cheerful few minutes.
SKULDUGGERY: And, as we were leaving, we were attacked by a group led by Gepard, an American mage I knew. The Supreme Council had declared war on the Irish Sanctuary, and their first order of business was eliminating the greatest threats.
VALKYRIE: That was us, baby.
SKULDUGGERY: Indeed. This attempt on our lives failed.
VALKYRIE: I honestly don't think you needed to say that last bit.

The Supreme Council now consisted of twenty-two Sanctuaries, and Skulduggery and Valkyrie were but two of the names on their list of targets they wanted assassinated.

Attempts were made on the lives of Anton Shudder, Finbar Wrong and nine others, including Fletcher Renn, who was badly injured, and China Sorrows, who was hunted across the country by Vincent Foe and his gang of murderous bikers.

We now know that Madame Mist had been scheming with this man whom nobody could remember. Their plan appeared to be provoking Charivari into assembling an army of Warlocks and Witches in order to go to war with the mortals. The sorcerers would then swoop in and stop Charivari and be hailed by the mortals as heroes. From there, they could take over with the minimum of resistance.

While being transferred to another jail, Dexter Vex was broken out by Tanith Low and Billy-Ray Sanguine, who took him to Ireland as a peace offering. Tanith, still possessed by that Remnant, viewed Valkyrie/Darquesse as her messiah, and wanted to help in whatever way she could.

The Dead Men re-formed, this time consisting of Skulduggery Pleasant, Erskine Ravel, Ghastly Bespoke, Anton Shudder, Saracen Rue, Dexter Vex and Valkyrie Cain. Their mission was to recover the Engineer, which was being held at the French Sanctuary.

VALKYRIE: The Supreme Council planned to use the Engineer to shut down the Accelerator if we started supercharging our sorcerers.

SKULDUGGERY: Whereas we needed it to stop the Accelerator from

overloading. So, either way, we were going after the Engineer – and they knew it.
VALKYRIE: See, it was a trap. The Supreme Council were trying to lure us in, but, instead of using that knowledge to our advantage, we decided to just walk into their trap anyway, because we're dumb.
SKULDUGGERY: That's not why we were going to walk into it. We were hoping that the ambush would motivate the African and Australian Sanctuaries to come to our rescue and then fight by our side. It was risky, but it was the only way we were going to win this war.
VALKYRIE: See? Dumb.

While the Dead Men embarked on their mission, Tanith and Sanguine teamed up with the Monster Hunters to disable the Midnight Hotel, the only remaining way for the enemy to enter the country. Despite encountering General Mantis and getting captured, Tanith's team completed the mission and got away.

The Dead Men entered the sorcerer town of Wolfsong.

VALKYRIE: It was quiet and it was friendly and we went to the tavern and everyone told war stories and... But there was this fog that'd roll in, and it bound magic, but apart from that it was nice. Lovely people.
SKULDUGGERY: But they'd been dead a hundred years. It was a town cursed by the Warlocks, by Charivari, the inhabitants cursed to be killed and then come back, only to be killed again the next night. We found a friend of ours, Trebuchet, who used to be the French Grand Mage. He was the only one alive. He showed us a secret way into the French Sanctuary, but he didn't leave with us. He stayed to endure his punishment.

Madame Mist sent Fletcher and the Monster Hunters to apprehend Zona, a Mexican mage who had the expertise

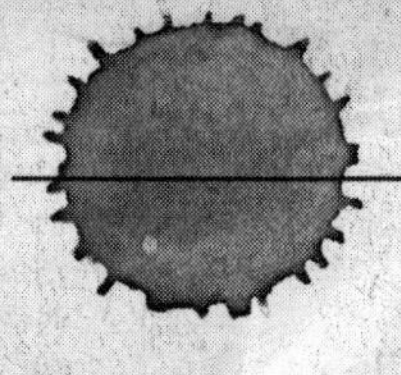

required to dismantle the (supposedly) impenetrable shield dome. When they brought her back to Roarhaven, they discovered that Mist had personally released Portia and Syc from their cells, and that two more Children of the Spider — the Terror and the Scourge — were on their way.

Infiltrating the French Sanctuary that held the Engineer, the Dead Men sprang the Supreme Council's trap.

SKULDUGGERY: They thought they had us.
VALKYRIE: They did have us.
SKULDUGGERY: And then our friends in the Australian and African Sanctuaries came to our rescue.
VALKYRIE: Can you believe that our entire plan hinged on whether or not other people came to save us?
SKULDUGGERY: Calculated risks, while risky, are still calculated.
VALKYRIE: Whatever that means.

They placed the Engineer in the Keep,[1] confident that its presence would lure the Supreme Council's forces, under General Mantis, into the Keep itself — at which point the enemy would realise the facility was empty. They would find themselves trapped there, as the Dead Men led an army against them. Surrender would be Mantis's only option. In theory.

1. A fortified location bordered by a cliff wall and dense woodland.

Another problem arose: the Engineer's memory-processing

unit had been damaged, and the only possible replacement was being kept at the Sanctuary in London.

SKULDUGGERY: We needed those memory files. Without them, the Accelerator was going to overload in a matter of weeks.

China led Foe's gang straight to the Church of the Faceless, and let Eliza Scorn try to deal with the assault while she escaped out the back. Which was pretty sneaky of her.

The Dead Men infiltrated the London Sanctuary and retrieved the memory-processing unit — but, while they were doing this, the Councils of Elders at both the Australian and African Sanctuaries were assassinated. The new English Grand Mage, Cothernus Ode, swore this was not the work of the Supreme Council.

Scapegrace and Thrasher, out on one of their usually uneventful night-time patrols, saw Madame Mist consorting with a Shunter, Creyfon Signate (remember that name for later). Their little adventures would eventually get a trio of thugs sent out to Scapegrace's pub to kill them. Lucky they had Grandmaster Ping there to come to their rescue.

Mantis and his army attacked the Keep, and Fletcher teleported Nye, the Engineer and the Monster Hunters away. Once Mantis had the Keep occupied, Ravel's army revealed itself, effectively surrounding the facility. Mantis's army had no choice but to fight its way out — at which point, Moloch's vampires would attack from the rear. It was all planned out so perfectly.

Charivari, meanwhile, had asked both the Crones of the Cold

Embrace and the Maidens of the New Dawn to join his army, both of whom declined. Then he travelled to Africa to recruit the Brides of Blood Tears, who were a lot more receptive to his ideas. It was while he was here, it is believed, that he worked out that Department X wasn't real, that it wasn't the mortals who were moving against the Warlocks, but the sorcerers.

Fletcher and the Monster Hunters teleported to Mozambique to investigate what Charivari was doing there. They met Ajuoga, who they didn't know was actually one of the Brides of Blood Tears, and, at her earliest opportunity, she abducted Fletcher. The poor guy.

Utilising both roadblocks and an energy shield, Madame Mist sealed off Roarhaven from Grand Mage Ravel's forces, and sent assassins after both him and Ghastly. The assassins failed.

Ravel, Ghastly and Shudder took a contingent of loyal sorcerers and Cleavers to Roarhaven, while Skulduggery, Valkyrie, Saracen and Dexter stayed to fight Mantis's army. Mantis and his soldiers engaged with Skulduggery's forces. According to the plan, this was the moment when Moloch was to unleash the fifty vampires – but none came.

VALKYRIE: I got up to the hill, found Moloch dead. Dusk had broken the most sacred of rules – he'd killed another vampire. From the hill, though, I could see across the battlefield, and I saw what I thought were our reinforcements. For a few seconds, I actually thought this was going to be an easy victory.
SKULDUGGERY: But they weren't our reinforcements. They were the other half of Mantis's army, and they attacked our rear and we didn't have a chance. We had to retreat.

Ghastly, Ravel and their team managed to get through the shield surrounding Roarhaven, and sneaked into the Sanctuary. Inside, they found China, exhausted and wounded, and got her to the Medical Bay before carrying on.

SKULDUGGERY: They came upon Madame Mist and some other Children of the Spider. Mist admitted to her part in the attempt to get the Warlocks to attack the mortals, and revealed that Nye had managed to stitch the White Cleaver back together, and put him in a brand-new uniform. He even had a new name – the Black Cleaver.

Ghastly and Shudder attempted to arrest them all, but Mist... she wasn't in charge. She had never been in charge. There had always been someone else making the plans, pulling the strings – a man who had used that amethyst crystal to make people forget his involvement. My old friend Erskine Ravel.

The Cleavers that Ravel had brought as back-up killed Anton Shudder. Ravel himself killed Ghastly Bespoke.

The shield that had been erected around Ireland fell. Mantis's army surrounded Roarhaven. The individual Sanctuaries that made up the Supreme Council began squabbling among themselves.

VALKYRIE: And I went home, to Haggard. I had to. Our great trap had been sprung and we'd been outmanoeuvred. Ghastly and Shudder had been... Ravel had betrayed us. The bad guys were winning. I needed to go home, so I went, and that damn reflection had pretty much figured that she'd be better off living my life than I would, so we had a bit of a fight. She was no longer an *it*. She was calling herself Stephanie now. She showed me how she'd killed Carol; she showed me

Fletcher Renn

the Sceptre. She tried to kill me. I tried to kill her. Then my mum came home and I had to run.

Ravel's mages found Kenny and Slattery asking questions about magic, and brought them in. Ravel saw an opportunity for a documentary that could help convince the mortal world that not all sorcerers were a threat.

Skulduggery's forces needed a Teleporter to have any kind of chance, so Skulduggery and Valkyrie travelled to the home of the Brides of Blood Tears, sneaking inside to hunt for Fletcher.

FLETCHER: I didn't need rescuing. Valkyrie might tell you I did, but I was doing fine on my own. I had my escape plan, I knew exactly what to do, and I was just biding my time. I did not need to be rescued.

They were discovered, however, and Valkyrie was badly injured.

VALKYRIE: Going up against the Brides was... intense. I'd never really fought Witches before and they came pretty close to killing me. But I had Darquesse in my head the whole time, talking to me, goading me... I didn't have a chance against the Brides and I was panicking. I was desperate. I was weak. She offered to take over, and I let her.

When Sanctuary operatives surveyed the scene weeks later, their reports detail absolute carnage. Death and destruction on a massive scale.

Valkyrie Cain, it seemed, was gone, and now there was only Darquesse.

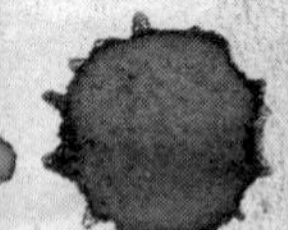

VALKYRIE: Don't worry, I come back. Or do I? Yes, I do.

SKULDUGGERY: We regrouped at Grimwood, where we prioritised Charivari as the most immediate threat. Once the Warlocks were taken care of, we could turn our attention to Ravel.

They were joined by the reflection, Stephanie, who had what appeared to be the only weapon capable of killing Darquesse — the Sceptre of the Ancients. Tanith and Sanguine, who had only been a part of the team because of Tanith's devotion to Darquesse, decided to leave after making an attempt on Stephanie's life.

Skulduggery and his team teleported into Roarhaven, co-ordinating with China, in time to watch Ravel make his speech. He announced that he had reached out to the Supreme Council and had brokered peace. The Sanctuaries of the world were now in agreement: their duty was to defend the mortals from the Warlock threat. To do that, magic would have to be revealed to the world, and the mortals would need to understand that the Sanctuaries were their friends and guardians. His plan, to effectively dominate the world, was received by an enthusiastic audience. He revealed that he had commissioned the architect and Shunter Creyfon Signate to build a massive city in another dimension. The construction of this city had taken years, but now it was ready. At Ravel's instruction, Signate shunted the entire city in, on and around those gathered — and the city of Roarhaven came into being.

It was an impressive achievement.

SKULDUGGERY: Ambitious. Audacious. Astonishing.

A few days later, Skulduggery and his team got word that China was in trouble. They suspected it was a trap, that China had been forced to contact them, but they went anyway.

It was, in fact, a trap.

SKULDUGGERY: And then the Warlocks arrived. Ravel had left a trail that led straight to the mortals, but Charivari was no fool. He knew Roarhaven was behind it all, and he turned up with his Warlocks and Wretchlings.

Putting their differences aside, Skulduggery and Ravel decided to work together to defend the city.

The details of the siege and conflict can be found in ***The Battle of Roarhaven*** by Gracious O'Callahan and Donegan Bane (available in your local Sanctuary bookshop), but there was a whole lot of death and screaming and blood flying everywhere, and guns and swords and magic and fireballs and heads being chopped off, and there were a bunch of Roarhaven mages who, having had their power boosted by the Accelerator, were as much a danger to their own side as to the bloody Warlocks.

And through it all was Charivari, this ten-foot-tall mass of muscle and savagery. I wasn't there when any of this happened (I was recovering from Archivist's Elbow, a debilitating yet very mild sprain) and so was on holiday in Barbados at the time. But I've seen the footage and Charivari was a terrifying man to behold, and he remained a terrifying man to behold

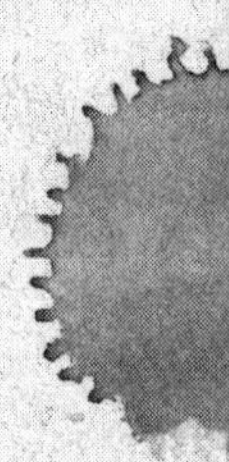

until Stephanie used the Sceptre on him. Then he was just a terrifying mound of dust.

Ravel, Skulduggery knew, would turn on him the moment that the Roarhaven forces began to dominate the battlefield, so he'd decided that he needed to strike first.

Outside, the Warlocks were still fighting, and people were still dying, and then Darquesse appeared, and she started destroying her enemies with waves of black flame.

Back in the Sanctuary, Skulduggery and China closed in on Mist and Ravel. China killed Mist, then had her own life saved by Darquesse, who proceeded to deliver to Ravel twenty-three hours of agony each day as punishment for what he'd done. Then Darquesse left. Just flew away.

SKULDUGGERY: The battle was done. It was over. The only thing left to do now was ask the Engineer to shut down the Accelerator.
SARACEN: But there was one element to shutting it down that no one had told us about. A soul must be willingly sacrificed for the Accelerator to actually turn off. If this wasn't done within twenty-three days, the Accelerator would self-destruct.

China declared herself the new Grand Mage and charged Skulduggery with the task of finding Darquesse and stopping her – killing her if he had to.

KENNY: Patrick and I, we got the hell out of there in the middle of the battle. It was chaos. It was beyond chaos. We got as much footage as we could and then we ran. Somehow we made it, you know? But we... we saw what happened. Or... we thought we did. We thought we saw Valkyrie's reflection – who we thought was *actually* Valkyrie – get attacked. What we didn't see was that English kid grabbing her and vanishing. We thought she died. And suddenly it all changed. I didn't care about the documentary, or revealing the truth, or becoming a big-shot journalist. The only thing I cared about was that this brave girl had died for us all. So I edited the footage we had and... and gave it to her parents. I figured they deserved to know that their daughter had died a hero.

REFLECTION

An individual's exact copy, capable of replacing them in social settings for limited amounts of time. The subterfuge becomes apparent to a mage within minutes, but arouses little more than a vague sense of unease in the minds of mortals.

Summoned with a SIGIL and an incantation meant to focus the minds of those without-or-inexperienced-with magic: "Surface speak, surface feel, surface think, surface real."

Once it has left the mirror, the reflection must consciously reverse its physical image in order to pass as the original. Upon returning, the reflection's memories merge with those of the individual.

An individual can only operate one reflection, and it is advised that the reflection operate out of the same mirror each time. Summoning the reflection from more than one mirror may lead to complications.

RIPPERS

Ex-Cleavers who hire themselves out to paying customers.

Known for wearing a variation of the Cleaver uniform – with a jacket instead of a coat, black instead of grey, and twin sickles instead of a scythe.

ARBITER CORPS

Before the Sanctuaries came into existence, law and order in the magical communities were handled by the Arbiter Corps, a group of elite sorcerers endowed with unlimited authority to investigate and arrest. The Arbiters operated on a global scale, and no matter, organisation, or individual was outside of their jurisdiction.

"Embrace
your inner
LUNATIC.
FUN TIMES
GUARANTEED"

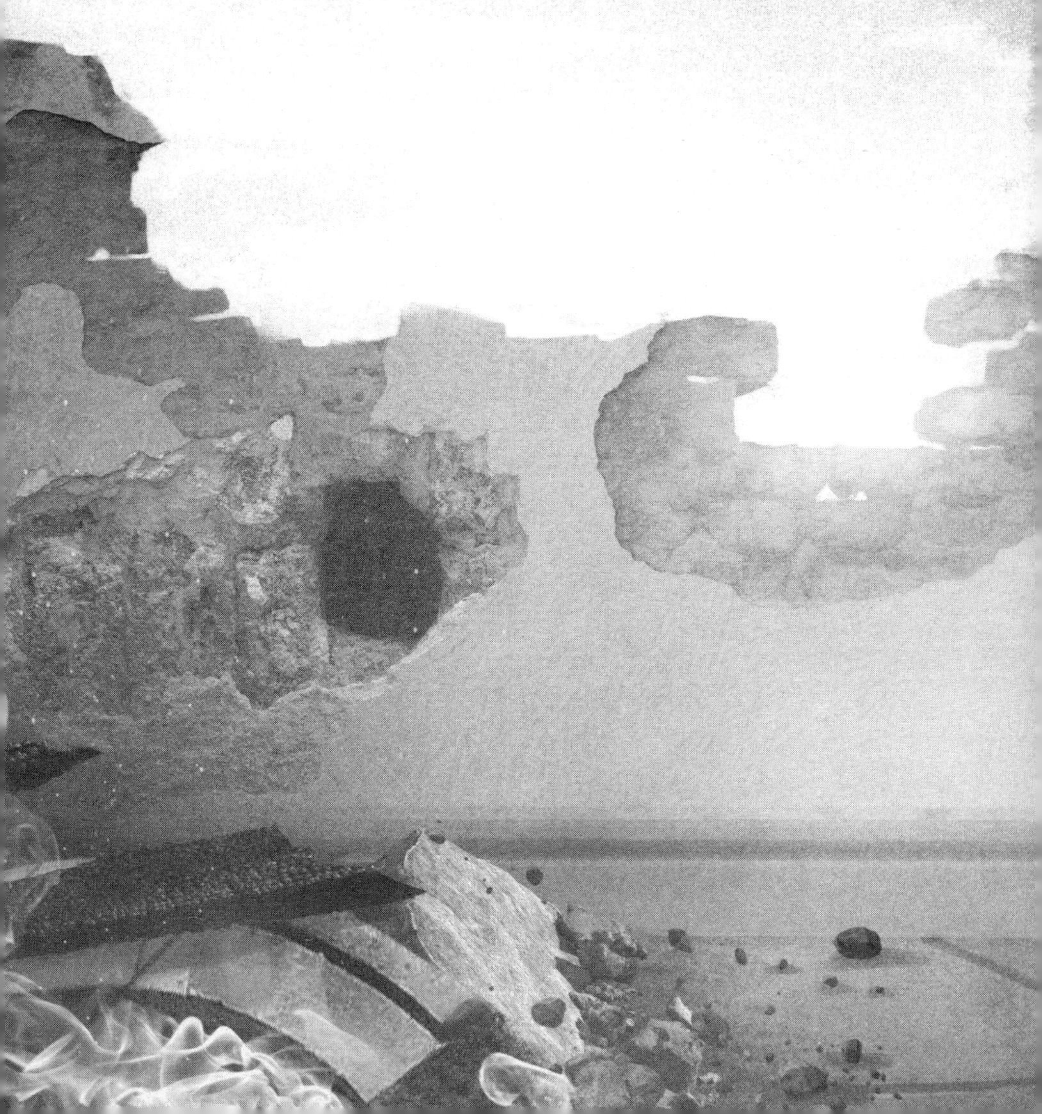

A NOTE FROM THE ARCHIVIST

I am Archivist Mordant. Archivist Rux has failed to turn up for work for three days in a row. Calls have gone unanswered. I have requested that the Archive Department investigate the matter, but those in charge are dismissive of my concerns. I have known Archivist Rux for fourteen years and, while we have never been friends, I do know that simply failing to turn up for work is not a part of who he is.

Please excuse the brevity in what is to follow: this project is behind schedule and I shall be cutting corners where necessary.

Thank you for your understanding.

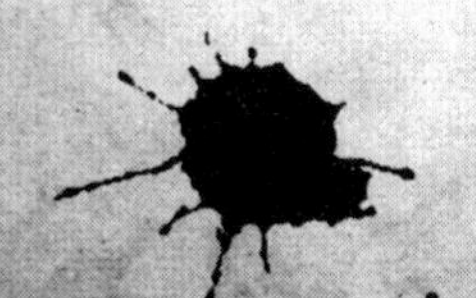

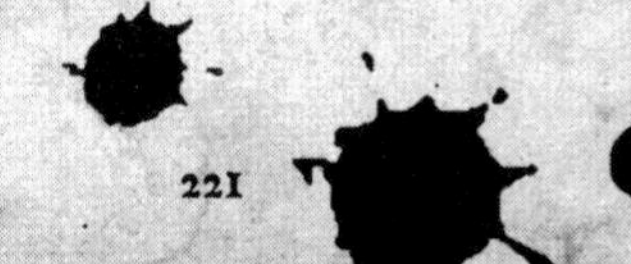

ABROGATE RAZE

PART TWO BY TAWDRY HEPBURN

In 1608, a man named Septimus Revere joined the Approaching Dawn, an obscure religious order for mages, what we would today call a cult, led by a sorcerer known as the Rector. They worshipped Kalomet, a deity with no fixed form or gender, who represented happiness through knowledge of the self.

By 1615, the Rector was dead and Revere was in charge. Under his leadership, the Approaching Dawn expanded in size and influence, involving itself in mortal affairs and amassing a steadily increasing fortune.

In 1636, taking advantage of the war against Mevolent, the Approaching Dawn plundered and stole and collected a wide array of magical tomes, which Revere devoured voraciously. One of the new converts to the cult, however, recognised Revere to be Abrogate Raze. Abrogate was forced to abandon the cult and everything he'd built up when the Arbiters arrived, and once more faded from history.

In 1646, a man called Wolfric Dredge was jailed for murder (no details found on the victim) in Italy. Dredge spent fourteen years in Carcere di Miseria. He escaped, was recaptured, and spent a further eighteen years in Carcere di Suora Oscura. While he was there, he admitted to being Abrogate Raze, and arrangements were made for his transfer to Ireland to answer for the murder of Quinlan Forte.

In 1678, a team of Arbiters came to teleport Abrogate to Coldheart Prison. Records show that they teleported out of Carcere di Suora Oscura at 11:29 on the morning of May 8th, but failed to arrive in Coldheart, where Skulduggery Pleasant was waiting to confront his father, seventy-one years after Raze had killed Quinlan. The bodies of the Irish sorcerers were found a week later.

Skulduggery Pleasant learned that Abrogate had been rescued by the Approaching Dawn, led now by Bertol Lucifugul. Lucifugal, however, had freed him as both a demonstration of his strength – in defying the Arbiters – and proof to his followers that he was superior to their "idol", Abrogate. He held a rigged trial that was supposed to convict Abrogate of blasphemy – but, when it came to a vote, all except Lucifugal found Abrogate innocent. Abrogate took over, and Lucifugal was put to death.

By 1686, the Approaching Dawn had lost all of its wealth and resources, mostly thanks to the efforts of Skulduggery Pleasant. That year, Abrogate and all but one member of the cult drank poison, killing themselves so as to join with their god, Kalomet. The only cult member not to drink was Susurrus Fallow,[1] who backed out at the last moment. He described being in a room with eighteen corpses, and then watching Abrogate Raze sit up. Distraught at having survived (Susurrus disputes this, claiming that Abrogate had died and come back to life), Abrogate ran into the woods and disappeared.

1. Susurrus Fallow turned his back on Kalomet and all religion at that point, and later became an operative at the Irish Sanctuary.

The Dying of the Light

The Accelerator had two weeks until it reached critical mass, potentially supercharging the power of every sorcerer twenty times over. The Engineer needed a soul "willingly sacrificed" in order to deactivate the machine.

Skulduggery Pleasant and Stephanie, Valkyrie Cain's sentient reflection, divided their time between searching for Darquesse and taking down the nineteen Accelerator-boosted mages who were making trouble.

Doctor Reverie Synecdoche tried to give Stephanie the Deathtouch Gauntlet – a weapon that, theoretically, had the potential to destroy Darquesse – but Stephanie declined to take it.

VALKYRIE: I wasn't there for any of this. I was trapped in a corner of Darquesse's mind while she shared a house with Tanith and Billy-Ray. That situation just didn't have the makings of the sitcom I thought it might.

Skulduggery Pleasant and Stephanie met with Grand Mage China Sorrows, discussing the link between Darquesse and Erskine Ravel, who was experiencing twenty-three hours of agony each day as punishment for his crimes. That link, Skulduggery reasoned, could be broken by shunting Ravel to another dimension, which would then draw Darquesse to them. The other option was tracking Darquesse's companions, Tanith Low and Billy-Ray Sanguine.

Skulduggery and Stephanie recruited Creyfon Signate, who was in a cell for his part in Ravel's plans, to shunt Ravel into another dimension.

VALKYRIE: At this point, I reckon that Darquesse and Tanith were releasing all the Remnants from the Receptacle, where'd they'd been for, what, almost two years? She used one of them to possess this guy, Nestor Tarry, an expert in quantum physics. He told Darquesse that to truly understand magic she'd have to speak with Argeddion, but Cassandra and the others had completely rewritten his personality to make him a totally different person, and not even Darquesse knew how to find him. But Nestor, the idiot, told her she could learn how from a book called the *Hessian Grimoire*. Darquesse turned him into a chair after that.

Skulduggery and Stephanie found out about a house Sanguine owned in Dublin and, while waiting for him to arrive, discovered the God-Killer weapons that Tanith thought he'd destroyed. When Sanguine arrived he co-operated immediately, claiming to oppose Darquesse's plans.

He told them that Darquesse was seeking the *Hessian Grimoire* in her goal to acquire darker magical knowledge. Now that he was actively working as a double agent, he kept the God-Killer dagger for himself, should he need it in an emergency.

Grand Mage Sorrows sent Vincent Foe and his biker gang of nihilists to join the Church of the Faceless. Jajo Prave, the Church's secretary, allowed them membership, thereby breaking the law prohibiting those with criminal records from being a part of the Church. Much to Eliza Scorn's fury, Sanctuary mages raided the headquarters, finding a list of secret Faceless Ones worshippers who were backing the Church financially.

Fletcher and Dai Maybury had joined Gracious O'Callahan and Donegan Bane in the Monster Hunters, tracking and apprehending the super-charged sorcerers around the world. Fletcher, at this point, was also Stephanie's boyfriend. They were diverted from their assignment into tracking down and trapping Remnants. The first one they found, however, hinted that perhaps his fellow Remnants had re-evaluated their opinion of Darquesse as their messiah.

Finbar Wrong informed Skulduggery and Stephanie about a vision he'd

had of Valkyrie asking for help. Cassandra Pharos conducted a seance and Valkyrie communicated with them through Finbar.

SKULDUGGERY: We spoke to Valkyrie. Darquesse was occupied with expanding her knowledge of magic, so Valkyrie had a short window in which to speak to us without being detected. We told her of the plan, to separate her personality from Darquesse's, and then drag Darquesse out of her, into a Soul Catcher.

Grand Mage Sorrows set about designing and setting a trap – a circle inscribed with Talveh Sigils, designed to use a sorcerer's magic against them. Once the circle was in place, Skulduggery and Stephanie broke into the Vault in the Dublin Municipal Art Gallery and stole the *Hessian Grimoire* and were, as they expected, suddenly confronted by Darquesse.

Keeping the grimoire with her, Stephanie led Darquesse into the trap. Stunned by a blast of her own magic, Darquesse didn't struggle as Cassandra, Finbar and Deacon separated the two aspects of her personality – and Darquesse was drawn out and trapped in a Soul Catcher.

SKULDUGGERY: Or so we thought.

VALKYRIE: She was just too smart for you.

SKULDUGGERY: She was.

VALKYRIE: Which meant I was too smart for you.

SKULDUGGERY: I wouldn't go that far.

VALKYRIE: They thought they had me back, and they thought that Darquesse was in their Soul Catcher. But it was the other way round. They'd managed to pull me all the way out of my own body, which was now completely controlled by Darquesse.

SKULDUGGERY: What was it like, actually, being in that Soul Catcher? How did it feel? Could you even feel?

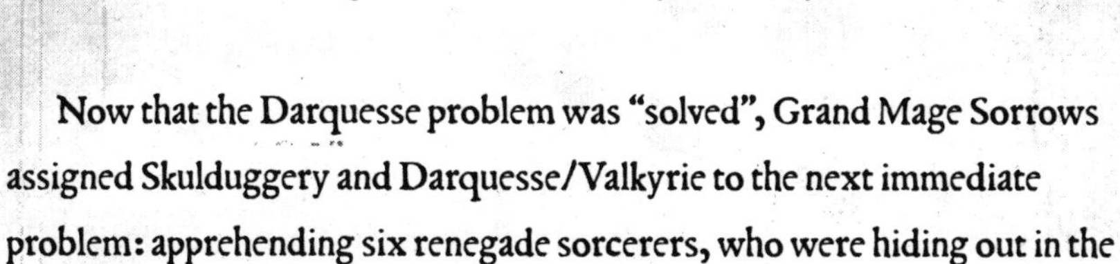

VALKYRIE: It was...

SKULDUGGERY: Yes?

VALKYRIE: Very round.

SKULDUGGERY: I despair, sometimes, with you, I really do.

Now that the Darquesse problem was "solved", Grand Mage Sorrows assigned Skulduggery and Darquesse/Valkyrie to the next immediate problem: apprehending six renegade sorcerers, who were hiding out in the New York Sanctuary.

Before she left, however, Darquesse asked Deacon Maybury for Argeddion's new identity. When he told her only Erskine Ravel knew, she killed him and walked away.

When they arrived at the New York Sanctuary to round up the renegade sorcerers, Darquesse took a detour, killing both the American Grand Mage and the Gnarl, a creature from the Caves of the Void. When Fletcher teleported them home, however, Grand Mage Sorrows was waiting to kill her.

SKULDUGGERY: There was a subtle difference in how Valkyrie and Darquesse behave – a confidence that only a truly immortal being could possess. I called ahead, got China ready to use the Deathtouch Gauntlet. We only had moments.

When the entity that was Darquesse left Valkyrie's corpse and departed, Grand Mage Sorrows allowed Valkyrie's life force to re-enter her body. Skulduggery used a Sunburst device to revive her – but upon awakening, Valkyrie discovered that Darquesse had taken all her magic with her.

Fletcher, Saracen, Dexter, Dai and the Monster Hunters' hunt for the Remnants was curtailed somewhat by the Remnants possessing both Dai and

Vex, and telling the others that they weren't following Darquesse's plans any more. Now they had their own plans.

Darquesse was possessing human bodies, but her power level was burning them out within hours. She approached Vincent Foe and his gang, offered them a role in the apocalypse to come – which they eagerly accepted – and possessed Obloquy.

VALKYRIE: I got back home and argued with Stephanie because, like, she killed Carol and tried to kill me, but then... I don't know. We started talking, and I realised she'd changed. She'd evolved. She was with Fletcher and, honestly, I knew that she'd be a better girlfriend to him than I ever was. And I could see that she loved my family just like I did. Oh, and Tanith popped by just long enough to kick us both in the heads, but when we told her that Darquesse was floating around somewhere as an untethered entity, she kinda lost steam. She didn't seem to be that into the idea of the apocalypse any more. Then she left, and Stephanie decided to give up the Sceptre and go back to a normal life and we agreed to, basically, share. That was the plan, anyway.

Stephanie's body was found the next day.

SKULDUGGERY: She'd put up a fight. Put up a hell of a fight. But sometimes that isn't enough. Sometimes you can't stop what's coming.
VALKYRIE: We didn't know why she'd done it. Darquesse, I mean. Why kill Stephanie? What did it get her?

FLETCHER: I really liked Stephanie. The thing is, she wasn't Valkyrie. I mean, you'd think that she'd just be another version of Valkyrie Cain and she really wasn't. There were huge similarities, of course, but... she was a completely different person. I don't know what would have happened if she'd stayed alive. Maybe we'd still be together. I think we would.

Valkyrie went home to retrieve the Sceptre – as a Deadlocked object, it would now bond to the next person who touched it.

VALKYRIE: Stephanie had hidden it in Alice's cot, and Alice... she must have touched it, because it had bonded to her. I couldn't use it. No one could use it. Not without killing Alice and then bonding with it themselves.

That night, Vincent Foe, Mercy and Samuel stole Stephanie's body from the Sanctuary morgue. When Valkyrie heard of this she drove to Grimwood and spoke to Echo-Gordon, who agreed with her conclusion – that Darquesse was going to soak Stephanie's body in the Source Fountain in the Caves of the Void. Just like it had done with the four God-Killers, those waters would imbue Stephanie's body with magical properties, allowing Darquesse to possess it without destroying it from the inside.

The detectives took the Echo Stone down into the caves with them. Echo-Gordon's directions led Skulduggery one way and Valkyrie the other, and it was she who came upon the Source Fountain, in which Stephanie's body was submerged. Foe's gang watched over it, and thanked Valkyrie for bringing Darquesse down with her.

VALKYRIE: Darquesse had taken over the Echo Stone. She'd stolen Gordon's appearance, his voice, she had access to his knowledge, and she got me to deliver her right to the place she needed to be. Then she left the Echo Stone, possessed Stephanie, they used the Sunburst on her, and up she sits. Darquesse, in the flesh.

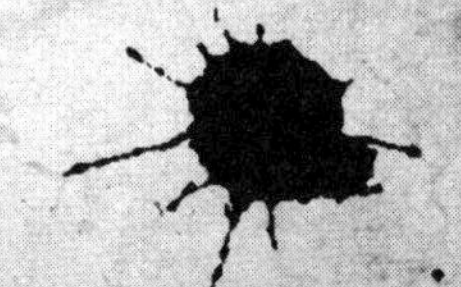

When Mercy went to restrain Valkyrie, Tanith arrived and killed her, allowing Valkyrie to run, rejoin Skulduggery, and escape the caves. Despite Foe and Samuel demanding Tanith's head, Darquesse merely extracted the Remnant from inside her, and swallowed it herself. This was the Remnant that had been inside Kenspeckle Grouse, and she needed the knowledge it had absorbed in order to track down Argeddion.

The physical trauma that she experienced would have killed Tanith if Darquesse hadn't immediately healed her.

Creyfon Signate and a team of Cleavers shunted Erskine Ravel to the Leibniz Universe, thus breaking the link with Darquesse that delivered twenty-three hours of pain every day. Now that they were preparing the lure, they needed the trap, and so they brought Melancholia St Clair out of her induced coma to act as reinforcement.

When Valkyrie returned to Haggard, she discovered that her parents had watched the documentary that Kenny Dunne had given them almost three weeks earlier.

VALKYRIE: They knew. They saw me on screen, throwing fireballs, using Necromancy. They saw the battle with the Warlocks and they saw me and Fletcher fighting Caelan in his vampire form... There was no denying it.
SKULDUGGERY: I arrived to explain things. I think I did a really good job.
VALKYRIE: They wanted me to stop, and right then I didn't have any magic, so it wouldn't have been impossible... but I couldn't. I had to do my part, whatever that ended up being, to keep them safe. To keep everyone safe.

Now free of the Remnant, Tanith returned to Roarhaven just as Signate arrived back from the Leibniz Universe with the news that Ravel had got free.

Using the knowledge she had absorbed from the Remnant that had once

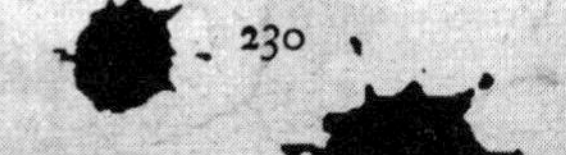

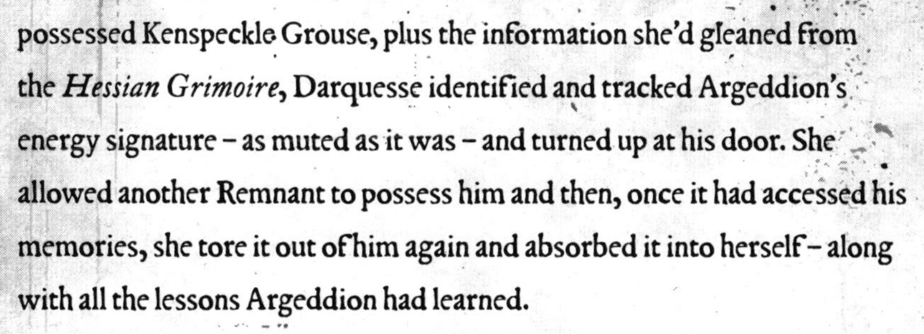

possessed Kenspeckle Grouse, plus the information she'd gleaned from the *Hessian Grimoire*, Darquesse identified and tracked Argeddion's energy signature – as muted as it was – and turned up at his door. She allowed another Remnant to possess him and then, once it had accessed his memories, she tore it out of him again and absorbed it into herself – along with all the lessons Argeddion had learned.

The detectives were shunted to the Leibniz Universe where they tracked Erskine Ravel to a church where the Children of the Spider had taken to worshipping the Faceless Ones. They found Ravel, but had to fight their way out – and were confronted by Mevolent, Lord Vile and a brought-back-from-death Baron Vengeous.

VALKYRIE: We were gonna lose. Skulduggery and Ravel were good, but I didn't have any magic and even if I did... Naw, we were gonna lose. And then Darquesse arrived.

Now that she knew how to shunt, Darquesse had picked up Ravel's trail and she was here to take him back.

Mevolent, however, had been waiting to face her again, and he revealed a weapon no one had seen before.

VALKYRIE: The magic-sucker.
SKULDUGGERY: That's not what it's–
VALKYRIE: The magic-sucker.

The Nullifier rifle was capable of draining a sorcerer's magic for seconds at a time.

VALKYRIE: Darquesse didn't like the magic-sucker. After getting shot with it a few times she was, like, I'm outta here. So she shunted away and the rest of us were grabbed and I was handed over to Professor Nye – in the Leibniz universe, Nye's a bit of an overachiever. It examined me, told me that when Darquesse took my magic she left me as a completely empty vessel, waiting to be filled.

Nefarian Serpine – now leading the Resistance – rescued Valkyrie, promising to free Skulduggery and Ravel if she helped him take the Nullifier rifle from Mevolent.

VALKYRIE: I did my best impersonation of Darquesse and, amazingly, we got away with both our lives and the magic-sucker.

SKULDUGGERY: Nullifier.

VALKYRIE: Magic-sucker.

Lord Vile tracked them down and when he attacked, the Nullifier rifle was destroyed in Valkyrie's hands, triggering her Surge.

VALKYRIE: The Surge? Yeah. The Surge sucks.

Skulduggery, Valkyrie and Ravel returned home, and Ravel was immediately put into a circle, carved with sigils to hide him from Darquesse.

Dusk reached an agreement with Grand Mage Sorrows: the vampires would help in the upcoming battle against Darquesse, and in return they would be made citizens of Roarhaven.

Even though her magic had yet to manifest, Valkyrie joined the others once her Surge had passed.

SKULDUGGERY: We had Ravel as bait, and we had the God-Killer weapons, but we needed every advantage we could possibly get. Then Wreath told us about the Meryyn Sigil.

The Meryyn Sigil was a tattoo that would make Valkyrie invulnerable for twenty-three minutes, but it needed to be activated by Skulduggery once he underwent three tests at the Necropolis.[1] Valkyrie agreed to let Grand Mage Sorrows carve the sigil into her arm.

1. Necropolis: Maryyn Ta Uul. The City Below. The City Beneath.

VALKYRIE: While we were using the Accelerator to super-charge Lord Vile's armour – just in case Skulduggery needed it – I realised that the reason Darquesse was so keen to expand her understanding of magic was because she wanted the ultimate challenge. She wanted to take on the Faceless Ones.
SKULDUGGERY: She also had another goal that we didn't know at the time: she wanted to kill and absorb Valkyrie. Apparently that would make her whole again, and she'd be ready to hunt the Dark Gods.
VALKYRIE: Don't see why she couldn't just be happy with a protein bar like the rest of us...

The next morning, Dai Maybury attacked Valkyrie in her house, took the Sceptre and kidnapped Alice. With her parents insisting on accompanying her, Valkyrie followed Maybury to the Remnant-infested town of Thurles, where the Remnants offered her their help. Dexter Vex would accompany Valkyrie and her family to Roarhaven, where Valkyrie would ask Grand Mage Sorrows to accept the Remnants as part of her army.

On the way to Roarhaven, Vincent Foe and the vampire, Samuel, intercepted Valkyrie and the others. When Foe promised her that he was going to kill her loved ones, her magic manifested itself in white lightning, and she killed both Samuel and Foe.

Skulduggery, Fletcher and Wreath arrived at the Necropolis in Scotland. Skulduggery, being dead, was the only one able to pass into the death field. He was confronted by figures in black robes with porcelain faces – the Inquisitor, the Validator, and the Guardian – who each presented him with a test.

The second test saw him meet with the entities that were his wife and his child, and the entities that once were Ghastly Bespoke and Anton Shudder and many other people who had died along the way. They told him that, to the dead, all moments exist simultaneously, and that they had seen him "when the worlds collide and when the darkness falls. We see you surrounded by blood, and fire and rotting flesh."

SKULDUGGERY: They tried to pull me deeper into the Necropolis, into a hole from which I'd never return.
VALKYRIE: Tell the people what happened.
SKULDUGGERY: I got out.
VALKYRIE: And then what did you do?
SKULDUGGERY: I pushed in the Validator.
VALKYRIE: Because that's how we roll.

The third test was personal combat but, after realising that the twenty-three minutes of invulnerability would begin immediately once the Guardian was beaten, Skulduggery knew he had to delay the fight until just before Valkyrie faced Darquesse. He left the Necropolis, and Skulduggery reunited with Valkyrie and the others in the High Sanctuary.

In the morning, they would take Ravel from the circle that hid him from Darquesse. Once she could sense him again, she would come for him – so Ravel would, once again, be fighting by their side.

Scapegrace, meanwhile, volunteered himself and Thrasher to go to the Necropolis to fight the Guardian, allowing Skulduggery to remain in Roarhaven and battle Darquesse. After undergoing an experimental mind-transplant back into their original, rotting-zombie bodies, they were ready to pass into the death field.

Darquesse arrived in Roarhaven at precisely 11:03 am. She was attacked with God-Killer weapons and a helicopter gunship, followed up by vampires and Cleavers.

VALKYRIE: We had the God-Killers, but we couldn't tag her. She caught each arrow Saracen sent her way. Dodged every swipe of the sword, every stab of the spear...
SKULDUGGERY: She broke the sword.
VALKYRIE: I watched her do it. I realised I could see people's auras, see their magic, and I saw her power just reach out, snap the blade. I knew I didn't have much time before it was just her and me – and all my hopes rested on Scapegrace and Thrasher beating the Guardian.

SCAPEGRACE: We didn't beat the Guardian. I fought well, and Thrasher flailed dramatically, but the Guardian beat us easily. Then he told me that, because I had a genuine pure-at-heart moment, I'd actually won. I'm still not sure of the rules, to be honest with you, but I wasn't about to object, so I activated the Meryyn Sigil. Then they asked me to be the King of the Dead. I said no, but... it's nice to be wanted.

Seeing wave after wave of Cleavers, vampires and sorcerers fall before Darquesse, seeing Saracen injured and Wreath killed, Ravel abandoned the spear and ran. Having no other choice, Skulduggery donned Vile's armour.

Suddenly invulnerable, Valkyrie succeeded in slowing down Darquesse until reinforcements arrived – in the form of Melancholia and Lord Vile. Together, the two Necromancers almost succeeded in killing Darquesse.

SKULDUGGERY: Almost.

Unleashing a blast that obliterated the East Quarter, Darquesse killed Melancholia and took Skulduggery out of the fight – at least temporarily.

The invulnerability that the Meryyn Sigil provided Valkyrie ended, and Tanith helped her back to the Sanctuary, where she finally donned the Deathtouch Gauntlet. It was then that the Black Cleaver moved against Grand Mage Sorrows.

VALKYRIE: OK, this gets slightly complicated. Eliza Scorn wanted China dead for what she'd done to the Church of the Faceless, and she asked herself, what better time to get her own back than right in the middle of a battle to save the world?
SKULDUGGERY: Eliza instructed one of her Church's members, Keir Tanner, to allow Nye to escape Ironpoint Gaol, where Tanner was warden.
VALKYRIE: And in return, Nye agreed to instruct the Black Cleaver to kill the woman he was supposed to be protecting.
SKULDUGGERY: Because the Black Cleaver had a tendency to obey whoever brought him back to life – in this case, Nye.
VALKYRIE: All that clear? Good.

Coming to Grand Mage Sorrows's defence were Tanith and Sanguine.

VALKYRIE: Sanguine couldn't let Tanith face the Cleaver alone. Don't get me wrong, Billy-Ray was a murderer and a psychopath... but he genuinely loved Tanith, and he ended up giving his life for her.

Tanith killed the Black Cleaver.

Believing that enough Remnants could overwhelm Darquesse and successfully possess her, Dexter Vex had made a grave miscalculation. Darquesse burned what is estimated to be over two thousand Remnants from her system, absorbing their strength and their knowledge as she did so. She also removed the Remnant from Vex's body, causing him grievous harm in the process.

With all of her opponents subdued, there was no one left to challenge Darquesse, and the only weapon that could destroy her was the Sceptre, which was bonded to Alice. In order for Valkyrie to use it, Alice would have to die.

VALKYRIE: Yeah, I really don't want to talk about this part.

In a state of great distress, Valkyrie killed her sister with the Deathtouch Gauntlet – reviving her moments later with the Sunburst.

FLETCHER: That messed Valkyrie up. I mean... she had to kill her own sister. Yeah, she managed to bring her back but... she still had to kill her.

Despite now wielding the Sceptre of the Ancients, Valkyrie failed to destroy Darquesse – but she did succeed in distracting her long enough for Cassandra Pharos, Geoffrey Scrutinous and Philomena Random to surround her and implant a suggestion into her mind.

They made her see what she wanted to see. She wanted to destroy the

world, so they let her destroy the world. She wanted to roam the universe, so they let her roam the universe. While years were passing for Darquesse, it was only mere moments for everyone else.

VALKYRIE: It was nerve-wracking. We were all standing around, no one saying a word. We had no idea what was happening in her head, and we had no way of knowing if she'd snap out of it and realise she was in a psychic virtual-reality thing.

CASSANDRA: We gave her everything she wanted, and once she thought that she'd obliterated all life in this universe, she got bored, and went looking for other universes. She found the reality in which the Faceless Ones had been trapped and she thought, *Oh, there's a challenge for me*, so she opened a portal. Now this she actually did in real life, just opened it up and flew up into it and disappeared from our lives forever. It was quite beautiful, really.

Time, however, was running out in the Accelerator room. With only one way of stopping catastrophic failure, it seemed as if Skulduggery Pleasant was going to sacrifice himself to save the world.

VALKYRIE: I knew you'd never do it.

SKULDUGGERY: You thought you were saying goodbye to me forever.

VALKYRIE: Naw. I knew what you were gonna do.

SKULDUGGERY: You were so sad.

VALKYRIE: It was pretty obvious.

SKULDUGGERY: I'm sure I saw a tear.

VALKYRIE: The Engineer told us a soul had to be willingly sacrificed but he'd never said anything about the soul having to be your own.

SKULDUGGERY: I think I see a tear in your eye even now, at the memory of it all.

VALKYRIE: God, you're annoying.

Skulduggery sacrificed Erskine Ravel's soul, and this shut down the Accelerator destruct sequence.

VALKYRIE: And we all lived happily ever after.

SKULDUGGERY: Did we?

VALKYRIE: Well... OK, I spent the next five years in Colorado, breaking off pretty much all contact with Skulduggery and my family. I couldn't face them, not after what I'd done to Alice.

I took on a combat instructor full time but I pretty much stayed away from everyone else. I got myself a dog. I read books. I worked out. I barely did any magic. It was... lonely.

And then these two killers – Cadaverous Gant and Jeremiah Wallow – came after me, which was a nice reminder of what I'd been missing. They'd been sent to kill me by an old, shall we say, associate, of Skulduggery's, just in case I decided to interfere with her plans at some stage in the future, but they screwed up, and had to take this guy who delivered my groceries, Danny. They took Danny to Gant's home, which was a nightmare of fire and chains and whatever, in which Gant was invulnerable. Wallow wasn't so lucky, and he fell off one of those bridge things and died, which made Gant so, so angry. I managed to lure him out of his house, and hit him until he ran away, and that's that. I gave Skulduggery a call, told him I was ready to come home.

A good man lies here,
Loved by all,
Pity his coffin is shared by Paul.

The Age of the Maggot Part Four

Valkyrie Cain had been living in Colorado for two years when reports came through of a Maggot attack in New Delhi. Skulduggery Pleasant and Temper Fray travelled to India to investigate.

TEMPER: By the time we got there, the Maggots were long gone. The local Sanctuary had made sure the witnesses remembered events differently from how they happened, but the clean-up crews had yet to move in.
SKULDUGGERY: We traced the Maggots' point of origin to a condemned building nearby, where we discovered the remains of twelve people – all in advanced stages of decomposition. What piqued our curiosity was that there were signs that something large had, essentially, burst out of them. Judging by what Valkyrie and I had seen emerge from the Bull Maggot in Poland, I hazarded a guess that the Maggots who went on the rampage had been born here, in the bodies of the victims, and then, due to some significant accelerated development, had grown to the size of the creatures we'd encountered.

It is at this point that Skulduggery and Temper found themselves confronted by a demon.

TEMPER: You ever met a demon? I don't mean the kind of demons you get in mortal religions, with the horns and the hellfire and whatever. These demons, they're the offspring of gods, but they're not gods themselves. What else you gonna call them, you know? They're definitely not angels, I'll tell you that much. This guy was tall, wearing flowing black robes made of leather or skin or something. Like vestments. Like something a seriously disturbed priest would wear – a priest who was into some weird stuff. His head was... I've no idea how to describe it. His head was large, and pale, and he

TEMPER FRAY

had these big, blinking eyes, and he wore a long mask on the lower part of his face that kinda looked like a feed bag – for horses, y'know? Except it was black and made of metal. I really didn't want to see what was under the damn thing, that was for sure.

The demon identified himself as Tarron, the head of the Rakhirrian Secret Police.

Tarron explained that maggots were agents of change. They hatched in the festering rot of the dead, becoming new life that sprang from the remains of the old. Tarron's people believed that it was their sacred task to be the link between evolutionary stages. They had done this countless times before, on countless worlds in countless realities. Millennia ago, they had arrived on Earth, shepherding humanity through its development, and now they were preparing to usher in the next evolutionary stage.

But something had gone wrong. The Maggots who had attacked the sorcerers were a subversion of the natural way of things, and Tarron believed that Bemmon's murder was only the beginning. It was his belief that Gog Magog had rediscovered his powers and had returned to declare war on his old enemies, the Order of the Maggot, by corrupting their "beautiful" natures and reshaping them into agents of violence.

SKULDUGGERY: I'd read Gog Magog's name a few times over the years, but I'd dismissed it in much the same way as I'd once dismissed the stories about the Faceless Ones.

Before Tarron could take his suspicions to his god Rakhir, however, he needed proof.

SKULDUGGERY: I told him that the evidence he sought probably lay in Hosanna

Fortune's notebook – currently in the possession of Remember Me – so Tarron agreed to help us track it down. Then he sent out his flies.

TEMPER: It was a hell of a sight. He opened the bottom of that mask of his and there was suddenly this incredible buzzing sound. A moment later, a... a... I don't know how to describe it...

SKULDUGGERY: A torrent.

TEMPER: A torrent, yeah. A moment later, a torrent of flies emerged – this buzzing black column that became a cloud over our heads – and then off they went, all these nasty little flies, searching for Remember.

A day later, Tarron visited Skulduggery and Temper again, with news that his flies had indeed found Remember Me. As they journeyed, Tarron confessed to believing that someone in the Order of the Maggot was working with Gog Magog.

Upon arriving at their destination, Remember Me sent a Bull Maggot to attack them while she made her escape. Temper left Skulduggery and Tarron to deal with the monster, and pursued Remember. She managed to get away, but Temper retrieved the notebook.

TEMPER: I was pretty proud of that, have to be honest with you.

He returned to the others as they were slaying the Bull Maggot, but before they could open the notebook the demon Shevennu, the Princess of Death, arrived. She confiscated the notebook and ordered Tarron to leave with her. Tarron complied.

TEMPER: That right there? To have our only lead snatched away right before we learned what that lead was? That sucked.

A NOTE FROM THE ARCHIVIST

Archivist Rux has been missing for over a week. Sanctuary detectives have searched his home but found no evidence of foul play. It is their opinion that he simply walked away – just like Archivist Palaverous did.

I have my doubts, but must continue my work.

Resurrection

A lot had changed in the last five years.

Roarhaven was now the First Capital City[1] of magic, having seen an influx of tens of thousands of sorcerers clamouring to live in a place where they didn't have to hide who they were. A school had even been established, Corrival Academy, that covered all "mortal subjects", plus a wide range of magical ones.

1. For an opposing viewpoint, read *The Mystical Cities* by Yonten Shinnlainsaw, published by Twelve Eye Books.

China Sorrows had installed her own puppet Grand Mages into the majority of the Sanctuaries around the world, and had awarded herself the position of Supreme Mage. Only the Australian and African Sanctuaries had been "allowed" to maintain their independence.

Skulduggery Pleasant had set up and commanded the City Guard, the Roarhaven police force, but had resigned his post following an incident in which a prisoner had died while in custody. The African Grand Mage, Naila, had appointed him as an Arbiter,[1] and for a time he partnered with Temper Fray. But when Temper went missing, Skulduggery had to enlist Valkyrie Cain's help.

1. See "Arbiter Corps", page 217

SKULDUGGERY: This was not easy.

VALKYRIE: I didn't even know if I wanted to come back. I'd returned to Ireland, like, three months earlier, which was a huge step, but I was doing my best to avoid everyone. I didn't even want to spend time with my family – who still had no idea what I'd done. There was no way I could ever tell them that I'd had to kill my own baby sister, even if it was only for a few seconds. How do you explain that to someone? No, I was back in Ireland, but I was a long way from being back in the game.

SKULDUGGERY: But the universe didn't care.

VALKYRIE: No, it didn't, so, when Skulduggery asked for my help, I helped. I became an Arbiter. But I was seriously considering packing it all in and just becoming a hermit for the rest of my life.

Temper had gone undercover, infiltrating the so-called anti-Sanctuary, a group of mostly Neoteric mages of which Cadaverous Gant was a member. The rest of the group consisted of sorcerers Richard Melior, Razzia, Memphis, Quibble, Nero, Azzedine Smoke and Lethe.

SKULDUGGERY: We'd encountered one or two others from this group over the years – Bubba Moon, for instance – and I'd been hearing rumours that they were now operating out of Roarhaven.

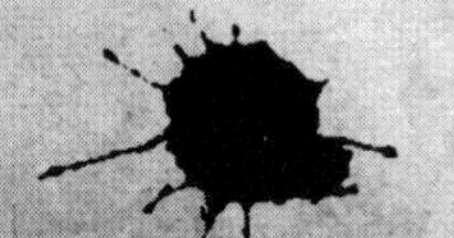

Omen, Auger, and Never

Temper believed that the anti-Sanctuary had someone inside Corrival Academy, recruiting students – and so the Arbiters approached Omen Darkly, in his third year at Corrival Academy, to be an undercover spy. Omen was the twin brother of Auger Darkly,[1] the Chosen One, and all that was required of Omen was to keep watch for suspicious activity and not actually involve himself in what was going on.

1. The Darklands Prophecy: at age seventeen, Auger Darkly would face the King of the Darklands in a battle that would decide the fate of humanity.

OMEN: Hello. My name is Omen Darkly. I'm fourteen years old. I'm–

ARCHIVIST: You don't have to do that.

OMEN: Sorry?

ARCHIVIST: You don't have to introduce yourself. You're just here to provide additional information or personal insight into the reported events.

OMEN: Right. Yes. Sorry. So do I talk now, or...?

ARCHIVIST: Do you have anything to say?

OMEN: Not really.

ARCHIVIST: Then no.

Nero teleported the anti-Sanctuary group on to Coldheart Prison.[2] The Cleavers, guards and officials were subdued or killed and close to 326 convicts were released from their cells. Security footage showed Cadaverous exploring the lower depths of the prison. Anti-Sanctuary operatives described hearing Abyssinia's voice in their heads, telling them what to do. I can only assume that Cadaverous was being guided by her now, because he went straight to Cell Zero, in which the box was kept that contained her heart.

VALKYRIE: This was all coming at me fast. I wasn't used to that any more. I was suddenly talking about bad guys and threats and meeting all these weird new people – including a guy dressed as a Plague Doctor who seemed, I don't know, nice enough, I suppose. But still – he was dressed as a Plague Doctor. That's pretty weird.

Believing that Valkyrie's untested powers included significant Sensitive abilities, the Arbiters visited the cottage belonging to the late Cassandra Pharos.[3] The cottage, still infused with psychic energy, allowed Valkyrie to conjure up a vision.

> **2.** A maximum-security flying island.
>
> **3.** The Night of Knives had claimed the lives of Pharos, Finbar Wrong and nine other prominent Sensitives as part of the anti-Sanctuary plot to remain undetected.

VALKYRIE: We saw a city in flames, we saw Omen and Auger Darkly covered in blood, we saw that Plague Doctor guy, we saw a girl getting killed with an energy stream, and we saw China and Saracen, both lying dead. So that was a fun vision to experience, y'know? Then to top it all off, I saw myself. I saw my own death. I was on my knees and... Oh, and we also saw a woman with silver hair, the Princess of the Darklands, telling me that she knew my secret. I hadn't a clue what the hell she was on about. Anything you want to share about that, Skulduggery?

SKULDUGGERY: Not really.

VALKYRIE: Nothing at all?

SKULDUGGERY: Nothing that I can think of.

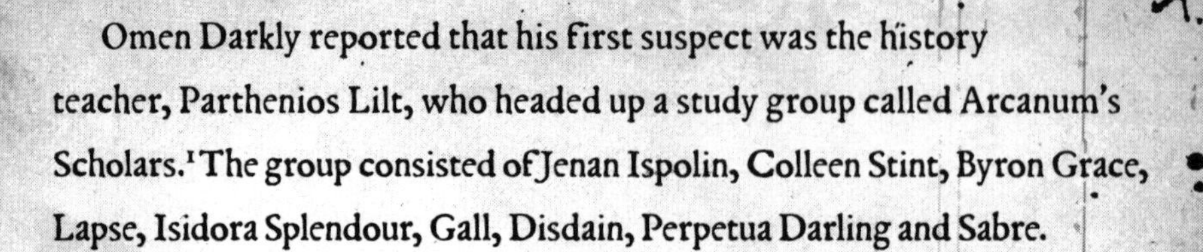

Omen Darkly reported that his first suspect was the history teacher, Parthenios Lilt, who headed up a study group called Arcanum's Scholars.[1] The group consisted of Jenan Ispolin, Colleen Stint, Byron Grace, Lapse, Isidora Splendour, Gall, Disdain, Perpetua Darling and Sabre.

ARCHIVIST: Well?

OMEN: Sorry?

ARCHIVIST: Do you have anything to add to that? Why did you suspect Lilt?

OMEN: Oh, uh... I suspected Mr Lilt because he was suspicious.

ARCHIVIST: Could you elaborate?

OMEN: Sure, yeah. He was... very anti-mortal, you know? And the Arcanum's Scholars were kinda, I suppose, selective, in the type of people they liked – Jenan, especially. They just... they seemed quite prejudiced against anyone who wasn't a sorcerer.

The Arbiters' investigation uncovered the Neoteric Report, a dossier that Lilt had written forty years earlier for the French Sanctuary. The Report included profiles on some of the Neoteric sorcerers[2] whom Temper had suspected of being anti-Sanctuary operatives, including Melior and Smoke.

1. Named after Rebus Arcanum, the probably-dead sorcerer.

2. See "Neoteric", page 17

The Report detailed Smoke's ability: one touch eradicated the conscience and forced obedience for forty-eight hours.

When the Arbiters visited Melior's house to speak with him, they were attacked by Melior himself and the rest of the anti-Sanctuary group.

VALKYRIE: We went up against a load of people who were wielding magic we weren't used to. Melior was a healer, but he could somehow use that power offensively. Razzia, she had these tentacle things that shot out of her hands. Destrier slowed time, just like Jeremiah Wallow did. And then there was Lethe.
SKULDUGGERY: Lethe was dangerous. He learned fast – broke down my fighting style in a matter of moments and worked out how to beat me. I hate people like that.

Fletcher Renn teleported the Arbiters to safety – but Nero teleported after them.

FLETCHER: That's not supposed to be possible, but he was somehow able to track me. He cheated, basically, and stabbed me, but next time... next time I'll be ready.

With Fletcher recovering, Supreme Mage Sorrows tasked Commander Hoc with arresting Parthenios Lilt.

SKULDUGGERY: After he had broken my arm and pulled my jawbone off, Lethe said the reason they had Melior was to breathe life into the lifeless – meaning they were planning on bringing someone back from death.

OMEN: I spied on the Arcanum's Scholars and stole one of the golden masks they wore. Oh, and I heard Mr Lilt say they'd probably have to kill Byron, probably because he wasn't that into the whole thing. When I reported back to Skulduggery he thanked me and, like, that was it. I was to go back to my life.
ARCHIVIST: Were you upset?
OMEN: It sounds so stupid, but I thought they'd make me a part of the team. I thought this was my chance to be a hero, like Auger was. But they didn't want to put me in any more danger.

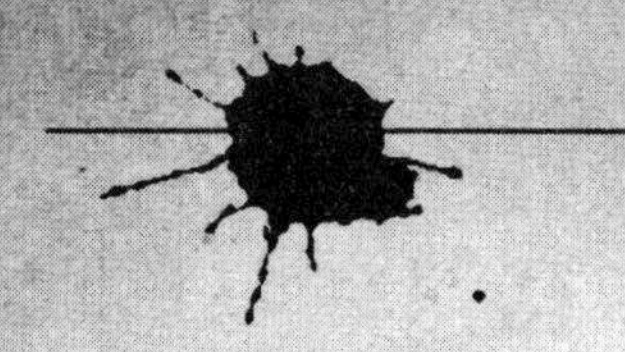

ARCHIVIST: So what did you do?

OMEN: I put myself in more danger.

Disguising himself with the golden mask, Omen infiltrated an Arcanum's Scholars' meeting that was visited by Nero, Razzia and Lethe. Lethe told the group – whom he dubbed First Wave – that they would bring terror to the American heartland and start a war between sorcerers and mortals. Before Lethe could get to the details, Omen was discovered and pushed off the balcony.

OMEN: Mr Peccant caught me as I fell and saved my life. I mean, I was wearing the mask so nobody knew who I was, so he probably wouldn't have saved me if he'd known it was me, but...

At the High Sanctuary, Supreme Mage Sorrows met with her Council of Advisors: Grand Mage Aloysius Vespers of the English Sanctuary, Grand Mage Gavin Praetor of the American Sanctuary and Grand Mage Sturmun Drang of the German Sanctuary. They discussed, among other things, the difficulties they were having in getting the First Bank of Roarhaven up and running, the fact that Coldheart Prison had gone quiet, and the possibility that the American president, Martin Flanery, was employing a sorcerer to force his agenda through Congress.

From what I have been able to ascertain, President Flanery had arranged, through his Personal Aide Bertram Wilkes, for a Sensitive – Magenta – to influence senators into agreeing to his controversial policies. There was also a link with Parthenios Lilt that I need to explore.

Security footage showed Nero teleporting into Coldheart Prison, unaware that Omen Darkly had accompanied him.

OMEN: I'd been spying on Jenan when Nero had, I suppose, reprimanded him? For allowing a spy into the meeting? Jenan said he suspected that I was the spy and Nero told him he'd have to kill me. Jenan didn't seem too upset at that idea. Then Nero was about to teleport and I was close enough to reach out and touch his shoe.

ARCHIVIST: Why did you do that?

OMEN: Why did I touch his shoe? I suppose I didn't exactly think it through. I mean, it wasn't the smartest thing in the world to do.

ARCHIVIST: It was incredibly stupid.

OMEN: Some people might say brave.

ARCHIVIST: No. Stupid.

OMEN: Right. I mean, yes, it was stupid. I didn't know what I was thinking, and I didn't know where I'd end up. I certainly didn't expect to end up in a prison.

Footage from Coldheart showed Omen conversing with Immolation Joe, a convict who was thrown back into his cell for starting fights with other convicts, who now freely roamed the prison. Occupying the next cell, however, was Temper Fray. Omen released him and, soon after, they encountered Lethe, Nero and Razzia.

OMEN: I'm not entirely sure how it happened, but somehow I ended up saving us.

TEMPER: Omen was brilliant. That kid doesn't give himself nearly enough credit for the sheer bravery of what he did that day. He forced Nero to teleport us back to Roarhaven, for God's sake. The boy's my own personal hero.

Richard Melior, meanwhile, had managed to arrange a meeting with the Arbiters.

SKULDUGGERY: Melior told us about his time in San Francisco, living with his husband, Savant Vega. Melior was a healer, and Savant absorbed knowledge at a glance, and back then–

VALKYRIE: OK, here's the short version of what he told us. Back in the 1960s, they fell in with a crowd of Neoterics like Lilt and Smoke and Bubba Moon, and then they left them behind because they were all weirdoes, and Melior and Savant move to another state and for forty years everything is cool. Then five years ago, Lilt and a few others kidnap Savant. Two months after that, this guy called Lethe turns up, dressed head to toe in a Necromancer suit, and tells Melior they'll kill his husband if he doesn't resurrect a woman called Abyssinia, a super-powerful mage who absorbed people's life forces. You wanna take over at this point?

SKULDUGGERY: This is a sensitive subject, so thank you for being so–

VALKYRIE: She was his ex-girlfriend, you see. They met when he was, shall we say, at a low point in his life. He was a lonely skeleton who didn't have any friends–

SKULDUGGERY: I had plenty of friends.

VALKYRIE: ... and it would still be another few hundred years before I came along, so he made a bad decision or two.

SKULDUGGERY: Thank you for that. Yes, Abyssinia and I had a relationship. She was the one, actually, who gifted me the armour that I would pour my Necromancy into.

VALKYRIE: She forced him to become Lord Vile.

SKULDUGGERY: No, she didn't. I went down that particular path on my own... but she didn't discourage it. We joined Mevolent's army together, where she planned to kill him and take over. But I betrayed her, thought I'd killed her – but she survived. Once I'd left Vile behind and I was back to being... me... I hunted her down as part of a team that consisted of both the Dead Men and the Diablerie. We, essentially, threatened her son until she agreed to let us kill her. Then I cut out her heart, locked it in a box and we built a prison around it. That's where Coldheart gets its name.

VALKYRIE: What a charming story.

SKULDUGGERY: It is, isn't it? Apart from the bit where everything happens.

Melior explained that, in order to resurrect Abyssinia from her current state (a heart), he would need the life forces of three Neoterics with specific energy signatures, and a modified Soul Catcher to harness it all. It is at this point that Azzedine Smoke corrupted Skulduggery.

VALKYRIE: Out of all the anti-Sanctuary operatives, Smoke was probably the most dangerous. A single touch and every dark impulse you possessed rose to the surface. Decent people were instantly turned into psychopaths. You can only imagine what effect it had on Skulduggery.
SKULDUGGERY: What do you mean by that?
VALKYRIE: I just mean, you know, you were already someone who'd gone down that path. You were familiar with it. You had tasted the darkness.
(There follows a prolonged silence in the recording.)
VALKYRIE: Anyway...

Fully aware that he had been corrupted and not caring one way or the other, Skulduggery chased down and shot Valkyrie in the leg.

VALKYRIE: Remember that? Remember when you shot me?
SKULDUGGERY: I remember.
VALKYRIE: I bet you do. I bet you remember.
SKULDUGGERY: I just said I did.
VALKYRIE: I bet you said you did.
SKULDUGGERY: I'm not sure what–
VALKYRIE: Shush. You shot me. Shush.

The Plague Doctor that Valkyrie had already encountered – whose actual name was Sebastian Tao – arrived in Roarhaven with a mission: to bring back Darquesse in order to avert some unknown catastrophe he believed was coming. To accomplish that, he befriended Bennet Troth – the father of Kase, one of Auger Darkly's best friends – and helped him track down his kidnapped wife, Odetta. As it turned out, Odetta hadn't actually been kidnapped – she had merely run away with Conrad, a Hollow Man whom she insisted was sentient.

Although Bennet didn't get his wife back, he held up his part of their deal, and introduced Sebastian to the other members of the Darquesse Society, a group of like-minded individuals who had witnessed Darquesse's power and had taken to worshipping her. The Society consisted of Bennet, Tantalus McGovern, Lily Amica, Kimura Kimora, Ulysses Aubade, Tarry Forsooth, and Shiloh Forby.

Valkyrie visited Supreme Mage Sorrows, who tattooed the Auxilium Sigil on to her skin for use in an emergency.

VALKYRIE: I was feeling insecure, to be honest, but China pointed out that if I helped prevent Abyssinia from coming back then I'd be saving the world from a war that the sorcerers would win. So, really, my own feelings of guilt and self-loathing didn't mean a whole lot in the grand scheme of things.

SKULDUGGERY: Meanwhile, I was having a great time. It is endlessly amusing to me how easily people are to rile up, so that's what I was focusing on. Lethe was clearly in charge, and I respected that, but I was having so much fun annoying everyone else that I really didn't care. While the others were tasked with breaking Lilt out of his cell in the High Sanctuary, I was to accompany Cadaverous to obtain one of the three life forces needed to resurrect Abyssinia. His name was Tanner Rut, and he was a serial killer.

When Valkyrie described to Militsa what Lethe had been wearing,

Militsa took her to the Museum of Magical History, bringing her to the exhibit of a necronaut[1] suit.

1. These almost indestructible suits were used by Necromancers for Deep Venturing – visiting the realms of the dead.

VALKYRIE: It was a different style, some different materials, but Lethe had been wearing something like that suit. It was bulletproof and stab-proof, and it looked cool.

An Incident Report filed by Arabella Wicked describes how she came upon Jenan Ispolin attacking Omen Darkly and had to step in to break it up.

OMEN: Jenan knew it was me – knew I'd been the one spying on them – so he did his very best to kill me. He seemed quite excited about the idea. But then Miss Wicked came along and she kicked his ass. Which, you know, was awesome.

Never teleported Valkyrie, Temper and Omen to San Francisco, looking for the house of Richard Melior and his husband. The house itself had been demolished but Melior's neighbour had kept some of their possessions, amongst which was a photo from the 1960s.

VALKYRIE: You know who was in that photo? There was Lilt, there was an old friend of Temper's called Tessa Mehrbano, and there was a traitor, a man who had – only a few minutes earlier – allowed Lilt to escape from his cell at the High Sanctuary. Tipstaff. Bloody Tipstaff. I should have known. This was the second time an Administrator had betrayed the rest of us. I should have known.

But before Valkyrie could return to Roarhaven and arrest the Administrator, Never had to teleport Temper to New York so that he could track down Tessa. The moment they'd teleported away, Valkyrie and Omen were attacked by an invisible man – Gleeman Shakespeare, otherwise known as the serial killer Mr Glee.

SKULDUGGERY: There are too many serial killers in the world, there really are.

Sent by Lethe in an attempt to stop them in their tracks, Mr Glee failed to kill either of his targets, but managed to escape capture himself. Valkyrie and the others returned to the High Sanctuary, where Tipstaff was arrested.

Temper tracked down his old friend Tessa Mehrbano. They had both helped Damocles Creed with his "experiments", but hadn't spoken since Temper abandoned them all in the 1930s. He asked her about the photograph and she admitted to associating with Lilt and Smoke in 1965.

TEMPER: Tessa told me that Smoke had been working on a "freaky black rubber suit" – Lethe's Necromancer suit – and suddenly all the pieces started to fit together.

Skulduggery and Cadaverous secured Tanner Rut and brought him back to Coldheart Prison.

SKULDUGGERY: We did our part with the utmost professionalism. Sadly, not everyone shared our work ethos, as Memphis managed to kill the person he was meant to bring in. This meant that Melior was one life force short for Abyssinia's resurrection procedure – so he suggested that Valkyrie's unique power signature would be a suitable replacement. That's where their plan started to go so amusingly wrong.

Because of his attack on Omen, Principal Rublic and Vice-Principal Duenna felt they had no choice but to expel Jenan from Corrival Academy. By this stage, however, Jenan had already departed, and had all but one of the Arcanum's Scholars with him. Valkyrie and Omen visited Byron Grace at his parents' home. He told them that, while he disliked many mortals, he couldn't rise to the level of hatred that had radicalised his friends.

OMEN: And then suddenly Nero and Skulduggery and Smoke were there. Smoke corrupted Byron and they teleported Valkyrie away and I was left to defend myself. I must have got in a lucky punch or something, because I'm still here to talk about it, I suppose.

Byron Grace was later treated for a fractured jaw and concussion.

VALKYRIE: I was brought to Coldheart, where I tried to get through to Skulduggery. It didn't work. He told me Cadaverous still blamed me for Jeremiah Wallow's death, so he wanted to kill me – but Skulduggery was determined to do it himself. I wish I could say this was the first time two people had argued over who got to end my life, but it tends to happen with alarming regularity. Then I was taken from my cell and hung upside down with two others. The first guy was killed and his life force was drained and Abyssinia's heart, it... it started to grow itself a body. The second guy was killed, Abyssinia's body grew more, until all it needed was skin and that last jolt. That was what I was for – that final dose. Skulduggery was about to kill me himself, but...
SKULDUGGERY: Valkyrie finally got through to me.

Skulduggery freed Valkyrie and they defended themselves against the Neoterics and the convicts, until they had only Lethe left to face. Working together, they managed to defeat him.

VALKYRIE: OK, this isn't entirely true. The cameras didn't pick up anything, and nobody else knew about it, but we had help – we had Darquesse.

SKULDUGGERY: I wasn't told about this until a few years later, I hasten to add.

VALKYRIE: When Darquesse left this reality, she left behind a piece of herself – what's called an Aspect – who called herself Kes. Only I could see and hear her, but Kes could interact physically with our world, although only slightly. She helped us beat Lethe. She turned out to be pretty cool, actually.

When Lethe realised he'd lost, he tried to provoke Melior into killing him so that Abyssinia could absorb his life force. He told Melior that he'd been responsible for keeping Savant Vega away from him for the past five years. Melior came very close to granting his wish, and then Never teleported in with Temper and Omen.

TEMPER: I told Melior what I'd found out – that Smoke had poured his corruption into Lethe's necronaut suit years ago. I didn't know why he'd have done this, but then it occurred to me that it'd be the only way to keep a person corrupted. So Lethe wasn't Lethe – not really. The question became, then: who was he?

SKULDUGGERY: Lethe was unbeatable. Once he saw you fight, you couldn't take him down. He learned and adapted in mere moments. Who else had that ability?

Omen told Melior that Lethe was his husband – Lethe was Savant Vega.

VALKYRIE: I realised I'd seen this before – this was a part of the vision I'd had at Cassandra's, where I'd watched one of the convicts kill Never. I got to her just in time but I was hit – and Abyssinia grabbed me.

Abyssinia managed to absorb enough of Valkyrie's life force – enough to restore her body to its former strength – before Never managed to teleport Valkyrie and the others back to Roarhaven.

The First Wave students received counselling and, once they proved themselves able, returned to Corrival Academy.

OMEN: That was awkward. I mean, they were on the bad guys' side, you know? But I suppose the school board and the principal and everyone figured they must have been led astray or something. It was a pretty traumatic time.

ARCHIVIST: And what about you? How were you coping with recent events?

OMEN: I was doing OK, actually. It was my first taste of what it must be like to be a hero, you know? What it must be like to be Auger. And I liked it. I liked making a difference, I liked... being somebody. I wanted more of it.

ARCHIVIST: Looking back, do you think that was a mistake?

OMEN: Oh my God, yes.

ABROGATE RAZE

PART THREE BY TAWDRY HEPBURN

Abrogate's trail picks up again in 1717 – 110 years after he killed Quinlan – when he joined Mevolent's army. Although a skilled fighter, Abrogate proved more useful doing what he loved best – researching. Given access to Mevolent's vast library, he helped keep Mevolent one step ahead of the Sanctuaries at all times, reporting only to him and eschewing all other contact.

It would appear that any and all references that the wider magical community has found to the god known as Gog Magog stem from Abrogate's research at this time. He first found mention of him, it would seem, in the *Sumerian Parchment*, which led him to the various obscure bibles of various obscure religions. Some of his notes survive to this day, and it was during his early investigations into who and what Gog Magog was that he felt "some dark thing stirring in my soul".

Abrogate, who by all accounts had been searching for a deeper meaning all his life (or at least all that he could remember), seems to have finally found something to believe in.

He emerged from this library only rarely. One of these rare occasions was in 1735, when he met Mevolent's Three Generals for the first time. According to the contemporaneous notes Abrogate took, Nefarian Serpine was brash and dismissive, Baron Vengeous was courteous and charming, and Lord Vile was, surprising no one, silent.

Given what we now know about Skulduggery Pleasant, however,

this meeting must have been, at the very least, something of a shock to Lord Vile. An argument could be made that being in the same room as Serpine – the man who'd murdered his wife and child – and his own father – the man who'd murdered his mother – may have led to the "epiphany" that shook loose Skulduggery Pleasant from the Lord Vile persona – as Vile walked away that very year and Skulduggery Pleasant returned.

In 1739, Abrogate betrayed Mevolent in return for amnesty. All charges against him were dismissed, and he supplied the Sanctuaries with plans for an attack that would have devastated their forces and destroyed their command structure. In retaliation, Mevolent sent out his top assassins, who all failed to kill their target.

By the end of the following decade, Abrogate had recruited two mages to help with his research into Gog Magog, known to us only by the initials FJ and RA. The notes these mages took start off as reasonable and precise, but become, by 1751, erratic and, in some places, nonsensical. They describe a darkness overcoming them – "a darkness of mind and body" – and even their magic being altered. The mage known as RA posits the idea that Gog Magog himself was infecting them through their research. In the margins of her notes, FJ casually mentions the fact that Abrogate had to kill RA the previous day because he'd become too unstable. She seems amused and outraged in equal measure. Three days later, FJ's notes abruptly stop.

While the Arbiters ceased their pursuit following the amnesty deal, and the Sanctuaries instructed all operatives to cross Abrogate's name off their Wanted lists, Skulduggery Pleasant had renewed his search, eventually tracking his father to an abandoned farmhouse in Russia, in 1798. Before storming the farmhouse, he alerted his siblings, three of whom managed to join him on the raid: Petulance Ruin, Mirror Grace and Respair Kempt.

They stormed the building just before dawn on the eighteenth of August. Nine hours later, Skulduggery Pleasant fled the farmhouse alone.

A NOTE FROM THE ARCHIVIST

I have found Archivist Rux's personal journal, where he complains of a "voice" in his head. I have taken this information to the Archive Department. It is in their hands now.

Midnight

Abyssinia's return meant that the vision the Arbiters had seen was now closer to becoming reality. They needed to find her and stop her before she could put any of her plans into operation.

Some in the anti-Sanctuary, however, were growing disillusioned with Abyssinia since her resurrection. Instead of focusing all her energy into her Big Plan, they saw her become distracted by the search for her long-lost son, Caisson.

For eight months, the Arbiters had been trying to find Abyssinia, but there had been very little sign of her, Coldheart Prison, or the rest of the anti-Sanctuary. Then they got word that she had visited a research facility set up by Serafina Dey, or Serafina of the Unveiled,[1] where she had killed many people.

1. The Unveiled siblings – Serafina Dey, Rune, Kierre, Strosivadian – were prominent figures in the 300 Year War. Only their brother, Damocles Creed, did not support Mevolent.

ABYSSINIA

VALKYRIE: It was a secret lab, up in the Alps. Under orders from Serafina, Eliza had broken Doctor Nye out of Ironpoint Gaol and it had continued its work here, and when we got there it told us that Abyssinia had indeed paid them a visit two days earlier.
SKULDUGGERY: She'd been looking for her son, Caisson, who had been tortured since 1929, predominantly by a doctor named Quidnunc. Unfortunately for Abyssinia, someone must have known she was close, because Serafina had already ordered that Caisson be moved into, essentially, a mobile torture chamber. Serafina wanted him to be kept moving to make it harder to track him down.

Nye's bodyguard, a Necromancer known only as Whisper, prevented the Arbiters from taking Nye into custody.

VALKYRIE: But Nye did give us one lead – it told us that Quidnunc suffered from liquefying new-grossness.

Liquefactive necrosis is a disease, weaponised by Mevolent during the 300 Year War, that rots flesh, meaning that Quidnunc would need a regular dosage of serum in order to stay alive.

Back in Roarhaven, a portal to the Leibniz Universe had opened outside the city walls, and mortal refugees were flooding through, fleeing from Mevolent's tyranny. This had caused huge disruption and great controversy in Roarhaven itself, and the complaints were growing as a makeshift Tent City was established.

OMEN: Everyone was talking about it. A lot of people were saying how terrible it was, those poor people, all that suffering, stuff like that, and a lot of other people were saying how terrible it was, why did they come here, why don't they go back to where they came from, that kinda thing. So no one was happy, basically.

Temper Fray, now an officer in the City Guard, was part of a team that was sent through the portal to report on the situation.

TEMPER: What is there to say? Maybe twenty or thirty thousand people, all starving, exhausted, and as terrified of us as they were of Mevolent.

The Arbiters asked Temper to use his City Guard credentials to find out who had been providing Doctor Quidnunc with the serum for his liquefactive necrosis. Temper passed them a name: Gravid Caw.

School records show that Omen Darkly's grades were slipping.

OMEN: You have my grades? Are you allowed to do that?
ARCHIVIST: This isn't for general publication. No one's going to see this.
OMEN: But still, I mean, aren't those private?
ARCHIVIST: Why don't you tell us why your grades were slipping?
OMEN: Well... I had a lot going on. I'd asked out Axelia (Lukt), and she'd said no because, obviously, and I wasn't enjoying the classes, and my parents were being their usual selves, which is never good for me, and compared to Auger's grades, of course mine were going to be bad.
ARCHIVIST: Your grades are bad compared to most people's.
OMEN: Oh. I mean, I suppose Never had a point too. He said I was obsessing over whether or not Skulduggery and Valkyrie were going to call me up to go off on another adventure.
ARCHIVIST: Did they say they would?
OMEN: They said they'd call, yes. They said I was part of the team now. Although maybe they were just being nice.
ARCHIVIST: What about Jenan Ispolin?
OMEN: Jenan and the rest of them (First Wave) hadn't been seen since Abyssinia

came back. His dad blamed the school, and me, and also Miss Wicked, who had, um, subdued Jenan when he'd attacked me. I was called in for a meeting. Jenan's dad was the Grand Mage of Bulgaria, so he was a pretty important guy, but my folks... my folks were the Darklys, you know? Because their son is the Chosen One, destined to fight for the fate of the world, they tended to get their own way.

ARCHIVIST: But they were on your side. Surely that was a good thing?

OMEN: They made sure the Darkly name was unblemished.

ARCHIVIST: And afterwards?

OMEN: They mentioned that I wasn't doing as good as Auger. And they had a point! So I volunteered to help Miss Gnosis distribute food and blankets to the mortal refugees. I got talking to a mortal girl my age, Aurnia. She told me about her world and I told her about this one. She was cool.

VALKYRIE: With Kes's encouragement, I was trying to delve deeper into that vision I was having. I saw soldiers, I saw Tanith, I saw the Whistler – that's what we were calling him, because he kept bloody whistling. I saw Cadaverous Gant holding a doll with a blue dress, saw Auger Darkly being shot, China lying dead, and I saw the Plague Doctor. The Future's Greatest Hits, basically.

Footage recovered from Coldheart Prison showed a ceremony in which one of the First Wave, Isidora Splendour, was killed as punishment for trying to leave. Although Jenan Ispolin was the one to kill her, there is reason to believe that Abyssinia had given him, at the very least, a psychic "nudge".

Shiloh Forby, of the Darquesse Society, was also an engineer for the High Sanctuary, and he had an opportunity to examine the box. He believed that it could be used to open a portal to the dimension that Darquesse had travelled to – a dimension full of the Faceless Ones. In order to find that dimension, they decided to try to track the Faceless Ones' energy signature – which meant they needed some Faceless Ones blood.

A Cleaver's scythe, stained with the blood of a Faceless One, had been recovered from Aranmore and was now held in the Dark Cathedral.

With his poll numbers at a record low and accusations of corruption coming at him from multiple angles, President Martin Flanery was losing his patience. He instructed his Personal Aide, Bertram Wilkes, to inform Abyssinia that he wanted the "operation" moved up. Wilkes reminded him of the delicate timetable they'd already agreed to, but Flanery was insistent.

It has since come to light that Bertram Wilkes was actually Vox Askance, an Elemental who was working with Abyssinia to steer the American president in the right direction.

Serafina's people were keeping Caisson sedated and constantly moving, but Abyssinia had sent Avatar to find their route and intercept them. Cadaverous, at odds with Abyssinia over what he believed was her preoccupation with getting her son back, conspired with Razzia to kill Avatar and fetch Caisson themselves.

Gravid Caw, the chemist who made Quidnunc's serum, was among those protesting the refugees who were still filing into Tent City. It was Caw's opinion that the refugees should be made to go back to where they came from, a view shared by many of his placard-wielding friends. When the Arbiters threatened him with arrest for the manufacture of a number of illegal drugs, he hoped that by helping them, he would stay out of prison. He told them that the only thing he knew about Quidnunc was that he was a member of the Sadists' Club. He was arrested immediately afterwards.

SKULDUGGERY: Quidnunc had been renting a room at the Sadists' Club, and the moment he saw us he gave up, asked to be taken into protective custody. He was terrified of Abyssinia finding him.

VALKYRIE: He told us what Caisson had told him. Basically, when he was a boy, the Dead Men and the Diablerie had hunted him and his mother down. China grabbed him, Abyssinia surrendered, and Skulduggery killed her.

SKULDUGGERY: Not my finest hour, but it was the only way to stop her.

VALKYRIE: But it doesn't end there, because Quidnunc also told us that Caisson's father was none other than...

SKULDUGGERY: You've gone silent.

VALKYRIE: I was waiting for you to jump in there.

SKULDUGGERY: Quidnunc was relaying the kind of second-hand information we cannot possibly–

VALKYRIE: Lord Vile! Lord Vile was Caisson's father, which meant Skulduggery was his father, which meant a skeleton got Abyssinia pregnant! I didn't think that was even possible!

SKULDUGGERY: You haven't forgiven me for spoiling the Darquesse thing earlier, have you?

VALKYRIE: Apparently, if a skeleton really loves someone who happens to possess a womb, he can make them pregnant. With magic.

SKULDUGGERY: It is theoretically possible.

VALKYRIE: So incredibly stupid.

SKULDUGGERY: Quidnunc was murdered a few minutes later, by the way – just in case we want to get back on track here.

Quidnunc died at the hands of Abyssinia as retribution for the decades of torture he'd put her son through.

VALKYRIE: She was different from what I'd expected. Nicer.

She told the Arbiters that she was royalty, descended from the Faceless Ones themselves, and that her father had been the King of the Darklands, also known as the Unnamed – a great leader who was murdered by his most

trusted warrior, Mevolent. She said that her son was destined to become the King of the Darklands and face Auger Darkly in a battle that might kill him – so she offered them a deal.

Once she had found Caisson, they would abandon the anti-Sanctuary, abandon all of her plans, and leave – and in return, Skulduggery would convince Auger Darkly to let the prophecy die.

SKULDUGGERY: But she was too powerful. We couldn't let her walk away. This had to end.
VALKYRIE: When she came for me, I looked into her mind. I went into her memories. I saw her with Skulduggery, and I saw Skulduggery become Vile, and I saw her at a feast in Mevolent's castle.
SKULDUGGERY: Abyssinia was to make a speech and then I was to kill Mevolent, at which point she would finally have her revenge on the man who'd murdered her whole family, and then she'd take over his army.
VALKYRIE: But she'd just found out that she was pregnant and that... that changed everything. She realised that revenge meant nothing. She now had a chance to start her own family, away from all the killing. She decided not to give the signal to kill Mevolent.
SKULDUGGERY: But she hadn't told me, and I betrayed her, stabbed her in the back, and tossed her through the window on to the rocks far below.

When Valkyrie broke off the psychic connection, Nero arrived to teleport Abyssinia away – after which he joined Cadaverous, Razzia and Destrier as part of their plan to rescue Caisson themselves.

The vehicle containing Caisson was on schedule, the guards Serafina had assigned were killed, and Caisson was unhooked from the machines keeping him unconscious.

But Cadaverous had never intended to bring him back to Abyssinia. He believed she had betrayed the anti-Sanctuary, fooling them with promises of a war between mages and mortals, when all she really wanted was the opportunity to rescue her son. If she wanted Caisson back, he told Razzia, at gunpoint, then she could come and get him.

Although she had agreed to mind Alice for the day while their parents celebrated their wedding anniversary, Valkyrie had to draft in Omen when an opportunity rose to meet with Supreme Mage Sorrows.

OMEN: Valkyrie had asked me to babysit. I'd never done any babysitting before and I wasn't looking forward to it, even though Alice was the nicest kid ever. I was just worried. Worried that I'd let her watch the wrong thing or eat the wrong thing or I'd say the wrong thing... There were so many ways it could have gone wrong. To have Cadaverous Gant just walk in and kidnap her, though, that was probably the worst thing that could have happened.

During the meeting between the Arbiters and the Supreme Mage, she told them that, in order to get the First Bank of Roarhaven off the ground, she'd had to go to Arch-Canon Creed. Creed had encouraged the members of the Church of the Faceless to move their finances to Roarhaven, and in return, Supreme Mage Sorrows introduced the Religious Freedom Act, which made the property of a religious organisation a sacred and autonomous zone, outside the jurisdiction of any investigative body – including the Arbiter Corps.

VALKYRIE: Then she told us about the deal she'd struck with Abyssinia to ensure her son's safety, right before she died, a deal in which China agreed to raise Caisson.
SKULDUGGERY: Mevolent would have had the boy killed if he knew he was really Abyssinia's son, so China made a deal with Meritorious and defected.

ARCH-CANON DAMOCLES CREED

VALKYRIE: Caisson grew up hating Mevolent, whom he blamed for forcing his dear old dad – Lord Vile – to kill his mum, and also hating Skulduggery, for killing the aforementioned mother.
SKULDUGGERY: He came after me about twenty years later, apparently, though a lot of people were trying to kill me around then, so I don't know which one was Caisson. I injured him and he was nursed back to health by a woman named Solace, and they fell in love. I like to think of myself as something of a matchmaker.
VALKYRIE: Solace used to be one of Serafina's handmaidens. She lived happily ever after with Caisson for something like 160 years before Serafina found her and brought her back to Mevolent's castle to punish. Caisson went after her.
SKULDUGGERY: And he killed Mevolent, drained his life force, and escaped with Solace.
VALKYRIE: Serafina thought it was Solace who'd killed her husband, and she tracked her down to China's home. China – for whatever reason – told her the truth, that it had been Caisson. And then she handed Caisson over.

Sebastian led Tantalus and Bennet into the Dark Cathedral via a secret tunnel. Once inside, they split up to look for the scythe, and Sebastian was saved from the Cathedral guards by Tanith Low. Tanith had rejoined the Knives in the Darkness, and she was here to assassinate Supreme Mage Sorrows, who was arriving for a meeting with Arch-Canon Creed.

TANITH: Yep, I was there to kill China. What of it?
ARCHIVIST: Well, I suppose the question I have is... why?
TANITH: She deserved it. She's deserved it for a long time. You don't think she deserves it?
ARCHIVIST: I... we... As an Archivist, I don't let my personal views–
TANITH: Yeah yeah. She deserved it because of what she was doing as Supreme

Mage. Anyway, yeah, I met the Plague Doctor there and we came to an arrangement: I'd kill China, and in all the confusion he could steal the scythe and get out of there without anyone noticing him. But then he had to go and save her life, didn't he? Git.

Tanith let him live, despite his interference, and Sebastian took the scythe and fled. On his way back through the secret tunnel, Tantalus tried to kill him and take the scythe back himself.

BENNET: Tantalus had never liked him, never liked the fact that Sebastian couldn't remove his mask or whatever... He didn't trust him, whereas the rest of us could just tell that he was a good guy. And the fact was, we liked him a whole lot better than we liked Tantalus, so we voted Tantalus out and voted Sebastian in as our leader.

Valkyrie returned to Haggard, where Omen told her that Cadaverous had kidnapped Alice. She called the number Cadaverous had left.

VALKYRIE: He was playing with me. He'd set up this game of challenges that I had to complete before midnight. Told me if I alerted Skulduggery or anyone else, if I deviated from his instructions, he'd kill my sister.

OMEN: We went to this place so she could have sigils carved into her eyes, which would let Gant see what she was seeing. That was her first challenge. Her second challenge was to kill me. That was my least favourite of the challenges.

VALKYRIE: I was lucky. I got Kes to stand in front of Omen as I pulled the trigger, so I shot her instead of him. Cadaverous didn't know I'd cheated.

The third task was to visit Rosemary Grody and Pādraig Vole, who gave

her a bracelet that locked round her wrist, binding her magic. They tried to eat her, then, but she got free and left them to tend to their injuries.

Valkyrie's fourth task took her to a country house, where she joined thirteen people being hunted down by riders on horseback. The object of the Wild Hunt was to reach a massive hedge maze, then get to the centre of the maze without being killed.

VALKYRIE: I had to dump my armoured clothes, the clothes Ghastly made for me. Man, I didn't want to leave them behind.

She'd almost made it to the centre when two Hunters caught up with her.

VALKYRIE: I figured that I was always solving these problems by beating people up, so I tried something else: I offered them a truckload of money. The woman, Hypatia, agreed to it. I promised to pay her, and she let me go.
ARCHIVIST: And did you pay her?
VALKYRIE: Of course.

At the centre of the maze there was a card that instructed Valkyrie to go to the Midnight Hotel.

Cadaverous had Caisson and was drawing Valkyrie in, so Skulduggery and Temper teamed up with Abyssinia to get them back. Their investigation took them from Cadaverous's cell in Coldheart to his apartment, where they found the remains of Satrap Beholden, an old boyfriend of Anton Shudder's. Skulduggery reasoned that Satrap may very well have inherited the Midnight Hotel after Shudder died, and if Cadaverous had killed him for it, that meant that the Midnight Hotel was now Cadaverous's home.

SKULDUGGERY: Cadaverous's power lay in his home – he could change the dimensions, the geography... In his home, Cadaverous was God. The only downside to that was that homes tend to be static. He wouldn't have that problem with the Midnight Hotel.

Valkyrie and Omen arrived at the Midnight Hotel, and Valkyrie drove her car right through the garage door.

VALKYRIE: It's hard to explain. Outside, it was night, OK? But inside, it was still outside, except it was day. The sky was a ceiling, and the sun was a clock, and I could see a town in the distance, and the sea, and mountains, but I was still only inside the hotel. Then Cadaverous called me on this payphone, said I had half an hour to get to his house, somewhere in this world that he'd built. So I got back in the car and I drove.

OMEN: I was in the back seat the whole time, and I had no idea what was going on.

Skulduggery, Temper and Abyssinia arrived at the hotel, but entered through the front door, finding themselves in an exact reproduction of the Carpathian Mountains, where Cadaverous had spent the first eight years of his life. Abyssinia sensed Caisson nearby, and led the way.

Valkyrie found herself in a town where everyone was Cadaverous Gant.

VALKYRIE: Yeah, this was weird. I don't know how much of that he meant me to see, but I got talking to a younger version of him, back when he was a boy. He told me Cadaverous had built towns like this to store the thoughts he didn't want to think, stuff he didn't want to deal with. The boy was Cadaverous's goodness, I suppose – which explains why he was so small. I was, essentially, peeking into his mind – but he was also peeking into mine, because the next town over was a version of Haggard that was a

distorted version of my own memories and experiences. It came close to overwhelming me, actually. I was lucky Omen was there to save me, just in the nick of time.

OMEN: I just want to repeat that I had no idea what was going on.

They reached Cadaverous's house and found the room where Alice was being held, but before they could break down the door, Cadaverous appeared.

Once Skulduggery, Temper and Abyssinia had overcome what appeared to be a symbolic representation of Cadaverous's own violent history, Abyssinia found Caisson. This drew Cadaverous away from Valkyrie and Alice.

SKULDUGGERY: Out in the real world, Abyssinia would have snapped Cadaverous in two. But in there, he was God, and she didn't stand a chance. None of us did.
VALKYRIE: When I was talking to the younger version of Cadaverous, he told me not to play Cadaverous's game, so I decided I wouldn't. I decided to run. Cadaverous caught up with me and beat the hell out of me, but I managed to get out of the hotel, back into the real world. Cadaverous... he wouldn't come after me. He wouldn't risk it.

Confident that Valkyrie would return for her sister, Cadaverous went back to the house. The sun had become a moon, and the moon struck midnight, and Cadaverous prepared to kill everyone.

SKULDUGGERY: But, of course, that didn't happen. Of course, Valkyrie Cain came to our rescue.
VALKYRIE: I grabbed a few of those seeds – from the bushes that grow at the base of the hotel? I grabbed one and returned to Cadaverous's house and planted it. You're

gonna want to pay attention here, because it gets confusing. I grew a new Midnight Hotel inside the old Midnight Hotel, and as it grew, everyone inside the old Midnight Hotel was teleported into the new one. So the new hotel, the small one that we were watching grow? We were *watching* it, but we were also *inside* it. So when I broke through the roof and dropped down into it, for a few minutes I was a giant, and I actually posed a threat. To fight me, Cadaverous had to grow until he was a giant too. Does that make sense? I'm pretty sure it makes sense.

They fought as giants, smashing into mountains and trampling over buildings. But as the hotel grew, Valkyrie got smaller, and weaker, and Cadaverous began to reassert his dominance. Valkyrie's last chance was to attack his mind, the same way she had attacked Abyssinia's.

VALKYRIE: I went into his memories, experienced his childhood traumas, and saw what a cold, unloved life he'd had. I figured that, maybe, by splicing his experience with my own childhood, I could, kinda, overwrite his murderous personality with love. Amazingly, it worked, and for a few minutes he didn't want to hurt anyone.

By that stage, however, Razzia, Nero and Skeiri had entered the landscape and recovered Abyssinia. Absorbing Skeiri's life force to heal her wounds, Abyssinia took Caisson and left – but not before shattering Cadaverous's newfound tranquility.

Faced with Cadaverous's rapidly returning murderous impulse and the power to go along with it, Valkyrie planted a second seed – but as yet another Midnight Hotel began to sprout, it became clear that they had run out of time.

SKULDUGGERY: And then the sky broke and a giant hand reached in, picked up Cadaverous and pulled him out through the hole–

VALKYRIE: ... and we looked round and saw that it was Alice who was now holding a teeny-tiny Cadaverous Gant in the palm of her hand. And then she squished him. Which was gross.

The death of Cadaverous Gant returned the Midnight Hotel to its former self, allowing those inside to seek immediate medical assistance.

OMEN: That was enough for me, as far as adventures went. I thought I wanted a life of action and whatever, but I really didn't like seeing people get hurt all the time. I realised I wanted to be normal. That's what Auger wanted as well – once all this Darkly Prophecy stuff was finished with, he wanted a normal life. In the meantime, of course, he was saving people and saving the world every week, it seemed like, only now he had Never joining him. Having a Teleporter is, like, super handy.

The refugees from the Leibniz Universe – the 18,257 of them who had managed to pass through before Supreme Mage Sorrows ordered the portal device shut down – were moved into an uninhabited part of the city, what became known as the Humdrums.

OMEN: I asked Aurnia out. I was pretty proud of myself for that. She said no, obviously, but that's not the point. At least, I don't think that's the point. It's not the point, is it?

When Valkyrie's parents returned from their night away, Alice kept her promise and didn't tell them about what had happened.

VALKYRIE: The thing was, Alice didn't seem upset by any of it. The kidnappings, the chasing, the violence, the fact that she squashed Cadaverous Gant. She was happy. She was always happy.

SKULDUGGERY: And that was the problem.

VALKYRIE: I turned on my aura-vision which, you know, lets me see a person's aura, life force, soul, whatever you want to call it – but I turned it on and I couldn't... I couldn't see Alice's soul.

Thanks to private recordings later recovered from the Oval Office, I have been able to ascertain the exact circumstances that led to the death of Vox Askance. Still posing as "Bertram Wilkes", Askance was unaware that President Flanery had been alerted to not only his true identity but also his role as undercover agent for Abyssinia. After Flanery revealed to him that he knew the truth, Askance was killed by a man identified as Crepuscular Vies. Crepuscular seemed to have a vendetta against Skulduggery Pleasant, and planned to use Flanery to destroy everything he held dear and, ultimately, kill him.

One good turn
Deserves another,
And one good urn
Deserves a brother.

The Age of the Maggot Part Five

Following another Maggot attack, Skulduggery Pleasant and Valkyrie Cain came to the decision that they must bring an end to this whole Order of the Maggot affair. Finding and questioning Remember Me became their focus.

Archivist Palaverous told them that Sunas, as the Governess of Souls within the Order, was in charge of recruitment, and therefore ideally placed to provide information regarding Remember. The Arbiters performed a summoning ritual and Sunas appeared before them.

VALKYRIE: It was my first time seeing one of the Order of the Maggot and, I have to be honest, I'd have had sweeter dreams if I'd called in sick that day. Did Temper tell you what they looked like?

ARCHIVIST: He did.

VALKYRIE: With the robes and the big head and the huge eyes and the long mask?

ARCHIVIST: Yes.

VALKYRIE: The fact that they've got the head of a giant bald fly?

ARCHIVIST: He didn't go that far, no.

VALKYRIE: Well, Sunas looked like someone had stuck a giant bald fly-head on a tall, gangly woman-body, and she was not happy about it.

SKULDUGGERY: Actually, I think the reason she wasn't happy was because she was trapped in the summoning circle, which also had the effect of binding her magic.

VALKYRIE: Looking at her, I could feel all the flesh rippling up and down my spine.

Sunas refused to answer any of their questions. Unbeknownst to the Arbiters was the fact that once an Order of the Maggot demon was trapped,

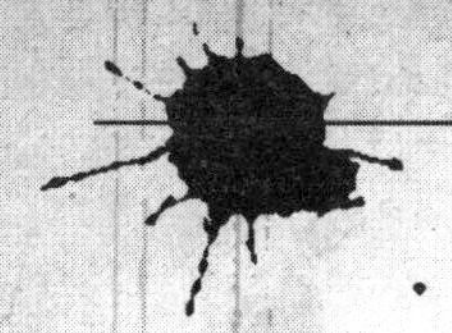

her brethren were alerted. Sunas knew all she had to do was wait. She didn't have to wait for very long.

Byshio and Hallick arrived, freed Sunas and overpowered the Arbiters. They were about to end their lives when Tarron appeared. He promised the others that he would handle the execution of these "insolent humans" once he had extracted the information he needed regarding Bemmon's murder.

VALKYRIE: They left, and I'll be honest with you, I kinda did think he was going to kill us. This was my first time meeting him, in all fairness, and I'm quite used to people trying to kill me the first time they meet me, so I didn't see why this would be any different.
SKULDUGGERY: When he was sure they were gone, Tarron told us that, because he was still operating under the assumption that there was a traitor in the Order of the Maggot, we were the only people he could trust. He revealed that he had tracked Remember to an alternate reality, accessible through a particular door opened with a particular kind of key. Tarron himself couldn't leave this dimension without alerting the traitor, so he gave us one of the keys and told us where to find the door.

On their way to the door – located in the basement of a department store in Dublin City – they saw Remember Me carrying a bag of groceries. They followed her through the door, into the alternate world.

VALKYRIE: You know the way there are, like, a supposedly infinite number of alternate worlds? Some are like our world, some are like Dimension X, some are populated by monkeys or Nazis or aliens or talking geese or whatever? Well, this alternate world wasn't one of those alternate worlds. This was the other kind – the kind that's boring.
SKULDUGGERY: Remember had been hidden away in a parallel reality, on an Earth that was devoid of higher life forms. We followed her through a door that acted as

a portal, emerging into a valley in a vast forest, the breathtaking beauty of the scene spoiled only by the camper van parked ahead of us.

VALKYRIE: It was a good camper van, though. Fancy.

SKULDUGGERY: What was fancy about it?

VALKYRIE: It had a porch.

With nowhere to run, and no Bull Maggots to call upon, Remember was subdued quickly, and without fuss. The Arbiters shackled her and arrested her and took her back into our reality.

When asked about Gog Magog's involvement in her activities, however, Remember laughed.

VALKYRIE: She told us that her time was up. Now that she'd been captured, he wouldn't allow her to live.

SKULDUGGERY: We sought clarification, obviously, regarding the individual she was referring to. We were so close to getting our answers, after all this time. But, before Remember could respond, Tarron appeared. He attacked us, grabbed Remember and left.

VALKYRIE: And we figured, yeah, we have our bad guy.

Bedlam

A drug called Splash was circulating in Roarhaven, quick hits of magic that temporarily boosted a sorcerer's own power level while also providing a general feeling of well-being. An Arbiter investigation found a link between the production of Splash and Doctor Nye, and the distribution of the drug by Roarhaven crimelord, Christopher Reign.

Skulduggery Pleasant and Valkyrie Cain paid a visit to Reign's nightclub, where he denied being anything but a legitimate business owner.

Upon leaving, they arrested three City Guards – Sergeant Yonder, Officer Lush and Officer Rattan – engaged in trashing a mortal's shop as part of a protection racket. The officers did not come quietly.

18,257 mortals – refugees from the Leibniz Universe – had been housed in the city's West District, in an area now known as the Humdrums. Many of them had found jobs in the service industry, and some had started businesses of their own – businesses that were targeted by criminal sorcerers and corrupt officers of the City Guard.

Omen Darkly was a regular visitor to the Humdrums, along with classmates including Axelia Lukt, to distribute leaflets aimed at helping the refugees assimilate further into Roarhaven life.

OMEN: I liked volunteering because helping people is good, and it got me out of some classes. I was in Fourth Year now, and I was supposed to start deciding what I wanted to concentrate on in Fifth and Sixth Year, and I hadn't a clue. I didn't know what kind of sorcerer I wanted to be or what kind of career I wanted... I didn't know anything. Oh, and we were also in the middle of the telepathy module, taught by Miss Wicked. I teamed up with Auger and we were shown how to

communicate with each other using our minds. Or, Auger's mind. My mind was taking a bit longer.

In delving deeper into her visions, Valkyrie started to focus on what she saw of Omen and Auger. In the vision, it was night, and they were on American soil, running from heavily armed, black-garbed soldiers. They didn't make it very far, and so when Valkyrie spoke with Omen she made a request: no matter what happened in the next few weeks, he and his brother needed to stay out of America. Understandably puzzled by the request, Omen agreed.

VALKYRIE: Those visions were plaguing me, but I figured if I could just make sure Omen and Auger were safe, maybe I had a chance of solving my other problems too. Right there on the top of the list was my little sister. I was checking in on Alice pretty regularly, but it was kinda like when you have a mouth ulcer, y'know, and you can't stop probing it? It hurts, but you have to do it. Every time I saw her, every time I saw how weak her soul was, how it was barely visible to me, it hurt. But I kept going back, because... I don't know. Oh, I also failed spectacularly to come out as bisexual[1] to my folks, so that was cool too.

1. It is unclear how long Valkyrie had been seeing Militsa Gnosis by this stage.

The Personal Aide to President Martin Flanery, Bertram Wilkes – otherwise known as Vox Askance – had been revealed to be a spy working for Abyssinia, and killed in the Oval Office by Crepuscular Vies, four months earlier. Wilkes's real name and untimely demise were unknown to Supreme Mage Sorrows, who only knew that Wilkes had once been associated with the anti-Sanctuary group, and that he had gone missing. She asked the

Arbiters to investigate the American sorcerer, Oberon Guile, who had been seen leaving Wilkes's apartment three days prior.

President Flanery had taken to recording everything that happened, both in the Oval Office and in his private residence. Exactly why he was doing this and what he planned to do with the footage, I do not know. Thanks to the footage, however, we can see that he accused Vies of not helping to maintain his public image as promised. Vies dismissed this concern, saying all that mattered was Whitley naval base [2] and the people who were due to die there in ten days' time.

VALKYRIE: I got a knock on my door late at night and Tanith's standing there. I hadn't seen her in years. She visited once, when I was living in Colorado, but neither of us were coping well with what had happened, so she went off to deal with her trauma and I stayed to deal with mine. But it was so good to see her standing there, you know? Like a blast of happier times.

Tanith revealed that she was the leader of the Black Sands[3] resistance group, fighting – in her view – to prevent Supreme Mage Sorrows and the High Sanctuary from taking control of the other two Cradles of Magic. She planned to give herself up in return for the release of dozens of friends and families of suspected Black Sands members, but Valkyrie insisted that she take some time to consider her actions. Tanith finally relented.

2. In Oregon, USA.

3. Labelled a terrorist organisation by the High Sanctuary, the Black Sands group operated mainly on the African continent.

Adam Brate, a member of the Church of the Faceless, told Temper, Skulduggery and Valkyrie that, thanks to the recent Religious Freedom Act, Arch-Canon Damocles Creed's search for the Child of the Faceless Ones[1] had resumed, resulting in the creation of more Kith.

1. See "The Child of the Faceless Ones", page 317

The vampire, Dusk, approached Valkyrie with a message from Caisson.

VALKYRIE: My first instinct was to call in Skulduggery and go arrest this guy – but then Dusk pointed out that Caisson and I weren't actually enemies. Yeah, he was Abyssinia's son, but so what? And, because he'd been the one to kill Mevolent, he could probably have been considered a good guy. So I said yeah, I'd meet him. But before that, we had to figure out how Oberon Guile fitted into all this.

Very little was known about Oberon Guile at the time. According to Sanctuary records, he had just been released from Ironpoint Gaol after serving three years for stealing the Staff of Gahruun from the Devils Museum. He had been married to Magenta Blithe and had one child, a son called Robbie.

When confronted by the Arbiters, he told them that Robbie had been kidnapped two years ago, and held by a revolving team of mages. In order to see her son, Magenta had been forced to work for President Flanery.

The Arbiters helped extract information from a mage named Sleave, one of the sorcerers who had been recently holding Robbie hostage. It was he who told them that the person who had hired them all was Crepuscular Vies.

This is, I believe, the first time either Skulduggery or Valkyrie had heard that name.

Serafina of the Unveiled undertook an official visit to Roarhaven as High Superior of the Legion of Judgement,[2] ostensibly to establish a presence in the city in the form of a place of worship. Her actual motive, however, was almost certainly rooted to the fact that Caisson was free, and she wanted him back.

VALKYRIE: Right before I met Serafina, I'd met Caisson, but I wasn't going to tell China that. On the one hand, she'd pretty much raised him since he was ten, but on the other, she'd already given him up to Serafina once before, so her track record wasn't too great on this.

ARCHIVIST: How had Caisson seemed?

VALKYRIE: He was... jumpy, and clearly traumatised by all that time spent being tortured. He'd heard that we'd been looking for Doctor Nye, and he was willing to trade Nye's location for the location of Greymire Asylum.[3] I'd never heard of it before, but apparently something at Greymire – K-49 – could help him.

2. One of the two leading religious organisations that worship the Faceless Ones, the Legion of Judgement follows Mevolent's interpretation of the *Book of Tears*.

3. A psychiatric institute for the treatment and rehabilitation of wayward sorcerers.

Skulduggery informed Valkyrie that only the worst of the worst got sent to Greymire and, as its location was beyond top secret, they couldn't tell anyone where it was. They could, however, sneak in themselves, take the K-49, and deliver that to Caisson instead.

One of the First Wave, Colleen Stint, approached Omen and asked him to

forge papers for her, Perpetua, Sabre and Disdain, so that they could start a new life with new identities elsewhere.

OMEN: She told me Isidora had been killed. Executed. She said Jenan did it, but maybe with Abyssinia in his head, a little. Anyway, she looked terrified, and they needed help to get out and just disappear. I'd never been very good at forging mortal documents, but I couldn't say no, could I? So I said I'd do my best.

The Arbiters visited Mellifluous Golding's Clockwork House,[1] where secrets were stored, used and traded. In return for the secret of Kes's existence, Valkyrie received the location of Greymire Asylum, on the supposedly abandoned island of Inishtrahull.

1. A building, constructed in the shape of a sigil for an as-yet-unknown purpose, which will ultimately be powered by the secrets stored within its walls.

VALKYRIE: The asylum itself was within a cloaked zone, so it's completely invisible until you get close. It's run by these oddball monks in masks, call themselves the Order of the Void. They wouldn't give us any of the K-49 – wouldn't even tell us what it was – so I slipped away to look for it on my own. Not one of my better ideas.

Doctor Derleth, one of the psychiatrists running experimental treatments on his patients, viewed Valkyrie as an interesting test subject due to her trauma and guilt over her actions as Darquesse.

VALKYRIE: I'm still not sure what they did to me there. I don't know if it was a gas that made me hallucinate or if my mind just... quit. I was seeing all kinds of things, people from my past and general weirdness – the worst of which was the Nemesis of Greymire.

From what little there has been written about the Nemesis, she seems to be a physical manifestation of one's own guilt, conjured to deliver punishment for past misdeeds, and can continue the pursuit long after the individual has left Greymire.

With the Nemesis now in pursuit, Valkyrie realised that K-49 was not a serum or a pill, but a room, a small room at the top of a tower, where she found an old woman, a powerful psychic, who was being soothed by a music box.

VALKYRIE: The music box. The moment I heard it, all the bad thoughts went away, and it was obvious that this was what Caisson needed to ease his pain. So I took it.
SKULDUGGERY: You stole a music box from an old woman.
VALKYRIE: If it makes things any better, I was conflicted about it, so...

The Darquesse Society had located Darquesse's energy signature – now they needed a Shunter to open a portal to that dimension, and a volunteer to go through and find her. Sebastian volunteered to go through, and Ulysses knew a Shunter. That Shunter, unfortunately, was Silas Nadir.

BENNET: We didn't exactly love the idea of working with someone like Nadir – you know, an actual serial killer – but we didn't have much choice. And then the portal was open and Sebastian... Sebastian just walked on through. One of the bravest things I've ever seen.
ARCHIVIST: I could find no details on what this other world looked like, and have been unable to locate Sebastian Tao for comment.
BENNET: Yeah, Sebastian values his privacy. It's why he wears that suit, you

know? But he did what he went there to do – he found Darquesse. She was this huge, giant version of herself, bigger than a mountain, he said. And she was fighting huge, giant Faceless Ones. He asked her to come back with him, to come back home. She didn't listen. He was crushed. This was his mission, this is what he was here for, and he reckoned he'd failed, so he turned round, headed back the way he'd come.

Skulduggery and Valkyrie met up with Oberon after he'd found a link between Crepuscular Vies and a mortal mercenary called Thomas Bolton, who was part of a private army called Blackbrook. They travelled to Arizona, apprehended Bolton, and left him with Oberon to interrogate.

VALKYRIE: I met Caisson to hand over the music box, which is what I thought he wanted. I'd tried it out – it was amazing. It soothed me right down, stopped all the horrible things I was telling myself... I was sorry to part with it. Turns out, I didn't have to, because he wasn't interested in the music box. Caisson wasn't after what was in room K-49, he was after *who* was in K-49. He wanted the old woman – he wanted Solace. I didn't know it right then and there, but she was his wife. She'd aged in that room while he'd stayed young. I didn't have a choice – I told him where Greymire was, and in exchange, he told me that Nye was in a laboratory. Underwater. I felt bad that I told him this really dangerous secret, but, I mean, an underwater laboratory, man. Sometimes my job is cool, and other times it's even cooler.

Abyssinia and the anti-Sanctuary helped Caisson break Solace out of Greymire – and then the couple left.

The Arbiters hitched a lift on the *King's Fury*, a cursed ship crewed by ghost pirates and captained by Captain Edgar Dudgeon.

VALKYRIE: Then they tried to kill us. I swear, most of my stories these days have "And then they tried to kill us" in them at least once. TTV, right? Things Turn Violent.

SKULDUGGERY: It does happen an awful lot. Thankfully we were saved by the arrival of another cursed ship, the *Savagery*. Things were getting pretty exciting – and then the Sea Hag snagged Valkyrie.

VALKYRIE: The bloody Sea Hag. Again, after all these years. So, yeah, she tried to kill me, but I was saved by a hot mermaid[1] called Una, who took me to Nye's laboratory. Now, as it turned out, Una wasn't so great, because her and the other hot mermaids tried to kill the Sea Hag, and while I wasn't a big fan of the Sea Hag, I wasn't just going to sit back and watch the hot mermaids murder her. So we saved her, and the Sea Hag gave me a bell that I can ring if ever I need her help. Presumably only for water-based emergencies, though.

SKULDUGGERY: You've digressed.

VALKYRIE: Sorry?

SKULDUGGERY: You've digressed. It usually happens when you start talking about the mermaids.

VALKYRIE: Oh... OK, so where was I before the hot mermaids tried to kill the Sea Hag? Yes, they'd just brought me to the underwater lab, and Skulduggery joined me and we told Nye what we were after. It explained that, because I'd killed Alice using the Deathtouch Gauntlet, her soul was shattered, so it gave us a device to retrieve the two missing parts.

1. Maiden of the Sea.

They found and recovered the first soul fragment – which had attached itself to a mortal "medium" – and discovered that the second fragment was in the Necropolis.

While Valkyrie recovered from the exertions of separating her sister's soul fragment from the soul of the medium, Skulduggery and Temper broke into the Dark Cathedral for proof of Creed's further attempts at finding and Activating the Child of the Faceless Ones. They discovered a vast cavern filled with Kith.

TEMPER: They were just standing here, thousands of them. Tens of thousands. People without faces. Living but... but not living. Creed found us, told us to get out.
SKULDUGGERY: He knew he was protected by the Religious Freedom Act. He knew that even if China hadn't been in his debt due to the First Bank of Roarhaven deal, there wouldn't have been anything she could have done.

Once Valkyrie had sufficiently recovered, she decided she couldn't wait for Skulduggery to go hunting for the remaining fragment of Alice's soul – but in order to access the Necropolis she needed the necronaut suit, currently on display in the Museum of Magical History.

Security footage shows Valkyrie, along with Tanith and Militsa, breaking into the Museum and absconding with the suit.[1] Valkyrie then travelled to the Necropolis.

1. Criminal charges brought by the Museum were later dropped when Valkyrie apologised. She did not, however, return the suit. The Museum remains annoyed.

VALKYRIE: I found it. The last fragment of Alice's soul. I found it. But there was someone there, the Sentinel, and she wouldn't let me leave. She wanted me to bring Alice to the Necropolis, to let her die to bring her soul peace, instead of bringing the

last fragment to her and allowing her to live. I'd already killed my sister once – there was no way I was gonna do it again. Something happened. I lost control of my power and there was a flash and next thing I know, I'm flying away and I have the soul fragment.

When she got home to Grimwood, Valkyrie was in a state of great distress and confusion. The Nemesis of Greymire appeared and attacked her again before disappearing. I still have no way of knowing if the Nemesis was anything more than a figment of Valkyrie's imagination or a real, physical threat.

VALKYRIE: What, it can't be both?

Tanith met Oberon in a London bar.

TANITH: I walked in and saw him there in all his grizzled glory and I was, like, hellllo, nurse...

He told her what Thomas Bolton had told him about Blackbrook Services, the private military company run by Crepuscular. He said that Blackbrook knew about the existence of sorcerers.

With the forged papers in hand, Omen travelled to Dublin to meet with Colleen. It was, however, a trap, and although he managed to evade the members of First Wave, the arrival of Parthenios Lilt ended his escape attempt.

OMEN: They brought me to Coldheart and Jenan told me what Abyssinia's plan was. They were going to attack Whitley naval base in America and First Wave were going to kill a whole bunch of military personnel. It was going to be Pearl Harbour, you know? When the Japanese attacked the base at Pearl Harbour, and it drew America

into World War Two? See, Abyssinia was going to attack Whitley, which would expose sorcerers to the world, and then, in retaliation, President Flanery was going to bomb the American Sanctuary. Jenan said I was going to be left at Whitley and framed for the attack – but that was never actually going to happen. See, Jenan didn't have the full story.

Valkyrie revealed to Supreme Mage Sorrows that she told Caisson where Greymire was located, and the Supreme Mage had her thrown in a cell.

VALKYRIE: Did you see the video? They didn't even bother deleting the video after the City Guard came in and almost beat me to death. Yonder, Lush and Rattan – three fine, upstanding officers. Doctor Whorl knew what had happened but he hated me because of what Darquesse had done, so he fixed me and sent me back to get beaten again. Y'know what? I hated myself so much at the time that I was actually OK with it. Can you imagine that? I reckoned I deserved it.

While Valkyrie was incarcerated, Skulduggery, Tanith and Oberon visited the Blackbrook military compound, where they were attacked by mortal soldiers carved with the same sigils that were inscribed on each hit of the sorcerer drug, Splash.

SKULDUGGERY: At first, I'd assumed that Splash was merely a drug designed for recreational use for mages – but this had never sat right with me. Doctor Nye wouldn't have cared about something so small. It isn't concerned about making money on criminal enterprises. But when I saw the same sigil carved into the soldiers' skin, it all made sense. Splash was the experiment. Splash was the controlled test. The real goal was to adapt it for mortal use – although more work clearly needed to be done.

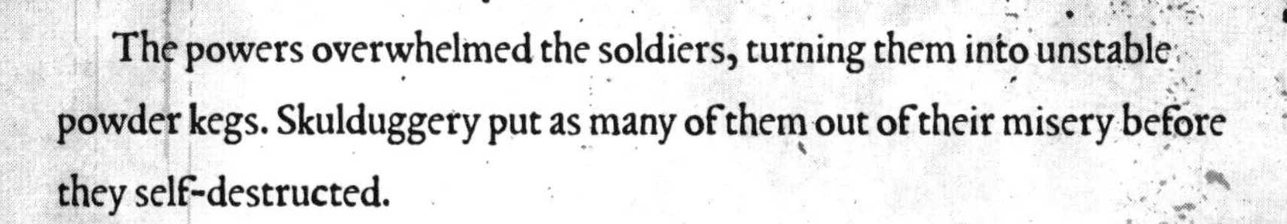

The powers overwhelmed the soldiers, turning them into unstable powder kegs. Skulduggery put as many of them out of their misery before they self-destructed.

SKULDUGGERY: The question then became – why? Why would Doctor Nye even want to give mortals these temporary powers? And what did all this have to do with the sorcerer we'd been hearing about, this Crepuscular Vies? Questions, questions, so many questions...

But Skulduggery was captured before he could follow Tanith and Oberon out, and teleported to the cave where Abyssinia was nursed back to health all those centuries before. The anti-Sanctuary group was waiting for him, and Destrier trapped him in the Eternity Gate,[1] where Skulduggery would be held for seven days – keeping him out of the way while Abyssinia's plan was enacted.

1. Designed and built by Destrier, the Eternity Gate is a prison cell that slows time – essentially trapping its victim in a single moment for however long the Gate is active.

President Flanery played a big part in that plan – or he thought he did, at least. The day had come, and he was ready to become a legendary hero and the saviour of the mortals. Once First Wave attacked the naval base, he would broadcast the footage, make a speech, and then lead the attack on the Sanctuaries – at which point Abyssinia would assume control of the magical communities around the world and a truce would be called. From that point on, Abyssinia would control the sorcerers, and Flanery would build a political empire to last for generations.

But Crepuscular arrived to tell him that Abyssinia had no intention of sharing power like that. Once Flanery broadcast the footage, she planned to use a life-force bomb to kill him while he made his speech. This would start the war she wanted – the war she would win.

She planned to double-cross Flanery, so Crepuscular told him how to double-cross her first.

Temper visited Valkyrie in her cell.

TEMPER: It was pretty obvious what had happened to her, so I set off for Commander Hoc's office, all ready to demand she be placed under protective custody. Instead, I was intercepted by Yonder and his buddies. Officers Lush, Ferule and Rattan took me to a deserted part of town and tried to kill me, and I was forced to release my gist.

ARCHIVIST: And you were reluctant to do so...?

TEMPER: Very. Any day now I'm gonna release it and it's gonna take over and I'll be gone and it'll be here in my place. But... I didn't have much of a choice. I told China what was happening, then spoke to Bejant, a friend of mine and one of the few City Guard officers I could trust. But he was killed right in front of me and I was grabbed. Not a good night for me. Not a great night for Bejant, either.

VALKYRIE: China rushed over, got Doctor Whorl to fix me up. I hurried it along by latching on to his magic and, kinda, improving on it. I healed myself, basically. It was pretty awesome. But then a bunch more people tried to kill me.

Abyssinia sent an army of Coldheart convicts into the High Sanctuary, armed with advanced weaponry powered by magic. Sanctuary forces reacted quickly and decisively, denying the Coldheart army a foothold.

FLETCHER: This is the part where I fought Nero. It was such a cool fight. Pity nobody else really saw it.

The Eternity Gate that trapped Skulduggery malfunctioned,[1] allowing him out earlier than planned, and he joined Valkyrie, China and Serafina as they confronted Abyssinia, Caisson and Razzia.

1. Destrier later admitted that he had programmed the Gate to malfunction.

Caisson was here to exact his revenge. He wanted to kill Skulduggery for killing Abyssinia when he was a boy. He wanted to kill China for betraying him and handing him over to Serafina. And he wanted to kill Serafina for torturing him for ninety years.

But Valkyrie had looked into Abyssinia's head and she'd learned what had really transpired all those centuries ago. Abyssinia was forced to admit the truth.

SKULDUGGERY: Abyssinia worked hard to get close to the man she hated, but things got complicated, as things tend to get. Mevolent was Caisson's father.

VALKYRIE: I never asked you, actually – were you disappointed?

SKULDUGGERY: Why would I have been disappointed?

VALKYRIE: Well, for a few days we thought you might have had a son.

SKULDUGGERY: I knew Caisson wasn't mine.

VALKYRIE: You were a hundred per cent certain?

SKULDUGGERY: I was ninety per cent certain.

VALKYRIE: So was the ten per cent of you that was thinking maybe this kid is mine... was that part of you disappointed?

SKULDUGGERY: I don't know. I try not to dwell on disappointment so I haven't examined my feelings about the subject too deeply.

VALKYRIE: Is that healthy?

SKULDUGGERY: Yes.

VALKYRIE: Oh, OK, then.

Following this revelation, Abyssinia and her followers teleported out, and Supreme Mage Sorrows extracted the location of Coldheart Prison from one of the recaptured convicts.

If the news got out about Caisson's true father, the devout followers of Mevolent would abandon the Legion of Judgement and flock to him. In order to maintain her authority and her church, Serafina needed Caisson killed, and so she sent her sister – the assassin, Kierre – to remove the problem.

Creed arranged for Caisson and Solace to visit the Dark Cathedral as he was preparing to Activate Temper.

OMEN: It was night, and I was taken to Whitley naval base along with First Wave and the rest of Abyssinia's forces. They went off to start the killing, but I managed to get free – more by luck than anything. I didn't have a phone so the only thing I could do was try the telepathy thing we'd been practising in school. And it worked. Amazingly, it worked. For the first time ever, something I learned in school was actually useful. I contacted Auger and told him where I was, and he went and got Never and they teleported over and we just, we had to stop them, y'know? We had to stop First Wave. We couldn't just run away. Thankfully, we weren't the only ones there.

Following their escape from the Blackbrook military compound, Oberon followed a lead that took him to the safe house where his ex-wife and son were being held, while Tanith followed another operative to the naval base.

TANITH: I'd picked up Dexter Vex on the way, and we arrived just in time to punch some people that desperately needed the punching.

The Arbiters entered Coldheart Prison and found Destrier, who told them about Abyssinia's target being Whitley Naval Magazine. He also told them that a life-force bomb had been planted beneath the White House, just waiting to go off.

VALKYRIE: Then we turned round and Abyssinia was standing there, looking... sad. After finding out who his dad was, Caisson had abandoned her, and she blamed Solace, for some reason.

She allowed Valkyrie to see into her memories.

VALKYRIE: I saw back to when she was a kid, when Mevolent had attacked her father. There was the prophecy, that the King of the Darklands would face the Chosen One in a thousand years and they'd battle, and one of them would die. The king, the Unnamed, he knew that the only way the Chosen One could kill him was with the Obsidian Blade, a knife that wipes whatever it cuts from existence, so he got Mevolent to find it and destroy it.
ARCHIVIST: But Mevolent found it and stabbed him with it.
VALKYRIE: Which is, admittedly, really funny. But the king was so powerful that he managed to slow down the effect the Obsidian Blade had on him. He slept, apparently, until Abyssinia grew up and became a badass and got pregnant. Then he woke, and when Vile threw her out of that castle window, he was there to nurse her back to health. Before he allowed himself to die, he transferred his magic to Abyssinia and his soul into a Soul Catcher. The plan was for Abyssinia to transfer his soul into the body of her son – which is messed up. Obviously, Abyssinia couldn't bring herself to do it, and then she was killed and her heart was cut out and that's where the story ended. Except not really.

Nero teleported Abyssinia and Razzia to the naval base.

SKULDUGGERY: We tagged along without them knowing because that's exactly how I planned it to happen.

VALKYRIE: You are such a liar.

SKULDUGGERY: If life is a game of chess, I am a grand master.

VALKYRIE: Pure luck, is what it was.

SKULDUGGERY: Grand master.

The Arbiters joined up with Tanith, Dexter, Omen, Auger and Never, and proceeded to take down the Coldheart convicts wherever they found them.

Abyssinia had told First Wave that they would be required to kill the Navy personnel on the base – currently sleeping in the barracks – and that the footage would then be used to start a war. But when the Blackbrook contractors appeared, Abyssinia informed First Wave that the contractors would be the ones killing *them*. The army of Coldheart convicts would then slaughter the mortal sailors when they rushed out to investigate the gunfire.

But then the Blackbrook contractors turned their weapons on Abyssinia and her people.

TANITH: I just wanna get this straight: Abyssinia made a plan with Flanery that would involve First Wave and then double-cross them, and then she planned to double-cross Flanery, but Flanery got in his double-cross before she got in her double-cross. That's three double-crosses, right there.

More Blackbrook contractors arrived, some armed with rifles that fired so-called binding bullets which, while not harmful, restricted a sorcerer's magic on impact. Abyssinia was injured and Valkyrie took her to safety.

VALKYRIE: This is where I started seeing elements of that vision I had, the one where Omen and Auger were hurt.

OMEN: We were dead. Those Blackbrook guys were right behind us and Auger was hurt and we were... It was the end. And then Valkyrie flew down and they all started shooting her. She saved us.

VALKYRIE: Omen and Auger saved me.

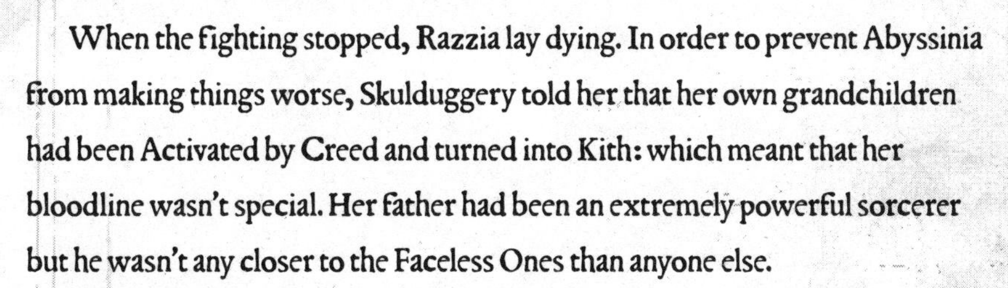

When the fighting stopped, Razzia lay dying. In order to prevent Abyssinia from making things worse, Skulduggery told her that her own grandchildren had been Activated by Creed and turned into Kith: which meant that her bloodline wasn't special. Her father had been an extremely powerful sorcerer but he wasn't any closer to the Faceless Ones than anyone else.

Abyssinia proved resistant to that idea.

OMEN: They fought her. They all just attacked and she threw them all back. Only Valkyrie was able to continue.

VALKYRIE: She pretty much threw me around the place.

While this was happening, Creed had brought Temper out on to one of the larger balconies at the top of the Dark Cathedral.

TEMPER: I was strapped to a table and generally not having a great time, and Caisson and Solace turn up. Creed says that if they join the Church of the Faceless, he'll be able to protect them from Serafina. Of course, if they join his church, a load of worshippers will abandon the Legion of Judgement and join his church too, so he's not offering this out of his heart. Solace wants to see how the Activation works, but Caisson tells him to stop. That's when Kierre arrived.

Kierre of the Unveiled delivered a mortal wound to Caisson before disappearing, and Abyssinia felt this from the naval base. A truce was called, and Nero teleported Abyssinia, Razzia, Skulduggery and Valkyrie to Caisson's side.

TEMPER: Skulduggery cut me loose and I went straight over to Razzia. She was always my favourite, and she was dying. She asked me to take care of her pets when she was gone. I mean, what could I say?

Caisson died of his wound, and Abyssinia allowed her father's soul to pass into her son's body, thus fulfilling her long-ago promise. Caisson, his form now inhabited by the life force of his grandfather, returned to life, and the King of the Darklands took back the power he had once given Abyssinia, and departed.

With Flanery as the focus of all of her rage, Abyssinia instructed Nero to take her to Flanery, and here I need to switch from eyewitness testimony to security footage. Abyssinia and Nero's sudden arrival seemed to terrify Flanery, but Crepuscular Vies was waiting to wound Nero and debilitate Abyssinia. When Flanery started to gloat about the war to come, Crepuscular informed him that the war wouldn't be going ahead – he had, effectively, changed his mind about that whole thing. Flanery was outraged that such a decision was taken without him. Crepuscular didn't appear to care.

Nero teleported Abyssinia back to the Dark Cathedral, where Abyssinia died in Skulduggery's arms.

In the aftermath, Skulduggery persuaded China to release the friends and family of the Black Sand members, which meant Tanith no longer had to turn herself in.

TANITH: Then he asked me to get a few people together and go find the Obsidian Blade. He figured since the King of the Darklands had returned, Auger Darkly was going to need all the advantages he could get. So off I went.

Sebastian returned through the dimensional portal – and he didn't come alone.

BENNET: All I know is that I was on the toilet and Demure started shrieking and I ran into the living room and there she is, standing beside Sebastian. Darquesse. Darquesse had come back.

All of First Wave were arrested at the naval base – all except Jenan Ispolin, who managed to escape in all the confusion.

OMEN: Auger and I went home for the summer holidays and I spent the first few weeks drawing comics and reading and not getting into trouble. I suppose I let my guard down. Then one day he turns up and tries to kill me. He would've done it too, but Auger came running in... and Jenan stabbed him. Nearly killed him.

The Darkly brothers were found ten minutes later and immediately teleported to the Medical Bay in the High Sanctuary. Jenan Ispolin received treatment for a fractured skull, jaw and cheek, and concussion.

According to sources that wish to remain anonymous, Solace appeared in Supreme Mage Sorrows's private chambers one night and told her she was going to take all her power away from her. This source also claims that

Solace had called Supreme Mage Sorrows "mother".

Valkyrie restored her sister's soul.

VALKYRIE: And pretty much immediately afterwards I had a psychic flash into the future, where I actually talked with sixteen-year-old Alice. That would have been so cool if she wasn't just about to go and face her arch-enemy in the final battle between the Child of the Ancients and the Child of the Faceless Ones.

SKULDUGGERY: You're still upset about that.

VALKYRIE: She's not meant to have an arch-enemy. I'm the one who has ridiculous stuff like that happen to her. Alice is supposed to be safe.

SKULDUGGERY: It wasn't all bad news, though, was it? After all this ended? Some good things happened too. You told your parents about Militsa.

VALKYRIE: Yeah, and they were as cool about it as I knew they would be. And hey, at least I had the music box, right? Whenever all that guilt and all that sadness and all that self-hatred threatened to drag me down, I just opened up the music box and I let my mind drift away. It saved me, it really did, especially after Dusk came to see me. He told me a story of when he was a young vampire out in the world, and he stumbled across one of Creed's cellars full of Kith. And what's a young vampire to do when confronted with a cellar full of weird faceless bodies? He took a bite. Took a sip. He spat it out, of course. There was something mixed with the human blood – something he realised later was the blood of the Faceless Ones.

Remember when he bit me? At Croke Park, with the Revengers' Club and everything? He bit me and said he could taste something different? My blood... it was Faceless Ones blood.

The family legend was wrong. The Edgleys aren't descended from the Last of the Ancients. We're descended from the Faceless Ones.

We're the bad guys.

DUSK

Rest in peace,
Our sister Claire,
Who saw the future,
Just not the bear.

ABROGATE RAZE

PART FOUR BY TAWDRY HEPBURN

The following is taken from the journals of Fransic Catawampus:

I said a funny thing at dinner tonight, but for the life of me I can't remember what it was – only that it struck me as hilarious, astute and quite poignant, given the circumstances. It was wasted, of course, on the company I was keeping. Out of my siblings present, Carver was pensive, Confelicity was taciturn, Bayard was reserved, Apricity was quiet, and only Uther was expressing anything that could roundly be considered an emotion.

(The emotion was anger, by the way.)

Skulduggery stood silently while Uther berated him, called him stupid and childish and rash. He carried on, but I lost interest and diverted my attention to coming up with new words for things, as has been my hobby of late. I think I shall call an apple a "crunch-shnuckle".

The dinner had been a disaster. The soup was cold, we'd just lost two sisters and a brother, and when the meat arrived it was overcooked.

Forgive me if I paraphrase the following exchange:

UTHER (QUITE ANGRY): Of all the irresponsible acts you have perpetrated over the years, this is undoubtedly the most deranged!
SKULDUGGERY (FINALLY SPEAKING UP): I would agree with you.
UTHER (REALLY, REALLY QUITE ANGRY): And what's worse – what is worse – is

that you involved the others! I'd wager they didn't even question your plan, such as it was. I'd wager they listened while you spun your web of words because you knew exactly what to say, didn't you?

SKULDUGGERY (SOUNDING TIRED): *Abrogate was at the farmhouse alone. If we didn't go in then and there, he would have escaped.*

UTHER (REALLY, REALLY QUITE ANGRY INDEED): *And yet he escaped anyway! He escaped and he took our brothers and our sisters with him!*

SKULDUGGERY (NOW SOUNDING QUITE ANGRY HIMSELF): *And, if the rest of you had come when I'd asked, he could very well be in shackles right now.*

UTHER (FURIOUS): *Don't you dare blame this on us!*

SKULDUGGERY (A MOMENTARY PAUSE): *I'm not. It's my fault.*

CONFELICITY (SLUMPED IN HER CHAIR): *How did it happen? How did he best all four of you?*

SKULDUGGERY (NOT AN OUNCE OF HIS USUAL BRAVADO ON DISPLAY): *He was using a magic I'd not seen before.*

CARVER (RIGHT, AS USUAL): *Our father is an Elemental.*

SKULDUGGERY (CONTRADICTORY, AS USUAL): *I know that – but it wasn't Elemental magic that repelled our attacks, or Elemental magic that countered and struck back. This isn't – and you need to understand this, all of you – this isn't the same man we knew. Abrogate has changed in ways I find difficult to describe.*

APRICITY (SHAKEN): *Try, Skulduggery. Start with what can be described. The magic.*

SKULDUGGERY (UNUSUALLY HESITANT): *The things he was doing, they were too varied to be of the same discipline.*

BAYARD (BORED): *Does that surprise you? We're all a little magically ambidextrous in this family. We have to get it from somewhere.*

SKULDUGGERY (PREOCCUPIED): *This wasn't that. This wasn't two disciplines, or* even three. This was many. For every move we made, he had a countermove. It seemed as though the only limit to what he could do was his own imagination.

CARVER (RIGHT, AS USUAL): You're being ridiculous. That's not how magic works.

SKULDUGGERY (CONTRADICTORY, AS USUAL): I know that. But it's what happened.

BAYARD (CLAPPING HANDS, SITTING FORWARD): So it's something we'll have to look out for – fair enough! The only question now, and I can't believe I'm the one to point this out, but the only question is where did our dear father take his new hostages, and when are we going to take them back?

SKULDUGGERY: (UNCHARACTERISTICALLY SILENT)

BAYARD (ANNOYED): Skulduggery. Where are they?

SKULDUGGERY (UNCHARACTERISTICALLY SOMBRE): I don't know yet.

BAYARD (INSISTENT): Well, what does he want them for? What's he going to do with them? You were in that damn farmhouse for nine hours – surely he must have said something.

SKULDUGGERY (DISTRESSINGLY SERIOUS): He said a lot of things. He talked about this god he was worshipping. He said he'd finally found what he'd been looking for. The gap in his soul, he said, it was being filled. Gog Magog. Have any of you heard of him?

MY SIBLINGS (EVERY HYPER-INTELLIGENT ONE OF THEM):

SKULDUGGERY (STRANGELY RELIEVED): Good. So Gog Magog, that's who he's worshipping. That's his saviour. He told us about him. It's... it's hard to remember this right for some reason, but after the fighting, after he'd beaten us, we all sat down and... talked. Abrogate told us that Gog Magog was the God of the Apocalypse, that he was imprisoned somewhere. He said there was something about him – the more you learned about who he was, the deeper you fell into worshipping him.

CONFELICITY (STATING AN UNDERSTATEMENT): That sounds dangerous.

SKULDUGGERY (BEING A SKELETON): The more he spoke, the less the others *interrupted. Two hours in – and he hadn't stopped speaking the entire time – they were absolutely silent. Watching him. Barely blinking. They were being infected. This Gog Magog, whatever else he is, he's a virus. Abrogate read about him, learned about him, and I think that's all he had to do to be infected, and now he's doing what he can to infect others. He's telling the story. It didn't work on me because I'm not like the rest of you.*

BAYARD (SERIOUS): *How do we get them back?*

SKULDUGGERY (SERIOUS): *I don't know.*

CARVER (STANDING): *We'll come up with a solution between us. We're not going to go running into another confrontation without knowing what it is we're facing. We're not going to be that irresponsible again, are we, Skulduggery? When we've got Abrogate in shackles, we'll see what needs to be done with Petulance and Mirror and Respair. But we will get them back.*

He says that like it's a certainty, but of course it isn't and he knows it. I don't think he can help it, though. Carver's been the hero for so long that I don't think he can bring himself not to promise the world, and then spend every waking moment trying to make it happen. He is tough on Skulduggery, though, and Skulduggery is tough on himself, but it takes neither a towering intellect nor a supernatural understanding of human nature to understand why: my brothers simply haven't forgiven themselves for what they see as the one monumental failure of their lives, when neither of them were there to stop our dear father from killing our dear mother in front of our dear younger siblings.

Of course, I wasn't there, either, and neither were Confelicity or Petulance, and so we all share some degree of regret, shame and self-loathing. Confelicity may be darkly witty these days, but she is merely a hint of a shadow of the verbal duellist she was back then. Petulance had a bold temper as a child, and a fiery temper in her teen years, and a vicious temper in her early twenties, but ever since our mother died she's been positively volatile.

And I, you ask? Dear old Fransic? Why, I was a fool back then, and I am indeed a fool now – but these days I at least have the good sense to be a conflicted fool. Besides, there is only so much self-recrimination to go around, and I quite like to fill my time with other pursuits, such as the aforementioned effort to find new names for things.

(That feeling you get when something nice happens and you are pleased, for example. I think I shall call it a state of being wevelly, after Alexander Rupert Wevella, the inventor of the wevel.)

Carver, of course, had a second monumental failure to weigh upon his shoulders: Skulduggery's death. The war had reached a new phase of intense conflict and Mevolent had targeted the leaders and the generals and the people running our side of the show. He had set his sights on the top soldiers, the best operatives, the most dangerous warriors. He had targeted Skulduggery. And he had targeted Carver.

(He'd also targeted me, but everyone seems to forget that little detail because I'd dealt with it by being rather wonderful at sleeping in, thereby missing the explosion that was supposed to kill me.)

Skulduggery had been singled out for a particularly unpleasant (ha) death by virtue of being Nefarian Serpine's most hated enemy.

I wish I could explain why this were so. I wish I could relate to you, oh reader of my most private of journals, the hidden truth that Skulduggery and Nefarian were once childhood friends! Or they'd fallen in love with the same woman! Or they'd fallen in love with each other! Or any one of a thousand reasons why two people would choose to hate each other with such unending ferocity!

Sadly, there is no such hidden truth. The only truth is that they met as enemies, and they just became better enemies as time went by.

Sometimes it happens thusly.

And why should Carver blame himself for Serpine's single-minded obsession with torturing Skulduggery, with robbing him of everything before finally ending his life? I have no idea, but it probably has something to do with what he sees as his duties as the big brother to us all. Possibly also because of a promise he'd never been asked to make to our mother, a year before our father killed her.

THE CHILD OF THE FACELESS ONES

Before the Ancients affected the environment, the Faceless Ones were able to roam the Earth in their natural forms. Once the environment was altered, however, the Dark Gods had to inhabit human bodies to survive. Some of these humans, if they'd survived the Faceless Ones moving on to the next vessel, passed their genes to the generations that came after them.

It is estimated that, today, one in seven human beings have a trace of Faceless Ones DNA in their system.

Damocles Creed, in an effort to find someone with a strong-enough strand of this DNA and thus bring them to their full power so that they could facilitate the return of the Faceless Ones, began a process of Activating potential candidates. Each Activation, though a failure, helped him refine the process. The failed candidates underwent a physical transformation, insofar as their faces were seen to "melt" as their skulls sealed over, removing such generally accepted facial features such as the eyes, nose, ears and mouth, and shedding all hair. Despite this, the candidates, now known as the Kith, continued to breathe normally, and they no longer required sustenance to survive. As their skulls sealed, so too did their minds, proving resistant to psychic probes, MRI scans and stimuli of any kind. Although the Kith appear, for want of a better term, "brain dead", there is currently no way for us to accurately make that determination.

A NOTE FROM THE ARCHIVIST

My name is Archivist Gamel and I've been brought in to finish this book because Archivist Mordant has gone missing. As of yet, my request for a twenty-four-hour security team has not been approved, despite the disappearance of all three Archivists who were working on this project before me. Apologies for any mistakes I might make, but I haven't been sleeping well since coming onboard, and I'm having difficulty concentrating.

I have been assured by the Archive Department that I am perfectly safe and that nothing untoward is going on. I'm not altogether sure that I believe them.

Seasons of War

VALKYRIE: I'd been having a full-blown existential crisis for about four months. I used to think I knew who I was: I was Valkyrie Cain, descended from the Last of the Ancients. The good guy. Now I realised, oh, not the good guy, as it turns out. Actually descended from the Faceless Ones, so pretty much the bad guy, and the only person I could talk to about it was Kes, the splinter of Darquesse who remained on Earth while she went travelling through dimensions, murdering entire universes. Probably should've seen it coming, now that I think about it...

A group of actors had taken to performing human sacrifices for their "Master", and giving him a percentage of their income. It was all a scam, and the "Master" was nothing more than a low-level sorcerer who barely put up a fight when Skulduggery Pleasant and Valkyrie Cain came to arrest them all.

The Darquesse Society were still debating on what they should do with Darquesse now that she was home.

BENNET: Sebastian told us that the first part of his mission was complete – he'd found her and brought her back – and now the second part would begin. Darquesse, he said, was the only one who could save us from what was coming.

ARCHIVIST: Which was?

BENNET: Sorry?

ARCHIVIST: What was coming?

BENNET: I haven't a clue. He wouldn't tell us.

Omen Darkly had recovered well from the injury he'd sustained when Jenan Ispolin had attacked him. His brother, Auger, was experiencing complications, though none that were thought to be life-threatening.

OMEN: I visited Jenan in prison, just to try to understand his hatred, you know? He still seemed really angry with me.

Alice was finally able to experience emotions, but they veered wildly between utter joy and the deepest despair.

VALKYRIE: I didn't know how to handle this. All I wanted to do was make her better, make everything OK... but I suppose that ship had long since sailed by this stage – sailed and then sunk. With the loss of everyone on board. Who were all eaten by sharks.
SKULDUGGERY: I was eaten by a shark once.
VALKYRIE: No, you weren't.

The High Sanctuary received an anonymous warning, advising them to prepare for a full-on invasion from the Leibniz Universe before the end of the year – seven months away. The Arbiters tracked the warning back to the Humdrums, where the mortal refugees had settled. There they found Nefarian Serpine.

SKULDUGGERY: He had been the leader of the Resistance, but had abandoned his post when Mevolent's forces were closing

in, and came through the portal disguised as a refugee.
VALKYRIE: Such bravery. Such nobility.

Serpine's warning was taken seriously, and Supreme Mage China Sorrows gave the Arbiters a mission: to assemble a team, shunt over to the Leibniz Universe, and assassinate Mevolent before he launched his invasion.

VALKYRIE: *We weren't assassins.*
SKULDUGGERY: *But...*
VALKYRIE: *Sometimes you have to do horrible things to protect the ones you love.*

The first person they went to was Tanith Low who, along with her new boyfriend, Oberon Guile, had been searching for the Obsidian Blade.

TANITH: "New boyfriend."
ARCHIVIST: That isn't accurate?
TANITH: We just weren't putting a label on it, you know? I try not to put labels on things. Apart from jam. I do like labels on jam. It's just handy, apart from anything else.
ARCHIVIST: Regarding the Obsidian Blade...?
TANITH: We were closing in on it, but I'll be honest: when Val asked me to head off to an alternate world for a few weeks to kill a bad guy, I did not hesitate for one moment to leave the searching to Oberon.

They also recruited Dexter Vex and Saracen Rue. There had been some tension that had grown between the two friends over the last few years, stemming from Saracen's reluctance to share the nature of his magical discipline. In order to move forward and re-establish their friendship, Saracen told everyone what his power was.[1]

They agreed to take Serpine along to act as their guide, and a young American Shunter named Luke Skywalker[2] joined the new Dead Men line-up. Arming themselves with God-Killer weapons and automatic rifles, they shunted, planning to spend no more than two months away at the very most.

1. No one, unfortunately, would tell me what it was.
2. Not the Jedi Master.

VALKYRIE: I took the music box with me. I mean, I had to. My head was... It wasn't a quiet place, and the music box calmed me down and let me think straight. I was going to be away from my family and Kes and from Militsa – I needed all the comfort I could get.

They started walking for Dublin-Within-The-Wall, where Mevolent had his palace.

TANITH: It was pretty barren. Dirt roads, empty settlements, no one around. Not sorcerer, and not mortal. We were starting to wonder if anyone was still in the country.

Valkyrie and Luke rescued a man from a pack of draugar.[3] The man, Proinsias, told them of the infection that had swept across the world, affecting mortal and sorcerer alike. Whole countries had been wiped out.

3. A draugr (plural, draugar) is a reanimated corpse, not known for biting/eating flesh.

SKULDUGGERY: Typically, a draugr does not transmit infections through its bite. These draugar were a hybrid, though, a cross between draugar and zombies.
VALKYRIE: Draugr and draugar still sound like the exact same word.
SKULDUGGERY: There's an extra A in draugar.
VALKYRIE: I have no idea which one that is.

Draugar roamed Dublin-Within-The-Wall. Evidence showed that the city had been under siege, and then abandoned. Serpine suggested that Mevolent had either gone to Tahil na Kurge, in Morocco, or Tahil na Sin, in Transylvania. They decided to sail for Belgium the next day, and begin the long trek to Tahil na Sin.

VALKYRIE: I suggested shunting home, travelling to Transylvania like civilised people, and then shunting from *our* Transylvania to *their* Transylvania. That would have been smart, but no one listens to the hot girl.

SKULDUGGERY: I told you about this. Mevolent had ways of detecting unauthorised shunts.

VALKYRIE: Absolutely no one.

SKULDUGGERY: Luke would only have been able to shunt two or three more times before Mevolent's Shunters would have been able to track him.

VALKYRIE: Nobody listens.

The team stayed overnight at Mevolent's palace, where an infected Necromancer attacked them. While not quite a draugr, the virus had greatly increased the Necromancer's power, and he was only killed by the God-Killer sword.

This encounter led Skulduggery to posit the idea that the Necromancers decided to go to war with Mevolent. By releasing the draugar virus, they would have given themselves an ever-increasing army, and by infecting themselves with a version of the virus, they would have increased their own individual strength.

SKULDUGGERY: If they planned to go up against Mevolent and Lord Vile, they'd have wanted to be as strong as possible.

Back in this reality, Darquesse had made copies of herself and sent them out into the world to experience and record everything they could.

BENNET: She needed all the information she could get, she

said, in order to make her decision about whether or not to save the world, or end it and start again. Which is a pretty scary proposition.

Darquesse merged with Kes – the splinter of herself that she had left behind years before – absorbing her ability to process emotions. This is what she had been searching for: the missing element that was preventing her from experiencing, and judging, the human condition.

BENNET: She, uh, she made herself pregnant. Please don't ask me how she did it, because I can't wrap my head around it. All I know is that as odd as it was, and as scary as things got, I still loved her, you know? She was my god, and I worshipped her.

According to multiple sources, Supreme Mage China Sorrows had taken to worshipping again at the Church of the Faceless, centuries after walking away from the religion. She prayed in the Dark Cathedral and went to Damocles Creed for support and counsel as the responsibilities she had taken on began to make themselves known. Her situation was not helped by the assassination of one of her Council of Advisors, Grand Mage Sturmun Drang, by an unknown killer wielding a spear. Commander Hoc assigned the murder investigation to Temper Fray.

TEMPER: It was a high-profile case with a lot of pressure and no resources, and Hoc wanted me to fail. China would have realised that if she'd had a moment to think about it, but she was being kept busy. Way too busy, if you ask me.

The last person Temper had seen to use a spear had been Kierre of the Unveiled when she'd killed Caisson, so he met with Serafina Dey, otherwise known as Serafina of the Unveiled, the High Superior of the Legion of Judgement. He also met with her bodyguard and sister, Rune, and her brother, Strosivadian. None of them could, or would, help him track down their younger sister, and Temper's authority was limited by the Religious Freedom Act, which protected religious organisations from scrutiny.

The Dead Men sailed to Belgium and began walking.

VALKYRIE: Luke died pretty soon after that. We were in this cave and he... It was full of them. Full of draugar. I couldn't save him. So he died.
SKULDUGGERY: And without wanting to sound callous, our lift home died with him.
VALKYRIE: And without wanting to sound even more callous than that, my music box was smashed. Smashed to bits. I'd been listening to it a few times a day, whenever the bad thoughts started to crowd around in my head. I was depending on it. And then it was gone.
SKULDUGGERY: And still we walked.

Omen was taught by Miss Ficus over the summer to make up for the time he'd missed both having and recovering from adventures.

Kierre of the Unveiled sought out Temper. Despite all evidence pointing to her, she denied murdering Strom. She did, however, admit to killing Caisson. Temper believed her. The question now was, who would gain from framing Kierre? The only person he could think of was Damocles Creed, who could use the murder to pile pressure on Serafina and the Legion of Judgement.

VALKYRIE: The music box was gone and I was spiralling, so Skulduggery forced me to focus on something else – my magic. I practised with the lightning bolts, I practised latching on to other people's abilities... It helped. It kept me occupied. And the longer I was away from that box, the clearer my thoughts became, and the happier I got.

He also got me to talk about what I'd done to Alice, to put it into words, to face it, I suppose. Deal with it. It was like therapy, except... Actually, no, it was like therapy.

Darquesse's pregnancy continued, and she declared that all the help she would need could be provided by Sebastian. The Darquesse Society took a step back.

Serpine led the Dead Men to a farm owned by an old acquaintance, Lorien, who had once betrayed him. Serpine killed him during the night, but revealed that Lorien had a habit of torturing and killing

NEFARIAN SERPINE

innocent travellers who crossed his path. Sure enough, they found his next victims in his cellar, and set them free. Then they took his horses.

VALKYRIE: Things got easier after that, in some ways. The bad thoughts had eased off. The nightmares had stopped. My mood had stablised. I was getting healthy again. Man, I'd missed that feeling. I was so used to hating myself and allowing that to colour everything around me... I didn't have my family and I didn't have my girlfriend and I didn't have my dog, but even so – I was doing good.

Ninety-four days in the Liebniz Universe and they reached Tahil na Sin, besieged by hundreds of thousands of draugar. Posing as agents of Mevolent's who were bringing Serpine in for execution, they hitched a lift with a pair of merchants, Mulct and Hapathy. Entering the city via a hidden supply tunnel, they learned that Mevolent was in Tahil na Kurge, building giant portals that he planned to use to invade our reality.

Once inside the city, they met with Governor Gratio Erato, who informed them that the plan was to evacuate to Tahil na Kurge in four months, and then for the combined might of Mevolent's army to march through the portals.

OMEN: Our folks were worried about the Darkly brand losing its prominence once Auger fulfilled the prophecy. They wanted to know what I was planning on doing once we left school.

ARCHIVIST: And what did you say?

OMEN: I really wanted to say art college, but I didn't think they wanted to hear that.

ARCHIVIST: So what *did* you say?

OMEN: Honestly? Nothing much.

Temper told Adam Brate to ask around about why Creed would want Sturmun Drang dead, but his investigations soon led to him being called before Supreme Mage Sorrows and Damocles Creed. Sorrows, under intense pressure, allowed Hoc to take over the murder investigation himself, and within two hours, the City Guard raided the Legion of Judgement buildings.

TEMPER: So with the whole city looking for her, whose door does Kierre knock on and ask to stay? This guy's.

ARCHIVIST: Was that an inconvenience for you?

TEMPER: Hey, I believed her when she said she hadn't killed Sturm, but to have a wanted fugitive hiding out in my house? Yeah, it was an inconvenience.

ARCHIVIST: According to my notes, she stayed with you for at least four weeks, maybe longer, before her siblings found her and took her back.

TEMPER: So?

ARCHIVIST: Four weeks, or longer, with just the two of you... Did any feelings develop between you?

TEMPER: Seems to me like you already know the answer to that question.

After an unfortunate incident in which Hapathy tried to kill Valkyrie because he believed she really was an agent of Mevolent's, he revealed that he was working for the Resistance, and offered to set up a meeting. Before any meeting could happen, however, the Necromancers attacked and the draugar breached the city gates.

TANITH: In all that mess, in all that confusion, I had a chance to kill a bad guy. Like, a really bad guy. I could have left it. The draugar would've probably killed him, but I couldn't do it. I had to know he was dead. I had to do it. This place... it was getting to me.

An explosion separated Valkyrie from the others, and she was pulled from the rubble, unconscious, as the draugar swarmed the streets.

VALKYRIE: I woke on this bus, crammed with magical aristocracy and protected by a squad of soldiers. We were travelling to Tahil na Kurge, and I was hurt and needed to recover, so I wouldn't have been able to get away even if I'd wanted to. Which I didn't. I thought I'd have to try to sneak in, but it looked like I was gonna be driven right through the front gate. I figured once I was there I'd meet Skulduggery and the others when they caught up. It was perfect, you know? Unfortunately, after a few weeks of driving, our little convoy got hit by a draugar horde. One of the soldiers, Assegai, and I were the only ones to escape. Our partnership lasted until she murdered some mortals, at which point I blasted her and left her in the dirt.

ARCHIVIST: And this was the last you saw of her?

VALKYRIE: No. God, no. She tracked me down and bonked me over the head and next thing I know I'm waking up in a dungeon in Tahil na Kurge. I ever tell you how much I hate waking up in dungeons?

Hector, a Resistance fighter, encountered the team on the road and arranged for them to be teleported to the Resistance camp, where Eachan Meritorious was in charge. Now that Tahil na Sin had been overrun, Tahil na Kurge was the last secure city in the world – but even that title looked like it wouldn't last for very much longer. Hundreds of thousands, perhaps millions, of draugar surrounded the energy shield that protected the city.

While he needed his troops to stay close, Meritorious had a mission for the Dead Men.

SKULDUGGERY: Ten months earlier, Mevolent had sent Baron Vengeous to a fort in America. The virus had started there and he wanted to know why and how. Vengeous never returned, and Mevolent became too focused on the portals to follow it up. But Meritorious needed to know what happened, so I assured him we'd take care of it.

Skulduggery and his team travelled to America. They found the fort that Vengeous had entered and went in after him, battling through dozens of draugar.

TANITH: Saracen... Saracen was bitten. We didn't know how long he had until he turned into one of them, but we held out hope that we could find someone to help him. If we could find Valkyrie in time, we knew she'd be able to latch on to a healer's abilities and improve on them. I felt sure she'd be able to do something.

Despite his injury, Saracen fought on with the others. Inside the fort they battled Warlocks until they found Baron Vengeous – injured, unable to leave, but alive. Even though his situation was dire, he refused to tell them what he'd learned about the origin of the virus.

SKULDUGGERY: With his permission, I put him out of his misery.

Before they could depart, they were surrounded by Necromancers. Solomon Wreath, who referred to the Warlocks as "pets", claimed that his master was the Death Bringer and intended to end all suffering. Once this world was dead, he planned to pass through the portals and kill our world.

SKULDUGGERY: It wasn't the Wreath that I'd known. This one was like the other Necromancers – he'd allowed himself to be infected with the virus, so he was... dulled. The only interesting thing about him was that he was prepared to allow us to walk away, so long as we left behind the gift that the Necromancers had given Serpine – his red right hand.

Although Serpine objected most strenuously, Skulduggery allowed the Necromancers to cut off his hand.

In Roarhaven, Oberon Guile approached Omen, informing him that he had found the location of the Obsidian Blade.

OMEN: It was owned by a sorcerer called Devon, in Scotland, so me and Never and Axelia went to, uh, borrow it. We were a little late, though, because two hired killers had already killed Mr Devon and taken the blade.

The killers in question were Reznor Rake and Tancred Bold. Their employer – whoever had hired them – planned to sell the Obsidian Blade at an auction, a little under two weeks later. Until then, Rake and Tancred were tasked with standing guard over the weapon, which they did at an abandoned hotel.

OMEN: We watched them for twelve days, waiting for one of them to leave. Finally, Rake drove off and we tried to sneak up and take the Blade. Tancred saw us, though, and he would have killed us if Crepuscular Vies hadn't shown up. Crepuscular asked me not to tell anyone about him. His bosses wouldn't approve, he said. I didn't know anything about him, but he was obviously working for one of the Sanctuaries, and this was an off-the-books kind of thing.

By this stage, Crepuscular had already informed President Martin Flanery that he would no longer be helping him in his bid to get re-elected. While Flanery handled the news with his usual grace and dignity, this part of his life was not something Crepuscular shared with Omen.

OMEN: We were becoming friends, you know? It was kinda cool. I suppose I needed someone to talk to and I didn't have anyone else. When I saw Auger kissing Never, I didn't quite know how to handle that. I genuinely didn't know if I was OK with it, or hurt, or, like, jealous or whatever. But I could talk to Crepuscular and Crepuscular could talk to me. So... yeah, he told me he had once been Skulduggery Pleasant's partner.

Under a different name, Crepuscular had accompanied Skulduggery on the kind of adventures he would later have with Valkyrie. On their very first investigation as official partners, however – on the trail of a murderer "with big plans – schemes within schemes" – Skulduggery was outmanoeuvred and Crepuscular was left behind, presumed dead. His captors tortured him, removing his face. Once Crepuscular escaped, he took a new name and became a new person.

Mere days after Temper had mentioned to Adam Brate

that he suspected that Damocles Creed was involved in Grand Mage Drang's murder, Hoc had taken him off the case.

TEMPER: Right there and then, I thought Adam was the one who'd tipped them off, but I wanted to make sure. Now that Kierre wasn't living with me any more, I figured I could take a chance, so I told Adam that Drang had been investigating ties between Creed and Drang's colleagues on the Council of Advisors – something I had absolutely no evidence of, that just existed in my head as a vague suspicion. I figured, if anything weird happened now, I'd know for definite that Adam Brate was working for Creed and I'd also know that there was some validity to the suspicion.
ARCHIVIST: And did anything weird happen?
TEMPER: A serial killer broke into my house and tried to kill me. Does that count?

Mr Glee's attempt on Temper's life failed due to the fact that he didn't know about Hansel and Gretel, Razzia's so-called Parasitic Murder Tentacles, that now lived in Temper's arms. Injured, Mr Glee departed.

During a rather vicious interrogation session in which her thumb was severed, Valkyrie escaped her captors.

VALKYRIE: I was not in a good way. My nose was broken, my jaw was fractured, my thumb had been cut off, I was pretty sure I'd peed myself – but I managed to find Professor Nye and I knew I was gonna be OK. I latched on to its magic and used it to heal all my injuries until I was strong again. One of my first priorities was to get my necronaut suit. Assegai had it. I wanted it back.

Alone inside the walls, Valkyrie began to plan for how she was going to complete her mission, while outside the walls, the draugar had started to press themselves against the shield, draining its power.

TANITH: Something was finally happening, and, boy, did we need the distraction.

After almost a month, the draugr infection had spread through Saracen Rue's system. With no hope of a cure and no sign of Valkyrie to heal him, Saracen's friend Dexter took him away from the group and eased his passing.

Skulduggery reasoned that now would be the perfect time for him to tunnel under the shield, into Tahil na Kurge, manipulating the earth to mimic Billy-Ray Sanguine's ability. Once inside, he would be able to assassinate Mevolent.

TANITH: With Saracen gone, I needed to do something - even something stupid. Which, as it turns out, is what this was.

They tunnelled into the city. They both got captured.

TANITH: I woke up, chained, beside Skulduggery, in Mevolent's office. We were there for days. He barely spoke to us. God, it was so boring. And then one of his soldiers, Assegai, came in, told Mevolent that Valkyrie had attacked her the previous night and taken her suit back. I was just hanging there, grinning. Typical Valkyrie.

SKULDUGGERY: That's when I realised why we were displayed in Mevolent's office. We were bait, to lure Valkyrie in.
VALKYRIE: I talked with this technician, Bucolic Kildare, who told me that they'd smuggled a communication device into our world. It had been brought in by a spy, hidden among the mortal refugees, who gave it to Serafina Dey. She'd been coordinating with Mevolent ever since.

Nye had created the devices, because of course it had, so I went back there, and it was delighted to see me. I told it I wanted to listen in. Nye told me to come back the next day. Naturally, it attempted a double-cross, and sent two guys with axes after me. After that, it promised me a way to deactivate the portals, but...
ARCHIVIST: But what?
VALKYRIE: But it double-crossed me again. Professor Nye, it turns out, is not remotely trustworthy.

In Roarhaven, it was almost Christmas. The principal of Corrival Academy, Hugo Rubic, had been made Grand Mage of Ireland[1] and elevated to the Council of Advisors, replacing the late Sturmun Drang. Ada Duenna took his place as principal, and one of her first problems to deal with was the disappearance of the Chosen One.

1. A somewhat meaningless role, drained of most of its authority by the very existence of a Supreme Mage.

Reznor Rake and Tancred Bold had managed to catch Auger by surprise. They took him hostage, and told Omen that he had three days to bring the Obsidian Blade to them.

OMEN: I couldn't do it. They told me that if I gave them the Blade, they'd let Auger go, but I just couldn't hand over the weapon that he'd need the following year to save his life.
ARCHIVIST: So what did you do?
OMEN: I agreed to the deal, then called Crepuscular and double-crossed them. I got Auger out while he took care of the bad guys.

In the Leibniz Universe, the day of the invasion had arrived.

SKULDUGGERY: To celebrate the occasion, in much the same way that a bottle of champagne is smashed against the hull to launch a new ship, Tanith and I were going to be executed onstage to launch the portals. I have to admit, it was just a thrill to be included in the festivities.
TANITH: We were chained up behind this massive curtain.

On the other side was Mevolent's army and thousands of onlookers, all ready to watch our execution and then invade our reality. Things were not looking good.

SKULDUGGERY: I wasn't worried.

TANITH: Care to say why you weren't worried?

SKULDUGGERY: I'd realised that Valkyrie had been disguising herself as Captain Assegai, using a façade to hide her face. I knew she knew the details of our execution day and knew she'd be able to stop it from happening.

TANITH: Care to say why you hadn't told me any of this beforehand?

SKULDUGGERY: I thought it would be funny.

As Valkyrie freed them, she explained that she had taken a bomb from Nye's workshop that was powerful enough to destroy the portals. Her plan to force the crowd to scatter so she could use the bomb, however, fell apart when the curtains opened.

VALKYRIE: We looked up and Mevolent and Lord Vile were there, hovering over the heads of the crowd – all eyes on us.

TANITH: The portals opened and the army started marching through.

And then Lord Vile killed Mevolent.

TANITH: He was the Death Bringer. I don't know why I didn't see that coming. He'd created that new type of draugr, he'd released the virus, he had the plan to kill everyone on that world and then move into ours and keep going, killing world after world...

In fighting back, Skulduggery once again drew on his Necromancer power and became Lord Vile.

TANITH: I saw it happen. Skulduggery was Vile. Valkyrie didn't seem too surprised, though, so it started me wondering if I was the only one that didn't know this particular piece of juicy gossip.

But the other Lord Vile proved to be the stronger, and he absorbed Skulduggery's armour into his own, which made him even more powerful.

It was at this point that the gates were breached and the draugar swarmed the city.

SKULDUGGERY: We decided it was probably time to go home.

What happened next is of public record.

The Cleavers, City Guard and Sanctuary operatives met Mevolent's army as they emerged from the portals, which had appeared on the edge of the Circle Zone, between the High Sanctuary and the Dark Cathedral.

Footage clearly shows Dexter and Serpine coming through the portal and fighting their way through to join Skulduggery and Tanith.

Valkyrie and Serpine both went for the Sceptre, as passing from one dimension into another would have meant that it would bond with the first person to touch it. Valkyrie got to it, and used it to destroy Lord Vile when he appeared.

Lord Vile's obliteration had a detrimental effect on the other Necromancers. They lost control of the draugar, who needed the Necromancers' focus in order to work effectively. Serpine threw the bomb into one of the portals. It exploded on the other side, destroying the machinery, and the portals disappeared.

The Roarhaven forces dispatched the last of the draugar and accepted the surrender of everyone else. The captives were later returned to their own dimension, where Meritorious and the Resistance had taken control.

VALKYRIE: We'd been gone for seven months, and I'd spent my twenty-fifth birthday in an alternate reality, but at least we got back just in time for Christmas. What are the odds, eh? I spent a week with my family, with Militsa, with my dog... Oh, and sleeping. I spent a lot of that week sleeping. Then someone looked over the camera footage and noticed that Mevolent's body had been taken through into this dimension. That wouldn't have been a problem, except for the fact that Mevolent had a habit of allowing himself to be killed just so he could come back – to prove to death that he was its master.
SKULDUGGERY: We needed China to allow us to take the Cleavers in and raid Serafina's property. If anyone was working on resurrecting Mevolent, it was her.

VALKYRIE: We didn't have much time, but we could still get on top of things. We just couldn't afford to let anything else go wrong.

Supreme Mage Sorrows delivered her New Year's Day speech, and was the target of a devastating psychic assault that left her comatose. Valkyrie identified Solace as the one responsible, and an hour later, Mevolent appeared on the streets of Roarhaven.

VALKYRIE: I was the one with the Sceptre, so I was the one who blasted him. I didn't have a choice. He was just too dangerous. So I made the decision.
ARCHIVIST: You made the decision to kill him.
VALKYRIE: Yeah.
ARCHIVIST: And what happened?
VALKYRIE: It wasn't him. It was a damn reflection. Another few moments and Skulduggery would have realised, but I wanted it over with. If I had to execute someone, I didn't want to hang around, you know? So I blasted his reflection, let my guard down, and the real Mevolent took the Sceptre and snapped it in two.

Skulduggery attacked him with the God-Killer sword but Mevolent took the sword for himself, and the Arbiters retreated.

Panicking and seeking guidance, the Council of Advisors appointed Damocles Creed as acting-Supreme Mage.

SKULDUGGERY: This was a major problem, but we had a bigger one.

Creed granted permission for Skulduggery, Valkyrie, Dexter and Tanith to go hunting through the deserted streets. When they found Mevolent, he had the Unveiled with him. They confronted and overcame Skulduggery, Dexter and Tanith, and Valkyrie was severely injured by Mevolent himself.

VALKYRIE: And all of this commotion caught the attention of the King of the Darklands, who probably thought to himself hey, what a great opportunity to exact my revenge on the man who had betrayed me all those centuries ago – even though this wasn't that Mevolent, not really.

The King of the Darklands engaged Mevolent in a battle above, and through, the streets of Roarhaven, stopping only when he sensed the presence of Auger Darkly.

OMEN: He broke through the walls of the school and went after Auger, even though the prophecy clearly stated that Auger would be seventeen when he faced the King of the Darklands, not sixteen. Bloody prophecies, always getting things wrong. Anyway, Auger fought him, and I did my best to help, and so did Never, and Kase, and Mahala, and Miss Gnosis and Mr Hunnan and Peccant and loads of the staff and students.

Auger stabbed the King with the Obsidian Blade. The blade itself snapped off when he withdrew it.

OMEN: It was like he was being erased. He just disappeared, bit by bit. It must have only taken a moment, but I can remember watching the emptiness spread out from where he was stabbed, and spread and spread until all of him was just... gone.

Now that the unnamed was no longer a threat, Mevolent returned to Valkyrie.

VALKYRIE: He was all set to kill me, and then Creed walked up with an Eternity Gate and a knife held to Serafina's throat. He told Mevolent to step into the Gate or he'd kill her.

Evidently, Serafina couldn't abide the thought of Mevolent imprisoned for the next few thousand years, so she plunged Creed's knife into her own throat to save him from making that sacrifice.

VALKYRIE: It didn't save him from anything. He'd already seen the Serafina on his world die, and he wasn't going to go through that again. So he picked her up and stepped into the Gate and that's where they both are now: trapped together in a never-ending moment.

TANITH: It'd almost be sweet if they weren't utter psychopaths.

Temper and Kierre left Roarhaven, but not before

confronting Adam Brate for his treachery. Brate confessed, apparently finding the whole thing quite amusing.

TEMPER: He said that there are people who play the game you see, and there are other people who play the game you don't see. He was one of the latter.

Brate teleported from the scene, and there has not been a sighting of him since.

Darquesse gave birth to herself, and left the baby for Sebastian to raise.

Here lies a man of dubious nature,
Whose charm was thinner
Than this portraiture.

The Age of the Maggot Part Six

Two weeks after almost dying by Mevolent's hand, Valkyrie Cain returned to Roarhaven.

VALKYRIE: I'd just spent the last seven months in Dimension X – I wasn't ready to get back into the swing of things quite yet. I was enjoying spending time with my family, spending time with my girlfriend, walking my dog, rediscovering what a shower was... But the day I go back to Roarhaven to meet Militsa for a coffee, there's Remember.

Remember Me surrendered to Valkyrie, and immediately requested a meeting with Skulduggery Pleasant. When Skulduggery arrived, Remember told them that after Tarron had taken her away, he'd carved a sigil into her skin, a sigil that shielded her from the eyes of the Order of the Maggot. He also put her in touch with an ex-Archivist, Arden, who steered her away from the Order.

Now out from under their control, Remember was allowed to finally speak the truth.

She told the Arbiters what she had told Tarron: that Tunnrak Rakhir himself had been responsible for everything that had happened.

For so long, Rakhir had been happy to nudge entire species to take the next evolutionary leap. His entire existence was in service to life itself, and as such he was content. But, as he took his Order from planet to planet, from one universe to the next, he began to grow disillusioned.

The Order had helped humanity once before, and was preparing to do so again. But the world's population had become so large that evolution no longer needed him or his demons – there were, simply, enough human beings around to guarantee that the next step would be taken.

The Order was weak. The rewards for its tireless work had always been meagre, but in the twenty-first century it found that it had virtually no worshippers to feed it. So Rakhir decided to instigate his own evolutionary change upon humanity ahead of time, and populate the world with creatures modelled after himself – creatures who would worship him and his demons, who would make them strong through their prayers and their souls. He planned to usher in the Age of the Maggot.

SKULDUGGERY: To achieve this, he needed to sabotage his own system. That meant killing the demon in charge of ensuring that evolution happened in accordance with the natural laws of the universe. So, in 1908 in Tunguska, Rakhir murdered Bemmon.

He kept it secret from the other members of the Order, fearing they would not understand this seismic shift in his vision. But, while he was pretending to be shocked and enraged at the loss of the Overseer of the Enduring Way, he needed someone to act as his agent of destruction on the ground.

VALKYRIE: Remember told us that she used to worship the Faceless Ones once upon a time, until Sunas visited her and won her over to the cult of Tunnrak Rakhir. He was looking for someone of her talents to see his plan through, so she faked her death and Rakhir set her up with a new life and a new mission: to protect his grand vision. But since Tarron and the ex-Archivist guy, Arden, went to work on her, she was now seeing clearly for the first time in a century or so.

While Remember wasn't privy to Rakhir's overall plan, she had one more piece of information: Tarron, along with his fellow gods Hallick and Byshio, had gone missing.

SKULDUGGERY: It all clicked into place at that moment. If Rakhir wanted his new species to grow from the meat of the old one, he'd need a whole lot of dead bodies. Murdering three of his demons would certainly accomplish that – depending on where they died, tens of millions of people could be killed in the blasts.
VALKYRIE: At first, we thought he'd be going for high population centres, but then Skulduggery realised that Rakhir would need to hobble any resistance as best he could, and so he'd probably be looking to take out Sanctuaries in the Cradles of Magic.

The Arbiters narrowed down the likely targets to Roarhaven, Melbourne and Johannesburg.

They alerted the other Sanctuaries.

VALKYRIE: But, obviously, we had a problem, in that we had to stop, and possibly kill, a god. And that's not an easy thing to do. Technically, we had access to the God-Killer weapons, but Creed was being a total-

SKULDUGGERY: He was being difficult. He'd sent the God-Killers off to be "secured", as he put it, and we didn't have the time to convince him to let us borrow one.

Cleavers had engaged Rakhir in combat in Melbourne, Australia, and the Arbiters were teleported over just in time to see that short battle come to an abrupt end.

VALKYRIE: OK, so Tunnrak Rakhir didn't wear a mask so, finally, we got to see what they really looked like.

SKULDUGGERY: And it wasn't that bad.

VALKYRIE: Excuse the bejesus outta me?

SKULDUGGERY: He wore a very nice floor-length black robe.

VALKYRIE: And?

SKULDUGGERY: And probably shoes, though I admit I can't be certain of that.

VALKYRIE: I meant, and what about his head? His giant head with his giant black eyes and that sucker-thing for a mouth?

SKULDUGGERY: You mean the proboscis?

VALKYRIE: Yes, Skulduggery. The long, gross proboscis with

all those fleshy tendril bits waving about? What about that?

SKULDUGGERY: I thought it was rather fetching.

ARCHIVIST: Maybe if we refocus on the events? You arrived to see Rakhir force Tarron to his knees among all the dead and broken bodies.

VALKYRIE: And we ran up.

SKULDUGGERY: And engaged Tunnrak Rakhir in a dialogue.

VALKYRIE: You mean, you insulted him.

SKULDUGGERY: It was a spirited dialogue in which both sides expressed strong opinions.

VALKYRIE: You kept on insulting him.

SKULDUGGERY: We had to keep him distracted, you see. We had to keep him from killing Tarron. The longer I could engage with him on an intellectual level–

VALKYRIE: You were calling him names.

SKULDUGGERY: – the better our chances of survival.

VALKYRIE: You were insulting his intelligence, his behaviour, his attitude, his whole entire plan – in fact, the only thing you weren't insulting him about was his giant fly-head, which was the most obvious thing to insult.

SKULDUGGERY: For us, perhaps, but as the god of all the fly-head demons, I assume he's widely regarded as being the most good-looking of his species, so I doubt it would have had any kind of lasting effect.

VALKYRIE: That… actually makes sense. Anyway, Rakhir got so mad at us that he forgot all about Tarron and marched over to, literally, tear us apart.

SKULDUGGERY: Fortunately, that's when the other demons arrived.

Shevennu, the Princess of Death; Wutt, the Prince of Rot; and Sunas, the Governess of Souls, accused Rakhir of betraying them, of betraying the Order of the Maggot and everything they stood for. They kept him occupied while Skulduggery freed Tarron. Tarron then vanished, retrieved Byshio and Hallick, and returned, and all of Rakhir's demons surrounded their god and attacked.

SKULDUGGERY: Rakhir had targeted Tarron, Hallick, and Byshio because he thought they'd be the three to oppose him – meaning the others, while they might disapprove, would be more inclined to go along with his plan. But when it had become obvious that Rakhir was the one behind it all, I contacted Shevennu and argued that a god who is overly eager for personal worship, who is willing to murder his own demons, is not someone she could ever trust. I also mentioned the fact that if Rakhir was dead, someone would have to take over. She went off to consider my words and discuss it with the others. Obviously, I had been persuasive.

VALKYRIE: We knew we couldn't hurt him ourselves, we knew he could kill us with a click of his fingers, but the plan was to go in anyway and keep him talking, and just wait for the cavalry to show up. That was the whole, entire plan.

SKULDUGGERY: Yes indeed.

VALKYRIE: And Skulduggery didn't bother to tell me about any of it.

SKULDUGGERY: I thought it would be funnier if you didn't know.

VALKYRIE: I honestly believed we were going to die.

SKULDUGGERY: I don't see how that makes it any less funny.

VALKYRIE: Added to that, there was no way of knowing if the cavalry would actually arrive. What would have happened then?

SKULDUGGERY: Then we would have been killed, and a marvellous joke would have gone to waste.

The demons overpowered Tunnrak Rakhir. At this point, Valkyrie constructed an energy shield around the Order of the Maggot.

VALKYRIE: I didn't really know what I was doing, and I really didn't know if what I was doing would be strong enough, but I knew that if Rakhir died in the middle of Melbourne, the city would've been flattened.

Rakhir was killed. The shockwave shook the ground, broke windows, and set off car alarms up to thirty-eight kilometres away, but Valkyrie's shield prevented further destruction and a catastrophic loss of life.

SKULDUGGERY: When it was finished, and the demons were standing around, silent and dwelling on what they had just done, we walked over. I picked up all that was left of Tunnrak Rakhir – a piece of twisted bone, like the one we found in Tunguska. Shevennu took that from me and they left, without saying a word.

VALKYRIE: Like, you're welcome, y'know?

SKULDUGGERY: And the world was safe, once again.

VALKYRIE: For another, what, four months? Five?

SKULDUGGERY: We have a busy schedule.

Dead or Alive

The Crystal of the Saints had managed to elude Skulduggery Pleasant since 1943. Rancid Fines, a fervent worshipper of the Faceless Ones, believed that the Crystal was powerful enough to call the Dark Gods home, and he had spent close to a hundred years trying to find out all its secrets.

To continue his work, however, he needed various sponsors – people with money who could bankroll his experiments. One of these potential sponsors, Kiln, had invited Rancid to demonstrate the Crystal's power. Much to Rancid's dismay, the attempt to bring the Faceless Ones home proved to be a failure.

Skulduggery Pleasant and Valkyrie Cain arrived to apprehend Rancid and retrieve the Crystal of the Saints. Distracted as they were by Kiln and the three ninjas he had brought with him, however, Rancid was allowed to escape. Again.

VALKYRIE: It was beyond a joke now. I no longer saw the funny side. I just wanted to catch him, to take the Crystal and put it in the Repository or give it to scientists to examine or destroy it if it proved to actually have any power at all... But no. The universe had other plans.

Militsa Gnosis was offered a job on a Research Team, specialising in the Source rifts. Due to Valkyrie's opposition to helping Damocles Creed in any of his projects, however, Militsa turned down the opportunity.

ARCHIVIST: How was Alice doing?
VALKYRIE: Good. Alice was good. She still had mood swings, you know? Pretty drastic mood swings. And, obviously, she was still set to become the Child of the Faceless Ones by the time she was sixteen, but she was doing good, all things considered.

Auger Darkly, on the other hand, had grown increasingly despondent.

OMEN: Everyone was talking about exams and Draíocht,[1] but Auger seemed to have just checked out, you know? Ever since he killed the King of the Darklands he'd been different. At first, I thought he'd just lost focus. He'd been the Chosen One for so long, and everything had been building towards this epic confrontation, but then it happened a year early, and then it was over. Yeah, he won, but... now who was he? He had to figure that out for himself.

1. Draíocht, or Féile na Draíochta (Festival of Magic), happens on 31 May every seventy-two years, celebrating a confluence of factors that boosts magic around the world.

Darquesse was growing and ageing rapidly. In four months, she was now approximately five years old.

BENNET: She was adorable. I mean, just the cutest little kid you've ever seen. Yes, the fact that she could kill everyone just by thinking hard enough made you hesitate to interact with her, but once you got past that, she was great.

Supreme Mage Damocles Creed made a speech in which he announced a curfew, mandatory worship at the Church of the Faceless, and the introduction of Sense wardens – officers who had the authority to read the minds of anyone they deemed suspicious – to keep the city safe from subversives.

Temper assembled a small team to act as a Resistance, striking back against Commander Hoc and the increasingly heavy-handed City Guard.

TEMPER: Kierre and the rest of the Unveiled were figuring out where they stood in a post-Serafina world, so I left them to it and sneaked back into Roarhaven to help out.

He recruited Corporal Aldo Ruckus, Tanith Low and Oberon Guile.

Skulduggery, meanwhile, had narrowed their problems down to one man – Damocles Creed – and set about convincing Valkyrie that the only way to ensure that Alice would not become the Child of the Faceless Ones was to kill him.

VALKYRIE: I understood where he was coming from, and I could see the logic behind it, but I've never been a huge fan of murder. Weird of me, I know. I figured I needed to talk to that future version of Alice again, and this time get some information. I thought that might help me make up my mind as to whether Skulduggery's plan was the right move, or if we should focus on exposing all of the people who Creed had turned into Kith. I thought, if everyone knew what he was up to, he'd have to step down from Supreme Mage, right?

The Arbiters enlisted the help of Jericho Hargitsi and Onosa Tsira, husband and wife Sensitives. Jericho believed that Valkyrie could send her astral self into the future to talk to her sister, so he set about teaching her astral projection.

Bella Longshanks, a friend of Axelia Lukt's, was caught out of her room after midnight. Even though she was with two other students, Bella was the only one expelled.

OMEN: I suppose I had enough to deal with, like with exams and Axelia and everything that was going on with Auger, but then this kid, Thiago, came up to me looking for Auger's help. What could I do, you know?

Thiago's uncle, Remington Venture, was a Sensitive who had had a vision in which he saw the Faceless Ones return in seven weeks. He planned to sacrifice a twenty-one-year-old American girl, art student Gretchen, in order to wake the Witch Mother, whom he believed would help humankind in the battle against the Faceless Ones.

Instead of placing this burden on Auger's shoulders, Omen and Crepuscular Vies stopped Remington themselves, with Omen saving Gretchen's life.

OMEN: I'd left behind any ideas of myself as an adventurer – I was just not suited to that life – but I have to admit, me and Crepuscular work well together. And it was nice being part of a team, you know? Having someone you could trust with your life. It's cool.

Crepuscular still hadn't told Omen about his connection to President Flanery – a connection that was ongoing. A British sorcerer – Perfidious Withering – paid a visit to Flanery, informing him that Crepuscular wasn't done with him yet.

VALKYRIE: I really didn't want to assassinate anyone, so I was hoping we could find some evidence that'd link Creed to the Kith. I needed to know more about Activations, so I asked Temper.

Temper told the Arbiters about Triton, a friend of his who, like Temper himself, had Faceless Ones' blood in his veins. Triton had volunteered to be

Activated, so he was strapped down and prepared. Creed used the Ensh-Arak Sigil, focused through a shard of a jewel or crystal, to generate a power that sought out the Faceless Ones DNA in his system and brought it to the surface. But Triton, like tens of thousands before him, did not have a strong enough strand to become the Child of the Faceless Ones, and so he was left as just another of the Kith.

VALKYRIE: I had been confident that Creed would have been forced out once people heard about the Kith, but suddenly I was feeling unsure. Leaving aside the fanatics, there were so many ordinary people out there, ordinary mages, who might be willing to forgive something like this if they were devoted enough to Creed as a leader. And it looked like they were.

After mastering the fundamentals of astral projection, Valkyrie sent her consciousness into the future. Her unique power interfered with the process, however, transforming her body into an energy that then mixed with her astral self – so that she arrived in the future in her physical form.

VALKYRIE: Yep. I arrived in the future, not as some kind of weird but definitely hot ghost, but as flesh-and-blood me. That was pretty trippy, but you know what was worse? The fact that I hadn't gone seven years into the future. I'd gone seventy-two.

SKULDUGGERY: Such an overachiever.

VALKYRIE: Right?

In the Roarhaven of the future, Valkyrie spoke with a young man called Izzaruh Rinse, who took her through the changes that had occurred.

VALKYRIE: Let's see... OK, Creed was basically the Pope, right? The Faceless Ones returned to Earth on Draíocht and, seventy-two years later, Creed was the Pope, sorcerers ran the world and mortals were divided into servants, slaves and food for the Faceless Ones. Izzaruh also mentioned the Seven Pillars, but I didn't know what they were at the time.

But Valkyrie's arrival had not gone unnoticed. Her future self, who had somehow been transformed into a winged, clawed harpy, killed Izzaruh and attacked Valkyrie herself.

VALKYRIE: I was a bird.

SKULDUGGERY: Harpies aren't birds, they're–

VALKYRIE: I was. A bird.

Valkyrie was rushed to the Medical Wing of the High Sanctuary and healed, but when the City Guard came to question her, she had to escape, and she returned to her own time.

VALKYRIE: The future, while heaven for a certain kind of

Skulduggery Pleasant

sorcerer, would be hell for mortals, so I couldn't see any other choice but to agree to the assassination.

Valkyrie met with Fletcher Renn, who was still teaching at Corrival.

VALKYRIE: We chatted. I asked him about his new girlfriend and how work was going and then I asked him to help out with the Creed assassination – just general small talk, really.
ARCHIVIST: And what was his response?
VALKYRIE: He said no. Obviously.

Skulduggery bought a high-powered rifle from Denton Peccadillo, a black-market dealer in stolen magical items, and set it up in the building across the street from where Creed was due to make his next speech. Once Creed started speaking, Skulduggery would fly up through the window and take the shot. When Creed was dead, the Arbiters knew they would have to go on the run – possibly for a very long time.

VALKYRIE: So we were waiting there. And talking. And it was getting closer and closer to the start of the speech...
SKULDUGGERY: And Valkyrie convinced me not to go through with it.
VALKYRIE: Because we're the good guys, dammit.
SKULDUGGERY: And then someone killed Creed anyway.
VALKYRIE: Brilliant!

The assassin had fired from the window Skulduggery was going to fire from, used the gun Skulduggery was going to use. Despite not going through with it themselves, all the evidence would still point to the Arbiters.

And then Creed's body was stolen.

SKULDUGGERY: We were in the morgue with Doctor Simon Dreadful and Detective Waverly Cardigan, and a Necromancer just walked in, said his name was Uriah Serrate, and that he was taking the corpse.

Footage showed Serrate dispatching the Arbiters with ease, and shadow-walking away with Creed's remains.

SKULDUGGERY: *"With ease." I resent that.*

Detective Rylent was assigned to the case, replacing Detective Cardigan, who went on immediate medical leave.

VALKYRIE: Rylent could have been trouble for us, so we had to forget about Serrate for the moment and find the assassin before he did. The killer had used our gun, our plan, so he knew what we were up to. That's what we focused on.

The events surrounding Creed's assassination rocked certain aspects of Roarhaven life – but there were other elements that continued as normal.

OMEN: Auger and I went to dinner with our parents and Auger... he lost his patience, I think. Our folks wanted to involve him in some other prophecy or something, just to keep his profile up for another year while their business ventures were being sorted out, but he told them to go to hell and walked out.

ARCHIVIST: Did he have a plan for himself?

OMEN: He was going to drop out of school, change his name, travel the world, become a healer. Isn't that nuts? Isn't that brilliant? Then he gave me his favourite shock stick. After killing the King of the Darklands, he didn't want to hurt anyone else ever again.

The Arbiters talked to Denton Peccadillo, who told them that he had procured the sniper rifle from the crimelord, Christopher Reign.

SKULDUGGERY: He also told us, in a roundabout way, that Rancid Fines was still trying to find a sponsor, and he was staying at the City View Hotel.

The Arbiters went immediately to arrest Rancid – but Silas Nadir had got there before them. In the confusion, Rancid escaped – with the Crystal of the Saints. Again.

Omen was becoming increasingly concerned over Axelia's apparent lack of interest in why her best friend Bella was expelled. Upon speaking to Ula, another friend, he learned that Bella had seen "something odd" the night she had sneaked out of her dorm room. She had asked Axelia to look into it, but Axelia couldn't remember what they had spoken about.

Omen took Axelia to see a classmate of theirs, Rangle Apt, who looked into her mind and uncovered a so-called "mind-mugging". Axelia had been called in to see Principal Duenna and, during that meeting, a memory had been suppressed – a memory where Bella had told her she'd seen something suspicious in the West Tower of the school. A suggestion had also been implanted to ensure that she remain disinterested in anything to do with Bella Longshanks from that moment on.

OMEN: Axelia was... can I curse here? Never mind. She was extremely, extremely annoyed.

The Arbiters arrived at Reign's nightclub, asking about the rifle he'd sold to Peccadillo. His response led them to believe that, not only was he not involved in the assassination, but also that he didn't know of their involvement, either. The conversation was interrupted by the arrival of Savoir Fair, the Business Liaison Officer with the High Sanctuary.

VALKYRIE: We left, and we were driving off and chatting, everything completely normal. We stopped at the traffic lights and this guy, a Ripper, walks out in front of us, takes out an automatic weapon, and opens fire.

Valkyrie was critically injured and Skulduggery was shot through the skull.

Valkyrie's life was saved by Doctor Locke in the High Sanctuary's Medical Wing, while Skulduggery replaced his damaged head with his original skull, which he had been cleaning.

While she was recovering, Valkyrie was visited by Savoir Fair who claimed that, years earlier, Skulduggery had confessed to the murder of a Sanctuary detective called Somnolent, and that since then, Savoir had been using that confession to blackmail him into investigating – and then arresting – Savoir's criminal associates that he wanted out of the way.

But the real villain, he insisted, was Christopher Reign who, among other crimes, hired the Ripper who made the attempt on the Arbiters' lives. Skulduggery had refused to kill Reign at Savoir's request, and so Savoir tried convincing Valkyrie to do it. Otherwise, he would be forced to release Skulduggery's confession to the relevant authorities.

Valkyrie confronted Skulduggery with this accusation.

SKULDUGGERY: It was entirely true – with some parts missing. I told her that when I first set up the City Guard, I helped China solidify her power by investigating those who opposed her. This wasn't strictly ethical, but it was strictly necessary. Rylent and Somnolent, two of the Sanctuary's best detectives, had heard people accusing China of misuse of power, and they were quietly looking into it. I went to talk to them but I found Somnolent, alone, and Somnolent misread my intentions. He attacked. It escalated. I killed him.

VALKYRIE: In self defence.

SKULDUGGERY: Indeed. I gave Savoir Fair an abridged version of the truth, just enough to make him think he had some leverage over me, and he started supplying me with all the evidence I needed to take down some notorious criminal figures. He thought, when it was all over, I'd allow him to stay out of prison, but there was a cell with his name on it – he just didn't know it yet.

Somnolent's old partner, Rylent, appeared again to question the Arbiters about their behaviour in the security footage taken the day Creed was killed, where it looked like they knew exactly where the assassin had been located.

VALKYRIE: He was determined to take us down, which seemed hugely unfair to me. I mean, he had reason to hate Skulduggery, but what had I ever done to him?

SKULDUGGERY: The thing I like most about you is your loyalty.

Valkyrie wanted to visit the future again, to make sure that Creed's assassination was enough to change things. It was Skulduggery's opinion, however, that she needed to practise her astral projecting in order to develop it to the point where she could avoid travelling physically. She agreed.

VALKYRIE: Then I went anyway.

But when Valkyrie arrived in the future for the second time, she discovered that nothing had changed. Then she was captured and brought before the Child of the Faceless Ones.

VALKYRIE: My now fully grown-up sister, who went by the name of Malice.

Malice explained that on Draíocht night seventy-two years ago, Creed performed a Mass Activation, sending out an Activation Wave that transformed thousands of people into Kith, and only stopped when it hit Valkyrie. But because she resisted the change, she was transformed into a harpy. Creed had then Activated Alice, and finally he had the Child of the Faceless Ones.

VALKYRIE: She was totally into it. She'd bought into the whole thing. My sister worshipped the Faceless Ones. Loved them. She *was* one, in a way. She was the most powerful sorcerer on the planet, and I tried to get her to see that she was on the side of the bad guys, but... it was no use. And then Cadaver blew a hole in the wall and got me out of there.

In the seventy-two years between Valkyrie's time and Malice's, the Source rifts had been widened, empowering sorcerers who quickly subdued the mortal population. Skulduggery helped train the Child of the Ancients to fight against Malice, but Malice emerged victorious, and brought back the Faceless Ones. Disillusioned, Skulduggery Pleasant abandoned his name and had taken a new one: Cadaver, named after Cadaverous Gant, the man who had kidnapped and nearly killed Alice as a child, and Cain, after Valkyrie herself.

VALKYRIE: And then he flipped. I thought he was the same Skulduggery I knew, but Cadaver was a... a different version, I suppose. Those seventy-two years, they'd broken him. So he sent me back to my time, but he attached his life force to mine.

Upon arriving back in her own time, Valkyrie found herself sharing her body with Cadaver Cain – with Cadaver in charge. He subdued Skulduggery, then assembled a new body for himself from Skulduggery's spare skeleton parts – including the skull that had been damaged during the Ripper assault – and departed Valkyrie's body for this new one.

Sebastian arrived home to find Tarry and Demure dead, and Darquesse missing. The Darquesse Society immediately blamed Tantalus, and he admitted to sending two violent thugs, Granton Bicker and Boaz Gobemouche, to retrieve Darquesse. They double-crossed him, however, and took her for themselves.

When Sebastian and the Darquesse Society confronted Bicker and Gobemouche, it was Darquesse who came to their rescue, revealing that she had never been in any danger.

BENNET: That made it worse, actually. It meant she'd allowed Tarry and Demure to die just so she could experience the kidnapping. We were very, very upset with her. They were our friends. They were *her* friends. She mightn't have completely understood what friendship meant, but she knew that she'd disappointed Sebastian, and she didn't like that. She didn't like that one bit.

Knowing that Bella had been expelled because of what she had seen at the West Tower on a Saturday night, Omen, Axelia and Never sneaked out of their dorms after midnight and took a look around.

OMEN: We saw our teacher, Mr Chicane, and a man he had in shackles. This secret door opened up in the tower and Chicane just - he pushed him through. We heard him scream as he fell.

Since the future was still due to happen, the Arbiters had to work out what they could do to prevent it. They knew, from what Temper had told them, that in order to generate an Activation Wave, a massive Ensh-Arak Sigil would be required.

SKULDUGGERY: This next bit is very impressive. Valkyrie?
VALKYRIE: Yes?
SKULDUGGERY: Explain the next bit.
VALKYRIE: Why don't you do it?
SKULDUGGERY: I prefer to listen to the awe that slowly creeps into your voice when you're reminded of just how clever I am.
VALKYRIE: You are...
SKULDUGGERY: Magnificent?
VALKYRIE: Unbearable. Anyway, right... So the genius here noticed that if you overlaid the Ensh-Arak Sigil on a map of Roarhaven, it lined up with streets and buildings and stuff. The seven points of the sigil were the Seven Pillars that Izzaruh was talking about. Pillars one and two were the Dark Cathedral and the High Sanctuary, and Pillar number seven was Corrival Academy. The other four Pillars were churches and boring places like that. Happy now?
SKULDUGGERY: I don't think you spent enough time complimenting me.
VALKYRIE: Oh, and for Creed to focus that kind of power, he'd need something a lot bigger than the little shard of the little jewel that Temper mentioned.

The Arbiters arrived to attend the memorial service for Creed, but sneaked into the bowels of the Dark Cathedral where, previously, Skulduggery and Temper had seen the tens of thousands of Kith. Now, the Kith were gone, but they found the first of the Pillars – resembling a chimney, or a gun barrel – rising the entire height of the Dark Cathedral itself.

VALKYRIE: We were figuring it out. The world was starting to make sense again. And then we stopped by the memorial service, and Damocles Creed and Uriah Serrate walked out.

To a rapturous audience, Creed explained how Serrate, a Necromancer and the new King of the Dead and leader of the Necropolis, had repaired and resurrected him to continue his great work in service to the Faceless Ones.

At a private meeting afterwards, Serrate apologised to the Arbiters for the violence in the morgue. He had brought Creed back to life and, in return, Creed agreed to establish a new Necropolis in the section of the city that was damaged on Devastation Day. The borders of this new Necropolis would be inscribed with the Gurahghul Sigil, to contain the death field.

VALKYRIE: We had, like, nine days or something until Draíocht. Creed had just come back. Things were looking bleak. We needed to meet, and we needed a plan.

The Arbiters, plus Militsa, met with Omen, Axelia and Never.

OMEN: We told them all about Chicane and the people he was pushing into the West Tower, and I was expecting them to tell us to focus on the exams and let them take care of everything – but that's, like, the opposite of what they said. They fully expected to be arrested at any moment, so they needed us to find the Pillar at Corrival and find a way to sabotage it. Then all those Cleavers arrived.

Detective Rylent and a squad of Cleavers and Sanctuary operatives attempted to arrest them, but the Arbiters escaped with the aid of Cadaver Cain, who arrived just in time. As they left the city without incident, Cadaver proceeded to explain just how he always seemed to be prepared for any eventuality.

VALKYRIE: I don't know why I'm the one who has to explain everything. I'm barely paying attention at any given moment.
SKULDUGGERY: You'll do fine.
VALKYRIE: So... When Skulduggery became Lord Vile and began his Necromancer training, he went Deep Venturing – exploring dead worlds in other dimensions. During one of these expeditions, he encountered a race of gods called the Viddu De. To the Viddu De, death was their natural state. They taught him their history and converted him to their... religion, I suppose. And they taught him a cool trick.
SKULDUGGERY: It was hardly a "trick".
VALKYRIE: In my explanations, I get to call things whatever I want.
SKULDUGGERY: Because time means nothing in death, they taught Vile to view all time at once.
VALKYRIE: Boring.
SKULDUGGERY: They taught him to see every possible path to every possible future, then sort through them until he had

VALKYRIE CAIN

a route laid out in front of him.
VALKYRIE: Borrrrrring.
SKULDUGGERY: When Vile stopped being Vile and I went back to being me, I had already blocked off certain memories from myself that I wasn't aware of, including everything to do with the Viddu De and what they had taught me.
VALKYRIE: And this is a perfectly normal conversation to have.
SKULDUGGERY: And so, at some stage in the future as it exists now, I am evidently going to stop being Skulduggery Pleasant and start being Cadaver Cain, at which point all of those memories will begin to surface – as I had foreseen, back when I was Lord Vile.
VALKYRIE: Oh my God, my life is so complicated.

Cadaver had come back to this time in order to stop Creed, and he assured the Arbiters that he was on their side. Skulduggery remained sceptical.

SKULDUGGERY: Very sceptical.

On Monday, the exams at Corrival Academy began. That night, Omen went to check on the West Tower to make sure all was quiet.

OMEN: All was not quiet.

He witnessed Chicane pushing another person into the hidden door in the West Tower. His attempt to prevent the murder failed, but in the struggle, Chicane himself fell through. Omen grabbed him, saving his life. Obviously conflicted between feelings of gratitude and the impulse to kill the eyewitness, Chicane walked away.

With five days to go until Draíocht, the Arbiters donned disguises and examined the new Necropolis. The Gurahghul Sigil, etched into the boundaries, successfully contained the death field that permeated the area. By chance, they also saw Uriah Serrate conversing with Savoir Fair outside the new Necromancer temple that Creed had instructed to be built.

VALKYRIE: If Savoir was somehow involved in all this, then maybe Reign was too.
SKULDUGGERY: Besides, we owed him for hiring that Ripper to kill us.
VALKYRIE: Oh yeah, I'd almost forgotten.

Valkyrie infiltrated Reign's nightclub but was attacked by both Acantha, Reign's assistant, and Reign himself, who ordered her to be killed. Valkyrie effected her own escape, aided by Skulduggery's arrival.

When the Arbiters questioned Savoir he admitted that Serrate had approached him months earlier, paying him to bribe Sanctuary officials so that they'd support the Necropolis being moved to

Roarhaven. For those officials and individuals that couldn't be bribed, Savoir gave Serrate a list of their names, and told him that he would have to remove them on his own. He also told them that the name of the Ripper who Reign hired to kill them was Coda Quell.

ARCHIVIST: You recognised the name, did you not?

VALKYRIE: "Did I not?" Yeah, I did.

ARCHIVIST: Do you care to–?

VALKYRIE: Coda was a Ripper I met back when I was in Colorado. I needed someone to train me, to train with, so I hired him. We became close, and he lived with me for a while. I thought I loved him, even though, as a Ripper, he wasn't really capable of loving me back. That suited me fine. At the time. Then, when he figured my training was complete, he left. Next time I see him, he's trying to kill me.

The Arbiters decided that, with all other avenues being exhausted, Valkyrie should travel into the future, find China and devise a plan to stop Creed.

Tensions had been steadily rising in Roarhaven. Supreme Mage Creed's new rules had not gone down well. Protests were organised, occasionally sparking off into small-scale riots.

Onosa told Temper of a vision she'd had in which the world was destroyed in less than a year.

TEMPER: Not gonna lie to you: that was pretty alarming.

When Omen enlisted Crepuscular's help in finding out how to sabotage the Pillar at Corrival, Crepuscular reasoned that Creyfon Signate would probably be the best person to ask. As the architect who designed the city, he would certainly have been the one to design the Pillars. Before they had a chance to make any plans, Cadaver Cain joined them. He introduced himself, overcoming Crepuscular's initial hostility by demonstrating that Cadaver and Skulduggery were two distinct individuals. He then offered them his help.

The three of them travelled to Signate's house to speak with him, and he told them that when Erskine Ravel had gone to him with his plans for the city of Roarhaven, Creed hadn't been far behind, forcing him to include the Seven Pillars in his designs.

He said that six Pillars, like the ones in the High Sanctuary and the Dark Cathedral, were boiling with the power that would then be used to power them – but he'd had to be sneakier with Corrival, because it needed some human sacrifices to get the power level up to where it needed to be. He'd turned the towers into Tempests – massive batteries – and when all the sacrifices had been made, it would be enough to power the Pillar.

But Signate had also constructed what became known as a Zeta Switch, a way to deactivate the Pillar. Before he could tell them where the Switch was hidden, Uriah Serrate shadow-walked into the room and killed him.

Cadaver, having already seen this version of the future unfold, led Omen and Crepuscular to retrieve the Zeta Switch. Along the way, he advised against killing Uriah Serrate, as this wouldn't bring them the future they needed.

Valkyrie confronted Coda Quell, who told her that after they had parted ways he had taken on the roles of assassin and bodyguard, depending on who was paying him. He had found himself missing her company, and came to the realisation that he did, in fact, love her. He travelled to Colorado but Valkyrie had already returned to Ireland.

When Christopher Reign hired him to kill Damocles Creed, Coda took this as a sign that he and Valkyrie were meant to be together. But when he arrived, he saw that she was with Militsa Gnosis.

VALKYRIE: He said that when Reign hired him to kill us, he deliberately left me alive.
SKULDUGGERY: That was sweet of him.

Valkyrie made her final trip into the future. She found China, asked her what she needed to do in order to stop the Activation Wave - but before China could give her an answer, Malice walked in.

She warned Valkyrie away from trusting Cadaver. She said the Viddu De wanted him to spread the death field throughout the universe, to kill everyone and everything, so that they could leave their reality and come to this one. Malice revealed that she was Cadaver's "lacuna", the element that didn't show up when he looked into the future. She was his weak point.

VALKYRIE: I had to go. My window to get back safely was closing. But as I went, China shouted something – she told me not to let Creed get the Eye of Rhast.

There was only one more day until Draíocht.

Temper's Resistance faced greater City Guard numbers than expected, and only the arrival of Kierre of the Unveiled saved them all from capture.

TEMPER: We had to leave Tanith behind. I was not happy about that.

TANITH: They had to leave me behind. I was not happy about that.

The only reference to the Eye of Rhast that Skulduggery could find led them to the *Book of Shalgoth*,[1] which in turn led them to a scholar who had imprinted his consciousness on to an Echo Stone that had been owned by Ghastly Bespoke.

1. One of dozens of grimoires that were destroyed by Mevolent hundreds of years ago.

With time running out, the Arbiters met with Uther Peccant, who had received Ghastly's collection after his death.

VALKYRIE: He gave us the Echo Stone and we talked to Oisin, who I hadn't seen since I was twelve.

Oisin talked to them about the *Book of Shalgoth* and the ways in which it contradicted, and corrected, the *Book of Tears*.[1] He told them that the Eye of Rhast had been known by a different name for centuries – and that it was now called the Crystal of the Saints.

1. See The *Book of Shalgoth*.

VALKYRIE: I hate my life.

At that precise moment, Rancid Fines was trying to interest Christopher Reign in to sponsoring his work with the Crystal of the Saints/Eye of Rhast, but Reign viewed it as far too dangerous for anyone to possess, and sought to destroy it or, at the very least, hide it.

He had the chance to do neither, however, because Uriah Serrate appeared and took it for himself.

Rancid Fines was, by all accounts, distraught.

Skulduggery suggested one final path to stopping the future from happening – they steal the Sceptre of the Ancients, which was being repaired in the High

Sanctuary, and destroy the Eye of Rhast before the Pillars power up.

Omen and his team – Crepuscular, Never, Axelia, Kase and Mahala – prepared to keep Creed's forces away from the towers so that they could use the Zeta Switch on the Pillar. Auger pledged to fight alongside his brother on one last adventure before he left it all behind.

China Sorrows broke Tanith out of her cell, and they went to help Temper.

As riots broke out in the streets around the High Sanctuary, the Arbiters used the confusion to sneak up to the research laboratories. They were stopped by Professor Reginald Regatta, one of the scientists who had been tasked with rebuilding the Sceptre. Instead of alerting the City Guard, however, Regatta allowed them to take the weapon.

The Arbiters used the secret tunnel to get into the Dark Cathedral, but on their way to the nave to destroy the Eye of Rhast, they were caught by Serrate. The Sceptre exploded, and Serrate defeated them in combat. They were brought into the cathedral to witness the Pillars being activated.

VALKYRIE: We were both, I think, fairly confident that Cadaver would arrive and stop it from going any further. But then Serrate appears with Cadaver in shackles and I remember thinking *oh holy* – wait, can I curse here? Have we established that cursing is allowed?

SKULDUGGERY: And then, of course, comes the reveal – that Serrate had been working with Cadaver from the start, that Lord Vile had sought him out hundreds of years ago and recruited him to the Viddu De's cause. That's why Serrate proved impossible to beat in combat – he could see the avenues of the future, just like Cadaver could.

Serrate shadow-walked to Corrival, where he fought alongside Omen's team against wave after wave of City Guard officers. When Omen found a chance, he used the Zeta Switch, and deactivated the Pillar, which meant the Ensh-Arak Sigil was lost.

And then the Pillars formed a new sigil.

VALKYRIE: The Gurahghul Sigil. The death field. Cadaver had planned on hijacking Creed's Activation Wave all along, except instead of a wave that would Activate whoever it hit, it was a death field that would cover the whole world.

Valkyrie's necronaut suit allowed her to keep operating as the Arbiters renewed their – ultimately futile – attacks on Cadaver.

VALKYRIE: Then the air tore. That's how it looked. It was the Viddu De, reaching into our universe, getting ready to pull themselves through. So what does Skulduggery do? I'll give you three guesses.
SKULDUGGERY: I did something incredibly brave and selfless.
VALKYRIE: If all three of those guesses are not "something

stupid", then I'm sorry, but we just can't be friends.

Skulduggery flew into the tear.

Silas Nadir led the next wave of City Guard against Omen's team and Serrate cut off his hand. But when Auger involved himself in the fight that followed, Serrate lost focus.

OMEN: He said "That's not how it's meant to happen," or something like that, and the next thing I know, all these cops stick their swords in him and he's dead. Idiot. But then Temper and Ruckus and Tanith and China came running up, so I was pretty sure we were going to win at that point.

Back in the Dark Cathedral –

VALKYRIE: Cadaver was being his usual confident self, and Skulduggery comes flying out of the tear again – and then the Eye of Rhast stops working. Cadaver doesn't know what the hell's happening – but it's Creed. Creed knew about Serrate. He knew they were working together. He knew what Cadaver was going to do. How did he know? OK, hold on to your heads, all right? Malice was with him – in the body of my little sister.

Malice had sent her consciousness with Valkyrie as she jumped back from the future, and had immediately sought out her younger self to possess her. Because Malice was Cadaver's lacuna, he had no idea what was coming.

And there was another lacuna at play, this one over in Corrival. Crepuscular worked out that Serrate and Cadaver couldn't see Auger in those future paths, either.

OMEN: Right there and then, I didn't understand how or why, but... but I do now.

Armed with the Obsidian Blade, which still had a sliver of the dagger attached to the hilt, Auger rushed over to the Dark Cathedral. He was their last hope against Cadaver.

Malice, in Alice's body, kickstarted the Corrival Pillar from where she stood in the Dark Cathedral, and once again the Ensh-Arak Sigil activated. Her plan then was to abandon Alice's body, allowing the wave to Activate her younger self, and return to the future, where she would carry on with her existence. When she left Alice, who collapsed, unconscious, Creed gave her life force a temporary home in a Soul Catcher.

The Arbiters, meanwhile, were busy making sure Cadaver Cain didn't reassert the Gurahghul death field. Auger came to help.

SKULDUGGERY: Cadaver could remember Auger right up until the moment when Auger killed the King of the Darklands. The moment the blade broke, we think, is when it all changed. A sliver must have broken off from the rest and went into

Auger's eye. If it had cut him, he would have been wiped from existence, so it must not have caused any damage... but it must have been absorbed into his system somehow.

Then, when Cadaver stabbed Auger with his own Obsidian Blade, it reacted. Instead of erasing Auger from reality, Auger absorbed the weapon's properties.

Footage showed the qualities of the knife – the density, the angular nature, the impossible blackness – spread to Auger, until it covered him completely. Auger – or Obsidian, as he came to be known – teleported away without a word.[1]

1. According to Cadaver's statement, made from his cell after he'd surrendered, in that moment he saw all the futures fall away until there was nothing left. "Oblivion is coming," he said.

Valkyrie flew into the Activation Wave, deactivating it before it expanded. In the immediate aftermath she seemed to suffer no ill effects, and the Arbiters assumed that her necronaut suit had somehow protected her.

Coda Quell seemed to think that it was Militsa who stood between him and a life with Valkyrie, and so he followed her as she toured the outer boundaries of the new Necropolis. He waited until she was alone, and then attacked. Militsa defended herself but, owing to the so-called Draíocht-boost, her counter-attack was far stronger than she'd anticipated, and Coda was thrown across the boundary, into the Necropolis, and died instantly.

Perfidious Withering introduced Flanery to Doctor Nye, who demonstrated the effect the drug known as Splash had on a mortal – giving the mortal access to temporary magic. Withering offered this drug to Flanery to use on his military, his police forces... whoever he wanted, and Flanery was pleased.

Sebastian, meanwhile, had been apprehended by the City Guard after Tantalus had gone to Commander Hoc and told him everything. At Supreme Mage Creed's orders, Hoc held Sebastian and the Darquesse Society as bait in order to lure in Darquesse.

She came, and she was captured and bound.

OMEN: I'm not sure what happened over the next few weeks. I don't really remember. I was in shock, I think. I'd just lost my brother. I didn't know what to do. My parents didn't know what to do. In one way, the world just stopped spinning, but... but at the same time it continued on as normal.

Creed was still Supreme Mage. China Sorrows was a fugitive, along with Temper and everyone who'd fought beside him. The protesters tried to keep marching but the City Guard just got tougher and tougher and protesters started to die. Eventually they stopped marching.

And then I met Valkyrie. I was out walking, trying to think, and there she was. I hadn't really seen her in a while and I was happy to see her. But she'd changed. She said she was the Child of the Faceless Ones. She was, like, a receptacle.

She said that they entered this universe through her. They left their universe, flowed into her soul, and a few weeks later, flowed out into our world. Then she showed them to me. They were right there. Standing over Roarhaven, standing over Dublin, standing over every major city on Earth, standing there, invisible... intangible... massive. They'd won. The Faceless Ones had come back.

My life, my love, my heart,
I thought we would never part,
But since I found you cheating
With that dimwit Keating,
A new life without you I must start.

ABROGATE RAZE

PART FIVE BY TAWDRY HEPBURN

Although it would take Skulduggery Pleasant two years to track down their father again, Abrogate Raze kept himself busy. Supported by Petulance, Mirror and Respair, he divided his attention between the search for new information on Gog Magog and recruiting others to this new religion, the Covenant of the Destroyer.

His three children were integral to this recruitment drive – charming enough to entice prospective members, powerful enough to safeguard their interests, and intelligent enough to stay one step ahead of their siblings.

They were also, by various accounts, dark sorcerers, and getting darker. Their magic was changing too, diverging from their chosen disciplines and becoming something closer to the power their father had displayed to Skulduggery in that Russian farmhouse. Over the next two years, they were responsible for countless robberies and over two dozen murders.

Meanwhile, their seven siblings split their time between fighting the war against Mevolent and searching for their wayward family members. Confelicity developed an intelligent virus, Malady, that was designed to pass through the world's population in eight months, bringing nothing but a mild cold to those it affected. Once it came into contact with someone of her bloodline, however, Malady would attach itself to their very cells and send out a signal that Confelicity could then trace.

The virus found their father and siblings.

On September 22nd 1800, when Petulance, Mirror and Respair were out of the country, the other seven descended on the grand manor in upstate New York where Abrogate was staying. Ignoring the reflection that Abrogate sent to distract them, they found their father and the ensuing battle tore the manor asunder and scorched the grounds, until, finally, they had him surrounded. Using a variety of techniques and weaponry, they succeeded in subduing him. Wary of his reputation for defying death, they bound his magic, chained him, and secured him in a black coffin, which was then [illegible]

While the Covenant of the Destroyer was quietly dismantled as a religious institution, their three siblings showed no signs of breaking free of Abrogate's influence now that he'd been taken off the board.

In the century and a half that followed, the two sets of siblings would have a series of violent encounters, most of which resulted in either widespread destruction, grievous injury, or a combination of the two.

The Malady virus, however, had not gone away as Confelicity had designed. Instead, it had evolved from an intelligent virus into a sentient virus, and inhabited the shell of a Wretchling. Malady just wanted to rest, but the continued existence of the Raze/Forte bloodline meant it – she – was unable to find peace. So she decided to eradicate the family.

Manufacturing a new virus within her own cells, she sent it out into the world. It found all of Abrogate Raze's children, attacking and draining their life forces. Only Skulduggery Pleasant was able to maintain the integrity of his life force long enough for the effects to fade. His siblings did not share his aptitude, and they died within twenty-four hours of each other, on November 14th 1958.[1]

1. Upon the establishment of the Corrival Academy in Roarhaven, Uther Peccant joined as Head of the English Department. The circumstances surrounding his apparent resurrection remain unclear as of the time of writing. The status of his siblings remains similarly unclear.

GAMEL JOURNAL ENTRY

Timestamp 3:49 pm

A sorcerer named Arden Gale has got in touch with me. He's heard what I'm doing and wants to help, claims to have done some research into Abrogate Raze himself. Probably be a waste of time, but at this point I'll take all the help I can get. Meeting him tomorrow.

Timestamp 11:52 am

Had to cancel the meeting with Arden Gale. Damn migraines starting up again.

TRANSCRIBED DIRECTLY FROM AUDIO RECORDING, DATED JUNE 10TH

GAMEL: Mr Gale, thanks for coming in.
ARDEN: Please, it's Arden. How're you doing?
GAMEL: I'm keeping busy, sir, that's how I'm doing. Any information you can give me to help me along would be

greatly appreciated.

ARDEN: That's why I'm here. We already recording?

GAMEL: Hope you don't mind. Have a seat. Do you want anything? Tea? Coffee?

ARDEN: I'm good, thanks.

GAMEL: Then let's get down to it.

ARDEN: Indeed. Well, I used to be like you – I was a researcher for the Sanctuary. The old Sanctuary, in Dublin, not this shiny new one. I was given an office deep, deep underground. No windows, a single light bulb, rattling pipes… It was cold, it was damp, it was miserable. But I had my books and I was happy.

GAMEL: (*indecipherable*)

ARDEN (*laughing*): Not quite! Not quite but close! No, but you have a much better set-up these days. I would've been dead jealous to see this.

GAMEL: When was this, by the way?

ARDEN: The 1980s. I used to have a tape deck in the corner and I'd play my music and despite the hard work, despite the long hours and the fact that nobody was appropriately grateful for any of the effort I was putting in, it was fulfilling. Really was.

GAMEL: You mentioned on the phone that you'd done some research into Abrogate Raze.

ARDEN: Yes, I had, so when I heard that you were going around, asking all sorts of questions about him, I thought this is a man I need to speak with. You know, I presume, the things that he's done? The crimes?

GAMEL: I'm aware.

ARDEN: Back in the 1980s, the Elders wanted a deeper understanding of some of the challenges that had been faced over the years. They'd just had some awful trouble with a serial killer that caught them completely unawares, and one of their operatives insisted that something be done. There was no point, he figured, in having these wonderful resources at our disposal – namely, me – and not making full use of them. So, down I go, into my office, and the first thing I open is a little notebook all about Abrogate Raze.

GAMEL: And you had a lot more information to go through than I've had.

ARDEN: Oh, yes. That notebook led me to official reports, files, diaries... I even had access to the Grand Mage Journals. I don't mind telling you, when I heard about that Desolation Engine being detonated in the Sanctuary, destroying all that history... I wept. I did.

GAMEL: It was a singular tragedy.

ARDEN: How have you been managing? It can't have been easy tracking Abrogate Raze down through the centuries without the files I had.

GAMEL: Actually, most of the work has been done for me. I'm the fourth researcher to come on to this project.

ARDEN: Oh? What happened to the others?

GAMEL: I don't know, actually. They've, uh, disappeared.

ARDEN: All of them? Isn't that, I don't know... scary?

GAMEL: I'm assured that the City Guard are looking into it.

ARDEN: Well, that's reassuring. So how long have you been at this?

GAMEL: A little over two weeks.

ARDEN: Still plenty of time.

GAMEL: Sorry? Plenty of time to what?

ARDEN: Hmm? To get it done. To get the work done. And I can help you with that! I wish I had a copy of my own work to just hand over, but the Desolation Engine would have destroyed that along with everything else. It's a lucky thing that I've got a great memory! I remember that notebook in particular. It was small, with tiny writing, crammed with insight, and that led me, of course, to finding out more about Gog Magog. You know of Gog Magog?

GAMEL: I know how important he became to Abrogate.

ARDEN: Oh, very important. Massively important. Cannot be overstated, that importance. His whole life, Raze had been searching for meaning, something to fill the part of him that was missing. You know that he couldn't remember anything about his early years?

GAMEL: I'm aware.

ARDEN: You know how old you have to be to not just lose details, not just lose faces and names, but to lose the memories of your parents? Your childhood? I have a theory that the human brain cannot retain memories that are more than nine hundred years old. I have met two sorcerers who are aged over a thousand, and they have much the same problem. Anyway, anyway, I'm digressing. So, this little notebook I found, all about Gog Magog, it was startling, it really was.

GAMEL: Wait, sorry, you mean the whole notebook was about Gog Magog?

ARDEN: Every last word. Why? Is that a problem?

GAMEL: I've just been... I've been noticing a pattern.

ARDEN: You have?

GAMEL: The more someone learns about Gog Magog, the more they fall under his spell, as it were.

ARDEN: Now that's interesting.

GAMEL: Did you find that?

ARDEN: You mean am I under his spell? Do I worship Gog Magog? (*indecipherable*)

GAMEL: Sorry about this – don't know what's happening.

ARDEN: Not at all, not at all. Technology is wonderful until it goes wrong.

GAMEL: There. I think that's... I think that's fixed. OK, good. Now, you were saying?

ARDEN: About...?

GAMEL: If you worship Gog Magog.

ARDEN: Oh my, no. No, no. I'm what you'd call cheerfully agnostic. I worship words, not gods.

GAMEL: So it didn't work on you?

ARDEN: This pattern you'd identified? I'm afraid not. Has it worked on you?

GAMEL: I... I'm not really...

ARDEN: Mr Gamel, as researchers, we are beholden to the truth, are we not? If we cannot be honest with ourselves, then what is it all worth?

GAMEL: I've been having... dreams.

ARDEN: What kind of dreams?

GAMEL: Dreams about Gog Magog.

ARDEN: And are you a Sensitive, Mr Gamel?

GAMEL: Good old-fashioned Elemental.

ARDEN: Well then, these dreams of missing gods are nothing

more than dreams! Mr Gamel?

GAMEL: I hear voices too.

ARDEN: Ah. That does sound more serious. So you believe you are falling under the spell of Gog Magog.

GAMEL: I think he's a virus and I've been infected.

ARDEN: Then why haven't I been infected?

GAMEL: Well, and no offence meant, but you might very well be infected, and you're just lying to me about it.

ARDEN (*laughing*): Very true, very true!

GAMEL: Are you?

ARDEN: Am I what?

GAMEL: Infected?

ARDEN: How would I know? Would I have to experience the dreams and hear the voices?

GAMEL: Maybe. I don't know if it's the same for everyone.

ARDEN: How long do you think you have?

GAMEL: Sorry?

ARDEN: Before you go missing too.

GAMEL: I don't know. Another few days, maybe. Palaverous lasted the longest - he was the first. Rux came second, didn't last as long. Mordant... Mordant knew something was up. She lasted three weeks.

ARDEN: And you're on week two. Yes, I wouldn't say you have very long left at all - providing your theory is correct, of course. When I worked as an Archivist, I got all sorts of fanciful ideas into my head, purely as a result of being down in that cramped, cold room all by myself for far too long. Do you take many walks? Some fresh air might do you good.

GAMEL: Yeah. That's a good idea. Thank you.

ARDEN: Not at all. We Archivists have to stick together.

GAMEL: Is it getting cold in here?

ARDEN: Is it? I got quite used to it, so I doubt I'd notice.

GAMEL: (*indecipherable*)

ARDEN: (*indecipherable*)

GAMEL: — about this. Don't know what's (*indecipherable*). Bear with me, I'll get a new one and we can continue.

ARDEN: No problem at all, my boy.

FIRST RECORDING ENDS.

TRANSCRIBED DIRECTLY FROM AUDIO RECORDING, DATED JUNE 10TH, SECOND RECORDING

GAMEL: And we're back. The temperature in this room has plummeted even though it's a warm summer's day outside. Mr Gale, if we could pick up where... Sorry?

ARDEN: I didn't say anything.

GAMEL: No. Of course not. Sorry. Um... if we could pick up where we... where we, ah...

ARDEN: Mr Gamel, are you having some difficulty?

GAMEL: No, not at all. No.

ARDEN: Are you hearing voices, Mr Gamel?

GAMEL: I'll be fine, thank you.

ARDEN: What are the voices saying, Mr Gamel?

GAMEL: If we could get back on track, that'd be great. I don't want to keep you any longer than is absolutely necessary.

ARDEN: It's perfectly fine. I'm not doing anything for the

rest of the day.

GAMEL: Even so, I...

ARDEN: You've gone quite pale. Are you aware of that?

GAMEL: Mr Gale, in your research into... into Abrogate Raze, did you find any... did you find...

ARDEN: Is that really who you want to ask me about?

GAMEL: No.

ARDEN: Who do you want to ask me about?

GAMEL: Gog Magog.

ARDEN: I'll help however I can.

GAMEL: You know about him, don't you? You know he's a virus.

ARDEN: Of course.

GAMEL: And you're infected.

ARDEN: Of course.

GAMEL: How long did it take?

ARDEN: To infect me? Months. Almost seven months. But that's because it took me so long to put the pieces together, you see. They have to be in order. Your mind has to recognise where everything fits so that it's in a proper state to take on the, ah, the virus, as you say. I was a completely normal person before I started reading about him. I never had any interest in violence, never had any grand ambitions to destroy anything. I liked my books. I liked solving puzzles. I was perfectly suited to be an Archivist.

GAMEL: I don't feel well.

ARDEN: That will pass, but by tomorrow morning you should expect to be feeling quite nihilistic. Are you married? Did I already ask you this? Are you married?

GAMEL: No.

ARDEN: It's for the best. When the nihilism started for me, I killed my husband. That made me sad. I really loved him. But these are the sacrifices we make, isn't that so? What are you doing, Mr Gamel? What did that do?
GAMEL: That button alerts the Cleavers.
ARDEN: In that case, it's probably time for me to leave.
GAMEL: You're not getting out of here.
ARDEN: It was very nice to meet you. I hope I've been of some help. Oh, I have something that may be of interest to you.

CCTV footage shows Arden dropping a notebook on the table, then opening the door and stepping out of the room. Almost simultaneously, the Cleavers rush in. They do not see Arden.

GAMEL JOURNAL ENTRY

Timestamp 8:41 am

I'm so tired. I'm at my kitchen table as I write this. Didn't sleep last night. Didn't sleep night before, either. Can't concentrate. It's hard to get my thoughts in order. There's a voice in my head and it's hard to hear anything else.

I haven't told anyone what's going on. They don't need to know. Too dangerous for them to know. The more people learn about Gog Magog, the further the virus spreads. I feel awful. My muscles are sore. Bones are tired. It's like there's something pressing down on the back of my neck. And the headaches. God, the headaches.

So can't tell anyone. I told the Cleavers and told whoever asked that Arden must have been a crank or a conman and he teleported out of there, but I didn't see him teleport. I didn't see him disappear the way Teleporters disappear. Don't know how to describe it, but he was there and then the Cleavers came in and he wasn't there any more. I don't know. Maybe he just teleported away and my eyes are playing tricks on me.

I have to figure this out. Arden left me a notebook and I haven't opened it yet. Need to get my thoughts down before I read it. Need to figure out what I'm thinking before I read what he's thinking. Does that make sense? Don't know any more.

So what am I thinking?

I'm thinking I need to figure this out and maybe, by figuring it out, it'll save me. Maybe I need to be armed with all the facts, or as many facts as I can get, in order to find a way to fight the infection.

See, there's something missing, something I'm not getting, not understanding. Something nobody's thought of yet. Abrogate Raze became, I think, Gog Magog's Herald, the Prophet who went among the people to spread the word of his god. Abrogate, maybe, had been waiting his whole life for this opportunity, only he didn't know it. Many people have remarked on the fact that he'd always felt he'd been missing something.

So, if Abrogate was the Herald, and the Herald is a sign of what's to come, then is Gog Magog due to return? The gods all got together to strip him of his powers, but what does that mean, really? Strip a god's power and maybe you still have a hell of a lot of power, at least compared to us mere humans. So, if he does return, would we be able to fight him? Would we stand a chance?

I have to know. I have to find out, and if he is coming back I have to warn people. Have to tell them what to expect. Tell them how to beat him. Going to read the notebook now as soon as the room stops spinning.

Timestamp 10:12 am

He'd worked it out. Arden had worked it out. Solved the mystery the rest of us hadn't even known was a mystery. He had the advantage, though. All those books and notes at his fingertips. All we had were scraps.

His notebook says he worked it out, and now the infection is inside him and all he wants to do is spread the word of his god, but he can't because the Sensitives are poking around, getting suspicious whenever he enters the Sanctuary. He wants to scream it from the rooftops, but they'll stop him, shut him up and shut him away, or more likely just kill him. Safer to kill him.

So he decides to be sneaky. Decides that it won't be his place to shout it from rooftops. No grand announcement - instead, he'll infect people little by little, over time, feeding them bits of information so they can watch it unfold.

The bit I find sneakiest, the bit I find the most perfect, is that the notebook doesn't even say what he worked out. No easy answer for anyone, oh, no. No cheating. No skip-to-the-last-page to find out how it ends. Instead, he gives all the same clues and bits of information that he got, and lets you work it out for yourself. See, I appreciate that! It's horrible and nasty, but at the same time so rewarding! That's what's missing in most viruses, I find. That sense of accomplishment.

But this here, what I'm writing, it's never going to see the light of day. All the work here is getting wiped. All the notes I inherited, all the books, all the journals and scraps of paper... the moment I reach the end, they're all going to go up in flames and this device is getting wiped then destroyed. I just need it for another few minutes. Just to get my thoughts down on the screen in a straight line.

Once upon a time, just after time was invented, actually, there was a god, and the god was called Gog Magog, and he was the God of the Apocalypse, and none of the other gods liked him very much, so bye bye, Gog Magog! They took his power from him and flicked him away like you'd flick a bug you'd found on your sleeve. And Gog Magog went spinning and tumbling, head over heels, and he crashed into the ground and he lay there and eventually he sat up, and do you know what? When the gods took his power, they took his memory too! So the God of the Apocalypse didn't know he was the God of the Apocalypse! What a jape!

So off he goes, this Gog Magog, and although he doesn't have his god powers any more he still has magic, so this absent-minded god wanders across the Earth and he thinks he's a person, just like you, and just like me, and he sees the sorcerers and he thinks to himself, *Hey-ho! I must be a sorcerer!* And he sees their magic and he thinks, *Hey-ho! That must be how magic looks!* and he changes his magic to suit! And he's thinking like a person now, so he picks a person's name for himself, and the name he picks is Abrogate Raze.

And lots and lots of years pass, and Abrogate Raze forgets all about the fact that his magic was once different from everyone else's, and before you can say, "Silly god!", he's living just like a sorcerer!

But there's something missing in poor Abrogate's heart, you see. Now, we know that what he's missing is who he really is, but he thinks he's missing something to believe in! The silly goose! So he searches and he searches and he worships and he worships, but it's never right! It's never quite right!

So he gets married, does Abrogate, because maybe the answer is love! Maybe that's what he's missing! And then he starts a family, because maybe a family is what's missing!

But he's not very good at being a husband, and he's not very good at being a father, and he kills his wife and goes on the run and spends the next 127 years looking for some vague spiritual awakening... and then he finds it. And guess what?

The thing he was searching for was inside him all along!

But of course silly Mr Raze doesn't realise this, so he plods along, reading and reading and reading, and all this reading about Gog Magog is stirring the part of him, deep inside, that *is* Gog Magog, and this is where the virus starts, this is where the infection begins, as his magic changes, as his old power comes back, and it mixes and stirs with all this nastiness, mixing and stirring, getting itself ready to go out into the world and replicate and spread and be beautiful.

But then tragedy!

His human failings come back to haunt him!

Two of his sons and two of his daughters, out for revenge after all these years, find him at last! And although Abrogate is stronger, and he infects Petulance and Mirror and Respair, Skulduggery Pleasant gets away and then comes back, a mere two years later, with all the children that Abrogate hasn't had a chance to infect yet!

And they attack him! And they shackle him! And they chain him and lock him in a coffin and [redacted]

Oh, the humanity! Oh, the...

no. What have I done this is wrong this is what...

the more people find out about Abrogate Raze and

Gog Magog the further the virus spreads but the purpose of the virus is not just to spread it's to FEED all worship makes gods stronger the virus feeds...

The virus feeds Gog Magog. Feeds Abrogate Raze. He's trapped in that coffin, but he's getting stronger. I can hear him in my head. He's getting stronger. I have to burn all my notes now, destroy this device now. No one can read...

They want this written they want it out there this isn't a record of events this is a spellbook to get everyone reading and thinking about him to bring him back it's a goddamn grimoire...

someone knocking on my...

A NOTE FROM THE ARCHIVISTS

Our colleague, Archivist Gamel, was taken suddenly ill before he could finish this edition. Rest assured, the very fine doctors here in the High Sanctuary believe he is on course to make a full recovery from whatever mystery illness felled him. In the meantime, Archivists Palaverous, Rux and Mordant have returned to their posts after some much-needed leave, just in time to assemble the book – as rough and ready as it may be – and see it to print.

Because of the sensitive nature of some of the information contained within, this book will, of course, only be accessible to the appropriate Councils of Elders. If you are not an Elder, please refrain from reading, and return this edition to your local Sanctuary.

But, if you have already read through it and are feeling unwell, or if you have developed a sudden headache, a sense of general nihilism, or if you start hearing a strange but undeniably attractive voice in your head, please do not worry. These symptoms will pass. What awaits you on the other side is a power the likes of which you have never known.

The God of the Apocalypse loves you.

Now go out and spread the word.

NOT TO BE REMOVED FROM
THE SANCTUARY ARCHIVE

INDEX

PROPERTY OF
THE ARCHIVISTS